CHAINED TO *Your Heart*

COLLIE MAGGIE

D1415849

OAKTARA

WATERFORD, VIRGINIA

Chained to Your Heart

Published in the U.S. by:
OakTara Publishers
P.O. Box 8
Waterford, VA 20197

Visit OakTara at
www.oaktara.com

Cover design by David LaPlaca/debest design co.
Cover images © iStockphoto.com/Bret Hillyard/stockphot4u/
Phil Morley
Author photo © 2008 by Lifetouch Church Directories and Portraits.
Used by permission.

Scripture is taken from the *Holy Bible,* King James Version.

ISBN: 978-1-60290-110-3

❦

I want to dedicate this book to **BONNIE BLUE**, my dear friend who first "pushed" me to write this story. I'll never forget your sweet spirit and grace.

AUDREY, without you I would still be staring at my computer like a deer in the headlights, trying to figure out where all the quotes and commas go.

MY FRIENDS AND FAMILY IN CHRIST AT LIVING HOPE CHURCH: your encouragement, love, and prayers have made this possible.

Most of all to my JESUS, thank you for my salvation and for adopting me.

1

Nightmare

It was the year of our Lord, 1864, and having just turned eighteen, Katie's future was a fearful thing now. Any hopes or dreams she once had were gone. She had heard about Newgate as a young girl and the horrors that dwelled there. People went in but never came out. Prisoners were treated horribly, and disease ran rampant. England had many prisons or gaols, as they were better known, but Newgate was the most notorious of all, and here she sat in the middle of it.

Never in her wildest dreams would she have believed she would one day be locked in a communal cell along with twenty-five other men, women, and children. The cell was almost twenty feet long and fifteen feet wide. Three small windows covered by metal grating were built high near the ceiling. Any fresh air that was available stayed at the top. A few lanterns burned, but proved useless. Off the large room were two smaller rooms, one of the areas for the women and one for the men. A few chamber pots and buckets lined the walls. In the three days the young woman had been there the rooms had not been cleaned. Most prisoners sat with their backs against the block walls. Others tried to sleep on the hard floor covered by filthy, matted hay.

The young woman scanned the prison cell. A rat scurried across the floor, forcing her to curl her legs up. She pressed against the dank wall. The small boy and girl lying next to her for warmth stirred in their sleep. Looking down on them, she was filled with compassion. She stretched her skirt over them in an attempt to keep them warm.

Leaning her head back and closing her eyes, Katie tried to deny her surroundings. She couldn't be here. She would wake up, and it would be a horrible nightmare that would only linger in her memory. Her other senses told her the truth. Her nose told her that she was still in the depths of hell. The smell of mildew, vomit, and human waste mixed with the scent of dirty bodies overwhelmed her. Words from her past came as if to soothe and comfort.

"All right, Katie, hold on. Hold on tight to what ya believe and who ya are."

They were the words of her beloved Gran, who could always ease her mind whenever she felt frightened. But now she needed more than just words. She longed for her home—for Papa and Gran.

The sound of the great iron doors opening caught everyone's attention. The gaoler mercilessly shoved a stout woman through them, causing her to sprawl, facedown, on the floor. A "whuff" came out of her. She lay there motionless until the gaoler closed the doors. Slowly lifting her head, she looked around with fire in her eyes. She appeared to be in her midforties with dark hair speckled with gray. She looked like she had lived a hard life. Her fiery eyes darted around the cell like a trapped animal's.

The children jerked awake, and started whimpering. Katie put her arm around them reassuringly. A man said something crude to the older woman while others snickered. In a quick movement that same man grabbed the woman. With a growl the woman reached up, grabbing the man in the most sensitive of areas. She proceeded to twist with all her might. The two of them rolled, kicking and swearing. With one good push the man freed himself.

"All right, ye old cow. If that's the way you want it!" the man yelled.

"Ya ever try an' touch me again, ya stinkin' scum, and ol' Mary will crack yer 'ead!" she screamed back.

Laughter erupted at her words.

"Ye better listen to the ol' girl, Pete, or we'll be diggin' your grave!" quipped another man.

The woman got to her feet facing the group of men. With her hands stretched into claws she braced herself for another attack. She knew she wouldn't win, but she would take a few down and leave a scar or two.

"Ah, she ain't worth it, Pete," another man piped up. "Besides, there be better tastin' fish in 'ere than that ol' whale." With that said, all the men turned to eye Katie.

The children pushed themselves flatter against the wall, clinging to each other as Katie slowly stood. Her heart tore at her ribs while her knees threatened to buckle.

Two of the men stepped closer. The dark one with matted beard led while the man with brown hair sneered at her, showing broken, black teeth. Their stench washed over them and anyone else near. The older woman ran to Katie, standing in front of her.

"Why, ya filthy blokes! It be not enough to grab poor ol' Mary, is it? Ya gotta try and put the hurt to this wee lass besides! Well, I ain't 'avin it; ya 'ear me?"

Katie was surprised at the sudden fear on the men's faces. She followed their gaze until it fell on the giant of a man standing behind Mary. Big Red, as the men called him, stood head and shoulders above the rest. His expression caught and held their attention. Without a word the men stepped back as their laughter died in their throats.

Red was not about to ignore such actions. In the two weeks he had been in Newgate all was quiet, but when this young woman came in, the other men took notice. He had felt trouble brewing.

The older woman straightened and smiled. "Ya blokes learn'd, did ya? Ol' Mary don't take nothin' from scum like ya. It be best ya learn it now if we be locked together in this 'ole of Satan's!"

Once the men were seated Red returned to "his" corner. Katie was amazed how quietly he moved in spite of his size. Even though no words were spoken the men heard Red loud and clear. There would be no more trouble of that kind with him in the cell.

Where Mary stood she had not seen the large man standing behind her. She felt very proud of herself indeed. Pushing her large bosoms up, she straightened her crumpled dress. Feeling quite smug, she brushed her hair away and proceeded to put her arm around the young woman. "No need for ya to worry, lass. Mary won't let them scruffs touch ya in any way. Ya be safe with me 'ere."

Katie felt lightheaded. Slowly she slid against the wall to the floor. Sitting next to her, the older woman turned a wary eye on the bunch of "foulers," just in case they needed another lesson.

Red watched as well until he was certain the trouble had passed.

Then he studied the girl. She captivated him. She looked to be eighteen or twenty with a slim build but looked fit. She seemed to have a delicate and gentle manner about her in the way she handled the two children. To Red she was of a ray of sunshine.

Red turned his gaze on the young ones. He guessed the girl to be four and the boy, maybe six years old. A week after he arrived, they came in with their mother, who seemed ill with a cough. Within days she died, leaving her children behind. He had tried to reach out to them, but they were too frightened of him. He was relieved when the young woman came to the cell. The children seemed drawn to her. She didn't hesitate to share her meager portions of bread and gruel with them. It was foolish of her to do so, but Red believed she knew that and gave anyway.

❧ ❧

Katie was finally able to breathe normally again. With her head on Mary's shoulder she listened to the older woman as she babbled on about her life. How fate had slapped her upside the head, landing her in this unfortunate situation. Katie's mind began to wander in spite of the chatter. Why had that man stepped forward to help? What did it matter? She was grateful he was there. Her attention came back to the woman. Smiling, she thanked her for her protection and introduced herself.

"My name is Katie. Did you say your name is Mary?"

Returning her smile the woman answered, "Aye, 'tis Mary, miss. Why, it was fittin' ol' Mary would step in. Us ladies got to stick together be what I am thinkin'."

Katie nodded in agreement. She wondered why Mary would talk about herself in the third person, but it added to her charm. Mary went on, "Ya seem too fine a lady to be 'ere. What would ya be 'ere for, if ya don't mind me askin'?"

Katie shrugged. "I was accused of stealing something I did not take."

Mary began nodding. "Aye, that has happened to meself once long ago. Now I 'ave done enough to make up for that one time of falsehood. I wish I could tell ya that ol' Mary be 'ere because of a falsehood now, but I cannot." Her shoulders seem to stoop a little with her confession. Katie didn't push for an explanation.

The two women stopped talking. Before too long, the older woman began dozing. Her head bobbed back and forth, threatening to hit the wall. She was about to slap at what she thought to be a rat, when she realized that two small children were wiggling in between her and Katie.

"What this be?" she exclaimed. "Why in this troubled world would ya be here for? Babes should be in their mum's bed. Just come betwixt ol' Mary and the lass. We keep yas warm as can be." Soon the young ones were snuggled in and sleeping as if they had no troubles at all. Mary looked at Katie with questioning eyes. Katie quietly explained about the children's mother and expressed her concern for them.

"When I first arrived, the children were petrified of everyone. I coaxed them a little and soon they came to me. When I asked about their mum they told me she had died here before I came. The poor wee ones. I don't know how long they've been here," Katie said. "I feel somewhat responsible for them now, but what am I to do? I don't even know what is going to happen to me."

Mary looked at the children with sadness. "Aye, what is to be done? I 'ear babes are given o'er to the workhouses. Terrible places they be. "Queen Victoria, bless 'er 'eart, be easier on us poor than ol' King George was, but they got to go somewheres."

Katie noticed a small, dirty piece of cloth in Mary's hand. The older woman stroked it as if to soothe herself. Katie wondered about it, but other things crowded her mind. Closing her eyes once more, she forced herself to think of other things besides her surroundings. Her mind turned back to her beloved Gran. She remembered how Gran loved to tell her about Ireland.

"It be the prettiest land ya e'er see," she would say, "but rocks grew where potatoes wouldn't. It be a 'ard life for sure. God made it up to us by making us Irish, and placing us in the most beautiful place except for heaven. County Mayo 'tis where all yer people come from, Katie. They were fishermen and farmers, the lot of 'em. Not a one owned 'is own land. It came to be that we all 'ad to leave our 'earth and 'ome. Still brings a tear to me eyes thinkin' on it." The dear old lady would wipe her eyes, loudly blow her nose, and sadly smile. "It be a 'ard thing to remember on."

Thinking on that, Katie began dozing, dreaming of the woman closest to her heart. Gran was rocking in her creaky old chair while talking softly of things that mattered most to her. "Ya know, Katie Elizabeth, life 'tis all about choices that are made. Whether by ya or someone else, it doesn't matter. What does matter is making good choices and how ya decide to live through the choices made. The biggest choice ya will e'er make is whether to be a-walkin' with Almighty God or not. You need Him in yer life, lass." Katie stirred in her sleep. Her sweet dreams of Gran disappeared and were replaced by dark shadows and the demon-like voice of the "black princess," Tess.

"Katie, where's my blue gown with the lace? Why do my things seem to disappear all the time? Get my pearl bobs over there and hurry. My hair is a mess! Fix it!" Katie felt herself running in circles trying her best to please her young mistress, but could not. "Oh! You are getting more useless as time goes on! Why can't you appreciate your position! My mother should never have allowed you here! You are useless!" the young woman screamed.

In Katie's nightmare, Miss Tess' mouth got bigger and bigger until only a massive, black hole remained. Tess turned to Katie, causing her to fall into it. Down, down she fell as slimy hands grabbed at her. Katie jumped herself awake. For a split second she couldn't remember where she was. As the fog lifted her mind, any sense of relief she might have felt was gone. She had awakened from one nightmare into another.

Closing her eyes she tried to remember her dream about Gran. The dear old lady's Irish brogue came back to her, but what were the words? What was it she had said about choices? It was something about God— that far-away being with white hair. She always imagined Him with one big eye that saw every sin, and a long finger to point it out. Almighty God, who never spoke to her or really seemed to acknowledge her existence, but then again, she never acknowledged His existence either. For the first time in her life she wanted to feel close to Him. She wanted to believe that He was real and could help her. There was no one else now. She had never felt as alone as she did that moment. The lowest time in her life had been losing Gran and Papa...until now. How she longed for that faith that seemed to come so easy to Gran. She longed for the faith in a Being that would love you no matter what. Katie wondered where Gran got all that faith. Where did it come from, and did God pick and choose who received it? With a sigh, Katie leaned back against the wall. What did it matter? She didn't have it. Katie tried again to think of Gran's words in her dream, but could not.

Her second dream was a different matter. She remembered it all too well. It was because of the "black princess" that Katie was here. How could Tess have done such a thing? As long as she could remember Tess seemed to hate her. Tess was capable of cruelty, but to this degree? How could she have told such a lie?

The fact that Lord and Lady Wilson would allow such disaster to befall her caused the worst pain of all. They must have known that she would never have betrayed their trust. Of course they had to believe their own flesh and blood over a maid...didn't they? Still they knew what Tess was like. They should have believed Katie when she told them she had not taken the necklace. It was obvious to everyone that Tess was jealous of Katie's relationship with Lord and Lady Wilson. Couldn't they see it too?

Katie remembered the day Papa had secured a position at the Brick House for her. Oh the excitement his news brought. Brick House was the name given to Lord and Lady Wilson's manor. It was huge and covered in red brick, thus the name. It seemed a palace with many large windows and beautiful lawns.

Papa was the head gardener and had taken great pride in his job. He made sure the grounds and gardens were at their best. He even had a staff of six men working under him. There was pride in that for sure. Papa was a hard worker. He worked as if Lord Wilson was looking over his shoulder, though he never did. Papa had proven himself to be an honest man. When Lord Wilson approached him about Katie working in the house, it only took Papa's word for Katie to get hired.

Yes, she had been excited, but frightened too, of course! To work at Brick House was an honor in itself. Employment was so rare for the

Irish, and being Katie's first job made it very special. She couldn't believe she would be making money of her very own. She found out through Papa that she would earn a farthing a week! Thoughts of all the grand things her earnings would buy consumed her. She would buy linen and a new bonnet for Gran. Papa could get a new plow along with a pipe. Oh the wealth they would have!

"Katie," Papa started, "Lord Wilson actually asked for you. His daughter is home from school and he wants you to be her maid. You're both the same age. Won't that be a fine thing?"

Katie never really had a best friend before, except for Gran. Did she count? Well, now she would have someone her own age to share secrets with, to run and skip. Gran wasn't very good at that part. "Papa," Katie asked, "what's a maid?"

"That's a girl who helps a lady get dressed and fix her hair and such."

"You mean that poor girl has no arms of her own to dress herself?" Katie's eyes nearly bugged out. Both Papa and Gran broke into laughter.

"No, no my Katie," Papa continued, "It's just that ladies don't work anymore than they have to, so they hire people to do their work for them."

"But Papa," Katie went on, "since when is getting dressed work?"

"Well, Katie, there is truth in that all right."

There was a lot to do to get ready. Gran went about scrubbing Katie's best dress. She only had two, so it was a mystery to her how Gran could figure out which one was the better. They were both worn but Gran would say, "We may be poor, Katie Elizabeth, but we are a clean people." So after her dress was scrubbed, Katie was scrubbed. Fear tugged at her heart along with the excitement.

"Gran," she whispered, "I'm afraid to go there. What if I don't do things right? Where do I go once I get to the Brick House?"

Gran looked at her granddaughter with great tenderness. "I know ya be afraid, Katie dear, but don't e'er let fear keep ya back from where God wants ya to go, just trust."

A sigh of frustration escaped. As much as she loved Gran it was hard to get a "real" answer from her. She always gave those tricky answers that Katie tried to figure out but seldom did. "Gran, I need a good answer!" Katie whined. "I don't know what you mean."

Gran just smiled and gave her a hug. "Simply, Katie, there be no need to worry about where God is taking ya, as long as ya trust in Him."

Katie just shrugged. She wasn't talking about the rest of her life. Gran was wonderful, but at times she was no help at all. Katie wondered if all old people talked like that. Was it because they knew they would be dying soon and needed to talk about God a lot so they could get to heaven? She didn't like to think about Gran "going to dust," as the old ones called it. Katie made her decision. She may be frightened a little, but no one would know. She would hold her head up and be brave...or at least try.

Early the next day she went to work with Papa. This was the first time she was allowed to go to the Brick House. It had always been a distant thing of beauty. Coming closer to it took Katie's breath away. *Grand* was not the word for it. She could not imagine the money a person would need to live in such a place. She always thought it looked like a castle. So of course it only made sense that her new, soon-to-be best friend must be a princess!

Papa stopped just before entering. Katie knew more instructions were coming. "Remember, Katie dear, to curtsey like Gran showed you, and be ever mindful of your manners. Oh, and don't forget to always say "sir", and...."

"Papa!" Katie loudly whispered, "I know, I know! You told me over and over last night!"

"All right, Katie girl, I guess you're ready. Now don't forget to smile." Katie rolled her eyes, causing Papa to chuckle to himself.

They stepped through the door into a large warm kitchen. Katie was amazed at the size of it. She thought that the whole of their little cottage could fit in this room alone. The smell of bread baking made her mouth water. At one end of the room were large windows and a table full of flour and bowls. "Flour fairies" danced in the sunshine pouring through the windows. A plump woman in a neatly pressed dress and crisp apron stood by the stove. She turned to see who was invading her kitchen, and broke into a big grin. "Well, look who's here. Mr. Brady, is this the wee girl you've been braggin' on?"

Katie shyly smiled at the woman. "This be my Katie," he said with pride. "She's here to work with Miss Tess. Is Lord Wilson here or out riding the grounds?"

Wiping her hands on her apron the woman went to retrieve two cups from the cupboard. "Sit, Mr. Brady, and have a cup of tea. Aye, Lord Wilson is out riding and Lady Wilson is resting, so you have a few minutes. Come Katie, have some milk and a warm slice of bread with jam."

Papa led Katie to the table, "Katie, this is Miss Maggie Gray. She's the best cook in the county."

Katie curtsied.

"Why, what a perfectly fine little lady you are. I can see why your papa would be so proud. Now Katie, you can call me Maggie. Come sit and rest yourself."

Katie liked her immediately. She seemed kind and was squishy looking like Gran. Her face was smooth and her cheeks rosy. When she smiled, which was a lot, her nose turned up a little, and she smelled good.

Suddenly a loud voice came from the next room. "I don't have to listen to you. You aren't my mother!"

"Oh-oh," Maggie whispered, "Brace yourselves. 'Tis the shrew coming."

With that, the kitchen door flew open. In stepped one of the prettiest girls Katie had ever seen. *I was right,* thought Katie, *there is a princess living here.*

The girl stopped dead in her tracks, staring at Katie. "Who are you, and why are you eating my father's food?" she bellowed.

Katie, with a bite of bread half in her mouth, froze. Lowering it to the plate, she turned to look at Papa.

Maggie, struggling to sound cordial, spoke up. "I invited Mr. Brady and his daughter, Katie, to sit a spell. She is your new companion, Miss Tess."

"I wasn't talking to you, Maggie. Can't she speak for herself?" the girl snapped. "And Maggie, she's not my companion; she's my servant."

"Now, Tess, ladies don't speak that way," corrected a very plain-looking woman who stood behind Tess.

The girl's ringlets bounced as she turned to glare at the woman.

With great flare, Tess walked through the same door she had just come from. That was the first meeting Katie had with her new—at least she had hoped—best friend. Disappointment flooded her heart as she realized the pretty girl wasn't going to be all that easy to like. She had no doubts now; she didn't want to stay. It had never entered her mind that any princess living in such a grand castle would be mean. Katie decided that the "princess" wasn't all that pretty after all.

"I apologize for our young lady," stated the plain woman. "She is quite high-spirited, and of course that's to be expected. It's just sometimes she seems to forget herself. Let me introduce myself. I am Miss Simms, the governess. I have been looking forward to meeting you, Katie."

Katie wasn't sure what to say but managed, "Thank you."

"I must attend to Miss Tess, but as soon as you are finished with your milk, Maggie can bring you upstairs to properly meet your new mistress." Miss Simms nodded then went out the kitchen door.

Katie couldn't help but think how the woman looked like she had swallowed a lemon whole after chewing on it awhile. All the excitement that had been building was gone, replaced with uncertainty.

Maggie noticed the wrinkle of concern on Katie's young brow. "Don't you worry yourself," Maggie cooed, "you will be just fine. You won't be alone here. I'll be here, and so will your papa." Pouring more tea, Maggie turned her attention to the man. "Miss Simms is new here too. It was decided that 'our' Tess would stay home from school, so a governess was hired. I suspect the school decided that."

Papa nodded in understanding.

Katie couldn't finish her treat of bread and jam. She couldn't swallow the lump in her throat, let alone food. Tears threatened as her disappointment grew, but Papa and Gran had been so excited. She could never disappoint them.

Katie's thoughts came crashing back to the present and the gaol. What if she had never stepped foot in the Brick House or met Tess? What if she had just stayed home with Gran? What good did it do to wonder what if? Again despair wrapped itself around her like a heavy cloak. Her life was now a never-ending nightmare. How could she ever feel safe again? Never again would she feel the security of someone taking care of her. Her beloved family was gone now. She was truly on her own…in the pit of hell.

Mary excitedly whispered to Katie, "Come, or it all be gone."

Katie went to jump up, but her body screamed its objection. Sitting and sleeping on the cold dank floor had stiffened her body. She was about to complain to Mary, but bit her tongue. If Mary, the old man across the cell, and the two wee ones didn't complain, she wouldn't either. By the time she got to her feet a crowd was already at the gate to get their meager portions. She doubted there would be anything left, but she had to try. She had to try for the children. They were so thin. Before taking a step she heard a deep voice.

"Get away; let me through!" It was the big man. The group of people parted out of his way. Katie felt disappointment. For some reason she had expected better of him, but what did she know about him?

Maybe he has motives of his own. Maybe…

Before she could finish her thought, the big man turned to hand her a wooden bowl. It was full of gruel, and there was a slice of bread as well. "For you, and the little ones," he said.

Then he turned to get food for the old man and the women. After they had their share, he went back for himself.

Katie noticed that his bowl wasn't nearly as full as the one he had gotten for her. It was funny how even the gaoler dishing the gruel seemed in a hurry to do his bidding. The other men in the cell glared at him, but nary was a complaint made. Katie watched as the crowd of people stepped aside for the big man as he made his way back to "his corner." He didn't speak to anyone, yet the people parted for him like the Red Sea for Moses. Katie smiled… the "red" man and the Red Sea. It was clear to Katie that the man's heart was just as big as his body. She felt shame for her earlier thoughts. Sitting, she gave the bowl to the two children. As they began to eat, Katie tore the bread into two pieces, giving half to Mary.

12

"Why, bless me soul. First ol' Mary has a lad waitin' on meself, and now a sweet lass gives me bread. Bless ya, darlin', for thinkin' of me. Ya have a good heart to go with that pretty face."

Katie smiled and slowly chewed her bread. Everyone grew still as they ate their meager meal.

Katie thought about the big man. He seemed gentle. His kindness to others touched her deeply. He wasn't loud nor did he demand any attention. He didn't complain or shout his innocence to anyone that would listen. He simply "served" others any way he could. By watching him, Katie felt hopeful in a strange way. His acts of kindness seemed to confirm that the future would somehow get better. Then and there she made a decision. No matter what she would hold her head up. This wasn't going to "best" her. She wouldn't let herself become bitter. No matter what the future held for her, she would be strong. She would be what she was raised to be and she would make it through—somehow. At least she would try.

2

Blood Red

Once everyone had a little food in their stomachs, all settled down to rest. Except for an occasional cough, and the faint trickle of water through the wall somewhere, it was quiet. Katie stole another peek at the big man. He was huge, bigger than Papa had been. She couldn't get over his large hands! There was no mistaking his red hair and beard, even though they were dirty and matted. One thing puzzled Katie. She saw the way the other men in the cell treated him. It was as if they were scared to death of the man. They kept their distance from him, and their eyes on him. She wondered if something had happened in the cell between the men before she got there. She had not yet heard the rumors about "Blood Red."

If you were to listen to the other men, Red was the foulest, most depraved man ever to walk the earth. It was said that he ate flesh! Word came down that a man and Blood Red had a fight. Before it was over, Red took a bite out of the man...and swallowed! It all made sense if you looked at him. He was huge, and all that red hair! After conferring with one another they had no doubts as to Red's liking of flesh. Taking no chances, they took turns watching all through the night. That man-eater wasn't gonna sneak up on any one of them!

Red had noticed the other men watching him. They would murmur amongst themselves, then nod towards him. He sensed their fear, but wasn't sure why they feared him. It really didn't matter as

14

long as they left him and the others alone. His thoughts turned inward. He thought about the mistakes he had made that landed him in Newgate. He was just one of many without a home or family. With shame he thought of how he had stopped trusting in the Lord and had taken matters into his own hands. There were hundreds without homes, families, or direction for their lives who had not ended up in a gaol. He had direction and hope in the Lord, yet here he was.

He had traveled all over working wherever there was a job to be had. Being large for his age and very strong, he never had problems finding work. As long as a body was willing to work hard, there was work to be found. James Patrick, or Red as he was called, was on his own since he was twelve years old. His parents died when their cottage caught fire. His father had taken him out and returned for his mother. He never made it out again. The boy was left alone with nothing. How old did that make him now? In his mind he figured about twenty-six or seven. He had done everything from harbor work to being a stable boy. The longest lasting job he had was working on a farm for over eight years. It had been the closest thing to having a home of his own after losing his parents. He now understood it was the Lord who brought him and his second family together.

He was fourteen and, once again, looking for work. He saw a man in the fields trying his best to hoist a boulder from the soil. As quickly as possible, Red ran to help, and before too long the rock was out of the way. When the farmer asked what pay he wanted, Red responded, "Just a bit of bread would be appreciated." With that, he was invited to a hardy meal. He was served beef, potatoes, fresh carrots from the garden, biscuits right out of the oven, and tea. When he thought it couldn't get any better, he was served hot apple slab! He hadn't eaten like that in months. Along with the food he was offered a job, and he thankfully accepted. Red wasn't sure how to respond when the farmer announced that the younger man was an answer to prayer. Since the man's only son was a toddler and his two daughters only seven and ten, he had been praying for help with the farm. Red had been called a few things in his short life, but never "an answer to prayer."

The kind couple shared what they had with him, as did their three children. Roy O'Malley worked hard on his farm, gladly teaching Red all he knew. Picket O'Malley was a wonderful Christian woman. She was a cheerful wife and gentle mother. She treated Red as one of her own.

Each night after chores, the children were given reading and writing lessons. There were times when Red felt uncomfortable being older, but he was thankful for the chance to learn. Just before bed they were told Bible stories. It was then that Red became a Christian. He probably would have stayed with them forever, except they lost the farm to a crooked banker. In the midst of being forced off their land, the O'Malleys had told Red of the plan God had for their lives. Oh, they were angry for sure, but once they sought the Lord, they asked for His blessing on the banker! They encouraged Red to do the same; to trust in the Lord as they would do. The eight years he spent with the O'Malleys rooted him for what lay ahead of him...or so he thought.

Red was a man of twenty-two when they lost the farm. Had that terrible day never occurred, Red would probably still be there. When they had to leave the farm, Red knew it was time for him to go out on his own. What a hard and sorrowful parting it had been. He was given kisses, hugs, and a small amount of money. After being sent on his way he found a large tree and lay beneath it, crying his heart out. When his tears were gone, he curled up and slept. Once he was awake he dusted himself off and found another job.

He wondered where his "family" was now. How disappointed they would be in him if they knew where he was. It had all started when he had stopped trusting in the Lord. It was after losing another job with no prospects that he began losing hope. It was bitter cold, and he found himself drifting once again. His belly had not been full for over a week. He happened across an open door, exposing a table with bread and cheese. Before thinking about it, he grabbed it and ran. It wasn't long before a few men had chased him down. He received a beating and a place of his own...in the gaol. Times were tough before, so why had he turned to stealing? He couldn't answer because there was no answer. At the time he was bone-weary, empty with loneliness, and weak.

Red shifted to ease the pain in his back. The wall wasn't nearly as hard as admitting his failure. Something stirred within him, a familiar longing. It had taken him awhile to figure out what that longing was.

Over the years he had tried to tell himself that one day he would have his own land and family. One day he would have a family that wouldn't leave him. Without money to buy the land or a family to give it to him, there was little chance of that happening. So he had given up... given up on himself, his dream, and given up on God. He had tried to save some money, but wages were small. He worked mostly for his food and lodging. Irritation replaced longing, irritation at himself. The world was filled with the starving and deprived. All he had to do was look around the cell to see that. Yet his mind continued to chase the elusive and impossible dream. The "wanting it" wouldn't go away. Shame came over him until he heard that wonderful, soft voice within, *Trust in me.* Red had to smile. The Lord was not about to let him sit there and feel sorry for himself.

Forgive me once again, Father, he prayed. He felt peace knowing the Lord would not leave nor forsake him. He would never feel alone again.

Another three weeks went by before the day of rescue came for the children. Keys rattling brought everyone's attention to the door. The gaoler unlocked the door and turned to look as if waiting for someone. A moment later a man and woman stepped through the door holding their arms out. "Patty, Michael, we're here!"

The two children looked up with the calling of their names. With squeals of joy and relief they ran as fast as they could towards the couple.

"You poor babies, we came as fast as we could. We just heard about your mother. Look how filthy you are!"

As soon as the children reached the woman they buried their faces into the folds of her skirt. By what Katie could make out, the couple was likely the children's aunt and uncle.

"Oh Arthur, let's get these poor children out of this horrid place. Who would lock innocent children in a place like this?" The woman questioned as she placed a hanky over her nose and mouth.

"I don't know dear, but I intend to find out. This is an outrage." Turning to the little girl, her uncle spoke softly, "Don't worry, you will never be left alone again."

Tears of relief ran down Katie's cheek. Knowing the children would have a place to live, and with people who seemed to love them, comforted her. Envy also tugged at her heart. How she wished someone would rescue her. She wanted to be brave, but what difference would it make? Who cared if she were brave or not? The memory of Gran filled Katie. Gran would have cared. How many times did she tell Katie to, "Be true to yourself and God"? No matter what circumstances surrounded Gran, she walked in peace. Katie didn't have that same assurance. *Well,* she thought, *maybe not, but I did have more than most.* She had come from a family of love, deeply rooted and solid. She may not know where she was going, but she knew from where she came. She still had more than most people. No matter what, no one could take that away from her. A surge of strength went through her that gave her a glimmer of hope; things would somehow work out.

"Get up with yas! Come on tarts, time to move into yer new 'ouse." The gaoler chuckled at his poor joke.

"What's going on?" one of the male prisoners asked.

"Nothin' tha' concerns the likes of ya. Sit back an' mind yer own business. All right, girlies, line up to be moved."

Looking at each other, they did as they were told. The gaoler and several other turnkeys took the ten women down to another cell. Fresh hay covered the floor while blankets lay neatly folded.

The women were relieved. They wouldn't have to worry about the men. The big man called Red seemed to protect the women, but they could never be sure of his intentions either. No one really knew him. After all, he was a prisoner too.

As the other women settled in, Katie tried her best to run her fingers through her long hair. The tangles were many and tight. Thoughtfully she turned to Mary. "What's to happen to us, Mary?"

Mary shook her head, "Not sure, lass."

"Mary, will we ever get out of here? What happens now?"

Mary's brow crinkled as if in deep thought. "I be 'ere twice afore. It be a 'ard thing to say. One time they jest let me out with nary a word said. The next time a gaoler 'isself said 'e would have me quartered if I come back, then 'e let me out again. I think they 'ave enough to worry 'bout sides an ol' woman such as I be, but now I be 'ere again. My mind worries a bit, Katie. If they know I be 'ere afore, they could keep me 'ere a long time."

This new cell became "home" to the women for quite some time. Other "good things" came their way. The women were assigned jobs, making the days more bearable. At daylight a bell would ring, and the women went out to another room to wash and dress. After they straightened up their makeshift beds, they were led to work. They were assigned to various jobs. Some worked in the kitchen; others cleaned corridors, sewed, or did laundry, depending on their capabilities. Some of the women were taken to factories, but Katie and Mary were ordered to do kitchen work. They were relieved to find they would be together. It was hard work but satisfying. It was such a relief to have something to fill the long hours.

Katie, Mary, and other kitchen workers were first to rise in the morning to get food ready. They worked through breakfast, which consisted mostly of gruel and dry bread. After breakfast and clean up they went to chapel for thirty minutes. Afterwards they went back to work through lunch...more gruel. When cleanup was finished, they were allowed to walk a bit outside in the "pen," taking in fresh air. There was a short rest period before the evening meal had to be prepared and served. Finally, after all the meals were done for the day, the kitchen was cleaned and set up for the next day. After the day's work, some of them had visitors, but most of them were locked up until the next morning.

Their routine was the same day after day. Sleep came quickly in spite of the harsh conditions. Time wore on endlessly, and the women forged friendships. They found strength in one another and safety in numbers. They took it upon themselves to pester the gaoler for brooms and buckets to clean up their areas. Once they were given those things, they insisted on getting clean hay.

The gaoler would complain but usually gave in to their demands. "Blimey, I gets 'his job ter get away from my ol' woman at 'ome cause she nags me ter death. Now I got ten more women naggin' after me 'ere! Be enough to drive a man to rum."

Katie experienced a strange sense of contentment in her daily life. She wasn't nearly as frightened as she had been. The days ran together, and time was of no significance. She had no idea what day or month it was. She focused on keeping fit but noted she was getting thinner. She knew that was because of the physical work, but mostly because of the lack of proper food. Although she worked in the kitchen, she was watched closely. No one received extra food...no one.

A good piece of time passed until a different day from the rest dawned. The women were not let out for work or chapel.

As they stood around speculating, they were startled when a man came to the gate and yelled out, "All right, come forward and step out! Step to; ain't got all day! Line up 'ere and stop that blabberin'."

The gaoler lined the women up, then led them down the long dank hallway. They made a sharp turn into another room. Everyone was surprised to see the room clean and bright. Sunshine washed over the walls, floors, and their faces. As soon as their eyes adjusted, they saw buckets of water on a heavy table. A second table held folded material. They stood together, not knowing quite what to do.

Again the gaoler barked, "Line up 'ter git yer 'eads shaved!"

"No!" one of the women shouted. A few others protested as well. They had been taught all their lives that their hair was their glory. Many of them never had their hair cut before.

"Yas ain't got no choice in the matter an' I ain't got all day. This be done whether yas wants it to be or not. Now somebody better go sit in that chair."

One of the older women slowly walked over and sat down. Another man stepped forward. He had scissors, razor, soap, and a razor strap in hand. After cutting the woman's hair short, he proceeded to shave her scalp. The room grew quiet.

"Why would they do that to us?" Katie whispered Mary.

"Ain't got no idea, Katie, girl. Ne'er 'ad it done afore the other times I be 'ere."

Katie wanted to bolt as panic seized her, but there wasn't anything she could do. How many other humiliations would they have to endure?

A few of the women began protesting again until the gaoler threatened them. Others just cried softly. One by one the women's heads were shaved. Once that task was completed, they were instructed to bathe and put on clean clothes.

"Ain't ya ever seen water afore?" the gaoler barked when the women didn't move. They were not about to undress with him there.

"Git away with ye now, ya filthy bloke!" Mary snapped.

The jailer sniffed, spit, then wiped his mouth on his sleeve. Turning to Mary, he snarled, "Tain't as though I want to be lookin' at an ol' heifer such as ye."

The women informed him they would only bathe after the men left. Once the women's heads were shaved, the gaoler began to walk out, only hesitating enough to make sure the women weren't already undressing.

"I be just outside the door if ye tarts get any ideas 'bout runnin'. Or could be yas want me 'ter wash yer backs fer yas?" His lips curled back in a sneer, showing his blackened teeth.

The women began touching their heads. It was true; their long locks were gone. The high pile of hair verified that. Their "glory" lay there in the hay. They stood staring at the pile for a time. Slowly one of the women kneeled to pick some of the hair up. "Seems like I've just lost an old friend," she whispered.

Mary, seeing a blanket, picked it up. "Come lass, and 'elp me 'old this," she spoke to the woman kneeling. "Katie, come and bathe while we 'old this up 'fer ya."

Each woman took their turn holding the blanket. There were only three buckets of water along with a sliver of soap to wash, so they had to share. Katie took great pleasure in feeling a little cleaner. She made a mental note never to take a bath for granted again. They found the material on the table to be clean shifts to replace their filthy dresses. All were the same size, causing some women to drown and some to squeeze into them. While milling around, one of the women found an extra shift. She began to tear some material from it for a scarf. Katie made herself a scarf along with a belt.

Time dragged by as they awaited news of what awaited them. They began discussing their fate, and what would become of them now. There had to be a reason for the clean clothes and bath.

"Could it be we are going to be set free?" one of the women whispered with hope in her voice.

"Nay," Mary said, shaking her head. "They not shave our 'eads or give out clothes and water last time I was 'ere. They jest open the door and shew ol' Mary out."

"Maybe we are to be taken to see the magistrate," another woman offered. That was the better guess, Katie thought. Just then the gaoler came back with two other men.

"All right, ya tarts; come this away and make it quick!"

The women formed a line, but this time they were shackled together. The gaoler led them out with two other turnkeys bringing up the rear. The women labored up some stairs, then turned out to a courtyard. Everyone visibly straightened once they stepped into the fresh air and sunshine. How sweet the air smelled. They had breathed in stench for so long their lungs couldn't seem to fill enough. Katie couldn't believe how chilled she felt without her hair. Turning, she looked back at where they had just come from. It was amazing to have such filth and freshness so close together. The soft sound of a bird singing caused a tear to fall. How she loved being outside. A deep longing gripped her heart as she once again thought of home...her home that was no more.

The women were instructed to get into a cart. It proved to be difficult with the shackles, but they helped one another. Once all were loaded, the horses began plodding along.

"Wesley," the gaoler barked, "watch the ol' lady. She's crazy and mean. She almost castrated one of the men with her bare hands a time ago."

The man called Wesley turned to eye Mary. "Don't worry; she gives me any trouble, and we'll rope an' drag 'er." Mary stared straight ahead.

The cart lumbered through tall gates onto a city street. People scurried out of the way. Katie would never get used to the noise of the city. The sounds of people and horse's hooves echoed off the stone buildings. Filth ran in the streets, but it could not compare to the gaol. Even so, this was a rare treat for the women. It would have been most enjoyable, had it not been for the situation they were in. Stares and jeers from some of the people didn't help either. One thing they did know for sure: they were going to find out what their futures held soon. Little comfort was found in that knowledge.

3

Victoria

"For heaven's sake, Peter," the woman quipped, "stop pacing the floor. You are truly working up my nerves."

The man turned to look at his wife. As long as he could remember she loved to make decisions regarding his business. He could sidestep her for the most part, but this time she had him against the wall. He took a long drag off his cigar and slowly blew the smoke before speaking. "I just don't think it is realistic, Victoria. You must realize that women placed in these gaols are not the caliber as yourself. Besides, my dear, you really do not need to worry your little head about such matters."

"Peter, why do you insist on talking to me as if I were a child?" The woman moved with grace as she approached her husband.

Peter knew "it" wasn't over by the lift of her dainty chin. "All I mean, Victoria, is that these women are not decent thinking. They do not live by the standards you do. The same rules do not apply to them as to women such as you."

"Oh, for heaven's sake, Peter," the woman repeated herself, "what does it matter if a woman has learned gentle and feminine ways? Women are women, so how can you even think of sending single women on ships? It just isn't decent. I can't believe you would even consider such a thing, let alone agree to it."

Peter ran his fingers through his hair. He could tell there would be no reasoning with her. He wasn't about to tell her that women had been shipped out unmarried for many years now. Victoria gave her husband *the look.* He knew he had two choices; he could do as she said, or lie and tell her he would do as she said.

"Must we speak of this right now? We'll be late meeting our guests for dinner." Hoping to divert her attention, he gently touched her cheek.

"All right, Peter. We can discuss this later, but be assured I will be satisfied on this matter." Turning, she called her maid to attend to her.

Putting up with his wife's self-righteousness was a source of great irritation to Peter. Her chin was raised, but not her morals. Oh, Peter wasn't the most moral man either, but he didn't pretend to be by dictating to others...except for prisoners of course.

∽ʘ∾

After leaving her husband's suite of rooms, Victoria headed towards her own. As her maid brushed out her heavy black hair, she thought of Peter. How she loved being married to him. He always gave into her wishes, but that was because she knew how to handle him. She enjoyed the attention and prestige that came with her husband's position. Being married to a Common Law Judge had benefits indeed. Peter had to travel to many different towns to sit the bench, giving her freedom to do as she pleased. She accompanied people she enjoyed instead of the many stuffed shirts they had to socialize with. With Peter's appointment on the bench and her inheritance there was more than enough money for the lifestyle she loved so much.

Yes, Victoria was very happy with her life. She only had two fears: growing old and boredom. It was the second fear that caused her to help the "needy." When she heard Peter talking about those wretched women, she just knew she had to step in. Men just couldn't understand what a woman needed. Every woman wanted a man to take care of them, to give them a home and some stability. Certainly she understood it would be difficult to marry a stranger, especially a criminal, but the women were criminals themselves. That fact made it "right." At least they would have someone to help them in their lives. Yes, it was the best way, the only way. Victoria planned on talking to her father to make sure he would "convince" Peter of that fact.

The ride to the dining hall was peaceful. Once arriving they spotted their friends and quickly walked over.

"So, Peter, how is the world of law and order?" Crowley stood and offered his hand.

"I think we are all safe for now," Peter answered.

The women hugged, then sat after their husbands pulled out their chairs. They ate a light dinner due to the theater date afterwards, but found they still had time before the opening.

"You see, Peter, Lydia agrees with me concerning the female prisoners." Victoria smiled at her husband.

"Now, Victoria, must we bring that up again? I was looking forward to a more uneventful evening. I prefer not to talk about prisoners or court matters of any kind."

Victoria could not be so easily swayed. "What do you think, Brent? Do you feel that women should be shipped off to…God knows where? They would have no safety in marriage with men all around!"

The man squirmed before answering. He hated to be thrust between the couple's disagreements. "Well, I'm sure Peter will have the right answer whatever he decides," he answered tactfully.

Victoria sighed. "Leave it to men to stick together on an issue that concerns the welfare of women."

Peter glanced at his pocketwatch. "It's time to be off. We don't want to be late, do we ladies?" Once in the carriage the talk again turned to crime.

"Did you hear that poor Mrs. Pike was accosted on Newberry Road, and the thugs got away?" Lydia stated.

Victoria looked at her friend, grateful for her bringing the conversation back to where she wanted it. "It probably wouldn't matter if they did catch them," Victoria jumped in. "There is no room to put any of these people. Our gaols are full, and so are the prison hulks in the harbor."

"It almost sounds like you have more sympathy for these ruffians than for the victims," Lydia stated harshly.

Bristling, Victoria bit back, "Don't misunderstand me. It's just that with so many criminals abounding, and nowhere to go with them, things could get much worse than they are now."

"Hallelujah!" Peter yelled. "Now, my dear, you have it: the reason we are sending these prisoners to Australia."

"Peter, I never said I didn't want these people sent away. It's just that we need to make sure the single women are sent out with husbands. I believe it's our Christian duty. I've never wanted to keep these prisoners here. I, like everyone else, want these people as far away from us as possible."

Peter scowled in the shadows. *So much for Christian duty.*

"Oh, what a wonderful idea!" Lydia exclaimed. "Can you imagine marrying a stranger, especially a convict who did only God knows what?"

"Lydia!" her husband jumped in. "Try to calm yourself. I'm not sure ladies should be discussing such things!" Lydia, properly chastised, sunk back against the seat.

"Oh, for heaven's sakes, Brent," Victoria said, "she is only stating a fact. These women are prisoners and have questionable character. They need our guidance in moral and spiritual matters. It may be difficult for them to marry a stranger but just think of the alternatives…Actually, I don't want to think of the alternatives."

Peter's dark mood deepened. Once his wife sunk her teeth into something, you couldn't get her to let go. He knew he would be forced to take steps to satisfy Victoria. That or suffer, and suffer he would.

Victoria, perhaps sensing she had overstepped when the only thing coming from her husband was silence, tried to smooth things out a bit. "These people can thank whoever it is they thank that Peter is their judge. At least you know they will get justice for their acts. If it were up to Earl Pierson, they would all be hanged. It's said he's hung more people than a woman hangs laundry."

Peter had to give her credit. She was good, but he knew his wife was "handling" him. She was a master manipulator and practiced on him constantly. He had realized this a long time ago, and hated it. He knew his wife had been taught by the best, his father-in-law. Every chance he got, the old man used his daughter to let Peter know what it was he wanted done in the court. Since he had "handed" Peter his position, the old man expected Peter to judge in accordance to his will.

Victoria continued her stroking. "Father knew when he stepped down that his recommendations would carry a lot of weight. He knew that Peter was the best man for the job."

There it was. Peter expected it to come sooner than this but knew it would come. Victoria had to remind him and everyone else that her father gave him his position. Deep down he felt envy for the men being shipped out. Given a second chance, he wasn't sure he would make the same choices he had, in business or marriage. The best thing about his position was the traveling, being away from the constant dickering of his wife. It brought him peace and a chance to explore the pleasures he wasn't able to when at home. Tomorrow he would be leaving again. It couldn't happen soon enough for him.

Victoria couldn't wait until tomorrow. Her husband would leave and be gone a couple of weeks. This would give her enough time to put into motion her plan. She would have satisfaction in regards to these women and their situation. This would also give her enough time to see her latest "male friend." A thrill sent shivers through her body. How she felt sorry for anyone who wasn't her. She had the perfect life, and all that went with it. She had beauty, intelligence, money, and power. Oh, and her Christian duty, as well. That was important too. Those women were lucky that she was looking out for their best interest. They should all be on their knees thanking her. Yes, life was good.

But after the rush of pleasure left her, she was left with a sense of emptiness. If her life was so perfect, why did she feel so empty? *I'm just being silly,* she thought. *I am the luckiest woman in the world.* And yet the emptiness remained...

The females were led to an underground floor of a large building where other women were already held. The gaoler turned, locking the heavy door behind him. One small lantern did nothing but send dark shadows across the room. The room itself was long and narrow with wood planks for them to sit on. Hay lay on the floor with a few blankets scattered about. The women snuggled together, trying to fight off the chill. The darkness matched their mood. Despair was their constant companion. The uncertainty about their future lay heavy on them.

Mary whispered, "Katie, I be hearin' the women talk and 'tis afraid I am. They be speakin' of ships and sailin' away to some far-off place."

Katie despaired even more. If Mary was afraid, Katie was petrified. "Before we get ourselves upset, let's ask them about it," she suggested.

Mary nodded.

"Aye, many ships have left already," one of the women shared. "Most of the ships don't make it, so I hear. Sea monsters get them for the most part afore they reach land."

"Why are ya frightenin' these women?" Mary said. "'Tis bad enough without ya runnin' yer mouth off!"

"'Tis true what I say! I be knowin' 'bout the sea. Me cousin sailed a time or two, and he told me of all the demons of the sea!"

Mary eyed the woman. "'ow can it be if yer cousin sailed a time or two, an' faced them demons, 'e came back ter tell tales?"

Shrilly the woman insisted her cousin had just barely escaped with his own life. Katie decided to listen but only believe about half of what she heard. Reality for Katie was frightening enough. "Where do the ships go, and who decides if you go or not?" she asked the woman.

"I 'ear different places," another woman spoke up. "Some call it Owstraler or something like that."

Another woman added, "I think it's called Australia. I know of no monsters except the ones who keep this prison, but I have heard it is a great and terrible journey. If you make the journey at all, you then go to this foreign land to face unknown dangers. I have even heard there are black, ferocious men there."

Mary shrugged and quipped, "Sounds like all the men aroun' 'ere. Sounds like 'ome." The women chuckled.

The same woman added, "I hear 'tis the magistrate who decides our fate to go or not." That made the most sense. The woman went on. "I do know that if you are married, your husband can't go with you. Your babes can, if your husband lets them. I know of a woman whose husband was sent out; she never heard from him again."

"Do you think if we get sent there, we'll ever get back home?" someone asked.

"Can't say, but from what I hear, I doubt it. I don't know if a lot of the ships make it. If they do, I don't know what happens next. I would guess those poor souls are worked to death." The woman seemed to forget that she was now one of those "poor souls."

Katie noticed Mary pull the old scrap of cloth from her pocket and begin to run it through her fingers. It seemed that whenever Mary was troubled, the cloth soothed her. Katie was about to ask her about it, but thought better of it. If Mary wanted her to know, she would tell her.

"Wha' if ya can't swim?" Mary spoke up. Katie thought she detected a quiver in her voice.

"What does that have to do with it? They don't care if we can swim or not," was the answer given.

Mary nodded.

Finally the women grew quiet. They faced another cold, damp, lonely night. Suddenly men showed up with extra blankets and food.

"'Ere be warm food for your bellies. I don't want no trouble tonight. Sleep 'cause yer gettin' hell on the morrow." No one had the courage to ask what he meant by that.

They ate in silence, then tried to rest. Sleep was lost to them, all except for Mary. Her snores would have made a sailor proud.

A thought had been haunting Katie since they left the gaol. What if she was to be hanged? In some ways it didn't seem any worse or better than being shipped off to the end of the world. Fear was fear, and Katie feared them both. What a strange name... Australia. It sounded as if it wasn't part of this world at all. Her mind could not comprehend how big the sea was, let alone another land. She had nothing to gauge her thoughts on, so was unable to soothe herself. Were there really sea monsters, and who were those ferocious black men? She gave up trying to sleep, but somewhere in the night she did. She slept deep and dreamless as if she did not have a care in the world.

Voices roused Katie, and for a split second she couldn't remember where she was. When reality hit, dread swept over her once again. Would she ever feel anything but fear and trepidation ever again? Katie stretched, trying to get the "kinks" out. Soon food was brought in. Most of the women stared at it, but Katie forced herself to eat. It was cold and tasteless, but there was no telling when she would get another chance. The others saw the wisdom in it and ate.

A gaoler barked out, causing the women to jump, "'Urry up with yas now. Day of judgment fer ya sins be 'ere, and the judge ain't takin' a notion to wait on ya, so git movin'."

The women stood quietly, not knowing what they were supposed to do. Fear in their faces seemed to bring about a lighter mood in the man. "Ah, don't want to face the music, does yas? Ya likes to play, but when it comes to payin' fer it, ya be afraid ain't yas?"

Mary was about to mention the fact that he didn't seem so innocent in life himself, but thought better of it.

"Line up now, and git yerselves ready to see the ol' judges. They don't take to ya being late so 'urry!"

The day Katie had been waiting for had finally come. She strangely felt relieved and fearful at the same time. Relieved, for the waiting was over. Soon she would know some of what lay ahead. Once again the women were lined up and shackled. The chains seemed heavier than before.

"The ol' men don't want no prisoners unchained in their courtroom neither. Especially wild women," the man scoffed. "Ya be a dangerous bunch. I can sees it fer sure. I like wild women even without any 'air on their 'eads." He snickered, pinching one of them.

The women were led out into the sunshine, but it didn't seem quite as bright as yesterday. They crossed a courtyard filled with flowerbeds of brightly colored blooms and an ornate fountain. *Why put things of beauty in such an ugly place?* Katie thought.

Arriving across the courtyard, the women were shoved into some kind of backroom. Other women were there as well so it was quite crowded and stifling. To Katie it seemed that they were either freezing or barely able to breathe. The turnkeys left them shackled and alone. Some of the women whispered among themselves, but most were quiet.

A woman Katie didn't know began sharing her pitiful story. How she had to steal food for her children after her husband died. Now she didn't know where her children were. She began crying bitterly and woefully. Katie wanted to comfort her, but she had no comfort to give. Someone else stepped forward to hold the pitiful creature. Even the hardest heart melted in the woman's brokenness. Without a word the women began joining hands as if to strengthen one another.

"Maybe we should pray?" someone offered.

Another shyly began praying a stumbling, sincere prayer. "Dear God, I ne'er talked ta ya afore. I don't know if ya can even 'ear me, but we are scared. We don't know what all is goin' ta 'appen, but 'elp us, God. We ain't got nobody else in the world. Please God, 'elp that woman, and 'er babes. Thank ya, God." Everyone whispered, "Amen." Many hours passed, giving them a lot of time to think and worry, but not Mary; she had fallen sound asleep. She never ceased to amaze Katie. Just about the time Katie thought she had Mary figured out, she would surprise her again. Mary had unquestionably lived a difficult life. Even so, Katie never heard her complain nor ask for anything for herself. The older woman seemed harsh at times, but her concern for others was apparent. Katie felt closer to her than anyone. With tenderness, she stretched her blanket over the sleeping Mary. Lying back, Katie tried to rest, but thoughts ran through her head. Most of the women had the same problem. There were many questions, but few answers. One thing was for sure: their day of reckoning was here.

4

Sentenced

Heavy shackles caused the women to hobble as they walked into a large room. Bright sunlight caused them to squint. Once their eyes adjusted, they could see the Victorian splendor of the room. Many had never seen such opulence. You could have told them they just entered Queen Victoria's court, and they would have believed you.

Ornate carved wood showed throughout. There were heavy red drapes elegantly hung on the four ceiling-to-floor windows. A beautiful chandelier hung in the center of the room. On each side of the room, tall lantern posts stood guard. In the front of the room a massive desk stood on a much higher platform, making it easier for the magistrates to look down on everyone. The two magistrates, wearing white wigs, sat side-by-side.

Two men dressed in red uniforms with gold braiding and black hats with feathers stood on each side of the high platform. Polished heavy wooden benches on one side of the room were filled with spectators. A large platform with a railing running the length of it held male prisoners. The women were led to stand behind the men.

Everyone stared as the women entered the room. Red, standing at the very front of the platform, watched Katie walk with her head held high. He felt strangely proud of her.

Katie was shaking head to foot. She had decided to be brave but forgot to tell her body. She hadn't thought about her shaved head until she saw the big man. Suddenly she felt her face flame. Strange that she would even care what he thought. She noted that he smiled, but she pretended not to notice.

The women looked around the room. A little man with a white

wig and specks on his nose stood in front of the magistrate's desk. Near to him was a table stacked full of papers. In the center of the room stood a small platform with railings on three sides. Katie guessed it was for prisoners.

Court was already in progress when the women came in. Only a few male prisoners remained to face their fate. The small man, wrestling with all the papers, seemed to know very little of what was going on. From time to time he would make some weak comments. He kept looking at his pocketwatch as if being held from something important. Katie figured he must be a barrister. *God help us all*, she prayed. If he was the only defender they had, the prisoners might as well grab the oars and head for Australia.

Peter Reeves was anxious to end this day. When the women had entered, it caused quite a stir. He cleared his throat, declaring, "Silence in the room."

One by one the men left were led to the smaller platform. Once a man was sentenced, Peter asked him whether he was married or not. The answer given depended on whether the man was put in the back room or led back to the gaol. The barrister wondered at the question of marriage but said nothing.

Calmly Red watched the proceedings until two turnkeys came to lead him towards the smaller platform. He tried his best to keep his calm demeanor. They released him from the "common" chains and put separate irons on him. They doublechecked to make sure he was secure.

Katie leaned forward to hear his name as one of the magistrates read it out: James Patrick Murphy. *A fine Irish name,* she thought.

Magistrate Reeves glanced at the prisoner being led forward. He was glad this man was chained. Usually one man guarded each prisoner, but they had two guards on this one. The size of the man was impressive.

After hearing the charge, Peter addressed the man. "Do you realize that by stealing that food you left those deserving of it hungry?"

"Yes sir," Red answered.

"Do you have anything to say in your defense?" Peter added.

Red simply stated he was wrong in what he did. "Do you have anything you would like to say, Barrister Boggs, in defense of this man?" Peter looked at the defender.

"No sir. This man has stated that he is guilty of the theft, so indeed there is nothing more to be said."

Peter conferred with his partner, Magistrate Mathers, before sentencing Red. He looked down at his desk as if going over some information, but in reality he was thinking. It was unusual for a man to state he was guilty. He was more accustomed to hearing lies, pleading, and excuses. Again, Peter was impressed with this man. "Prisoner, are you married, or do you have family in these parts or own property here?"

"No sir, no wife, family, or property."

Peter continued, "You are hereby sentenced to be transported to Botany Bay for no less than seven years. You will be given the privilege of making a new life for yourself there. At the end of your seven-year sentence, you can stay there or you may choose to be shipped back to England. I hope you will take advantage of this opportunity I am giving you to make a new home and life for yourself. Next prisoner, forward!"

Mathers was amused with Reeves's little speech. What had gotten into him? He was talking as if he really cared, and why in the world would he ask if the men were married or not? No one told him of it. Clearing his throat, Mathers leaned towards Reeves. "If it's not too much trouble, could you explain what this is about?"

Peter didn't like to explain himself to anyone. Trying to curb his irritation, he answered, "This is something new. We're allowing the single female prisoners to pick one of the men to marry. It's either that, or stay here in one of the gaols. We aren't transporting single women out."

"That's surprising to hear," Mathers responded. "When was this decision made, and by whom?"

"Can we discuss this later?" Reeves all but snapped.

"Certainly," Mathers stated.

James Patrick expected his sentence. It didn't matter that he stole because he was hungry; stealing was stealing. What did surprise him was the way he felt...completely at peace. He heard the journey was survivable at best. He knew the "new land" was not much better, but he had decided never to doubt his Lord ever again. He would have to face the consequences but knew the Lord would sustain him.

Katie's heart went out to the big man, but why? Why did she care about him? In any case she knew she was accused of doing the same crime as he, so her punishment would probably be the same. Anger filled her. Why was she even here? She looked around, only to blush when she saw many eyes turned in her direction. Why should she feel shame when she didn't do anything?

Lifting her chin, she stood straighter. Who were these people to judge her? How shallow were their lives that they needed to sit all day in a room, and see others judged and sentenced? Would she be able to convince the judge of her innocence? She had been shouting her innocence from the beginning, but no one believed her yet. Why would he? Only Tess and God knew she wasn't guilty. She certainly didn't expect either one of them to show up any time soon to speak on her behalf. She felt a longing in her soul...to be close to God like Gran had been. No, she wasn't going to do it; just call on God when she got in trouble. It wasn't right. It was too late now. She would have to get through this on her own.

Once the men were finished, the women were led, one by one, to the dreaded platform. Every once in awhile the barrister would make a feeble attempt to defend the prisoner, but each time the prisoner was found guilty anyway. Katie wondered if this man got paid for being there. The one thing that puzzled everyone was the question that had been asked of each prisoner: "Are you married?" It had never mattered before.

One of the women was found guilty of killing her husband and sentenced to hang. She tried to explain that her husband had beaten several of their children so badly that one of them had died. She explained how she tried to protect her children from him, but it didn't matter. She had committed murder. She would hang. Katie wondered sadly what would happen to the children. Why was there so much suffering in this world? The hysterical woman had to be half carried out of the courtroom.

The day wore on, causing a woman to faint from the heat. Just about the time Katie thought she would die of thirst, buckets of water were brought in. They were given a few minutes to sit and drink. The

36

women gave a collective sigh of relief as they sat leaning against the back wall. After ten minutes all prisoners were led out in small groups for personal breaks. When they returned, the lanterns and chandelier were lit, and proceedings resumed.

Mary's name was the first called. The common shackles were removed, replaced by a smaller set. As Mary was being led, Katie noticed she was hobbling. *Probably from the leg irons,* Kathie thought to herself. She sent up a quick prayer for Mary. She hoped God would listen, even if it was her doing the praying.

Peter barked at Mary once she took her place, "Your charge is prostitution. What do you say, guilty or not?"

Mary looked him square in the eye. "I be as innocent as yourself be."

A gasp was heard from the spectators. Katie's heart sank. Surely Mary had just sealed her fate with that remark. Everyone turned to look at the man who held Mary's future in his hands. They expected him to be scarlet with anger, but after a second of surprise he began to laugh! Everyone in the courtroom was surprised by his reaction, but soon most of the spectators were laughing along with him. Magistrate Mathers covered his mouth to hide a smile.

Barrister Boggs spoke up. "I find this lack of respect quite disturbing, sir!"

Peter leaned forward, causing the laughter to die. "I, on the other hand sir, find this woman quite refreshing," Peter turned his attention back to Mary. She squirmed a little under his gaze. He began ruffling some papers. "I see that you have been arrested before. What do you have to say to the court?"

Mary was surprised at this young man's response to her. Casting her eyes down, she responded, "Aye sir, I cannot lie 'bout that, yer Lordship. 'Tis truth told that it be a time or two I be locked up, but there be another truth, sir. I would ne'er be able to make it to that foreign land. I not be sayin' that I have not wronged anyone. It just be that I'm not strong to take the sea 'tis all." Mary had been afraid of water all her life. The sea was the most frightening thing imaginable to her. She would drop dead of fear if she had to sail anywhere. Only her stiff old corpse would be left.

In a gentler tone, Peter spoke. "You have repeated arrests, and it would seem clear that you have no intention of turning yourself around. I have no choice but to sentence you to five years in service of the gaols. You will serve at Newgate. At least you will have a roof over your head, and honest work."

Katie found herself holding her breath. She looked at Mary for her reaction. At first it seemed as if Mary had not heard the sentence. She stood there quiet, then looked up at the younger man and nodded. Five years in the gaol was far better than death at sea. Mary stepped down and was led out.

"Next!" the Magistrate called out.

Katie watched Mary until the pulling of her wrist brought her attention back. Her turn had come. Queasiness threatened. She fought the sick feeling. All this was humiliating enough without getting sick too. Katie tried to steel herself. No matter what, she had to remember that she was innocent. She refused to feel shame. She placed her hands on the rail to steady herself. Tears threatened to flow, so she closed her eyes and clenched her teeth. She had never felt so alone and scared. She comforted herself by thinking, *I'll cry later.*

Peter was getting tired. The heat was worse because of his robes and wig. He fought the urge to run out of the room. With resolve he looked down at the paperwork for the next case. Another thief…would this day not end?

Peter hated the way they shuffled their feet when they walked. He seemed to forget about the leg irons. Yes, indeed, his contempt was harder and harder to hide when it came to these cowards. They wouldn't think twice of killing or robbing, but they had no backbone when it came to facing up to their deeds. He was starting to believe that he was the one who had been given a life sentence. Having to face these miserable liars year after year was growing wearisome. His only reprieve today had been the old prostitute, and the big man. Prisoners usually didn't tell the truth. It was quite refreshing in deed. He looked up at a young woman standing on the platform. She was the one who held his interest when she first entered his court. She stood out from the others.

Katie looked back at him. Her eyes stayed fixed on him until he looked down, breaking the spell.

Peter spoke up. "It says here that you are a thief. Is that correct?"

Katie's tongue seemed twice its size, causing her words to stick in her throat.

"Well?" Peter questioned as he looked up from his papers.

Katie swallowed. "I have never stolen anything in my life, sir."

"So you are completely innocent then?"

"No sir," Katie came back. "I'm not innocent in my life, but I did not steal what I am accused of."

"Do you have any proof you can offer?"

"No."

Once again Peter looked down at the papers on his desk.

Katie tried to will her eyes off this man who was about to change her life. She wanted to look away, but could not. She heard the man let out a sigh, as if disgusted.

Peter picked up a paper and held it up for Katie to see. "I have sworn testimony here stating you did steal a necklace. Your word is of no value here. If that is all the proof you have, I am afraid I must find you guilty."

Without asking, she knew who had written the statement of lies and then sworn them to be true.

"Are you married, or do you have children?"

Katie shook her head.

"I sentence you to seven years. You will be transported out with the others. That is all."

Katie opened her mouth to defend herself, but what could she say in her defense? She offered no resistance as she was led to the back room. Seething anger filled her. Thoughts of strangling Tess touched her mind.

The day wore on, causing many of the spectators to leave. Evening fell, and all were exhausted. Hoping to speed things along, Mathers read the cases to Peter, letting him judge all the prisoners.

Finally the last woman stood before him. Even so this would not be the end to the day. Now he had to face the unmarried women, and ask them if they wanted to marry or not. Peter wasn't sure how this new procedure would work. He wondered how the female prisoners would take the ultimatum: work in the gaols or marry a stranger. He was sure some would think of it as a double sentence. Of course they could refuse to marry. What did it matter really? Marriage wasn't a sacred thing to people like these anyway. After the last prisoner was sentenced he had the gaolers bring all the unmarried prisoners back inside the courtroom. They were led to the benches since all spectators had left.

Mathers excused himself. If Reeves wanted to play the "who's married and who's not" game, then let him. He had better things to do.

As the women and men were being seated, Peter came down from his desk to stand before them. Katie had never been in court before so she had no idea what to expect. There was no way for her to know that this was highly unusual behavior for a magistrate. Peter slowly looked at each prisoner. They would visibly straighten when his eyes fell on them. He wasn't sure how to present his news, so he just stood there looking at them for a few moments.

Fear hung in the air. The prisoners wondered why they were brought back to court. Why hadn't they been taken out with the others? Something was amiss, but what?

Clearing his throat and placing his hands behind his back, Peter began pacing. He stopped at one point as if ready to speak but turned and began pacing again. Finally he decided to be direct. "I suppose you are wondering why you have been kept at court. As you can see, only those who have been sentenced to sail and are not married are here. It has been discussed at great length and decided that those unmarried women who have been sentenced to sail will need to be married."

A gasp could be heard throughout the group.

Peter continued, "I realize this is a surprise to you, but this has been decided for your best interest. To ship out single women is difficult on both them and the men. As you can see, there are only three women here that this applies to. We will not force this upon anyone. However, if you decide not to marry, you will be given the only other choice. You will have to serve your time in one of the gaols here."

Katie barely heard what was being said. Had she actually heard him say marry? Marry? Marry…who?

"Women, you will be allowed to pick out a husband from these men. If the man is not willing, then you may pick another. If no man here will marry you, then you will be sent to a gaol to serve your time. The time spent in a gaol will be the same amount of time that you would have served at your destination. You will be brought back here to voice your decision tomorrow morning. If you decide to marry, then you will be shipped out with your husband. You need to decide now, so look the men over well. Guards, give these people fifteen minutes to talk with one another. After that, take them back to the cells below to be held until court tomorrow. I want to remind all of you that this could be an exceptional chance for you. This is a chance to have your own family and home. I would hope that you take advantage of this opportunity, and make a good life for yourselves. You may find your life can be quite rewarding when what you obtain is from honest work. Guards, watch them carefully. Let them speak to one another no longer than the allotted time." Turning back to the prisoners, Peter added, "I would suggest that you don't let shyness hinder your time." With that, Peter turned and walked out. Tomorrow would be another long day.

Katie was still trying to make sense of his words. Everyone turned to look at each other. Some of the men had smirks on their faces, and some wore the same look of surprise as the women.

One of the gaolers shouted, "All right, snap to. Ain't got but a few minutes."

Katie was shaken. Fifteen minutes! How could a decision that big be given only minutes? She started looking at the men. Could she spend seven more years in that hell she had just come out of? Things were a little better since she worked in the kitchen but still…. She thought about the magistrate's words; of having her own home and family. She had always dreamed of that, but not this way!

One of the women jumped up and grabbed one of the men's arms. "This bloke is mine, so don't be thinkin' otherwise!" she addressed the other women. She had surprised the man, but he smiled and nodded, letting her know it was fine with him. A few of the other men chuckled.

Suddenly a soothing calm came over Katie. She knew what she had to do. Standing, she stepped forward and stood in front of James Patrick. He lifted himself off the bench with surprising ease as she approached. He towered over her. "Sir, I do not think I would live if I had to stay long in this place. I have seen your kindness and your compassion for others. It has touched me. If you marry me, sir, I promise I will be as good a wife as I can be. I'm strong, a hard worker, and in spite of being here, I am an honest person. I would not do anything to shame you." Katie couldn't think of anything else to say. Her mind raced. What if he turned her down? What if he accepted? What if...?

Red looked down at her. How small and fragile she seemed. Dark circles lay under her eyes. Her skin seemed almost translucent. It had been a shock to see her head shaved. Where there had been silky brown hair, little peach fuzz now appeared. A feeling of protectiveness swept over him, and his heart pounded.

For a second Katie thought he was going to turn away from her. What would she do then?

A loud voice interrupted her thoughts. "Don't be doin' it, miss!" a man with no teeth yelled. "He be a man eater! I 'ear say he eats the flesh of the innocent!"

"Shut up, ye crazy ol' goat!" the gaoler snapped.

Katie looked at the toothless man, then turned away.

The old man continued, "It be fine with me if you get kilt, and done eaten by the bloke. Serves ye right fer not taken heed of my words, lass. Cannot say ya wasn't told of it."

Red wondered what the man was raving about. He stepped closer to Katie, speaking in hushed tones. "What I say is to you alone. I'm not sure what the future will be. I have been alone most of my life and struggle to care for myself at times. I don't know if I can properly care for you. Especially in the situation I'm in right now."

Katie understood what he was saying, but felt he was her only hope. "I thank you for your honesty, sir, but I have no home or family left. I do not know what the future holds like you, but we could help

42

each other. I will try not to complain or be a burden to you. I know I don't look strong now, but I am a hard worker. Usually I'm cheerful, when not in such a difficult place as this." She held her breath, knowing what he was about to say would change her world forever...one way or the other.

Red admired her strength. The thought of having someone to care for, and have them care for him, filled him with warmth.

"Make up yer mind, man," the chainer spoke up. "Ya got a minute left."

Red felt something awaken within him; the knowledge that it was meant to be. She was meant to be his, and God was bestowing a rare and wonderful gift on him. Even though he didn't feel love now, he somehow knew that given time they would have it.

He reached for Katie's hand. There they stood, both in chains while everyone gawked at them. He smiled at her. "Then so be it. We will wed, and I too give you my word that I will be the best husband that I can be." His look of tenderness made Katie blush. He continued, "Maybe I should tell you my name if we're to be married. My Christian name is James Patrick Murphy, but everyone calls me Red."

Katie whispered, "Aye, I heard your name in the courtroom. I also heard others call you Red. I will try to do my best to make you glad for your decision. I would like to call you by your given name, James Patrick. My Christian name is Kathryn Elizabeth Brady, but almost everyone calls me Katie."

Red repeated, "Katie."

In a second their "moment" ended, and they were thrust back with the others.

"Ye be sorry fer it all, lass," hissed the toothless man. "Ye don't believe it now, but I 'ear he does eat the flesh. He will surely put harm to ya."

"Shut up ya ol' fool, or I'll take a bite outta ya meself!" the gaoler yelled. "What about yerself, woman?" He turned to the third woman. "Best to git up to grab yerself one of these fine gents afore time is gone."

Everyone watched the woman. She kept her gaze on the floor.

"Fine then. All ye prisoners on yer feet, and make 'er snappy. Me supper awaits me!" the gaoler barked.

5

Matrimony

Katie and the other two women were the only ones in the cell. Mary and the others must have been taken back to the gaol. Soon food was brought, and to their surprise it was hot and plentiful.

The other woman who had decided to marry came and sat next to Katie. "Tain't it something that we had to marry one of them blokes?" she asked with her mouth full. "My man was surprised I grabbed him, eh?" The woman giggled. "I had my eye on him afore, so the choosing weren't so hard."

Katie smiled at her, not knowing how to respond. She looked over at the other woman sitting by herself, noting she wasn't eating. Getting up, Katie grabbed some food to take over to her. "Aren't you hungry?" Katie asked her.

The woman was in such deep thought that she jumped at Katie's voice. "Oh, I nary saw you standing there," she sputtered. "Aye 'tis hungry I am, but I have my mind on other things." After thanking Katie, she took the bowl. Katie turned to walk away, but stopped when the woman began talking again. "Couldn't believe my ears when that judge said we would have to marry a stranger. Not me. I have had enough trouble from menfolk. At least here I know what to expect. How can you marry a stranger?"

Katie tried to sort her feelings out before answering. It was strange, but she wasn't afraid to marry James Patrick. In the depths of her soul she knew she would be safe. However, she was afraid of sailing far away to a land she couldn't even visualize. What amazed her was the fact that she had a sense of excitement about it all as well. She turned to the woman and spoke softly. "We have been given only two choices. I feel I have made the best decision for myself. I am afraid of sailing far away, though."

"Aye, 'tis a hard decision to be sure. Well, may the good Lord watch o'er all of us," the woman added.

Katie nodded, and then turned back to her food. Her mind went to the events of the day. After she finished eating, she laid back on a blanket. It didn't take her long to fall into a deep, dreamless sleep. She was exhausted.

⤺⤻

Red sat off by himself, resting his back against the cell wall. He couldn't keep his mind off his soon-to-be bride. He felt anxious to marry the gentle girl. Her name! What was her name? It was Kate, no Katherine, no Katie. Yes, that was it—Katie Elizabeth Brady. He felt everything from excitement to fear to shyness. When would they be married? Would she have picked him for her husband in different circumstances? What was he thinking? Of course not! She wasn't given much choice. Doubts filled him. How could he marry with nothing to call his own? Again he had to remind himself about the Lord being in control. He remembered how he felt peace with the decision to marry her. Soon sleep called him. Closing his eyes, Katie's face came to him, and once again he knew it was meant to be. She was meant to be his. He smiled in the dark.

⤺⤻

The morning found the women being led back into the courtroom to give their decision. Katie's mind raced. Had she rushed into it? She almost began laughing out loud. Of course she had rushed into it…she had no choice. She knew she could change her mind, but wouldn't. She looked around for James Patrick, but the men were not there yet. A few minutes later they could hear someone barking out orders.

"Git goin', blokes! Time be runnin' an' we best not keep the good magistrate waitin' on us." Everyone knew the gaoler was saying that for the magistrate's benefit, but he could have saved his breath. Peter wasn't in the room yet. The gaoler led the two men towards the women, then went to stand over by the other chainer.

"Ain't like 'im to be late," the one said to the other. "Hope this be o'er soon. Gonna be a hot one again today."

The other chainer joked, "Don't wan't no cryin' from ya when the wedding comes. I ain't got no hanky." The two laughed, slapping each other on the back.

Peter finally stepped into the room wearing his robe but not his wig. Katie thought he looked even younger without his hairpiece. Stepping up to his desk on the high platform, Peter spoke directly to the prisoners. "I see that you have made your decisions to marry since there are two couples in front of me. I would like all four of you to stand before me. Gaolers, remove their chains." After their chains were removed, they stepped up to the front of the room. Red moved next to Katie. He gave her a smile of reassurance, noting the scarf on her head.

Peter looked intently at the two couples. He then addressed the women. "Have you thought this through?"

Katie couldn't believe he would even ask them that. He had given them no time to consider anything and pretty much no choice in the matter.

Both women simply answered, "Yes, sir."

Peter then turned to the men. "What about you? Are you both in agreement to marrying these women?"

They both answered, "Yes, sir."

Then Peter asked all four of them, "Are you prepared to marry now?" They all nodded in agreement. Peter stepped down from his desk and instructed the two couples to step closer to the front. He married the two couples in one ceremony. Before they could say, "I do," it was finished. They stood looking uncomfortable, not sure what to do next. Peter stepped back up to his desk and spoke to the couples.

"Your marriages are legal and binding. I will have you sign these papers. If you cannot write, make your mark. You will not see one another until the time comes to set sail. I have decided to give you one hour to visit. Gaolers, take them to the back of the room. Let them sit, and bring them something to eat. Give them one hour before taking them back to the gaol. Do not chain them again until the hour is up, but I want them guarded well." He then led the two couples to a smaller table with official-looking papers.

James Patrick and Kathryn Elizabeth found that their new spouse could write as they signed their names.

Peter again turned to the couples. "I understand this must be difficult for you, but I want you to realize you have been given a wonderful opportunity. You now have family and will soon have a chance to make something out of your lives. It will be a hard life, but having someone to help you in your endeavors will make it easier. You are the first couples to marry by order of the court. I feel especially hopeful that you will succeed. God bless your marriages, and good luck." With that Peter turned, disappearing into an adjoining room.

The gaolers shuffled up to the couples in the front, sputtering all the way. "Blimey, ya would think 'e be speakin' to the Queen 'erself, God blessin' ya and all. All right with yas, 'urry up to the back now. We best get yer food so we can serve ya like ye be the royals and all. Yas won't be getting chained, but be mindful now, we be watchin' yas. Now sit yerselfs down."

The couples sat at opposite ends of the row for privacy. James turned to get a better look at his bride. He noticed how flushed she looked. "Are you all right?"

Nodding, she softly answered, "Aye, I am fine—just out of breath with everything happening." A pleasant feeling filled her, causing her to blush. Both sat quietly for some time until they heard a strange noise. Looking around, they saw the other couple engaged in a long passionate kiss. Now they both blushed.

Soon the chainers brought some food. Red wondered if he should mention how nice he thought Katie looked. She probably wouldn't believe him, not with her shaved head. Katie wondered if she should mention how brave she thought James was, but thought better of it. Both tried hard to think of something to say until they both began talking at once. They burst out laughing. Katie liked his smile. Deep dimples creased his cheeks.

After their meal they began speaking of everyday things. They discovered they had a lot in common. Neither of them had any family, except for each other now. They spoke of their fears and hopes for the future. They both confessed how they always wanted family of their own. Katie showed a great deal of knowledge in farming, which pleased James. They had another thing in common. Katie had lost Gran when their cottage burned to the ground just as James had lost his parents. All too soon it was time for them to part.

"Take care of yourself, Mrs. Murphy. I'm not sure when I will see you again." James Patrick smiled at the surprise on Katie's face.

"Oh, that's right! My name is changed now!"

They had only a moment more together. A strange sense of disappointment filled them as they were separated. The gaolers gruffly placed them in chains once again. It always amazed Katie how some people preferred treating people roughly when given any degree of power. It seemed to annoy the gaolers that the magistrate spoke to them as human beings.

The four were hoisted up into a cart and headed back to the gaol. During the ride back James would smile at Katie as if to let her know everything would work out. She realized she now had someone who cared for her. That knowledge gave her hope. *I will take care of you too,* she thought.

Once at the gaol, the men were led one way and the women another. James turned to speak to Katie. "I don't know when I will see you next, but you must eat as much as you can. You must take care of yourself!"

Katie nodded, keeping her eyes on him until he was out of sight. Slowly she turned, letting herself be led away. Funny how alone she felt once she was separated from him. It would be a battle to keep her spirits up, but now she had someone else to think of. Maybe she didn't know what the future would bring, but at least her life was moving forward.

What a difference a day made...married! Tears welled up as she thought of how Gran had talked about having a wedding for her one day. She had told Katie of the dress Mama had worn. It had been tucked safely away for so many years for Katie to use someday. Sadly it had been lost in the fire. *Now I'm married!* Katie thought. It was not a wedding of her dreams, but life was nothing she thought it would be. She had to make some plans. She was determined to do her best to keep herself as strong as possible. She had to prepare herself for what was ahead. The feeling of loneliness lightened. Suddenly she was given a future and a family.

Katie and the other "newly married woman" were led to a different cell once at the gaol. Mary and the other women were already there. The two friends hugged after seeing each other. Katie shared everything that had happened to her since they had been separated, surprising Mary to say the least.

"Can't say I e'er 'ear such a thing as that as 'avin' to marry some bloke. Ya picked a man did ya, Katie?"

Katie told Mary it was the man who looked after them in the communal cell. "His name is James Patrick."

To her surprise, Katie saw Mary's eyes tear up. "Aye lass, ol' Mary had a man such as that once. Surprised are ya? 'Tis true and 'e be a good bloke ta me. Died, 'e did, and then I had to go to the streets. Yer man seems to be of a kind heart, handin' out food to us an' all."

Katie didn't push for any information about Mary's past life. She simply held the older woman's hand as they both became lost in their own thoughts.

⊷🙑🙒⊶

Time seemed more peaceful since the men and women were separated. The threat of violence was gone until a new prisoner was brought in. She was a large woman with a loud voice to match. Her name was Bess. It was obvious to everyone that she wanted to rule the cell. Threats and coarse language were her weapons. They worked on just about everyone...except Mary. You could feel the tension in the air almost as soon as Bess came into the cell. She warned the others not to cross her. "Me name 'tis Bess, an' I be in gaols afore. I eat firs,t and if I want a spot then I get it. Ya 'ear me? Don't be crossin' me, or it be bad fer yas." Without warning, she kicked a woman out of her spot as if to emphasize her words. The others weren't sure how to react. Some moved further away from her while Mary just let out a "Humph!"

Room was given to the woman until she pushed Katie out of pure meanness two days later. Bess came at Katie. "Git away with ya, or ya hit the floor!" she yelled, making Katie jump.

Mary was on her feet in a split second. Everyone stood with their mouths gaped open at her speed and agility. Without any noise, she grabbed a hold of the woman's hair. Before the woman could even react, Mary spun her around and kicked hard. Bess was knocked against the wall. Mary grabbed her again, pushing her against the opposite wall. Just as the woman turned to defend herself, Mary slapped her. The sound of it echoed through the cell. "Want some more, tart?" Mary yelled. She braced herself for the counterattack.

After hearing the fight start, the turnkey watched through the gate. He was enjoying himself immensely. Fights, especially between women, were a rare treat. It added excitement to an otherwise boring day.

Katie couldn't believe her eyes or ears. Mary had changed into another person. The sweet, caring person she knew was gone, replaced with a wild woman. Her hair, what she had of it, looked like it was standing on end. Her face was distorted. The snarl that came from her sounded inhuman.

Once the surprise of the attack wore off, Bess lunged at Mary. The two women rolled on the ground. Hay, dust, and the other women scattered everywhere. It looked like Mary was going to be bested until Katie jumped in to help. Now three women were rolling, and what a sight it was. Five of the other women jumped on Bess as well. Before too long she was subdued and pinned to the ground. Mary got up, spitting and sputtering hay from her mouth. She spun around, looking for her opponent. After completing a couple of turns punching air, she finally stopped. It took a couple of seconds before she realized Bess was down with the others on top of her.

"That a way! Git 'er good! Let 'er 'ave it, lasses!" Mary yelled in excitement and anger.

"Git off me, ya bloody lout!" Bess yelled. "'Tis a sorry lot ye be 'ifin yas don't let me up!"

The women held her down. Katie was able to stand once the other women had a good hold. "Nay, you will stay there until you cool down," was Katie's reply.

Mary had to get in her two words. "Ya be bullyin' us women since ya got 'ere. I be sick of it, and so be the others it would seem. Ya want to be wearin' yer face on yer backside, keep it up, ya ol' hag!" Mary emphasized her words by pushing her bosoms up.

Katie was a little calmer. "Mary is right. We won't have you pushing us around any longer. You will wait your turn like the rest of us when the food comes, and no more pushing anyone out of their spot at night. If you start acting like a human being, we will let you up. Don't think of getting up to start more trouble. Do you understand?"

The woman glared but agreed. The women slowly let her stand. She swayed, having to brace herself against the wall. After catching her breath, she simply sat down. The other women sat down as well, keeping a keen eye on Bess.

Katie turned to Mary. "I've never been in a fight before. Are you all right?"

"I be fine and dandy. 'Tis been a long time since I ripped some 'air out! Good thin' she 'ad 'air to rip out. I be glad me 'ead be shaved so she cannot grab any of mine. Does the blood good fer sure, to ruckus." Mary laughed.

Katie smiled, shaking her head in response. There was only one like Mary. She seemed more like a child at times than a middle-aged woman.

Soon the women calmed down. Everyone was exhausted from all the excitement, except for the gaoler. He was disappointed it had ended so quickly. Hopefully he wouldn't have to wait long for the next bout.

Weeks passed, and the women thought they would go mad with boredom. They made up games to occupy themselves or exchanged stories. They came to know each other better. Even Bess began to participate. Excitement swept through when word came down that they may be given jobs again. It would be an easier time of it if they had something to do.

By now, Katie sported a hairstyle resembling a boy. Mary challenged Katie by betting whose hair would grow the fastest. Mary was losing, for her head was still covered more in gray fuzz than hair. "I earned all those gray 'airs, every one," Mary boasted. She then proceeded to take a broken old comb, running it through pretending it was caught in a snarl. Everyone laughed. Katie was proud of Mary. In all the time they suffered hardships, she never complained. Well, she did complain about one thing—the fact that Bess was a friend now, ending the possibility of another good fight.

All Red thought about was Katie. Now that he was away from her, he thought of all the things he wanted to talk to her about. He worried about her as well. Hopefully she would fare well. He prayed for her every time he thought of her. She seemed a dainty creature compared to some of the other women, but he knew he needed to trust in God for her safety. Since God had given her to him, He surely wouldn't take her away from him now. What a great comfort to know he could rest in the Lord.

Like the women, the men found they were in a cleaner cell than before. Boredom lay heavy in their cell as well. Most of the men's thoughts turned toward sailing out. When would they leave? How long was the voyage? Would they be able to work land for themselves once they were there, or would they be used strictly for slave labor? If that was the case, why would they need wives? There were so many questions and no answers.

Again Red took comfort, knowing the Lord had all the answers. He would direct their paths, and all would work out. Red had no qualms about going to Botany Bay; it was just the "getting there" that concerned him. He might not get land right away, but it sounded like hard work could earn him some land later on. He didn't care where the land was as long as it would be his to hand down to his children.

Children…what a strange thought. Just a few days ago he was alone in the world, except for the Lord of course, and now he had a wife. His thoughts turned back to Katie. He never thought about marriage much. He just figured he would meet someone someday, fall in love, and that would be it.

Weeks passed, and a few new men arrived in the cell. They were fair fellows, fitting in as best as anyone could. One of the men was a talker and openly shared his experiences with the others. The experience that seemed to interest everyone the most concerned the prison ships in the harbor.

"I was there fer 'bout three months, be my guess," he began. "Foulest place I e'er be in, rats crawlin' all over. Lice nearly eat ya alive." With that statement the others stepped back. "This place we be in now is a heap better. Why, they had small boys chained with the foulest of men. There were women crying mournfully, and some with wee ones to boot. Cells are in the dank belly of the ships, weavin' back and forth 'til a man empties his belly. Only clean air was up top. If the weather be foul, then we be left chained and locked below."

"How did ya e'er get out of it?" ask one man.

"Seems one of my ol' cronies be up fer 'is trial soon. Needs me as a witness, so I be brought back to shore. Thank Mary, Mother of God."

This was just one of the many fears the men in the gaols had to face day in and day out. At any given time they could be brought to one of the prison hulks. It was no secret the gaols were bursting at the seams.

As bad as Newgate was, it wasn't the worst. Not like Kirkdale, where gaol fever ran rampant these days. If that wasn't bad enough, it wasn't unusual for cat-o-nine tails to be laid to the back. As long as you minded your own business, chances were someone else would get it. Stories were told how some of the young boys had to give the men their food for protection. At Kirkdale you had a good chance of going out in a coffin. From what other prisoners said, "Newgate 'tis closer to Heaven, while Kirkdale shimmies up to hell."

Red couldn't imagine how bad it had to be to consider this place closer to Heaven. He prayed he would never need to find out.

The men asked the talker if he had heard about sailing out or what it was like in the new land.

"Only that if a body goes ter the new land, you don't 'ear of him no more. Seems they don't come back...ever. Don't know what be worse, the goin' or the stayin'."

The men all agreed on that. Finally they all settled in for the night. Snores, loud and soft, could be heard throughout the cell.

Red prayed well into the night, thanking God for His protection. Soon he slept, dreaming of his bride. He saw her sailing off without him. She was crying and trying to jump ship, but men held her back. Red wanted to swim to her, but he couldn't move. He fought to go to her. When he woke, he felt exhausted. When would he see Katie again? Had something happened to her? Why would he dream something like that? He had to remind himself to trust in the Lord.

As the days wore on, he felt pulled and agitated. No matter how he prayed, the uneasiness that settled around him wouldn't leave. He felt he would go crazy unless he heard something of his wife, but he had no way to contact her. That was the true torture, the not knowing....

6

Freedom

"**C**ome with me," was all Katie was told. She'd never been led out of the cell by herself and felt nervous about it. Grabbing her scarf, she looked back at Mary as she went out the door.

The gaoler fastened lighter chains on her wrist. She was led a few steps down a long narrow hall to a heavy door. The gaoler knocked. He opened the door wide, allowing Katie to see the magistrate who had married her to James sitting behind a desk. He wasn't wearing a robe or wig but was dressed casually. He was studying some papers.

Katie stood quietly in front of the desk, not knowing what to do. The man looked up from his desk and told her to sit down. She did as she was told, while trying to still her beating heart. *Now what is he planning to do to me?* was her only thought.

"Take those chains off this woman!" he barked at the gaoler. Once that was done, he had the gaoler leave. "Do you like tea or is coffee your preference?"

Katie hadn't had coffee in so long. "Nothing sir, but thank you."

"Nonsense, you look like you need some warming up. These gaols are damp. I'm having coffee myself, so would you like some or tea?"

She relented. "Coffee would be fine."

After calling the gaoler back in to retrieve their drinks, he began. "I'm sure you are wondering why I had you brought here. I was surprised by a visit a few weeks ago by a man and his wife named Lord and Lady Wilson. Their concern was for you. Do you know them?"

Katie was surprised by the news. "Aye, I know them."

"Well, it seems they found out you are not guilty after all. I explained you had been sentenced and also married. I guess you could say they were quite shocked by the news of your marriage. After they left, I instructed the authorities to investigate their claims. They have done that, and it seems you are indeed innocent. This puts me in a very uncomfortable position."

Katie's heart began beating irregularly. "They really know I'm innocent? You finally believe me?" Relief flooded her, questions filled her. "What changed that they now believe me?"

Peter explained how Lord and Lady Wilson had caught their daughter, Tess, in a lie. After a time she admitted she had taken her own necklace.

"I questioned them about the sworn affidavit I was given in regards to your case. Their daughter had signed it. I also asked them if they realized their daughter could have certain charges brought against her. They were aware of it, but at this point are more concerned about you."

Katie's heart soared with the news. Her mind raced. Taking a drink of her coffee gave her time to think. Setting the cup down, she looked at Peter. "What happens now? Does this mean I will be released?"

Peter had never encountered such a predicament such as this. Unfortunately innocent people were sometimes charged and found guilty. It was bound to happen with the vast numbers of prisoners. This was the first time, though, that a high-stationed citizen had come to him personally and pronounced a prisoner's innocence. If that wasn't enough, there was the fact that he'd had her married off. Yes, this was a very uncomfortable situation indeed.

"I guess that is pretty much up to you. Of course you will be released. I have been given a letter for you. I will leave you alone to read it. Can I assume then that you can read?"

Katie nodded that she could.

"Then please take your time. When I come back, we'll discuss what we will need to do then." Peter opened his desk drawer, pulling out the letter. After handing it to Katie he stood, leaving the room.

Katie slowly tore at the seal. She began reading.

Dearest Kathryn,
It is with great difficulty that I write. I cannot tell you what shame and pain we feel. I wonder if I can express to you how sorry we,

Lady Wilson and I, are. We want to talk to you personally to explain all that has transpired, and how we learned of your innocence.

Arrangements have been made to bring you to the Brick House whenever you are ready to meet with us...assuming, of course, you do agree to meet with us.

Please give us a chance to earn your forgiveness if at all possible. We will do all we can to make up for your horrible experience.

Lord Edward Wilson

Katie sat staring at the letter for some time. She found herself blinking back tears of relief. Finally they all knew she was innocent! That was so important to her. She would not have to stay in this horrible place any longer.

Suddenly she thought of James. James Patrick, her husband! What was she to do? Could it be she *wanted* to be married to him? What about going off to a new land?

She knew what to expect at Brick House. She would rather be at Newgate with all its filth than spend one more day under Tess's thumb. What was she to do? They certainly didn't expect her to live there again?

Peter stepped back into the room and cleared his throat. "Have you decided what you would like to do yet?"

"I'm not sure. How soon can I leave?"

"Today; there are papers that need to be filled out and signed. Do you have somewhere to stay, any family?"

It suddenly struck Katie that there was no home or family waiting for her. "No, sir, I have no family left. My father was killed in an accident, and Gran passed away almost five years ago. I lived at the Brick House with Lord and Lady Wilson after my father was killed. I was in their employment." Why was she telling him all this? Surely he wasn't really interested.

"Lord Wilson was informed that you would be released today," Peter said. "He has ordered a carriage to wait here, all day if necessary, if you decide to see them. Meantime I can make some inquiries into finding you temporary shelter." Peter surprised himself by offering his help.

Katie wasn't sure how to respond. Temporary shelter, where? How long? Once again her future seemed confused and frightening to her. She shrugged. "I guess I could speak to them." After hesitating, she added, "What do I do about my husband? I mean, I am married now, and we are to be shipped away. What is to become of him?"

Peter ran his fingers through his hair. "I'm not sure I have the answers, but why don't you meet with Lord and Lady Wilson and go from there? It will give you time to think of what you want to do. We surely will not force you to be shipped out since you are not guilty of a crime. As far as your marriage goes, since it hasn't been…well, a real marriage yet, it can be annulled."

Katie blushed, looking down at her hands.

Peter rushed on, "These decisions are the kind you need to think about for a time. Why don't I make arrangements for you to rest and change into some new clothes? Meantime I will send a messenger to Lord Wilson's estate to inform them that you are coming."

Peter called for his assistant to get a room ready for Katie and to ready clean clothes for her. Standing up, Peter stepped around his desk and leaned against it. "Miss, I cannot tell you what to do. I feel somewhat responsible for your predicament. I want you to know that I will do what I can to help you. You are not going to be left in the streets on your own."

A knock was heard as Peter's assistant stepped in to let them know a room was ready. As she was led out, she turned, giving a smile of thanks. He had been the only person who had shown any concern for her, except for Mary and James Patrick, of course.

Peter stared after her. The smile she had given him made his heart lurch. A feeling came over him that he hadn't felt in a very long time. Shaking his head, he turned his mind back to business. It was one thing to promise help, but now what was he to do? Maybe he had spoken too soon, promising too much. There was something about her that made him feel protective towards her. He admittedly confessed to himself that he felt attracted to her. Maybe he just needed one of his ladies's companionship tonight. He had a line of them from town to town. No it was more than that, more than physical. Well if nothing else, the young woman could stay in the room she occupied now. Rooms were available to the magistrate and their wives if the women chose to accompany their husbands. Victoria had yet to come with Peter, and probably never would.

Katie was amazed at how beautiful her room was. It looked like it belonged in a castle somewhere. Not even the Brick House held a room such as this. A large tub full of water was placed in the middle of the room, while a fire burned brightly in the fireplace. A huge bed with a large peach-colored coverlet stood at one end. There were two ceiling-to-floor windows with peach-colored drapes on each side of the bed. A clean shift and a pair of slippers lay on the bed. After the man closed the window curtains, he showed Katie where she could find all she needed. After he left, she went over to lock the door. She was used to being locked in, not locking others out. Only a few hours ago she had been in prison, and now here she stood in this grand room. Heaven and hell, guilt and innocence, beauty and ugliness all rolled together. *Have I died and gone to heaven?* As she sank into the tub filled with hot water she decided she was right. She definitely had died and gone to heaven.

Red paced the cell, flexing his arm and leg muscles as best he could. He needed to be strong with a long voyage and new life ahead of him. Unlike the others sentenced to sail, Red was more than willing. There was an expectancy within him that made the everyday humdrum life in that cell bearable. He dreamed of the voyage and adventure…to work for his own land. Sure, he would be working for others for the seven years of his sentence, but after that…. He could only shake his head at the wonder of it all.

Thankfully the men had a break from their cell a few days later.

They were given hard labor, breaking down an old stone wall just outside the city. Red welcomed the work and fresh air. His muscles ached, putting him in misery the next day, but he hoped for more work to come.

Slowly the other men began seeing Red in a new light. They saw how he worked and held himself. When others complained and cussed, he simply did his work. When others moaned and groaned under the pressure, Red kept his daily routine going. He prayed, exercised, ate, and exercised some more. The men witnessed this big man in prayer. At first a few snickered, but as time went on they saw a new strength that had nothing to do with the physical. One by one the men came to respect him and began following his lead. Even the gaolers noticed.

When there was work to be done, it was the men in Red's cell who were chosen because of the good day's work done without complaint. Days passed more quickly, but it was still difficult. They were given hard work, but not extra food. Heat and filthiness still surrounded them. Fresh water was not to be found, and danger of other prisoners was still a concern. The others watched Red pray and "walk" in peace. They watched him very closely.

Katie stretched her muscles and decided to leave the bath. She stayed in as long as possible but now felt chilled. Grabbing a towel, she stood before the fire. She had not had a bath like this in over two years. *Now what do I do? Am I supposed to stay here?* she asked herself.

Katie looked longingly at the massive bed. She was exhausted. Walking over, she "tested" its softness. Her body and mind wouldn't let her resist. Turning the rich coverlet down, she slipped under the soft blankets. Katie sank in its softness and warmth. She thought about James. What would happen to them, their marriage? The magistrate was right. It wasn't a "real" marriage.

It is too a real marriage! Katie thought angrily a minute later. *It was real enough yesterday before everyone found me innocent.*

Katie's head ached. In her mind she could see James standing in front of her, looking hurt and confused. What was she to do? Where would she go? Suddenly a new thought was conceived. What had changed? She was still married to James. She must certainly be able to go with him! They had to let her go with him. She may be free, but she was still married and wanted to be. Yes she wanted to be married to James. She held her breath, knowing in her heart that she loved him. When did it happen? It didn't matter. Her decision was made. She would find a way to stay with him. She would go to Australia with her husband. Katie hadn't planned on asking Lord and Lady Wilson for anything, but now they could help her. They had influence. Yes, they owed her that, didn't they? Smiling, she snuggled down, and soon she slept soundly.

❧☙

Lord Wilson took the note from the Butler. Opening it, he turned and smiled at his wife. "She is coming," was all he said.

"Oh, thank God!" Lady Wilson brought her hand to her bosom. "Thank God!"

Lord Wilson sat next to his wife and placed his arm around her. Bringing her closer, he kissed her cheek.

She smiled up at her husband, whispering, "I should never have doubted you, Edward. You said she would come, but I had my doubts."

He gently touched his wife's cheek. "To be honest, I doubted as well, but we don't need to worry now. She will be here tomorrow or so says the note."

His wife responded, "Thank God Tess isn't here. Is the cottage ready? Did you get the bank draft?

He chuckled. "Dear, you've asked me that several times now, and I keep giving you the same answer."

"I'm sorry. I guess I am being a twit. I just don't know what we'll do if she refuses. I don't know if I can ever forgive myself for what we did to her. She only served us with loyalty and with love. I cannot imagine going through what she did."

The man nodded sadly. "I know dear, but she's a very special young lady. I can't say whether she'll forgive us or not, but we will try our best to make it up to her."

And with that Lady Wilson spent the rest of the day in preparation. She needed to stay busy so her thoughts wouldn't overwhelm her. A special meal had to be planned, and she needed to meet with the cook, Maggie. She wanted every detail of Kathryn's "homecoming" to be perfect.

Lord Wilson paced in his study. He had comforted his wife with the right words, but doubts still plagued him. How could she ever possibly forgive them? What innocent, such as Kathryn, could ever get past her ordeal? He knew a little of what Newgate was like, unlike his wife. Could you say, "Oops, we were wrong," and expect her to forgive completely?

Opening his desk drawer he retrieved a cigar. Clipping the end, he lit it. This wasn't the first time Tess had gotten them into a mess. No, this was more than a mess. This had been the undoing of an innocent woman whose family had faithfully served his family for many years. The Brady named had been an honorable one, until Tess's lies.

Running his fingers through his hair, he drew on his cigar then exhaled. Oh, it wasn't all Tess. He had a lot to do with it too. By the time he and his wife had returned from their trip, Kathryn had been arrested. Tess had signed the affidavit stating the girl was guilty. It was too late to do anything. At the time he thought there might be a chance she had stolen the necklace. Deep in his heart he knew better, but he didn't want to expose his daughter for what she was, a liar and a cheat. It had all gotten out of hand so quickly.

You're a coward, Wilson. Tomorrow would be difficult to face, but face it he would. He only hoped he could make some of it up to the girl. He longed for her forgiveness. It was important to him because of her father. Brady had not only been a fine man and employee, he had been a true friend. Lord Wilson knew he had let him down. Thank God Brady wasn't around to see what happened, but things needed to be made right...if they could be.

Lord Wilson rose from his chair to gaze out the window. *Forgive me, Brady. Forgive me for what I've done to your daughter.* What more could he say?

7

Broken

Katie stepped in the waiting carriage to take her to the Brick House. It seemed so strange to be going there. She let her mind wander as the coach passed tree-lined streets heading for the outskirts of town. Now that she was out of Newgate, she felt amazed at how she had adjusted to the hardships. How strange to think her time spent there had passed so quickly. She clearly remembered how time crawled when she was sitting in Newgate instead of this comfortable coach. Smiling to herself, she knew much of her adjustment was due to Mary and the friendship they had forged.

Lifting her hand to her head, Katie adjusted the bonnet she was given. Her short hair poked out, and once again she fought to keep it neatly tucked. She wondered where the clothes she was given had come from. They fit a little loose but there wasn't much to fill the dress. Her bones seemed to jut out everywhere.

Sighing, Katie couldn't help think how wonderful it was to be outside. The carriage ride soothed her. Suddenly she sat up straighter. What if she was dreaming? What if she was still in the gaol? She pinched her arm hard. No, she was sitting on the red velveteen-covered seat of the carriage. Smiling at her own foolishness, she again sat back in comfort.

Would the Wilsons realize she wasn't the same person she was the last time she had seen them? She wasn't the young innocent with no idea of life anymore. She had to learn fast and hard in the gaol, and she did. Katie had learned well and chose to be the better for it. What happened to her could not be changed, but she could choose how she would react to it all.

Gran's words once again came back to her. "Ya know, Katie Elizabeth, life 'tis all about choices that are made. Whether by ya or someone else it don't matter. What does matter is how ya decide to live through the choices made."

"Aye, Gran, now I understand."

Her thoughts now turned to James and Mary. They had been her strength, her reason for going on. She was going to help them somehow. She wouldn't rest until she had done something to better their lives.

Before she realized it, Brick House loomed in the distance. Katie busied herself tucking her hair under her bonnet once more before the coach reached the front of the Manor. She felt somehow detached from her surroundings. She didn't feel anxious or fearful. She was strangely calm when the footman opened the carriage door for her.

Lord Wilson descended the front stairs. He hesitated at the sight of her. The young woman looked thin and drawn. Her hair stuck out in the front and bottom of her bonnet. Dark circles lay under her once bright eyes. Guilt for her suffering stabbed his heart. Lord Wilson extended his hand to her, and she took it. "Kathryn, we are so happy you have decided to come. Lady Wilson is in the parlor waiting for us."

As Katie entered the house, she felt the old familiar feeling of dread wash over her.

Lady Wilson rushed over to Katie as soon as she saw her and wrapped her arms around Katie's frail form. "Oh Kathryn, how wonderful that you would come visit us."

Katie stood motionless.

Just then a maid came in with a tray of coffee, tea, and cakes. Lady Wilson blinked back tears, "Thank you, Maud. Just put the tray on this table would you, please? I'll serve."

The maid curtsied, and turned to leave. Lady Wilson poured Katie coffee, remembering how she enjoyed the black drink.

Lord Wilson came to sit on the couch facing Katie. "My dear, it was with great sorrow and shame we found that we had accused you wrongly. Our daughter was caught in a lie. That does not take away from our own guilt. We are willing to do anything we can to make this up to you. We realize the ordeal you have been through can hardly be worth any amount of money, but we will do whatever we can to lessen the pain for you."

Katie sat quietly wondering if they had any idea of the fear, pain, and suffering she had endured. Of course all that, and the day-to-day humiliation of it all. Would they understand that her suffering began long before her imprisonment? That one prison had only been replaced with another? That their beautiful home had been a place of darkness and despair for her just as much as that cell she had been in? Because of their daughter's cruelty, and their blindness to it, she had suffered greatly. Oh, she knew they were sincere and caring people, but how could they not have seen their daughter for what she really was? What could they possibly give her that could make up for any of it?

At Katie's silence, Lord Wilson stood. He walked over to the mantel of the fireplace to pick up a sealed envelope. He promptly handed it to the young woman. "This is just a small portion of what we owe you, Kathryn. Please realize that we know in our hearts no amount of money could make up for this. We want you to have something to help you in your new life."

Katie slowly opened the paper. In her hands she held a bank note for a tremendous amount of money. Not in her whole life could she possibly spend it all. Stunned, she looked at Lord Wilson, waiting for him to say, "Oh Kathryn, this is just another cruel joke."

He quietly waited for any kind of response. When there was none, Lord Wilson again spoke. "Along with these funds we have the papers of ownership to your father's house." He handed her another envelope.

"Papa's house?" Katie questioned. "Papa never owned a house."

Lord Wilson explained, "We never told you, but this house was given to your father for many years of faithful and loyal service. Along with it, he received seventy acres of land. I don't know if you knew this, but he saved my life once. I fell off my horse when it bolted. My boot became caught in the stirrup. I was dragged a great distance. Your father jumped in front of the horse, putting himself in danger. He was able to grab the reins, and thus saved my life."

Katie vaguely remembered, as a little girl, hearing a lot of commotion about Lord Wilson getting hurt. She heard something about Papa being a hero, but Papa had always been a hero to Katie.

"Two weeks before you were supposed to move into the house is when he was killed. He was going to surprise you. We never mentioned it to you after he died because you were too young to live alone. By the time you were old enough we, well…" Lord Wilson looked down as if embarrassed. He went on, "By the time you were old enough to claim the house we were so attached to you. We couldn't bear the thought of you leaving us. That, and also we hoped some of your sweet nature would rub off on Tess. We kept your papa's house in good repair. We fully expected to hand it over to you, but the opportunity never came."

Anger filled Katie. So she was left to endure their daughter's abuse in hopes she would what? Teach their daughter to be a better person?

Lady Wilson added, "Kathryn, there are no words to tell you how devastated we are. We have always known that Tess is a troubled girl, but we never thought she would never be capable of this. We wore blinders when it came to our daughter. We cannot lay all the blame on her shoulders. I know we are just as guilty, like Edward said. We have come to realize how selfish we have been. We ask…no, we beg your forgiveness, and ask only one other thing of you. Please tell us if there is anything else we could do to try and make things right."

Katie felt overwhelmed. Money and a house! What did it matter now without Papa and Gran to share it with? Why now? Why at all? Could she so easily take these things and call it even? Was forgiveness bought and sold? Was a year of her life and the ruin of Papa's name worth all this money and a house? Papa's good name was all he ever had. He sealed bargains on his word alone. Isn't that how she first got this position, on his word alone?

Katie's throat burned; tears threatened. She tried blinking them away, but one slipped through. Lady Wilson noticed. Without hesitation the older woman knelt by Katie's chair. "Please forgive us, dear. The most painful thing for us above all was discovering our daughter was capable of such lies and deception. Not only to lie to us, but to have a heart capable of hurting you in such a terrible manner. We are not excusing our part in all this, Kathryn, but we were wounded in this as well. We felt it best to send Tess to her aunt's estate for a time. We are not sure what will become of her, but we are ready to face any charges made against Tess."

Katie nodded slowly and looked down at her hands folded in her lap. Did they really want her to feel bad for them because their daughter was a liar and cheat? Katie's anger grew a little hotter until she looked at Lady Wilson. The pain was so evident on her face. If Lady Wilson was guilty of anything, it was believing in her daughter.

Katie thought of Mary and James. Maybe there was a reason for all this. Gran used to say things didn't "just happen." Katie's anger cooled while her heart softened towards the matronly woman. Reaching her arms out to Lady Wilson, both women began to cry. Lord Wilson shifted uncomfortably, looking towards the ceiling. The two women clung to each other weeping bitterly. They had both lost so much.

Katie finally felt her throat relax enough for her to speak. "I guess a lot of people have been hurt by this. It was especially horrible in the beginning, but I forged friendships there. I became close to some of the other women. It is amazing how people can adjust when they have to. Gran used to say that unforgiveness was one of the quickest ways to hell. It is capable of killing a heart and putting disease on a body. I understand now what she meant."

Lady Wilson daintily blew her nose. "Kathryn, I must again confess we had selfish motives. We couldn't think of our home without you. We were very wrong for that. It's just that you were a ray of sunshine and laughter. We were hoping some of your wonderful qualities would rub off on Tess, as Edward has said. You had attached yourself to our hearts. We were so wrong to lay the responsibility of Tess's actions and attitudes in your young hands." Lady Wilson put her arm around Katie's shoulders. "We need to make plans. Do you think you will want to move into your own home?"

Katie looked into her kind face. "I'm not sure what to say or do. I can't believe the change in my life in one morning. My mind is spinning, and I don't know what to do." She thought about her beloved papa, how proud he would have been to have a home of his own. After losing Gran in the cottage fire, they were all that was left of their family. Papa had stayed in the men's quarters on the estate, and Katie had a small room of her own in Brick House. She closed her eyes to the memory of the most terrible time in her life except for the gaol. First Gran had died, then Papa was crushed while cutting down a tree.

Lady Wilson broke into her thoughts. "Then, dear girl, why not move into your new home? Stay until you decide what you want to do. Whatever you decide, we will be here to help you. We have also heard of the circumstances in which you were forced into marrying some criminal. Needless to say, we were appalled. You can have the marriage annulled. We are willing to help you with that as well."

Katie wasn't sure if she should tell them of her plans to stay married to James so she was silent.

"Enough for today. You look exhausted, dear. We'll have our carriage brought around to take you to Brady's Brick."

Katie's jaw dropped.

"Yes, that's what your father named his cottage. He thought you would like that. We had it prepared for you just in case you agreed to go there. Write down anything you require, and we will have it brought over to you. In the meantime try to rest, and think about what you want to do with your future. There is a maid there to help you, so you won't be alone. Her name is Sadie."

Katie remembered. "Magistrate Reeves agreed to help me find a place to stay temporarily. I should let him know I have a home."

"I'll have a message sent to him," Lord Wilson stated.

"May I ask you something?" Katie inquired.

"Of course, dear," Lady Wilson answered.

"Did you supply the clothes I'm wearing? They were brought to me just after my release."

The older woman smiled. "I took it upon myself to buy some things. I wasn't sure of your size. I hope you don't mind?"

Katie was relieved they weren't Tess's castoffs. "Not at all. I really appreciate your thoughtfulness."

Everyone rose to leave. Lady Wilson and Katie walked hand-in-hand to the carriage. Soon she was heading to her new home, Brady's Brick. Tears flowed freely once she was alone. Her life seemed surreal, a new life, a new home, freedom. Her life seemed to be pushed and pulled every-which-way and none of it by her own actions. Katie closed her eyes, letting her body rest in the gentle sway of the coach.

She decided not to make any decisions for three days. By three days she would be rested, and have some idea of where she was heading. For now she would just wait to see her inheritance. Brady's Brick was a gift from Papa, making her love it already. She could hardly wait to see it. Her own home, the home of Papa and of Gran too. It didn't matter if dear Gran never saw it. Given the choice they would have lived there together, but they were not given choices. They were just given hardship and death.

A stab of self-pity bolted through Katie, but she didn't let it take hold. She wasn't going to waste time on that. This time yesterday she was locked up, but now...no more sleeping on a blanket covering hay, no more hunger or cold. Katie felt exhilaration. She appreciated the sunshine like never before. She melted into the softness of the coach seats in which she sat. She rejoiced in the rhythmic clopping of the horses' hooves. She was thrilled at the femininity of her dress and bonnet. She felt weak with thankfulness for her freedom. Freedom she had not experienced since she had left her precious home with Papa after the fire.

The next time she opened her eyes she saw it...her home. The carriage pulled up in front. Her heart skipped a beat. It wasn't too long ago when she'd thought, *I'll never feel joy again.* She was wrong. Joy flooded her. She felt weak in the knees with it. For the first time in a very long time, she cried...tears of joy.

Red heard a group of men talking about the next voyage to Botany Bay. He stepped up to listen. He needed to learn as much as possible to prepare himself and Katie for the sail. He was disappointed, for there was nothing he hadn't heard already. The prisoners relied on new people coming in to give them any details, but few knew anything of the transport ships. Walking away from the group of men, Red began talking to others. They laughed and shared stories. It had taken a long time for Red to get people to trust him since that ridiculous story had come out about him. Now it seemed that God had given him favor in most of these men's eyes. Some treated him like their leader. Others resented it, but James just trusted in his Lord. Even those who didn't like him seemed to respect him. They saw gentleness and acceptance without being judged. In spite of their hard lives and hard hearts, they responded to Red's Savior without even knowing it.

Days went by until he was once again summoned to the heavy locked door. Unconcerned, Red stepped out...probably another job for him and the "crew." He was led into a room that was obviously an office and told to sit down. The gaoler stepped out, closing the door. Looking around, Red felt uneasy. He was alone with no chains or guard. That was unusual. He shifted to turn in his chair when the door opened. Red jumped to his feet at the sight of the man who had sentenced and married him and Katie.

"Why are you not in chains?" Peter Reeves barked. Before Red could respond, Peter opened the door shouting, "Gaoler!"

The man came running. "Where are his chains?" The man looked at Red's wrist, as if to find a clue to the answer.

"I be sorry, sir. I best forgot 'em. Big Red here be trusted, and we don't chain 'im none no more."

"Who told you to trust this man? Who made the decision to keep prisoners out of chains? I will be back in a few minutes, and this man will be chained! You will be guarding him! Understood?"

"Aye, sir!"

Peter left his office. It was amazing to him that more people didn't get killed around there. He reached in his pocket for his handkerchief so he could wipe the sweat of fear from his brow.

Red was amused by it all. The gaoler had run out to get chains, leaving Red alone once more. Before too long the man returned, and to Red's surprise the man started apologizing for having to chain him. "Sorry, but ol' man Reeves is boss. If he says to put chains on ya, then chains it is. Ya best sit in the chair."

Red stood quietly while he was shackled then sat as instructed. He tried to hide a smile for it was quite the sight. The gaoler stood all of five feet tall, and sitting down Red was still taller. He could overpower the man by just blowing on him.

Soon Peter reentered his office. Seeing the guard and chains in place he closed the door. "Stand up! Who told you to sit?" Peter barked.

Red stood. Even the gaoler straightened a little. Peter started reading some papers to himself, making the prisoner stand for some time. Red thought about what he had read in the Bible about Jesus standing before his accusers. He had stood and offered no resistance, and he was innocent. *Help me to be more like you, Lord.*

Finally Peter looked up with disdain. Red wondered if the man hated just him, or if he was like this to all prisoners. When they were in the court, Red had sensed fairness and compassion in this man. What had changed?

Peter was fighting a battle within himself. He was fighting jealousy, and he hated it. He was jealous of this prisoner, this nobody. It galled him. Kathryn Brady had picked this big lout as a husband, and Peter hated Red for it. Of course it seemed that he had forgotten it was his doing in the first place. He had forced the young woman into her decision. It had been years since he'd felt his heart stir for a woman. Peter had found himself fantasizing about her. He couldn't get her off his mind. When he finally looked up from his papers, he barked once more, "You are here out of my good conscience to tell you that your marriage has been dissolved. You are no longer husband to Kathryn Brady. You will need to sign papers when they are ready. That is all."

Red was stunned. It felt as if someone had hit him in the stomach with a hammer. He was frozen in place. It didn't take long for him to realize that he had been holding his breath. Once the words sunk in he responded, "Not married, but how…why?"

Peter looked up, annoyed. "I said you are dismissed. I need not explain anything to you." Peter wasn't about to explain that this was his decision. The girl didn't even know about this meeting. She had not made any decision as far as Peter knew, but no matter. He was positive she wouldn't have anything to do with this man, given the choice. Now he was making the choice for her, and how relieved she would be. He couldn't wait to tell her that she was not bound to this oaf any longer.

The gaoler stepped up, grabbing Red's wrist chains to lead him out. The look on Red's face softened the gaoler. Once out of the room the man whispered, "Don't worry yerself, man. There be nothin' I cannot find out. As soon as I 'ear anything I will let ya know of it. Ol' man Reeves seem to not take a lik'n to you. It makes me want to find out even more what flies in the air."

72

The other men in the cell stood when Red was let in. "We got ourselves another job, Red?" was their question. All Red could do was shake his head. Red walked over to his "regular" spot and sat down.

The men exchanged looks. Something was wrong. They decided to keep quiet.

Red was lost in angry thoughts and hurried prayer. *Why, Lord? Why would this happen? I believed in my heart you wanted me to marry Katie. You have made me feel for her, and now she is being taken away. Is this a test, Lord? Do you want to see if I will turn from you or stay on your path? Lord, was I placing my hopes for my future on Katie, and not you? Is this why you've taken her from me?*

The big man closed his eyes and rested his head back against the wall. The sigh that escaped him said it all. He found himself fighting tears. So much of his future, hopes, and dreams had been due to Katie after they were wed. He had not realized how much she meant to him until he heard he had lost her.

Why, Lord? Why? Once again Red felt the vast emptiness that came with being alone in the world. No family, yet he knew better. He did have a Father and a Lord who cared. He would cling to Him, for He alone would get him through. What did people do who didn't have the Lord?

Red settled it in his heart. *I will wait on you, and trust in you. I know that you will not leave me nor forsake me.*

But his heart still ached. He couldn't help but wonder what had changed Katie's mind. *Lord, why do I feel my heart breaking when I know you dwell within it?* A Scripture verse came to mind: *"When you are weak then I am strong. Lean not unto thine own understanding."* His life was not his own. He had no control over it. Red did the only thing he could; he surrendered. He surrendered the pain, the emptiness, Katie, and his broken heart, once again, to the Lord.

8

Home

Katie could hardly take it all in. She was unable to take her eyes off the little cottage. More tears fell as she thought how excited Papa must have been when he was planning to move into it. Emotions flooded her; excitement and sadness consumed her. Why, oh why, couldn't Papa and Gran have lived? How different things would have been. Papa had always been her champion, and Gran was just as tough when it came to protecting her. They would never have let her be put into prison. Papa would have been able to speak to Lord Wilson and convince him of her innocence. How wonderful it would have been if....

She was doing it again, the "what ifs." Sighing, she stepped down from the carriage. Only one thought remained in her mind. *Papa, I'm home.*

Katie slowly walked through an iron gate that was attached to a wooden fence covered with vines. The small stone cottage seemed to reach out to her, to welcome her. Color burst everywhere from the trees covered in their fall foliage. Mums and marigolds lined the fence. A stone path led to the arched front door. Small-paned windows graced each side of the front door. Under the windows hung little boxes with a variety of flowers adding to its charm. The stone path broke away from the main entrance curling around to the back.

Katie wasn't sure what to do so she knocked softly. Slowly opening the door she peeked in. Her eyes had to adjust to the dimmer light of the room. To the left of the entrance was a large fireplace that took up most of the wall. Two doorways stood on each side of it. Straight ahead were four cottage windows with criss-cross panes. Under them a table with four chairs was placed. Sunshine through the trees splashed onto the table and overflowed onto the floor. To her right were steps that evidently led to a loft area. Furniture filled the room, making it look cozy. Everything was neat and tidy like the outside.

Katie heard a noise and turned to see a woman enter the main room. She was wiping her hands on her apron. Suddenly the two women squealed at the same time, for in front of Katie stood her dear friend, Maggie. The women ran and grabbed each other in great delight. They were like two little girls jumping up and down. Once they calmed down they stood back, looking at each other.

"Oh Katie, I didn't hear ya come in! What a sight for me old eyes. How I've missed you, lass." Maggie hugged her again.

Katie was still in shock. "I can't believe you are here! When I was told there would be someone here to help me I never expected you! They said a girl named Sadie would be here. It's so wonderful to see you." Suddenly Katie's tears of joy turned into uncontrollable sobs. She had fought the onslaught of tears for so long. The dam she had built to hold them back broke. Tears freely flowed—tears of joy, sorrow, fear, and shame streamed down her face. Embarrassed, she turned away, covering her face with her hands.

Maggie held the girl in her arms. As if comforting a small child, she cooed, "It be all right, lass, Maggie is here. You go ahead and cry."

Sobs wracked Katie's body as Maggie led her to a chair. After a few moments Katie's crying ceased. She wiped her eyes, blew her nose, and began to apologize for her outburst.

"I won't hear of it, Katie!" Maggie exclaimed. "Had I been there in that place I would do worse than cry a few tears. So much has happened to you of late. No wonder you are overwhelmed. You are home now. I insisted on being here for you. I think Lady Wilson would give you anything, so she let me come. I wanted to surprise you. That's why I told Lady Wilson to tell you Sadie was here. I will stay until they call me back to the Brick House. Come, let me show you the cottage, and then you are to rest. After that I'll finish supper."

Katie followed Maggie. The room off to the left of the large fireplace was a small bedchamber. Rose-colored curtains around a bed with a matching coverlet caught Katie's attention first. A small fireplace graced one wall along with a desk and chair. On the mantle of the fireplace sat a small woodcarving of a dog. Katie gasped. She had forgotten about the little carving her father had given her one Christmas long ago. "Maggie! How did this get here? I thought it was lost in the fire!"

"I don't know, Katie. It was in the things Lord and Lady Wilson had kept for you. A few days ago I was told to unpack your trunks, and ready the cottage. That's when I found it."

Katie went over to pick up her treasure. She noticed it was scorched on one side. "Look, someone must have found it after the fire, but who? It was probably Papa." After placing it gently back on the mantle, she began to look around again. A wardrobe stood in one corner while a rose-colored rug lay beside the bed. The lace curtains that covered the double windows fluttered in the soft autumn breeze. Fresh-cut flowers and an oil lamp sat on a small table next to the bed.

The two women turned back into the main room. On the other side of the fireplace was another doorway. Stepping through, Katie found herself in the cook's room, where another fireplace with a baker's oven next to it occupied the farthest wall. Colorful rag rugs covered the floor for warmth. Two small criss-cross windows graced the outer wall. They were also open, to let in fresh air. Underneath the windows sat a small table and two chairs. Open-faced cupboards and shelves holding utensils and food occupied the wall opposite the door. The back door was divided into two halves with the top half open. Katie looked out to a beautiful flower garden planted on one side of a cobbled path. On the other side was a vegetable garden.

The two women turned towards the main room again. Katie walked over to the large table adorned with more fresh-cut flowers. Speckled sunlight danced on the high-gloss surface. Two overstuffed chairs, a small divan, and various-shaped tables were arranged to face the fireplace. Across the room was another door to a small room used for storage.

"How cozy!" Katie gushed. "Where do you sleep?"

"Up those stairs to the loft. It's warm up there. Come, I'll show you."

They went to the stairs that led up to Maggie's loft. It was a charming room with a low ceiling. A window was centered at the arch of the roof. A bed, bench, and a table with a lamp were all the room held. Wooden pegs for Maggie's clothes hung on the taller wall at the other end. A simple rag rug covered the floor.

After descending the steps, Maggie asked, "Katie, are you up to some tea, or would you rather lay down for a quick nap?"

"I feel wide awake. Do we have coffee?"

"Aye, I forgot you favor it. I can only imagine how you must be feeling, coming to your Father's house after all you have been through." Maggie stopped after seeing Katie's downcast face. "I'm sorry, lass; I didn't mean to upset you again."

Katie raised her hand towards Maggie. "No need to apologize. You did nothing wrong. It was so terrible in the beginning, but then I started to look forward to the future once I was married. Isn't it funny how a day can change a life? Now I'm not sure what I will do. I feel like I've been going from a dream to a nightmare back to a dream again. My life has taken on so many strange twists and turns."

Maggie hadn't seemed surprised about Katie's marriage. Most likely Lady Wilson had already told her about it. As she made the drinks, she listened to Katie without judgment or questions. The two friends sat at the table in the cook's room, enjoying each other's company.

Maggie began to reassure Katie once more. "'Tis no dream, Katie, you are home. No one can take it from you, and I will stay as long as you want."

They spoke of Papa, of old times, and the events leading up to Katie being arrested. Katie had always known Maggie had deep feelings for Papa. It would not have surprised her if Papa had asked Maggie to marry him, if he had lived. They would have made each other happy.

"Now drink your coffee, then lay down for a time while I fix our supper," Maggie ordered.

Katie did as she was told. She was used to doing that after all. She was sure she wouldn't sleep, but needed to rest. Climbing in her soft bed she curled up.

Within minutes Maggie could hear the girl's deep breathing. "Sleep the sleep of the innocent, lass," Maggie whispered as she began peeling potatoes.

9

Struggles

It didn't take long for Katie to become settled in her new surroundings. It was time for her to make some serious decisions now. The gaol seemed a distant bad dream, but her thoughts often turned to James Patrick. She saw his face everywhere. She should be feeling relaxed and comfortable, but instead uneasiness filled her as if something was expected of her.

It was a dismal day. Thunder crashed as lightning blazed across the sky. Maggie built a roaring fire to keep the dampness at bay. Katie curled up in her chair, staring at the same page of her book until Maggie interrupted her thoughts. "Katie, come get some fresh coffee."

Katie moved to the table to watch the rain. "Oh Maggie, I don't know how to help James Patrick." It was the first time Katie had mentioned her husband.

"No one will fault you if you turn from the marriage. People don't expect you to stay married to him, lass." When Katie didn't respond, Maggie went on. "You aren't considering staying married to him are you?" Before she could answer the clopping of horses coming up the lane caught their attention. Maggie went to look out the front door.

"Who is it, Maggie?"

"I don't know. Never seen the carriage around here before, but it's someone important. Sure is a fancy rig."

Once the horses pulled up, and the coachman opened the door, a gentleman jumped out. Wearing a black cloak with his hat pulled low, his identity was hidden. He briskly walked through the front gate and up the path. Maggie opened the door wide for him to step through. "Good day, sir." Maggie curtsied.

"Is your mistress home?" he inquired.

"Aye."

Lifting his hat, he stepped inside. Katie was surprised to see it was Magistrate Reeves. Apprehension filled her. *What in the world could he want? Was her release a mistake? Did he come to take her back to the gaol?*

"Forgive my intrusion, miss. I hope I haven't caught you at a bad time?"

"No...not at all. Please come and sit by the fire. Maggie, would you please get some fresh coffee?"

The man shook the rain from his hat and coat, handing them to Maggie, who scowled at the water on her clean floor.

Katie and Peter sat before the fire, nervously smiling at one another. Peter noticed how much the young woman had changed. She was attractive even in dirty rags and a shaved head, but now she was radiant. In this short span of time she glowed with health. Her simple dress only added to her charms.

He spoke first. "I just wanted to see how you were doing. I heard from Lord Wilson that you were living here, and the circumstances by which you acquired this home. It's quite a story indeed."

Katie didn't respond. She wasn't sure she liked the idea of this man knowing her personal business.

Clearing his throat, Peter pushed forward. "This is a very charming cottage. You seem to have started a new life. It suits you. I do have some news for you. It is of a delicate matter, so I felt I should speak to you myself." Peter felt irritated when his statement was met with silence. This one-sided conversation was difficult. "Since I was the one to perform your marriage, I took it upon myself to take steps to annul it. You are not obligated to the man. I have also informed the...ah...gentleman of these facts as well. I thought it best if you didn't see him again. You've been through enough. I thought it best to spare you any more discomfort."

Katie wasn't sure she was hearing right. Wasn't this the same man who had sentenced her, then forced her into the decision to marry a stranger? And now he wanted to spare her discomfort? Was *he* actually telling her that *he* had decided she shouldn't be married at all? Anger surged through her.

Peter thought it strange when he noticed how rigid she held herself. What was the matter? Didn't she understand what he had just said? Maybe he had not made himself clear. "What I'm trying to say is that…"

Katie held her hand up to stop him. She took a deep breath. This was a powerful man. She didn't want to anger him or take the chance that his wrath would fall upon James Patrick. Keeping her voice level, she started out slowly, picking her words carefully. "Sir, I cannot express how much I appreciate your concern for me. I appreciated how you came to my rescue when I thought I had nowhere to go and you offered me shelter. Again you show your thoughtfulness by coming to my home personally."

Maggie let out a "sniff" from behind the door, where she was listening.

"Things have been happening so fast in my life that I have not had a chance to think. I wish you would have informed me before taking any steps on my behalf. I have not been able to make decisions for myself for a long time now. I would like to begin doing so. I understand you were trying to save me from further distress, and I appreciate that. I hope you understand, but I must ask that you leave any changes regarding my life to me."

Peter felt another twinge of irritation. Wasn't she listening to him? He was doing all the dirty work for her. Smiling to hide his true feelings, Peter spoke. "I understand, Miss Brady; however I felt somewhat responsible for your predicament. I was only too happy to oblige myself."

Katie almost corrected him about her name, but hearing the edge in the man's voice, she continued to tread softly. "Again, thank you for all you have done for me. You have gone out of your way to help me, and I appreciate your kindness. I feel I have burdened you more than enough. Is it safe to say that my marriage is …erased then?"

"I have been only too happy to help a lady in distress."

Again Katie could hear Maggie let out a "sniff." Katie glanced towards the door to give her a "look."

He continued, "All I need is for you to sign this paper, and it will be over for you."

Katie looked down at the paper. There were two signatures required—hers and James Patrick's.

"I noticed that Mr. Murphy hasn't signed," Katie said a little too softly.

Peter gave her a quizzical look, then explained, "I tried to get the man to sign. He agreed to sign the paper if you were to sign first. I cannot fathom what the man was thinking."

Katie's heart leapt at Peter's words. "You mean to say he refused to sign?"

"Yes, he stated that if you wanted out of the marriage, then he would sign. It's not as if you had a real marriage, you know. I don't know why he had to make this more difficult for you."

Katie had to bite her tongue. The marriage was real enough just a few short days ago. Real enough that this man was willing to send them off together to a new land. "May I have the paper? I cannot think of this right now. There are so many new changes in my life. I do not want to make any important decisions about anything right now. I only hope you can understand."

Peter scowled. Why was she making this more difficult than it needed to be? "Of course I understand," he lied. He stood, handing the paper over to her. "All you need to do is sign, and I will take care of the rest. My intention was not to make you feel pressured into making any decisions. I know you have been through enough. Thank you for your hospitality. Here's my card, if you wish to contact me about anything." Maggie ran to get his coat and open the door for him.

"Thank you again for all you have done for me," Katie said, giving him her warmest smile.

"Good day," was all he said before going out the door.

Maggie was chomping at the bit. "Humph, what a dandy! Katie, are you thinking of staying married to that stranger?"

Katie sat down and stared at the papers. Looking up, she softly stated what was in her heart. "Yes, I am going to stay married to him...if he wants."

Maggie sat beside the young woman. Placing her arm around her shoulder, she replied, "You must think very highly of the man. Can you tell me of him?"

"I will tell you soon, Maggie. Suddenly I feel very tired. I think I'll go rest a bit before dinner." Katie stood to go into her bedchamber. Curling up under her blankets, she soon fell off to sleep. She dreamed about a large red-haired man with the bluest eyes, but there was something wrong. There were tears in those blue eyes. Katie stirred in her sleep as James Patrick stirred in her dreams.

Later that evening as Katie ate dinner, she went over what Mr. Reeves had told her. James Patrick would only sign if she signed first. Did that mean he wanted to stay married to her? It had to mean that. Her future was just as unsure as before. Katie put her fork down. She sat by the window gazing out into the garden. The season was turning cold. All the flowers were dying. The thought of a long winter ahead deepened Katie's gloomy thoughts.

Maggie came in to clear the table. When she finished, she sat beside Katie. "'Tis worried I am for you, Katie. I feel as if we are family. I don't know if you knew, but I had feelings for your father. He was such a gentle, kindhearted man. I believe, Katie, that had he lived we would have...well, who knows?"

Katie reached out to hold Maggie's hand. "I know he was very fond of you too."

With tears glistening Maggie explained, "The reason I'm bringing this up now is to let you know that if you would like to talk things over, I am here for you. Like I said before, I like to think of us as a family of sorts. I don't have a lot of answers about things, but sometimes it clears the mind just to let the words pour out."

As if given permission, Katie did just that. "Oh Maggie, I have come to love James Patrick. He protected me while I was in the gaol. I felt safe being his wife even when we were apart. I've grown to trust and respect him. There was even a sense of pride knowing he was my husband. He isn't an evil man or a thief, but someone who was trying to fill his belly to keep from starving. When Mr. Reeves told me James Patrick wouldn't sign that paper unless I signed first, I felt relief. I was happy he wanted to be married to me. It was only a year ago that I felt all alone in this world. When James Patrick came into my life, I felt I had family and a purpose again. Even when we were to be shipped out,

I felt secure, knowing I would be with him. I have seen him in a horrible place, and he proved to me how brave and compassionate he is."

Maggie listened quietly.

"I was told later," Katie said, "that when James first arrived everyone thought he was some kind of monster. Less than a year later a lot of people respected him. After we were married, a gaoler brought me news about James. He told me that James and some other men were given extra jobs on the outside. My heart would actually flutter thinking about him. Maggie, can you understand what I'm feeling?"

"Aye, Katie. Remember what I said about your father?"

Dabbing her eyes, Katie continued, "Then of course you know how I feel. I also met this woman named Mary. She became a dear friend. I feel so guilty leaving her there in that dreadful place. Here I am sitting by a warm fire with food in my belly. Oh Maggie, how can I help her and James Patrick while they're still in that gaol?"

Maggie didn't have all the answers, but she did have comfort to give. "Katie, I have listened, and you do sound like a woman in love. He fills your heart and your thoughts. That tells me how important he is to you. I don't think things just happen. I think they happen for a reason. If you want to stay married to this man, then don't let anyone tell you different. I guess the first thing you would need to do is go talk to the man…hear what he has to say about it all. You have after all, accepted him as your husband. Who better to talk to about your life together? As far as your friend in the gaol, you are in a better place now to help her. You have Lord and Lady Wilson. I think they would do anything for you. You could call on them for help. You also can take in extra food and clothing for her. I'm sure she would love you to visit."

It was as if a great weight was being lifted off of her. "Yes! I do want to stay married to him. I want to be his wife, Maggie. It will mean I will have to leave here. I would rather do that than stay in this lovely, safe home without him."

Yes, she cared deeply for him, and somehow she had gotten the idea that caring for him was wrong. It was all right as long as she had been in the gaol, but now that she was a free woman it wasn't acceptable. That was what Mr. Reeves had tried to impress on her without actually saying it.

"Tomorrow I will go and visit James and Mary," Katie said. "Can you put some food together for me to bring?"

"Aye, two baskets full I'll have for you. Now make sure you tell him how you feel. Do it first thing." Maggie stood. "I'll go and make some coffee. I have a feeling we're going to be up for a while talking."

It was indeed very late before the two women went off to bed. Katie found sleep impossible once she climbed into bed. The sun wasn't going to rise quickly enough for her this day. She could barely wait to see James Patrick...her husband.

⊰〜⊱

Red woke feeling stiff, but his mood was lighter. There was no reason for him to feel better, but he did. Maybe it was because he had poured his heart out to the Lord the night before. He admitted his love for Katie. He hadn't realized it until he found that she was taken from him. His anger and hurt had surprised him. There were no answers given to him, but he knew the Lord heard.

"Up and at 'em, Red. Ye got a visitor, and 'tis a fair lass to boot," the gaoler shouted for all to hear. "She be a-waitin' for ya, so up with ye now!"

Red knew it was Katie. His heart began to beat faster. He'd had all night to think it over and decided not to make this difficult for her. She had only married him because she was forced into it. He just wasn't sure he could sit and listen to her as she explained herself out of his life. He had faced many a fight, and even death a time or two, but this was a harder thing. He squared his shoulders and took a deep breath. If at all possible the only two who would know his heart was breaking would be God and himself. He couldn't stand the thought of losing her. The only way it could be worse was if she knew how he felt, and she walked away from him anyway.

The gaoler led Red to a small room that was bare except for a small table with two chairs. Red was told to sit, and that his visitor would be there shortly. The gaoler added that he would give them privacy since

84

he knew he could trust Red, but the chains would have to stay on. It wasn't but a minute or two when Katie stood in the doorway. Red couldn't take his eyes off of her. She was lovely in her simple gown. She had a healthy glow, and had even filled out some. The lump in his throat threatened to do him in. He stood without saying anything. He didn't dare. His voice would fail, making him look a fool. He sent up a quick prayer for God's will.

Katie walked in and sat across from him. She noticed he had lost weight. He was beginning to look a little gaunt. She tried to read his expression, but his face was hard. His eyes caused her to hesitate, but determinedly she began. "How are you, James Patrick?"

He just nodded.

"I know you heard that I was released. Would you believe it if I were to tell you Mr. Reeves came to see me? You remember, don't you? He was the magistrate?"

"I know who he is." Red almost snapped the words.

Katie faltered but went on. "He told me he felt it best to annul our marriage. I was angered because I felt no one had the right to decide that except you and me. He had brought the paper for me to sign. I...I saw that you hadn't signed it yourself."

"You mean you weren't the one who wanted to annul the marriage?" Red straightened in his chair.

Katie noticed a small vein pulsating at James's temple. "No James, I didn't know anything about it. We were thrown together by our circumstances, and I would understand fully if you feel it best for us to...well, not be married. I felt you and I had an understanding of sorts. I would never do something like that without talking to you first. I really don't know how to say things except bluntly. Gran always used to say, 'If ye need to say something, then say it.' I had no knowledge of this paper until it was brought to me. I didn't sign it when I saw you hadn't either. I thought it best if we talked about it. Like I said before, if you feel it best..."

Before Katie could finish Red jumped up from the table. Since he was chained at the wrists, he couldn't reach out to her but stepped forward. Katie's eyes grew twice their size, not knowing what to expect from him. "You mean you want to stay married to me? Is that what you're saying?"

Katie blushed scarlet. For a split second Red thought he had mistaken what she was trying to say and had made a fool out of himself after all.

Katie looked up at him with a twinkle in her eye. "I want you to know I hold no claim to you, James Patrick. You owe me nothing, and I understand that. I have found that I care about you deeply."

Red's heart pounded.

"Even though we were pushed into getting married, I chose you myself. I thought we were forced to marry but we weren't. No one made me marry you. I started to feel comfort in knowing that I had a family again. I felt safe knowing you were my husband, and pride too. I heard how people were talking about you. How the men respected you, and the ladies well, a few let me know how they envied me. James, I want to stay married to you if you will have me."

James grabbed her hands the best he could. The room they were in was barely big enough to hold the smile on his face. They started laughing and talking all at once. Katie told him of Papa's house, and of the lands given by the Wilsons. James could scarcely take it all in.

"Katie, I will be shipped out, but not soon because winter is coming. Now that you have a home, are you sure you want to go with me?"

Nodding, she said, "I have thought it through. I want to stay with you. Would there be any way you could stay here now that we have a home?"

"I don't know. I remember Reeves asked me if I had family or land before he sentenced me, but I don't know if it would make a difference now."

Katie's face brightened. "Why don't I talk to Lord and Lady Wilson? Maybe they can help us! They said if I needed anything, all I had to do was ask."

James thought about what Katie was saying, but it wouldn't work. "If I stay, I would be locked up here until I've served my given years. I would rather be working the land than sitting in a cell all that time. Even if the land I'm working won't be my own."

Katie crinkled her forehead in thought. "Then I will ready myself for the sail. I will also make arrangements for visits until it is time to go. What will we do with Brady's Brick?" After seeing the questioning look on James' face, Katie explained, "That's what Papa named our cottage. I don't want to sell it, James. I know Papa would want me to keep it."

Red smiled at his wife. "Then you won't sell it. We need to make plans."

Katie nodded in agreement. "Aye, you are right. I will see if I can come see you again in one week's time. Is there anything I can get for you while you are here?"

"Some fruit would be nice if you can get some," was his reply.

"As a matter of fact I already have that," Katie stated. Getting up from the table she walked just outside the door, stooping to pick up a large basket. It was loaded with food. "How about a picnic?" She smiled.

After the feast, James sat back, patting his stomach. They talked a little longer, but all too soon it was time for Katie to leave. She stood up as her husband came around to her. He placed his arms around her. He had to lift his hands with chains over Katie's head. "You have made me a happy man, Katie Elizabeth. I thought I had lost you."

Katie lay her head on Red's chest, listening to his heart. After a moment they stepped apart.

❧ ☙

After Katie left, Red was led back into his cell. He told the men some of what had happened.

"Ye don't say," sputtered one of the men. "Ye mean that ol' man Reeves hisself told the lady she could not be married to ya?"

The night was spent talking about marriage and the joy, or lack of it. It all depended on who was doing the telling. Laughter could be heard as they shared their stories of wives trying to tame them. Red, for the first time ever, felt a part of it all. They talked well into the night about their lives and wives. Red stayed quiet for the most part. After all, he lacked experience.

10

Bon Voyage

Lord and Lady Wilson arrived for a surprise visit at Brady's Brick just before the noon meal. Fortunately Maggie had made enough stew and biscuits for all. After greeting one another, Lady Wilson spoke first. "We hope you don't mind but we were shopping, and at the last minute decided to stop for a visit. We hope we aren't interrupting your lunch as I can see your table is set."

Katie smiled. "No, no, please...please stay for lunch. Maggie always makes more than enough, as you already know." The couple accepted her kind invitation. Afterwards tea and fresh berry pie were served. Katie was asked many questions about how she liked her new home, and if she was settled in. She thanked them for keeping her trunk with her few treasures. She also told them how grateful she was for all they had done and were doing for her.

Lord Wilson grew serious. "Kathryn, I was called upon by the magistrate, Mr. Reeves, a few days ago. He was distressed by some news. He heard you decided not to annul your marriage. He hoped I would talk to you and try to make you understand that you need not stay married. For some reason he feels you find yourself obligated to this man. You need not be. Mr. Reeves also informed me that he was happy to settle things for you so you wouldn't have to be involved. Then he heard that you insisted on visiting this person at the gaol."

Katie pushed her bowl away, knowing her meal was finished. Maggie all but ran into the next room for safety. Katie was a gentle soul, but this was a touchy subject. Anger threatened to rise until Katie looked at both their faces. They spoke purely out of concern for her. Gently she tried to explain her decision. "I know it is because you care that you are here. I have made some decisions that may surprise you, but I hope you understand. I want to stay married to James Patrick. I have found that I care for him deeply, and he for me. Without going into great detail I need for you to understand that being in the gaol was very difficult. This man cared for me and for others as well. He looked out for the weaker ones, and I came to respect and care for him. No, more than that; I have come to love him."

"Are you sure of that, or is it gratitude you feel?" Lord Wilson questioned.

"Yes, I am sure. I had every opportunity to walk away from him, but found I couldn't. I know it will be a hardship sailing to another land, but I feel I can face whatever comes with James Patrick. I want to be his wife."

Lady Wilson looked at her husband as if he could say some magic words to change the girl's mind. When he stayed quiet she jumped in, "My dear, do you truly realize what you are saying? Not only do you want to leave this comfortable and safe home for the unknown, but to leave with a stranger! Think about what you are doing!"

"I do not wish to hurt either of you; however I think you will understand when I tell you that I had to learn to trust strangers in my situation. I learned that just because people were locked up in a gaol didn't mean they were bad people. Many suffered from their circumstances. I saw horrible things, and I saw acts of courage and tenderness. My eyes were opened to many things. I found myself trusting people who were virtual strangers."

Lady and Lord Wilson did not have an answer to that. What could they say? They knew in their hearts it was they who had let this young woman down. They needed to trust in her right now, in her judgment. Even if she were to make a mistake it was her right to do so.

Lady Wilson spoke in a very contrite way. "Kathryn, you are right. We need to let you live your life. You know we are only thinking of you, but we really don't have any right. I guess we have been trying to control your life again. That needs to end. It's just that we have come to love you as if you were a daughter, and we want you safe." Lady Wilson then leaned over the table to place her hand over Katie's. "Please dear, I ask one thing: that you let us help you. We will keep your home open for as long as it takes for you to come back, even if it's for a visit. We will speak to the authorities, and try to make the voyage more comfortable. Since you are free and your...husband is not, we may be limited as to what we can do, but we will try. You will always have a home here. If you ever need anything, just ask. We have let you down once. It won't happen again."

Katie's heart overflowed from their kindness, but she knew she would not let herself completely lean on these people. She needed to lean on herself and James Patrick. It wasn't that she didn't trust them, but where she was going they would never be able to help her.

Katie thought of Mary. "There is one thing you could do for me if you would," she started. "There is a woman who is a great friend of mine. She's still in the gaol. She became as close to me as anyone could. She stepped in to protect me before she even knew me. I would wish that she could live here at Brady's Brick as long as she wants. Do you think we could meet with a magistrate on her behalf? Since she will have a home, they may let her leave. I believe she was given a hard sentence since she had nowhere to go. Mary is proud. She would never agree unless she could somehow pay her own way. She worked in the gaol kitchen with me. I can tell you she would be a great help to anyone given the chance. She is strong and intelligent, and even though she was in the gaol..." Before Katie could finish, Lord Wilson interrupted her.

"Dear Katie, you need not explain anything to us. Your friend will be welcomed. We would be happy to help. As far as her staying here at Brady's Brick, this is your home to do with as you wish. We will go tomorrow, and do what we can to have her released."

Katie jumped up with tears in her eyes hugging them both. "You will never know how happy you have made me," she sniffled.

The Wilsons promised to pick her up in the morning to submit a petition of release for Mary. With a job and a home waiting, they were very hopeful. Then they bid Katie good-bye.

Maggie closed the door softly after they left. She had to wipe her own tears. "Blimey, can't say I ever heard the master and his wife sound so sad in all my days. They sure take a shining to you. It nearly killed them when all this first happened. I believe they knew the truth all along, but Miss Tess cornered them. She forced them to choose her over you. Of course they sided with their own blood. That young woman has a way of making people do what they don't want to do."

"What has become of Tess?" Katie asked. "I was told she was sent away."

Maggie shrugged. "She was shipped off for a time. Hiding out, I guess. I heard it cost his Lordship a pretty copper penny to keep her from the gaol for falsely signing papers and lying about you."

That old feeling of bitterness washed over Katie. She knew it was wrong to hate. Gran had taught her that, but she couldn't deny her hate for Tess. She would fanaticize about getting even with her. Katie felt uncomfortable with this feeling. It seemed to have power over her. Somewhere in the back of her mind she knew it could overtake her if she allowed it. For the most part she was able to fight it off, but once in awhile it would raise its ugly head. Yes, hate was ugly, but at times it felt so good.

Victoria followed her maid to her room, throwing her hat and gloves on the bed. "Marie, put all my things on the table, and get my bath ready." Marie obeyed while Victoria began opening packages. Holding her new treasures, she admitted to herself that shopping was becoming a bore. She decided to get more comfortable by taking her hair down so Marie could brush it out.

Her thoughts turned to her husband and his moodiness. After he had returned from his court rounds, he still seemed distant from her. He seemed lost in his own thoughts lately, leaving little time for his wife. Sometimes he could be so aggravating. She didn't want him around all the time, but when she required attention he needed to be there. She smiled in the mirror. His mood really didn't matter. She knew how to handle him. A little flattery, a little extra feminine attention, and her husband would melt. Victoria only had one problem. She was getting as bored with her husband as with shopping. She needed something new in her life. She needed something exciting or someone; maybe a trip to America. No, there were wild Indians there. The thought of them made her shudder. Maybe Paris; it had been a long time since she and Peter had gone anywhere.

Just then Peter entered her bedchamber. He stopped to admire his wife's beauty. He would never get tired of looking at her. Yes, he had to admit she was a beautiful woman, but empty inside: no substance, no depth. She couldn't or wouldn't meet his needs. Their lives revolved around her. He had once loved her deeply, but his desire for her had waned. He felt nothing for her anymore. When she tried to demurely force her will on him, it angered him. He was no fool. Peter suddenly felt that strange, restless feeling again. Although he had just returned from a long trip, he wanted to get away again.

Victoria jumped at seeing him out of the corner of her eye. "Peter! For heaven's sakes, you scared me half to death! How long have you been standing there?"

"I'm sorry. You seemed deep in thought, and I didn't want to disturb you."

"Well, now that you have, I want to talk to you about something that's been on my mind. I would like for us to take a holiday to Paris. It has been so long since we have traveled anywhere exciting. You have been working so hard, and I hardly see you anymore. What do you think?"

Going to Paris was the last thing he needed. "You're right. It has been some time since we traveled hasn't it? I really can't get away right now, no matter how much I would like. Why don't you go? Ask Ruth to go with you and make it a shopping trip."

Victoria pushed her lips together in an exaggerated pout. "Don't you want to be with me?"

Peter could see Victoria needed stroking. "Of course, darling, but because of the shortage of magistrates, I have to help pull the extra counties. I couldn't leave them strapped right now. We could wait until next year, if you're willing."

Victoria stood and walked over to her husband. Slipping her arms around him she lay her head on his chest. "I don't want to wait that long. If you really can't come along, maybe I will see if Ruth can go. You wouldn't mind?"

Peter put his arms around her, setting his chin on top of her head. "Well, I guess I could let you go if you promise not to put us so far in debt that I would have to work the next fifty years."

"Oh thank you, Peter! Now you know I'll try to hold back a bit." Victoria lifted her head, considering him with a bright smile. "Now I must get in my bath before the water turns cold." Pulling away, she walked to the side room where her large tub was filled. She stopped and turned just before closing the door. "You realize, of course, I won't have as much fun without you."

Smiling, she closed the door, then climbed into the warm water. Yes, she knew how to handle Peter. She knew he didn't want to go with her, and she didn't want him to. She would be free to really enjoy herself.

Lady, you're not fooling anybody, Peter thought. He knew she didn't want him to go with her, but it worked out for him too. With Victoria gone for a time, he would have the freedom he desired, and that was something to look forward to. Even if it cost him a bundle with Victoria's spending, at least he would have some peace. The price was worth it. He hoped his lovely wife would be leaving soon.

⁂

The harbor was a mass of humanity. Everywhere there were men running around while ships were being loaded and unloaded. Huge crates were stacked everywhere, along with other materials. To one end of the harbor, carriages were dispatched to pick up incoming passengers, and drop others off.

A young woman in a maid's uniform stumbled on the plank descending from one of the ships.

"Be careful, you twit! If you drop any of my bags in the water, you'll follow them!" Tess Wilson hissed.

The maid turned red with embarrassment as she held on tighter.

Tess lifted her skirts to keep from tripping herself. At the bottom of the plank she stood waiting impatiently for her father's coach. "Where are they? You would think they would care if their own daughter came home."

The longer the young woman had to wait, the more agitated she became. Men carrying baggage from the ship brought the rest of her trunks. The two women stood, feeling quite uncomfortable in the middle of the noise and filth. If that weren't bad enough, a number of ruffians kept eyeing them.

The sound of harnesses and horses' hooves caused Tess to turn. She watched as a fine carriage, pulled by matching bays, stopped further down the pier. Fascination replaced irritation as she watched a man and woman stepping down. By looking at them, one could tell they were well off. The woman was dressed elegantly with a cape that matched her smart little hat. The man was handsome and dressed impeccably. All of his attention was on the beautiful woman.

Tess was mesmerized as she watched the couple. Jealousy crept in as she witnessed the tenderness between them. She wanted to be given that kind of attention. Tess thought she had a lot of baggage, but it was nothing compared to this other woman. Another carriage filled to the brim with trunks, boxes, valises, and other items followed. Soon several men were busy unloading the woman's trunks. Tess strained to hear what they were saying, but there was too much noise.

"I'll miss you, darling. As excited as I am, it won't be as fun for me without you. Are you going to miss me?" Victoria practically purred.

Peter held his wife, saying all the right words. He wondered why Victoria felt she had to "overplay" her departure. "Don't be ridiculous. You know how much I'm going to miss you. Please take care of yourself. Three months is a long time for you to be away. I just hope you don't forget me," he said, overplaying himself.

"Oh Peter! How can you joke about such a thing? Of course I won't forget you. Are you sure you won't change your mind, and come along?"

"Well, I expect we would end up with a chaperone once Ruth got here. You know I need to stay here to make some more money to replace all you plan on spending," he joked. They embraced once more, and turned to see the Crowleys' carriage pulling up.

After greeting each other the two couples walked the plank to the ship. With great fanfare all the good-byes were said, and kisses given.

Soon the men headed back to their separate carriages. "So, Reeves, what are you going to do with all this freedom now that the women are leaving?" Crowley smiled wickedly.

"I would suspect the same as you." Peter chuckled. Shaking hands they parted.

Peering out the window of his carriage, Peter noted an attractive, young woman by herself, except for a servant. Baggage was piled all around her. Frustration creased her lovely brow. Peter tapped the top of his carriage with his cane. "Digs, pull over," he ordered his driver.

"Yes, sir!"

As soon as the carriage stopped, Peter opened the door himself and jumped down. Stepping in front of the woman he tipped his hat, introducing himself. "Hello, you appear to be in need of assistance. May I offer you mine? My name is Peter Reeves." Peter bowed.

The woman gave a demure smile, offering him her hand. "Mr. Reeves, I'm Tess Wilson."

"Wilson? You wouldn't happen to know Lord and Lady Wilson would you?" he asked.

"Why yes, they are my parents! You know them? I must say I'm angry with them right now since they were supposed to pick me up. I can't imagine where they are. I was about to hire a carriage, but you don't know who or what has been sitting inside one of those."

Peter studied the young woman. So this was the daughter who had so coldly lied to send an innocent woman to the gaols. He would have to be careful. If she was capable of that, she could be capable of anything. "Actually I'm glad they aren't here. It gives me a chance to meet you, and offer you my assistance," Peter once again bowed slightly. "I have met your parents on several occasions. I'm sure they wouldn't mind if I give you a ride home. That is…if you want."

"So you can be trusted, sir?" Tess smiled.

"Well, I never said that—only that your parents know me." Tess laughed, stepping into the carriage as Peter held the door for her. "Digs, you and Sacks hire a public coach. Sacks, you load the luggage in it. Make sure to leave room for the maid."

"Yes sir, Mr. Reeves," the driver responded.

❧❦

Victoria stepped onto the deck to get one last glimpse of her husband. What she saw made her blood boil. At that precise time, her husband was helping a young woman into their carriage. She gasped, then turned back towards the cabin, rage contorting her face.

A sailor had to step out of her way. He would rather fight the sea than a woman in such a foul mood.

Pacing her cabin like an animal, Victoria hissed at the air, "I'm not even out of the harbor yet, and already he has a trollop! I'm not going to be made a fool of! Well, two can play that game." She had the time, and Peter's money to make sure she wouldn't suffer alone. "So be it. Let him have his fun now. He will pay dearly."

❧❦

The angry woman on deck was so loud the sailor could hear her berating the air. He was glad he wasn't the target. He walked off shaking his head. He didn't know who the man was she was muttering about, but by the look on her face…he was a dead man.

❧❦

Peter instructed his driver to head to the Brick House, then sat back to enjoy the ride. Tess was the first to start the conversation. "I hope you don't think me bold, but I noticed you were escorting a woman to one of the ships. You seemed close." Tess wondered if she was overstepping.

"Ah yes, she is my wife. She's traveling with a friend to Paris," Peter offered.

"Paris! Oh, I have always wanted to go there."

"Really? You obviously were traveling. Have you been gone long?" Peter questioned.

"Too long to suit me. I was just visiting my aunt for a time, and now I'm headed home. I don't consider that traveling, but I have been gone about six months. I was anxious to see my parents. That's why I was so disappointed when they didn't come. I appreciate your help, Mr. Reeves."

"Call me Peter. That is quite an extended visit. It would seem strange your parents wouldn't be here to greet you, but I'm happy to help a fair lady in distress." Peter could pour on the charm when he wanted to, as could Tess. They were a fair and well-matched pair.

"Tell me, Peter, you said you've met my parents, when?"

Peter shifted in his seat. He had to be careful how he answered her. "Why, there are few people in London who don't know your parents. When you said your last name, they just came to mind. Like I said, I've met them at several social occasions." Peter gave her a bright smile.

Tess nodded, smiling back. She seemed content with his answer.

They rode in silence until they stopped in front of the Brick House. Peter was always impressed with the wealth that gushed from the estate. He had only been there a few times before but appreciated the grandeur even more each time. As soon as the carriage stopped, the footman opened the door, helping the occupants down. They walked up the stairs to the entryway just as the door opened.

Lady Wilson stood with a look of surprise and question on her face. "Tess! How? Why? Mr. Reeves!" Lady Wilson was so flustered she couldn't get a full sentence out.

Peter grabbed her hand, speaking quickly, "Why Lady Wilson, how nice of you to remember me since it has been a while. Remember we met at the Grayson's Ball? I hope you don't mind that I offered your daughter a ride home. I was at the harbor seeing my wife off and spotted this young woman in distress."

Lady Wilson understood what Peter's intentions were and appreciated the fact that he obviously hadn't shared any information with Tess.

Tess stepped forward. "Mother, where were you and Father? I waited and waited. Thank goodness Peter offered his help, or I might still be standing there in that awful place."

"We thought you were arriving next week. We had no idea you were arriving early, but I appreciate *Mr. Reeves* bringing you home." Lady Wilson emphasized his proper name, sending her daughter a message. She did not appreciate Tess calling a man by his given name after just meeting him...especially a married man.

Tess scowled. She wasn't even in the house yet, and she was being corrected. Pouting, she asked, "You didn't get my letter explaining my plans? Aunt Marilyn wanted me to stay a little longer, but I missed you and Father so much. I needed to come home." Tess melted into her mother's arms.

Lady Wilson clung to her daughter. "I have missed you too. I'm so glad you're home. Thank you, Mr. Reeves, for all you have done for our daughter. Please, come into the parlor and have some tea."

"Where's Father?" Tess inquired. "Shouldn't he be home by now?"

"Your Father had business to attend to, and won't be home until dinner."

The trio sat having tea while discussing all the news and tidbits that Tess had missed out on. They were all careful not to mention Kathryn. When it was time for Peter to leave, Tess felt a sense of loss even before he was out the door. "Must you leave so soon, Peter?" Tess cooed.

Lady Wilson's brow arched, seeing her daughter practically throwing herself at the man. Surely Tess had heard him speak of having a wife. Lady Wilson was finding out more and more about her daughter that was disturbing.

Peter turned to respond to Tess until he saw the disapproval of Lady Wilson's face. He decided to distance himself from the young lady, at least for now. "Thank you, Lady Wilson, for your hospitality. I enjoyed my afternoon, but I really need to attend to business. It was nice to see you again." Peter took his coat and hat from the servant. Bowing, he stepped out the door.

Tess pouted once more as she turned to go back into the parlor. "Why, he didn't even say good-bye to me. What kind of gentleman won't even acknowledge a lady?"

"A married gentleman, Tess, especially when a young lady is falling all over him."

"I only asked why he had to leave so soon!" Tess shouted.

"Tess, let's not fight on your first day back," her mother pleaded. She had forgotten how quickly she could feel overwhelmed in her daughter's presence.

Tess lifted her head slightly, showing her defiance. Anger filled her. Her parents had no idea how she planned to make them suffer. She would never forgive them for forcing her to go away. How could they have stood up for that stupid servant girl over her?

Tess suddenly smiled at her mother. "You are right, Mother dear. Forgive me for being so curt with you. I'm tired from the trip."

Lady Wilson realized she was filled with regret, regret that her daughter was back. Peace was once again gone from her home. Sadness washed over her as she realized her true feelings for her daughter. Dread and anxiety filled her instead of happiness and joy. Lady Wilson excused herself from Tess's presence to rest before dinner. She suggested her daughter do the same. With heavy heart the grand lady left the room before Tess could see the tears forming in her eyes.

11

Mary Willow

Mary bent over the scrub barrel to wash the pots. In spite of her aching back, she felt content with her life. Once her talents were realized they were used. She was given the job as head cook shortly after she had started working in the kitchen. Some may have thought that a punishment in itself, but she was thrilled. She had never held a "position" before. It was a "proudful" thing to her. Mary was given more freedom in her job, and found the days flew by. She often fought to get decent food to work with but did the best she could with what was given her.

There was only one thing that caused her heart to ache, and that was the loss of her friend. Katie came to visit once a week. When it was time for her to go, it seemed to Mary that a small piece of her left with the girl. Mary was happy Katie girl was no longer made to stay in this "pit o' the devil," but how she missed her.

Sighing, she put the pot on the shelf where it belonged and bent her body backwards as if to get the kinks out. Talking to herself, she quipped, "Blimey, 'tis a better life in this 'ere kitchen than the streets. Who e'er think ol' Mary be 'appy in prison?"

Chuckling, she turned to check out "her" kitchen to make sure all was in place. The old girl hadn't felt pride in a long time, but she felt it now. She took great pride in her kitchen. She was first to work in the morning, and last one out at night. As time passed, she had proven herself trustworthy, earning the freedom she needed to do her job right. The other cooks could care less about cleanliness or how the food tasted. They thought Mary to be a crazy old woman, but they didn't mess with her. If she wanted to do all that extra work, then let her.

"Eh, ol' Mary!" the turnkey named Henry greeted her. "Ye be gettin' in big around 'ere. Ye need to check in at the boss's office in the morn. 'Tis said ye got some high-and-mighty gents to sees ya on the morrow!"

Fear gripped Mary's heart. Things were going good now. She didn't want any changes. "Me? What for they need to be a-seein' me?"

"Nobody be tellin' me nothin' round 'ere. I jus' do what is told to me, an' I be told to fetch ye in the morn," came the answer.

Henry let Mary inside her cell. Trying not to disturb the others, she turned to her "spot." She carefully hung her dress and apron on the peg. Fear kept rearing its ugly head at her. All sorts of unpleasant things entered her mind. Was something missing in the kitchen? If something came up missing, would she be blamed?

The night wore on for her as she tossed and turned. Sleep eluded her until she realized she was worrying for nothing. After all, what could they do to her? She was already in prison, and she hadn't done anything to get hanged over. They could take her kitchen from her. Now that indeed would be a great loss. Well, she had no control over her life or what happened around her. Others had her life in their hands. At any given time her world could be turned upside down just on someone's whim. Turning one more time to get more comfortable, she resolved that it would be a long sleepless night...and it was.

Finally the morning arrived. Why was it that sleepless nights were endless? Mary knew she was late in rising, but exhaustion ruled her. Bones could be heard creaking as she stood. Stretching, she reached for her dress and long apron.

"Mary! What are ye doin' 'ere so late in the morn?" one of the other women asked. "Ye always be in the kitchen long afore anyone."

Mary nodded in agreement. "'Tis truth ye speak. I slept hard fer sure," she lied.

The turnkey unlocked the door. "Are ye ready for yer visit today, Mary?"

Mary nodded. Once again, fear squeezed her heart. "When is it I go?"

"Not 'til later, but don't worry, I'll come to fetch ya when the time comes." The man smiled at her.

"Thank ye, 'enry," Mary nodded as she headed towards the kitchen.

"Ye got a visit from some other besides Katie?" one of the other women asked her as they walked together.

"Aye, but cannot say as to who it be. 'Twas told it be with gents."

One of the other women snickered. "Could it be that yer reputation followed ya 'ere? Could be the gents heard more than ye being a good cook."

Everyone laughed except Mary. She was afraid. Nothing good ever came out of people needing to see her. Life had taught her that...no good indeed.

Mary thought the night had dragged on, but it was nothing compared to the day. Knowing she would be summoned made her edgy. One look at her, and people stayed clear. Everyone knew by midmorning of her call to the office. Just like her, they all assumed it was bad news. Finally the word came down that she had been summoned. Slowly she pulled off her apron and went to wash her hands and face. Poking wisps of hair back into her cap, she slowly turned to leave the kitchen. The other workers silently stepped aside and turned to her as if she were walking to the gallows. They all took turns patting her shoulder as she passed.

Mary's feet felt like they were made out of lead. As she looked down the hallway it seemed to lengthen, and grow narrower. She wasn't sure, but she thought she had seen a noose hanging at the end of it for a split second. Finally she stepped up to the door. The gaoler lightly knocked. After being asked to enter she peeked in first. To her surprise she saw several men, and a fancy looking lady. Even more surprisingly, Katie was there.

Katie sprang to her feet to greet her friend. "Mary, I'm so glad to see you!"

"Wha...why?" was all Mary could muster.

"Come sit down, Mary. We have good news for you." Katie took her hand, leading her to the chair next to hers. "Mary, this is Lady Wilson."

Lady Wilson extended her hand to Mary. "I've heard wonderful things about you from Katie."

Mary could only nod. She was dizzy with relief. She didn't know what was going on, but Katie said it was good news.

A man behind a desk cleared his throat and peered down at his papers. Looking over the rim of his specs at Mary, he addressed her. "I take it that you are Mary Willow?"

Mary nodded affirmative. "I am, Magistrate Withers. I have been given your case to review. You have been here at Newgate for over two years now. Is that correct?"

"Aye," Mary mouthed, although nothing came out.

"It would seem, Mrs. Willow, that you have some very good friends. A petition has been brought before me. I have reviewed your case, as I said before, and found you to be an exemplary prisoner."

Mary bristled. What did he call her? Exempla what? What did he mean by that?

"During this year of confinement you have earned a position as top cook, and by the looks of this report, an excellent one. Praise for a prisoner is not easily found here, Mrs. Willow. I must say, I am impressed with your accomplishments."

Mary felt herself blush to her amazement. She hadn't blushed in over forty years. Not since that boy, Tommy McNally had...why, of all things. Even though she wasn't sure what all the words the man was saying meant, she knew they were good. He was actually saying what a good cook she was.

"I also reviewed the crime committed that caused your confinement. I know many women of your um...station, shall we say, has been victimized by society. That can cause a woman to go astray." Now it was the magistrate's turn to blush. Clearing his throat again, he went on. "I have a signed petition to free you at this time. I have been assured that you have a home and employment, so you can become a useful member of society. What do you have to say to that?"

Mary could scarcely breathe. Home, job, where? She looked around until her eyes fell on Katie. This couldn't be a joke. Katie wasn't cruel. She looked back at the man behind the desk.

"Well, Mrs. Willow, do you understand what I've just said?"

Katie laid her hand on Mary's arm speaking gently, "Mary, it's true. You can come home with me now!"

As their words sunk in, she began shaking her head. Loudly she exclaimed, "Aye, aye, would be a fine day to leave 'ere; a fine day indeed, but what of my kitchen?"

Katie laughed. "Let's worry about you for today. I'm sure they can work something out in the meantime."

Tears slipped down Mary's cheeks. Sniffling, she took Katie's hand. "Nobody e'er came ta 'elp me afore ya come along, Katie girl." Katie held out a hanky. Mary loudly blew her nose. "Blimey, would ne'er have thought it to be me last morn in the gaol when I awoke. Katie girl, 'tain't dreamin', am I?" She handed the used hanky back to Katie, who only stared at it with a bemused look. Mary quickly tucked it in her sleeve.

Katie laughingly assured her it was not a dream and hugged her friend. "'Tis true, Mary. You are free. Free to come home with me. All we need to do is get your things."

Mary grabbed her friend once more. "I 'ad it in me mind that I be stayin' 'ere a long time, so I try to do the best I can. Ter get out o' 'ere is a fine thing. Oh thank ye, Katie girl. Thank ye!"

Laughing, Katie hugged her back. "Lady Wilson is the one to thank. She fought hard for your release."

Mary turned to the other woman. "Thank ya fer yer help and kindness."

Lady Wilson beamed. "Mary, how could a good lady such as you ever be kept in such a place?"

For the second time in one day the impossible happened—Mary blushed from ear to ear.

As Katie and Lady Wilson signed papers, Mary went back to her cell to recover her meager belongings. Upon hearing her news, the others were excited but hated to see her go. "Blimey Mary, who's going to cook fer us?" That seemed to be the big question.

"I don't know. 'Twasn't told of that."

"Where ya be livin' now, Mary?"

"Not too sure on that either, but I s'pect it be a piece better than this place be." Mary hugged some of the women before leaving. Looking back she couldn't help but feel bad for leaving them there. She felt a little sad to leave her kitchen as well, but not bad enough to stay.

"Now ye girls be good, and don't go given' ol' 'enry trouble…'ere?"

Henry cleared his throat while shuffling his feet. "Don't ya forget us 'ere, Mary. Kinda got used to seein' yer face around."

"Why 'enry, yer face is all red," laughed a couple of the other women.

With a sniff, Henry led Mary back to the office. "God bless ya, 'enry," was all Mary could say for the lump in her throat.

Tipping his old cap, Henry turned and shuffled away. He was surprised at how sad he felt to have Mary leaving, but there weren't a lot of women like Mary. He would miss her for sure. Full of spit and fire, that one was.

After Mary had left the office to get her things, Katie and Lady Wilson embraced. "Thank you, for all your help getting Mary released," Katie cried.

Lady Wilson fought tears herself. "Oh Kathryn, did you see her face? What a wonderful day for both of you. Have you everything ready for her at the cottage?"

Nodding Katie wiped her tears, and turned to Magistrate Withers who stood looking rather uncomfortable, witnessing their emotional show of affection.

"Thank you, sir, for all of your help. We could not have succeeded without your recommendation."

Clearing his throat nervously, Magistrate Withers took Katie's hand. "You're very welcome, Mrs. Murphy. Good tidings don't come often enough with my job. I was greatly impressed with Mrs. Willow's record. It spoke volumes on its own. Now if you will excuse me, I must leave to attend other business. Good day ladies, gentlemen." Nodding to all, he left.

Katie and Lady Wilson turned to thank the others for all their help. Lady Wilson spoke to one of the barristers. "Mr. Jacobs, I appreciate all your time invested in this. I must say that Lord Wilson was pleased at how diligently you worked on Mary's release. I am to inform you that he will be stopping by your office to personally hand you a bonus."

A wide smile stretched the young man's face as he thanked Lady Wilson before leaving.

Mary timidly reentered the room, holding on to her pitiful bag of belongings. Once Katie saw her, she took Mary's arm and led her back out in the hallway.

"Come, Mary; let's get you out of here. Lady Wilson's coach is waiting for us, and I'm anxious for you to see your new home! There's so much to talk about! I can't wait for you to see your room, and Maggie has stew cooking on the stove."

"Where ya takin' me, an' why didn' ya tell me, Katie girl, ya was workin' to set me free?"

"I didn't want you to be disappointed if things didn't work out. It took longer than I had hoped. If it hadn't been for Lord and Lady Wilson, I don't know if you would have been released. As far as your new home, it's a surprise."

Mary turned to the "fancy" lady standing next to Katie once more. Tears threatened to fall once again, so Mary looked down at her shoes as she spoke. "'Tis thankin' ya again, I am. Katie girl told me of ya when she come to visit. She said ya 'ad a kind heart."

Lady Wilson appeared touched by the words. "I am so happy I could help, Mary. Katie speaks highly of you, too."

With those words, the three women walked out, arm in arm, as if leaving church instead of one of the most notorious prisons in history.

Maggie stirred the stew once more. She then checked her bread before going back to the spare room. All the boxes had been removed and were replaced with furniture. Heavy curtains hung on the window now that winter was on its way. The bed was freshly made up with a warm coverlet in bright patchwork colors to match the curtains. Rag rugs covered the floor while a small fireplace, with a cheery fire, warmed the room. The day couldn't be more perfect for Mary's arrival. She turned to check on her stew once more when she had heard a coach approaching. Glancing once more around the room, she nervously patted her hair into place. She stood at the door but didn't want to seem overanxious by opening it too soon. She turned back to stand by the fireplace, changed her mind, and ran back towards the door. *Blimey, I haven't been this nervous about anything in a long time,* she thought. She couldn't stand waiting any longer...she opened the door.

The coachman was helping Katie down. He then turned to give Mary his hand, but Mary wouldn't have it. "Been 'elpin' meself down all these years. Can do it now," was all she said. The poor man looked at Katie, not sure of what to do. He decided it was best to step back, out of Mary's way. Katie had to hide a smile as she observed Mary flounce to the ground on her own. Katie waited on the walk until Mary caught up. They turned to wave their good-byes to Lady Wilson.

"Here it is Mary, Brady's Brick. What do you think?"

Mary stood eyeing the cottage. A smile broke across her face. "'Tis one of the finest cottages I e'er see in me life, Katie!"

Seeing Maggie in the doorway, Katie turned to Mary to introduce the two women. After all the pleasantries, the three women went in. Mary's eyes nearly bugged out as she looked around. "Blimey, Katie girl, this 'ere cottage be fanciful."

The two women went from room to room as Maggie set the table for lunch. It was when Mary saw her own room that she let out a shriek. "Cannot be! Me own room with the curtains? I ne'er, I swear I ne'er 'ad me own place such as 'ere even when me poor ol' Percy brought me in to 'is house." That was the first time Katie ever heard the name of Mary's dead husband.

"Why don't you get your things settled before we eat?" Katie suggested. She watched as Mary carefully set her torn bag of belongings on the bed. She carefully lifted out the only other dress she owned. Looking around she found a wooden peg for hanging. With her rough, red hands Mary smoothed the dress out as best she could. Turning back to her bag, she took out the half-toothless comb she always carried, and set it on the table by her bed. Once again she turned back to the bag, bringing out the worn, filthy piece of material that Katie had noticed so long ago in the gaol. With great tenderness, she placed it next to the comb. Closing the bag, she pushed it under the bed announcing, "I be moved in now."

Katie's heart swelled as she watched her friend. Mary had shared only a little of her life. In so many ways Mary was a mystery. She was one of the toughest, yet gentlest women she had ever met. What could Mary have accomplished in her life if only she had been given the chance? Katie was going to give her that chance now. She vowed to do everything she could to help Mary live her years remaining more comfortable and worry-free.

Once settled in, the two women went into the kitchen. They found Maggie standing off to the side, wringing her hands in anticipation of Mary's arrival. Katie watched with an amused look. "'Tis a fine kitchen indeed," Mary chided. "So cheery with the wee windows. Smell the bread. Reminds me of the kitchen in me own house on Turnmill Street in East London. 'Twas not a fine place such as this, but to me 'twas a palace. 'Course it was not smellin' so sweet there even when the bread was bakin'. A stinkin' place 'twas the street we lived, but I 'ad me Percy. Why, Percy and me had a fine life there for a time." Mary lifted her apron she always wore to wipe a tear.

"Come sit and eat now. 'Tis been a busy day," Maggie stated. "Hope you like my stew. The mixin's have been in my family for a long time now." Maggie set about slicing fresh bread and mixing up some hot tea and honey for Mary.

Katie served herself and sat back, listening to the two women. They spoke of the old ways to making stew, and how mutton was the best of all. It was as if she weren't there, not that she minded. It was good to see her two friends together; did her soul good.

"Honey! Yer 'ave real honey fer the tea! 'Tis been a fine day fer sure. Ye bless ol' Mary with yer kindness. Why, Katie girl, 'tis been too long since I had me a speck of honey. 'Tis why ol' women such as I get crusty and sour. Never get enough honey." Mary laughed at herself.

As evening fell and dinner was put away, the three women enjoyed a crackling fire. Now that the sun had gone down the air turned very cold. Katie broke the silence that had enveloped them for a time. "Mary, you've mentioned your husband a few times today. In fact, I never knew his name before today. Can you tell us more about him, or would it be too painful?"

A faraway look came over Mary's face as she went back to the old times with her Percy. It was a special time in her life when the hardness was made softer for the love she had with him. How she missed him still. She felt the sharpness of her longing for him as if he had died yesterday, instead of twenty years ago. She took a sip of tea, letting her mind go back to him once again. His memories were her treasure, and she chose carefully who she shared them with. She hadn't spoken of him for so long. It was hard for her to begin.

"'Twas in Ireland where I met 'im. 'Twas a young lass when I first laid me eyes on 'im. Thought 'e was one of the most handsome men I ever did see. Black hair like pitch, and blue eyes that 'ad to be from an angel. No man could e'er have such blue eyes. 'Is laugh made me laugh too, and when 'e looked upon me 'twas if I was on fire. First time I e'er saw him, 'e was chasing down sheep for the shearin'. I member 'e was mad and swearin'. My Percy could put a red face on a sinner for the swearin' 'e did at times."

Mary chuckled at the thought of it. "I remember 'is big hands. Biggest I e'er saw on a man."

Katie thought of James Patrick's hands.

"Percy told me 'e was wantin' to leave the island fer all the hardships. Said 'e had the passage for 'isself an' spare fer me if I be willin' to follow. Told 'im I wouldn't be 'is whore. Needed to marry me first, and 'e did. Then we sailed. Seems to be a hundred years ago. Me Percy was a 'ard worker. Worked in a factory, 'e did, once we settled in London. 'Twas 'ard work, but 'e was thankful to 'ave it. Made nothing fer all the work 'e did.

Taking another sip of her tea, she continued on. "Weren't long afore he begin to 'ave coughin' fits. 'Twas bad spells 'e 'ad. Afore too long 'e begin ter spit up 'is own blood. They called it Black Lung. Killed 'im outright, it did. Me poor Percy, 'ardly drank the rum either. 'Twas a good man." Sniffling, Mary wiped her face on her apron.

"Mary, I'm so sorry," Katie said, laying a hand on Mary's arm.

Blowing her nose, Mary shook her head. "'Tis sad fer sure, but needs to be remembered. Can't forget my Percy. We 'ad a wee one, a boy. Tiny as could be. Poor little one not be strong enough to live in this 'ard world. Named 'im baby Jimmy, we did. Died small, but 'twas best that 'e did because 'e was sick from the start. Percy took it the hardest. I be glad 'e was in God's 'ands, and not in this cold world. I saw hardships fer the wee ones. They worked j'st as 'ard as the men did.

King George is said to 'ave blood on 'is throne from all the wee ones workin' in those cotton mills. 'Tis a fact, our babe's better off in 'eaven then 'ere. How it be fer me to care fer 'im, if I cannot care fer meself? All I 'ave of baby Jimmy now are the memories, an' a small piece of 'is blanket." So that was the tattered piece of cloth Katie saw in Mary's room. No wonder she handled it so tenderly. Katie thought it best to talk about something else.

"I forgot to tell you some important news. You did such a fine job as cook at the gaol that they are willing to hire you for wages to come back. You have a day or two to think it over before they select a prisoner for the job."

"Blimey, getting paid doin' what I was doin' afore? 'Tis a blessin' indeed. Was that the job the judge mentioned afore lettin' me out?"

"No," Katie answered. "Originally, Lady Wilson was going to offer you a position at Brick House. I received word from Newgate this morning about the job and meant to tell you sooner. I thought you might like 'your' kitchen back, but the choice is yours. Lady Wilson said that her offer is still open."

"'Tis a fact ol' Mary took pride in 'er own kitchen. Done, will do it I will! I like ter take me kitchen back. I 'ave friends there an' all. Ter 'ave a 'ome and place to work...God be good ta ol' Mary fer sure. Did the price to be paid get told?"

"Well, he said if you were willing to start out at half crown per month you could have the job," Katie said, smiling at her friend.

"Ne'er had half a crown afore. How much that be?"

"Two shillings and six pence."

Beaming, Mary finished her tea. "'Tis a rich one I'll be!" Suddenly her smile disappeared. "Won' be 'urtin' the Lady's feelin's iffen I take the other offer, do ya think? She be good ter me."

"Of course not," Katie assured her. "She is going to be happy for you."

"Praise be the Almighty! Then I'll take it fer sure!"

It had been an exciting day for all. It wasn't long before Mary's head began bobbing.

"Mary, why not head for bed?" Katie gently shook her.

"Aye, I think I will. Good night ta yas now." Mary headed for her room. Getting into the fresh gown she was given, she gently picked up baby Jimmy's piece of tattered blanket. Stroking it, she tenderly placed it next to her cheek. It was hard to remember back, but good too. It had been a magical day that Mary would never forget. Things would never be the same for her...thank God. After tossing and turning for a time Mary gathered her bedding and placed it on the board floor. Tucking Jimmy's cloth under her pillow she covered up and was soon asleep. It would be a long time before she would get used to a soft mattress.

The other two women sat by the fire a while longer enjoying their time together. They talked about Mary and the events of the day. "What of Mary once you leave the house? Have you told her your plans yet?" Maggie questioned.

"No, so much has happened today. If she wants, she can stay here to watch over Brady's Brick when I'm gone. She'll be able to make a living with cooking for the gaol. They don't pay anyone to cook there. Why should they? They have enough prisoners to do the work. I told a fib, but Mary is proud. She would never take charity. I had to make arrangements to pay her myself after the warden agreed to my plan. He said it was the best run kitchen he ever had when Mary was in charge. He agreed to keep my secret. I gave the bank instructions to give her a draft each month. She'll think it's from the gaol, and that's what I want. I don't like deceiving her, but she would never take money from me. This way I know she will be all right, and it gives her a sense of purpose. The money will pay for her looking after the place for me, but she won't know it."

"You are a good friend, Katie," Maggie stated quietly.

"I owe her my life. She is one of the bravest, kindest people I know, but you wouldn't ever want to get her mad. I saw her take a woman, much younger than herself, and teach her some respect." Katie's eyes crinkled with amusement at the memory of the fight. "Then one time she stood between me and two men. Defended me, she did, as if I were family instead of a stranger—and won! Of course James Patrick stood behind her, and that really was the reason those men backed down. She didn't know that, though. She was brave for just standing up to them."

"I don't think I could ever do that. I'm not that brave. It all sounds so awful. I cannot imagine being in one of those places; all those poor people. Mary has lived a hard life; yet look at her gentle and kind spirit. 'Tis a hard thing to hear of all her troubles," Maggie added.

"She is someone special, that's for sure," Katie answered as she headed to her room. "Thank you, Maggie, for making her so welcomed today. It was important to me."

"It was important to me too. I'll be heading for bed myself. Good night, Katie. Have sweet dreams."

Katie lay on her bed unable to sleep. Her thoughts churned around James Patrick. She had tried to speak to several people about her husband, but his guilt was without question. In fact, remembering back to their trials, James was the only one who confessed his guilt. Katie sensed that James wanted to leave England. It held nothing for him, and his heart was turned to the new land. He hoped to earn his own land one day. It was said ten acres would be given to a prisoner who was willing to work it. It wasn't a lot, but enough. Even though she had land from her father, it seemed important to James to earn his own. They both knew it would be years before that happened, though.

Katie got up and cracked the window open. Quickly she added more wood to the fire. Fall was her favorite time of year. She loved the crisp air. The curtains lifted at the breeze. She hurriedly jumped back into the bed. Watching the curtains move, and listening to the leaves rustle in the wind, she turned her thoughts back to James. She knew he held his belief in God very seriously. He didn't push her into what he believed but instead encouraged her and comforted her. Without realizing it, she began whispering a prayer to God. That unknown invisible God of James Patrick and Gran. *Please, watch over him and keep him safe. Let us soon be together, and thank you for bringing Mary home.*

Katie thought for a time about what she had just done. Why did she pray? It just seemed to come out of her without thinking about it. She was too tired to figure it out and snuggled down into her blankets. Without realizing it, she thanked the invisible God once more for her soft warm bed.

12

Kiss

The door opened to the room, and Red rose to his feet at the sight of his wife. She smiled and handed him a basket. Red grabbed it in spite of the chains.

"I wish you didn't have to be chained like that. I don't know what they think you're going to do."

"They probably know I would grab you, and not let you go." He smiled.

Katie blushed. Red put the basket on the table, then waited for Katie to show him what she had brought.

After removing a towel from the top, Katie handed him a package wrapped in brown paper. "Mary made you a fine shirt, and I knitted you more socks. I hope they fit. They look a little big to me, but try them and see." Next she lifted out cheese, apples, and slices of fresh bread. "I have some roasted beef here for you too."

Red's mouth watered. "Tom! Would you like some of this here food?" James asked the guard. "My wife brings enough to feed this whole place." The gaoler stepped into the room giving a sheepish grin and nodded to James. Katie placed some beef on a slice of bread, and handed it to him. He took it, tipped his cap to her, and stepped out the door. "I think the men get almost as excited as I do when you come to visit. They keep asking if my 'saint of a wife' is coming in. Are you sure you can afford to be bringing all that extra food each week?" Red inquired.

"Saint indeed! I have more than enough. I'm just thankful I'm allowed to give it to you."

"Speaking of being thankful...." James bowed his head in prayer.

"Heavenly Father, I thank you for all the wonderful blessings in my life and especially, Katie. Thank you, Lord, for bringing her into my life. Bless this food, and help us to always remember who our blessings come from. In Jesus' name, amen."

It always amazed Katie how a man in chains and locked in a gaol could be thankful for "all his blessings." Yet she had to admit that she felt her life being led by a power greater than herself. She had been aware of it for some time now. It gave her a strange sense of peace.

Red watched as Katie started eating an apple. She seemed lost in thought. "Where are you?" he asked.

Katie smiled. "Oh, I was sailing off to the New World on a mighty ship. Have you heard when we leave?"

"No, I would think you would be able to get more information than I would. Did you speak to Lord Wilson about sailing to Botany Bay?"

Katie hesitated in answering him. She didn't know if she should tell him her news or not.

Red saw the worried look and stopped chewing. "What is it? What's wrong?"

Katie looked at her husband. He had a right to know. He would have to know if they were to sail soon. "James, I talked to Lord Wilson a couple of days ago. He came over and brought two men with him. One was a marine and had been to Botany Bay. The other man worked on one of the prison ships in the harbor. Oh James, it was horrible what they told me, and I feel they were holding back some of what they told."

"What did they say?"

"The man who guarded prisoners gave me a short history of the prison ships. How the overcrowding of the gaols forced them to put prisoners on old ships in the harbor. Those ships quickly became so overcrowded that they decided to send the prisoners to Botany Bay. They used to send them to America, until the war. He said that it's not as bad aboard those prison ships now as it used to be years ago."

"Do you know what kind of ships they are?"

"Aye, they are old troop transports with their masts and riggings gone. He told me that Typhus has claimed many a prisoner and marine alike. Rats run the ships, and the men are chained together in the hulks. They are only brought up for fresh air when the weather is fair. Many die, and I heard the food is not sufficient to stay healthy. I never thought I would be truly thankful that you are in here, but I am. How dreadful to think you could be on one of them. If they consider the conditions better now, what must have it been like before?"

"It could still happen, Katie. You never know. I could be taken to one of those ships yet. Besides, look around. Gaol fever has struck here, but God has protected me. If it weren't for you, I would be getting a lot less food, and not near as good. You and the Lord take good care of me."

Katie wished she had his faith. At least she could see he was gaining weight.

He continued, "I will just pray for God's will. I can't ask God to spare me the hulks, and have others go."

Katie said nothing to this. She still couldn't understand her husband's relationship with his God. How could he easily dismiss the thought of being taken aboard one of those horrible ships?

"Was that all the man said?" James asked.

"He said if the men were lucky, they would be picked to do harbor work on shore or dredging. The men are usually so weak and cramped up from being chained for so long. James, what are we going to do? I didn't know what to expect, but I never dreamed anything like this. If being on a ship anchored in the harbor is that horrible, then what will it be like sailing thousands of miles on a rough sea? If that isn't bad enough, I have heard of many hardships once we reach the land. Hunger and danger threatens. People are struggling to survive in a place so far away that help is not to be found."

As Katie talked, her voice seemed to lift with agitation. Red could see her lower lip tremble.

Covering her hand with his, he tried to comfort her. "Katie, I knew all along it wouldn't be easy. I don't know all the facts, but I have heard that the colonies are better settled now. I've been thinking about all this, and need to ask you something. I've been asking myself if it's fair for me to put you through all of this. Why should you pay for my crime? I think it would be a good thing if you were to stay here. Maybe the magistrate was right about getting the marriage annulled. You have a home here, and friends. I think it would be best."

There was more Red wanted to say, but the look on Katie's face stopped him cold. Her expression turned from worry to anger within seconds.

She jumped up, knocking her chair over. With her dainty hand, she jabbed her finger into the big man's chest. "James Patrick Murphy! How dare you try and ditch me! Just because I may be a little afraid of the unknown, that by no means makes me a coward! And what makes you think you can tell me what to do? How do you know what is best? I have had men telling me how to run my life long enough. No more! Don't ever think you can tell me that I am going to stay here while my husband sails off! I am not going to have our marriage annulled! Whatever happened to all that faith you're always talking about? Is your God so weak he won't be able to watch over us?"

Red's eyes bugged out while his mouth hung open. With her chest heaving, and sweat on her brow, Katie retrieved her chair. She couldn't remember feeling so angry. Actually she couldn't remember ever talking to anyone like that before. Pushing loose hair from her face she took a deep breath. She felt dizzy. It was as if a dam had let loose, causing all her fears and frustrations to pour out.

The gaoler rushed into the room when he heard Katie's raised voice. After seeing everything was all right, he left. He wasn't about to step in between a man that size and a wife that mad. With a shaky hand Katie wiped her face with her hanky and proceeded to let out a loud sigh. Red was still sitting with his eyes bugged out. He looked so ridiculous; she couldn't help but stare at him. Without warning, she burst into laughter. Red jumped with surprise at the sound. He looked at her as if she had just lost her mind, which caused Katie to laugh even more. After a moment Red began chuckling. Soon his body shook with laughter. Even the gaoler joined in after hearing them. It made quite a scene.

Once Katie caught her breath, she spoke. "Oh James, I don't know what came over me. I am not a high-tempered person. When I saw your face like that, I couldn't keep myself from laughing. You looked so silly."

James chuckled again. "My face! You should have seen yours! It

116

was so red and puckered up! I thought you were going to throttle me."

"I was thinking about it," Katie stated before breaking into laughter again.

Laughter gave way to a more serious mood as Red spoke. "I want you to know that while I was saying the words, my heart was telling me to stop. I don't want you to suffer through all the hardships, but I hate the thought of losing you even more. I guess I'm selfish, but I'm greatly relieved you won't even consider it."

Without hesitation Katie stepped around the table and knelt before his chair. Placing her hands on his knees she looked up into his eyes and spoke from her heart. "You will never get rid of me, James Patrick. Not unless God himself decides otherwise." They both stood. Red lifted his chains over her head drawing her closer. Lowering his head, they shared their first kiss, a kiss of promise. Katie drew back for lack of breath and lay her head on his chest. She could feel his heart pounding, matching her own. They both spoke words from their heart.

"Mrs. Murphy, I love you," Red whispered.

"I love you too, Mr. Murphy."

A few moments later Katie walked back into the sunshine with her basket empty and her heart full. She decided then and there to start working towards the future. Part of that was doing what she could to make changes in that prison. Some changes had occurred, but too few and far between. There was much to do. Who else could better understand what the gaol needed than someone who had lived in it? She felt different—changed somehow from a girl to a woman. She felt stronger and not as afraid of the future. Hardships were coming—of that, she had no doubt. But people could live soft, and still have a hard life. Hardships were not something to fear, but to live and work through. She knew in her heart that somehow they would make it, for they had each other. Yes, they would make it. That was the promise of the kiss they shared.

"I can't believe you let those men tell Kathryn about all the horrors aboard those ships! I think that was cruel! That wasn't like you at all, Edward!" Lady Wilson scolded.

"My dear, I thought it best that she realize what she's getting herself into. It won't be easy and especially for an innocent such as Kathryn."

"But to let them give her gory details that only served to frighten the poor girl. She has been through enough. I thought you wanted to help her!"

"I do, but she needs to know what can happen. How else will she prepare for such a journey? I hear it's very difficult. I don't want to tell her otherwise. Besides, after hearing all this, she may change her mind. It would be best for her to do that now, rather than when she's halfway across the ocean."

Lady Wilson dabbed her eyes. Looking up at her husband, she felt overwhelmed with fear and grief. "Oh Edward, why in the world would she want to do this in the first place? I truly have tried to understand, but I can't. I told her differently, but to marry a stranger, and go off to some godforsaken place. At best all they can do is to scratch out a living—if they survive at all. It's beyond me."

"Now, now Barbara, there's no reason to get yourself all worked up. Have you forgotten that you and I were virtual strangers when we married? That ours was an arranged marriage? We have come to love each other deeply. I know that it isn't quite the same, but we need to let her make her own decisions. I wasn't trying to be cruel, but to prepare her for some of what she may face." Lady Wilson nodded in agreement while he continued, "She has her mind made up, so all we can do is try our best to help her. Since she is going to be so far away, it will be next to impossible once she is there. You will need to trust me, my dear. I promise you, we will do everything in our power to help her. Now, go rest before dinner. We don't want Tess to know that you've been crying. How would you explain it?"

Lady Wilson let her husband lead her to the staircase and obediently went to her rooms to rest. Sleep eluded her as her mind went from Kathryn to Tess. Once again she had to admit that she had enjoyed her relationship with Kathryn more than with Tess. This knowledge caused her much pain and guilt. She couldn't help it. She

118

had come to love Kathryn as much, if not more, than her own daughter. Her fear for the girl's future was very real. She knew she had no control over her own future, let alone anyone else's. It was futile to worry. Nonetheless, she felt panic whenever she thought of Kathryn sailing away. She decided to indeed trust her husband and promised herself something. She would watch to make sure as time passed that her husband's concern for Kathryn wouldn't ebb away. Once that was decided, she was able to rest.

Lord Wilson stepped out into the garden. Although the temperatures were dropping, the sun had not fully set, leaving the temperature still pleasant. Soon it would be time to close the house up and move to their summer home. He felt tired. His age was catching up with him. Knowing that made him feel melancholy. This should have been an easy time for him and Barbara. He had expected to have grandchildren by now. It had been his intention to see Tess married and settled into home life. He had hoped that would curb some of her wild nature.

He knew his wife was also feeling agitated due to their daughter's return. Her health seemed fragile. He needed to take steps to ease his wife's worries, but what could he do? He was a man of action, which was easy if you had the money. He did, but money wasn't the answer this time.

He had expected to hear from the detective he had hired any day now. He should have hired him sooner to check on James Murphy. He would have to know what kind of man Murphy was if he was to help them. It all depended on the detective's report. Kathryn may have decided to stay married to the man, but if he turned out to be a rogue, he would not spend his time or money on him. Being in the gaol in the first place was cause for mistrust. However, Kathryn had been in the gaol for no fault of her own; perhaps something similar happened to the man, though he doubted it.

Lord Wilson's brow creased as his thoughts returned to his daughter. He knew it was a matter of time before she, once again, got herself into a "situation." Barbara could never know what he knew about Tess. He had spent a lot of money keeping their family name cleared of any scandal. However, he was never sure of what Tess was up to. Barbara told him of how Tess had practically thrown herself at a married man.

Deep in thought he turned back into the house. After closing the French doors, he stepped over to the side table to pour some brandy. Arrangements to move to the summerhouse would have to be postponed. He had too many irons in the fire to leave and questions that needed to be answered. With resolution he decided that it was time to give George Day the answer he had been expecting. If George's son was truly interested in marrying Tess, then he would give his permission. If she wouldn't settle down on her own, he would arrange a good match for her. With that decision made, he belted down the brandy pouring another. Tomorrow would be a difficult day. He didn't want to face it, but face it he would, and so would Tess.

∽◈∾

"Lord Wilson, you have a visitor, sir. A Mr. Grimes." The servant stepped aside to show the man into his employer's study. A young man stepped over the threshold smiling, bowing ever so slightly.

"Grimes, thank you for coming, sit down." Lord Wilson extended his hand. The man took it. "Graines, fetch some tea, and brandy."

Once the two men were settled, the younger man took out a small notebook from his pocket, opened it, and began, "I have some interesting information for you. What do you want first?"

"What do you have on Murphy?"

"He was orphaned and traveled from job to job. Ended up with a family for about eight years, but they lost their farm. As far as I could find out, he was once again on his own. Seems he's a hard worker. Except for stealing bread and cheese from a shopkeeper, he was never in trouble before. He fared better than most of the gutter pups here in the city. I checked him out at Newgate. Seems when he first arrived most of the men were afraid of him. Probably from his size; he's huge.

The gaolers even use him on jobs with a team of men. Seems he gets the job done, and done right. I came across something quite interesting. Many of the turnkeys respect him. That's unheard of."

Lord Wilson listened intently.

The man went on. "I also found many of the other prisoners are quite loyal to the man. They treated me with great suspicion and were quick to defend him. I find myself quite amazed by it, really. They usually tell any and all if they think it will help them. Many times they offer information I don't ask for, but not on this man."

Lord Wilson lit a cigar and leaned back in his chair. Taking his time, he puffed, blowing the smoke over his head. "What was all the stealing business about?"

"I guess he was hungry. Stole bread and cheese, and got caught."

"That's it? I still can't believe they will transport a man for as little as that." Lord Wilson snorted.

"I hear tell of a lad, twelve years old, who was sent out for stealing pants for himself. He was cold and half-naked. They want these thieves gone. It doesn't matter what they stole."

"Taking food because you're hungry or clothes to cover yourself doesn't make a thief. If he worked all those years, it shows that it's not his nature. I can't fault anyone for trying to eat. Is that all the information you have on him?"

"Yes sir, I had trouble finding out anything since he has no family, and the tight-lipped cronies wouldn't talk."

"What other information do you have for me?" Lord Wilson picked up his ornate cigar box and offered one.

Taking a cigar, the man clipped it, and waited for a light. "Your daughter, well, has been seen on several occasions with Magistrate Reeves. Seems his wife is on an extended trip to Paris with a friend of hers. Reeves and your daughter have been seen at the gambling house, and out to a few plays."

"Gambling house! Her mother would faint dead away if she knew her daughter was frequenting such an establishment, *and* with a married man! What else?"

The man squirmed in his chair. He didn't feel comfortable telling a father of his daughter's loose actions. "That's about all. It seems they are…well, shall we say, becoming close friends? The man's wife is due back in another month."

"So there seems to be a marriage of convenience between Reeves, and his wife then?"

"I was told that Reeves got his title of magistrate from his father-in-law. Was a barrister making less than he is now. Met his wife and fell into money."

Lord Wilson leaned back in his chair once more. He had much to think about. "Anything else?" was all he said.

"That's about it for now. I'm still working on getting a meeting together for you with those men I told you about. Grayson is free now, but I am still having trouble getting in touch with Brice and Knotts."

"Contact me when you are able to set something up. If there are any new developments, contact me immediately." Lord Wilson rose from his chair dismissing him. "Good job, Grimes. You answered many of the questions I had. Thank you for coming."

The two men left the study, stepping into the massive foyer to the front entrance. Once again they shook hands before Grimes left.

Lady Wilson descended the stairs smiling at her husband. "Business, Edward? Seems a lot of people have been coming and going lately."

Lord Wilson took his wife by the hand and led her into the parlor to sit before the fire. "Nothing you need to concern yourself over, dear. I've decided to stay in London instead of going to the summerhouse. I have some important business I need to finish, and I thought it would be nice to have the holidays here this year. What do you think?"

"Of course, Edward, I don't mind if you need to stay. I will need to get word to the staff not to open the summerhouse."

"I've already taken care of that. Would you like to have a Christmas ball this year?"

Nothing could have surprised her more. Her husband was not one for such social functions. "It's been such a long time since we entertained like that, Edward. I would love it! It would give me a chance to show off the house dressed in its Christmas finest. Tess will be excited too, I'm sure of it."

"I think you will be the one most excited, my dear," the man said.

"Why, Edward? Is there more to all your surprising news?"

"Oh yes, but I'm not telling you yet. You must wait and see. I don't want to spoil it." He failed to mention to his wife that it would be more than a Christmas ball. She didn't know it yet, but she was about to plan her daughter's engagement party. "Start making the arrangements and make sure Tess helps. Spare no expense, Barbara. Christmas comes only once a year, and who knows when we will ever do this again."

Lady Wilson's excitement rose, and her eyes twinkled with merriment. "Oh Edward, what a wonderful ball it will be. Thank you!" Off she ran to make her plans. Lord Wilson smiled at his wife's excitement, and at his cleverness. Soon all would be set, and he would not have to worry over his daughter any longer. Let another man have the job.

13

Family

Mary held the back door of the cottage open for Henry as he pulled at the pine tree. Snow followed, leaving a wet trail on Maggie's clean kitchen floor.

"Blimey 'enry, Maggie will cuff ya if she sees that snow all over." Mary warned.

"Well, git a rag, woman, and wipe it up afore she sees it," Henry quipped. The fragrance of cookies baking along with the aroma of pine filled the warm kitchen. Mary was amused, watching Henry struggle with the tree. "Ya think maybe ya could help some, putting this monster up?" Henry leaned forward as his chest heaved.

"Are ya alright there, 'enry?" Mary jumped up from her chair in concern.

"Aye, just need some more breaths of air, and I'll be fine."

Between the two of them the tree was soon standing in front of the windows, ready to be decorated. Maggie had come in to check on her cookies and gave her approval. "'Tis a fine tree. Katie will like it. Come and have some tea now. Sit and rest yourselves."

"Don 'ave to ask me twice." Mary smiled, grabbing Henry's arm. "'Ave we any honey left, Maggie?"

The three old friends sat in comfortable silence for a time, sipping tea. The rest of the afternoon was spent sewing lace onto the cloth decorations they had made earlier. They strung cookies for the tree. As they placed all the decorations, Maggie asked, "When did Katie say she would be back from seeing James?"

"Don't know but won't be too long now. It be gettin' dark." As if to answer, a horse whinnied, and the sound of a carriage pulling up was heard. "I'm home! Anyone here?" Katie shouted breathlessly.

"Aye, in the kitchen, Katie. Are ya hungry?" Mary shouted.

"Aye, famished. What's on the stove?" Supper was pleasant and Katie raved about the tree.

Henry finished eating, then said his good-byes before heading home. "Let me walk a piece with ya, 'enry," Mary said before running for her cloak. The two old lovebirds left, leaving the house quiet.

"I think it's sweet that Henry started courting Mary after she left the gaol. The way they act, you would think they were kids." Katie laughed.

Maggie chuckled. "Remember the day the old rogue came to the door with that handful of wilted flowers, all red-faced and stammering? I thought Mary was going to bust with pride. She was more flustered than him, I think. Never saw her for a loss of words before. Probably never will again neither. Do you think he'll ask her to marry him?"

"I don't know. Would be grand if he did, but I don't know if Mary would go through with it. Still talks of her Percy a lot and says she's too old for such things. It's fun to watch, though."

"How have your meetings been going with the Lady's Society? Have you been able to help those poor souls in the gaol? Any more changes made?"

Katie shook her head. "Not really. It can be so frustrating. Trying to make any kind of changes in this old system is like dragging a dead horse. Everyone agrees the changes need to be made, but they seem to drag their feet. Laws are born, not written, and labor can be hard and painful. Elizabeth Fry has struggled for years for reform, but it comes slow."

"Who is Elizabeth Fry?"

"She's the one who has fought for changes for the women at Newgate. She visits them, brings them food and clothing. She has given them hope when they had none."

Soon the two turned their conversation towards other things, enjoying each other's company. Katie picked up her bag of knitting and began working on it.

"What are you knitting now, Katie?" Maggie questioned as she finished washing the dishes.

"Another sweater for James. You would not believe how damp it is in that place. I thought I was going to die from the cold when I was there. I wouldn't be surprised if James gives this one away too. He always says that he finds someone whose needs are greater than his."

"A rare man he is, Katie. A glorious find he is. Not too many men like him around. Wouldn't mind finding one such as him for myself."

"Who says you won't? You never know Maggie, just like Mary, you could get a man knocking on your door."

"Won't hold my breath—or anything else—waiting," Maggie joked. "Maybe if your papa had lived….well, you know."

The two sat lost in their own thoughts after that. Katie thought of her beloved papa, while Maggie thought of her lost love...the same man.

⇛⇝

Christmas was approaching fast. Katie needed to stay up late each night to finish making her presents for her "family." There was a sweater for James, warm socks for Henry, and a new warm covering for Maggie's bed. She had finished sewing the two new aprons for Mary the previous week. The hardest of all was what to give Lord and Lady Wilson. They had everything, and there was nothing they couldn't buy. Katie wanted so much to give them something special for all they had done. The Wilsons had more than made up for any past mistakes. Katie thought of them as part of her family. She never went to the Brick House because of Tess, but they came to see her on a regular basis. What could she make for them? Time was running out, and she was feeling panicky.

Suddenly it dawned on her. She would give Lord Wilson her father's watch. It had meant the world to Papa, for it had come from his father. It was one of her treasures, but she wanted him to have it. He had not only given her father a job when most people hated and mistreated the Irish, but he took her father into his heart. If it hadn't been for the Wilsons, her family would not have been able to have a comfortable life. Oh, her father worked hard earning what he made, but he was happy because of it. For that, she had to credit Lord Wilson.

126

Katie had thought of giving the watch to James, keeping it in the family, until she reminded herself that the Wilsons were her family too.

For Lady Wilson she would give her the most valued prize of all—a beautiful shawl made by Gran, given to her mother. It was a delicate knit, the color of cream, and made when Gran lived in Ireland. Gran had saved it for Katie, keeping it in one of her trunks. Thank God, the Wilsons kept Katie's things for her when she was locked up. It was because of them that she still had her treasures. She became very excited now that she had gifts for them. She knew they would like anything she gave, but it was important to her to give them something special. She was almost finished, and Christmas was only two weeks away.

There was only one thing that could have made her Christmas perfect—having James there with her. Sighing, Katie slipped out to the kitchen for some milk. Returning to the main room, she stirred the fire. She began thinking how much her life had changed since Gran had died. More changes were to come, and perhaps there would not be a time like this again. Would she ever sit at a warm fire on a cold night, and feel safe and secure again once she left? Katie felt apprehensive about the future, but it was too late to worry about it now. The decision to go was made, and go she would. Hopefully it wouldn't be the nightmare she kept hearing about. After all, she had heard terrible things about Newgate, too. While it certainly wasn't pleasant, she found she could endure.

Finally, as the clock chimed three in the morning, Katie lifted herself out of the chair, stretched, and headed for bed. As she lay watching the flames in her fireplace, she thought of her family. Family, yes, she once again had a family besides James, and it would be hard to leave them. She was as close to those around her now as she was to Papa and Gran. Blessed she was, and she knew it. As she lay in her bed she again whispered a soft prayer, *Thank you, God. Thank you for my family.*

"Father, you wanted to see me?" Tess came bouncing into her father's study.

"Come sit down, Tess. I need to talk to you. Where's your mother?"

"Didn't she tell you that she had to run to do some shopping for the ball?"

"Yes, but I wanted to make sure she was gone. I need to talk to you, and what I have to say may upset you. I do not want your mother to hear."

Tess leaned forward in her chair. "Is Mother all right? She isn't ill, is she?"

At least she still has decent concern for her mother, Lord Wilson thought. *There may be hope for the girl after all.* "No, she's fine. What I need to speak to you about concerns your future."

The hair on the back of Tess's neck stood up. She knew this wasn't going to be good. Her father never called her into his study. Something was wrong...wrong for her. She braced herself. "Tess, I hired a detective to look into your activities. What he found greatly disturbed me. You have forced me to make some hard decisions."

"You what? A detective? Who?" Tess blurted out.

As calmly as possible, Lord Wilson answered her questions. "He's a friend of mine. His name isn't important, but what he found out is. Seems you are 'seeing' a married man, and you have been frequenting some unsavory places. Tess, what are you thinking? Don't you know a lady doesn't go to the gambling houses?"

Tess stood to her feet, thundering, "How dare you! I'm not a child to be dictated to! You side with some servant, sending me off to Aunt Marilyn's, and now you have me followed? I'm not going to stand for it." Tess turned to storm out.

"If you don't sit down, you will never get another cent from me."

Tess stopped in her tracks. Pulled between her pride and greed, she teetered in the doorway. Finally greed won out. She turned back towards her father.

"Good. Now I want you to listen to what I'm going to say. First of all, we've been through all this about Kathryn. You lied, sending an

128

innocent person to the gaol. Your mother and I couldn't believe you would do such a thing. I had to pay a great deal of money not to have you arrested for falsely signing those papers, but that is past. I now have new concerns. The reason I told you about the detective in the first place was to avoid your denial and save time. I had hoped by now that you would accept one of the proposals that had come in for you. Instead, you decide it's more to your liking to run with a married man, and show yourself a loose woman." Tess opened her mouth to respond, but her father raised his hand. "I will have my say. I had hoped you would have settled down by now and possibly have a couple of children. It has been your mother's hope as well. Since that is not the case, I have taken steps to make it happen."

Tess's eyes widened. "What do you mean you've taken steps—what steps?"

"The party your mother is preparing for is going to be more than a Christmas ball. It will be your engagement party as well. Your mother doesn't know about this, but after our talk, she will." Lord Wilson waited for the words to sink in. His daughter's mouth opened, but nothing came out. He continued, "I have been corresponding with George Day. His son, David, has asked my permission to marry you. I said yes, and you shall also. They will be coming for a visit in a week, and I want you to be ready for it."

"You what! You can't do this, Father! Give me away as if I were a puppy! David Day! I've never met the man, and you expect me to marry him?"

"You have met him, but it has been years. His father is a ship builder. He owns a large estate just outside London. The family is old blood. Your future husband has his own estate in Kent. He has asked for your hand, and I am giving it to him. He will be taking over his father's business and feels it is time to settle down. I've had him checked out and found him to be an excellent catch."

Tess sat paralyzed. How could this be happening? She'd had her father wrapped around her little finger for as long as she could remember. What had changed? How could he even talk to her like this, as if she were some kind of harlot off the street? "I know who he is, Father, but I don't remember ever meeting him, just hearing about him.

I heard he was dull and dim-witted."

Lord Wilson lit a cigar. "Tess, I can see that you are in shock. You must realize I'm doing this for your own good. You are heading into disaster, and as your father, I feel inclined to take the necessary steps to secure you a future. David Day is far from dim-witted. He's a great businessman."

Tess spoke as if to herself. "I can't believe you're doing this to me. Have I been that horrible that you would throw my life away as if it meant nothing?" Tears threatened as she looked up at the man who had always been her protector.

For the first time, doubts clouded his mind. Maybe she was right. What if he was doing the wrong thing? No, he had to concentrate, and remember all that she had been involved in lately. Her tears were not going to work to change his mind this time.

"You have no choice in the matter. You have proved you are not capable of making your own decisions. Before you ruin your reputation, and our name, I will see you married! That is the end of it, except for this—your mother will be home soon. You will not say anything to her. *I* will tell her the news, and *I* will also let her know that you were in on the 'surprise.' She must think that you and I planned to surprise her as a 'Christmas' present. Do you understand?"

"And what if I refuse?"

"Then you will leave this house, never to return. You will have to rely on your lover's money and help, which I doubt will come after his wife returns."

Could he, would he really do that? Tess wasn't sure, so she nodded in agreement. Slowly she opened the door, waiting for her father to say, "I'm only joking," but it didn't come. She advanced the staircase, heading for her rooms. Locking the door, she disrobed, then curled up in the chair before the fireplace. Putting her hands over her face, she cried. Her life was over. She would marry some stranger and get fat having his brats. She would probably die in childbirth. Tess considered suicide for a minute, but not seriously.

A soft knock was heard at her door. "Miss Tess, 'tis Betsy. I 'ave a bit o' tea fer ya."

Tess threw on a robe as she unlocked the door. "Leave the tea, and

130

don't bother me anymore. Tell my mother when she gets back that I
have a headache and went to bed early. Make sure no one bothers me
anymore tonight. Now get out!"

Betsy quickly headed out the bedroom door after Tess locked herself in
once more. Going into the kitchen, Betsy couldn't wait to tell the
others that Miss Tess was in some kind of trouble again. Why else
would her eyes be red from crying? No one on the staff would feel pity
for the girl. It was always a time to gloat whenever she was in one of
her "tragedies." With great exaggeration and joy she proceeded to tell of
"the goings on" upstairs.

"Miss Tess is 'ard to work for, but she sure keeps things excitin',"
Betsy said gleefully.

All agreed before returning back to work. They couldn't wait to
see what was going to happen next.

"We 'ave a letter!" Mary shouted as she came through the door. "'Tis a
'ard winter's day out. Wind darn near blew the letter from me 'ands."

Katie smiled at Mary's excitement. As time passed, Mary seemed to
become more comfortable with her surroundings. It was fun to watch
her take such great pleasure in simple things…like a letter. Mary
handed it to Katie, then sat down waiting with expectation to hear the
news it held.

"Oh, it's from Lord and Lady Wilson. They will be able to come for
our Christmas gathering after all. Mary, we have so much to do. We
only have three days left!"

Katie's excitement at the news was contagious. Mary beamed at the
thought of planning something this important. "'Tis grand news fer
sure. Well, Maggie an' me put our 'eads together, and thought long and
'ard bout what ter be serving for Christmas. We 'ave decided on 'avin'

lamb and red potatoes. I can make me best puddin', some sausage, an' wine sauce. What ya think, Katie?"

"It all sounds wonderful. You have done a beautiful job at decorating already. I want to use the linen cloth for the table, and our best dishes of course. They may be Lady Wilson's hand-me-downs, but they are still beautiful. I also need to finish wrapping gifts. Do you think we should hang some pine boughs on the fence outside?"

The two friends talked over their plans for celebrating Christmas. "Ne'er thought I would be sittin' in such a fine cottage as this, 'avin' cider. Life is funny, ain't it, Katie girl?"

Katie smiled as she sipped her cider. "It sure is. It wasn't so long ago that we were sitting in filthy hay. Now look at us on soft chairs in front of a warm, bright fire." The women became quiet, lost in their own thoughts.

Katie broke the silence. "When I went to visit James Patrick last, he told me there was to be another hanging. Mary, that could have been us they were leading from Newgate. James said there will be three women hanged along with seven men next week. Remember the woman who killed her husband trying to protect her little ones? I suspect she'll be one of them. I wish we could do something for those poor souls."

"Aye, 'tis a sad thing indeed. I 'ad a friend taken' out and 'anged. Did I tell ya that?"

"Oh Mary, I'm sorry. When was this?"

"Oh, 'twas a long time now. 'Er name was Rosie Meggens, a good friend 'o mine, she was. Lost 'er man an' two of 'er babes to the fever. She became a Pure-finder after that."

"Pure-finder? What in the world is that?"

"Pickin' up dog turds. She got a few shillings a bucket fer 'em from the tanneries."

"Oh, how awful. What did the tanneries do with it?" Katie asked.

"Rosie told me it were used in makin' the bindin' of fancy leather books. Can ya believe it? Ole Rosie worked 'ard to find them turds. After a while it all got ta her. She took to stealin' an' got caught. They 'anged 'er. Couldn't go and see 'er 'anged meself. That's when I turned to the streets. 'Ard times hit me, but I weren't going to be no Pure-finder. All stealin' got yas was swingin' from the gallows."

Katie rose from her chair to go over, and put her arm around Mary. "Mary, I'm so sorry you lost your friend that way."

"Ya, it be a 'ard thing fer sure, but I wanna ferget it now. That's why I don't go to no hangin'. 'Enry does when 'e can, but I don't go with 'im."

Again silence fell in the room, leaving the women staring at the fire. The only sound was the ticking of the clock and the crackling of the wood. *Bang!* The front door flew open, startling them. "Blimey, ye scared ten years off me!" Mary shouted at Maggie.

"Sorry, I couldn't grab hold of the door. Wind is picking up."

Katie rose to take some of the packages from her. "Were you able to find what you were looking for?"

"Aye, it took me awhile, but it was worth the search," Maggie answered as she removed her cape.

"What yer lookin' fer, Maggie?" Mary asked.

"Never mind with you! I needed a gift for a friend, and you don't need to know more." Maggie spoke with a twinkle in her eye.

Mary crinkled her brow until she understood that Maggie was talking about her. Smiling, Mary got up, turning towards the kitchen. "Well, fine. Ol' Mary 'as some secrets of 'er own, ya know."

Katie poured Maggie hot tea. "Come and warm yourself. Mary and I were just talking about our Christmas gathering. Lord and Lady Wilson will be coming. We got a letter from them today."

"Good, did Mary tell you what we were thinking about serving for dinner?"

"Aye, and it sounds wonderful. I'm really getting excited. It has been a long time since I celebrated Christmas with family," Katie said.

"'Tis true of meself as well," Mary stated as she came back into the room.

"We are going to have a fine Christmas this year," Maggie added. "What are you giving James Patrick?"

"I've crocheted a blanket, a sweater, and more socks for him. He keeps giving his away, and I can't make them fast enough. Mary is going to bake a rum cake, and I'll pack a fine lunch. We'll make it as merry a Christmas as we can." The women talked into the night, of their plans for the holidays until Katie stood. "Well, I best be off to bed. We have much to do in the next few days, and I want to have an early start tomorrow. Good night."

The other two rose as well, saying their "Good nights." They all settled in, but sleep wasn't to be for awhile. Too much was left to do, and knitting was going on until the wee hours.

After much tossing and turning, Mary sat up from the floor, looking at her bed. *'Tis time ter try out this soft bed*, she thought. Picking up her blankets, she smoothed them on the mattress along with the coverlet. Setting her pillow at the head of the bed, she proceeded to lower herself down gingerly, as if on a bed of nails. Covering herself up, she lay there stiffly, quickly deciding she was not yet ready. She doubted she would ever be able to get used to a soft mattress. But since it was so cold, and the bed was beginning to warm from her body, she decided not to get up right away. She would lay a little longer before climbing back onto the floor…but soon she was fast asleep.

14

Christmas Eve

Christmas Eve was here! The cottage smelled of roast lamb, fresh pies, rolls baking, and the scent of the tree. Mary and Maggie were up early with all the excitement of the day ahead. A fire crackled in each fireplace, helping to warm the cottage with "Christmas Spirit."

Aromas reached Katie's nose, waking her. Yawning, she rubbed her eyes, and stretched. Realizing what day it was, she jumped out of bed, grabbing her robe and slippers. She flew into the main room, where Mary and Maggie were already waiting for her.

"Merry Christmas Eve!" all shouted at the same time. The three friends sat at the table laughing, eating rolls, and telling of Christmases past.

"Let's open some presents," Katie suggested.

"Ain't ne'er opened presents on Christmas Eve morn," Mary whispered as if they were all about to commit some mortal sin.

"I know, but let's just open one! I can't wait!" Katie laughed after seeing Mary's serious expression. Carrying their cups, they went by the tree and sat down. Katie sat cross-legged on the floor while Mary and Maggie pulled up chairs. "Here's one for you, Mary," Katie laughed as she handed the gift over.

"'Tis been a piece o' time since I got me a present. We were jest happy if'n we 'ad any food on Christmas Day."

Katie nodded in understanding. She watched as Mary opened the box.

"Blimey, 'tis two aprons! None so grand I e'er see! Don't know fer sure if I be wearing 'em. They be too pretty to mess up wearin' cookin' and cleanin'.""

"You better wear them, Mary Willow! The head cook at the gaol should look the part."

"'Tis a fine present, Katie girl. Thank ye." Mary blinked as her eyes misted.

"Here, open mine, Mary!" Maggie laughed.

"What? Thought we were to open only one!" Mary beamed, reaching for the gift. She carefully pulled back the paper and sucked in her breath as she stared at a new dress with lace at the collar. "Oh, I ne'er saw such a fine dress as this! Ya made it fer me did ya, Maggie?"

Maggie nodded as she helped Mary hold it up. "I snuck in yer room and copied the size from one of your dresses hanging there. I hope it fits."

"'Tis a pretty blue color, an' there be lace at me throat! Well, where will I e'er wear it?" Mary questioned.

"Don't forget that we're invited to several Christmas celebrations. I was going to ask you both to go to Chapel with me tonight," Katie asked.

"Blimey, Katie girl, 'tis you that people was invitin' to Christmas. Not ol' Mary."

"No, the invitations were for all of us, and I won't go if you don't."

"Then best we all go. Don't want ta ruin yer fine Christmas by keepin' ya at 'ome." Mary laughed. "I be thankin' ya, Maggie, fer the fine blue dress. I ne'er 'ad such a dress in me life! I want yas to open me gifts. Such fine gifts as these they are not, but I 'ope yas like 'em anyway." After both women assured Mary that her gifts were special to them, they began unwrapping. Katie received a beautiful linen hanky with her initials embroidered on it. For Maggie, there was a knitted hat that would keep away the winter cold. They were both thrilled.

"Now open your gift from me, Maggie," Katie said as she handed it to her.

"Oh, 'tis lovely. It's going to look beautiful on my bed. So much work you've done on it. Now I know what Mary means about not wanting to wear those pretty aprons. I'm tempted to hang this coverlet on the wall instead of putting it on my bed. Now ain't that a silly thought. Can you imagine anyone hanging their bed coverlet on the wall? Thank ya, Katie. Now open my gift to you."

Katie opened the package to find a soft nightgown with matching robe. Maggie was pleased when Katie stood, holding it up. She twirled around the room several times. After thanking each other once more, the women sat before the fire, drank their warm drinks, and talked. "Well, so much for self-control. Who said we had to wait to open gifts on Christmas Day anyway." Katie smiled.

"You did!" came the answer at the same time. All laughed.

"'Tis it time now?" Mary asked Maggie.

"Time for what?" Katie inquired.

"One more gift to be opened," Maggie answered. She nodded to Mary. "'Tis a gift from your husband."

Katie sat up straighter in her chair, setting her drink down. She watched Mary as she went into her room. After pulling the small package from its hiding place, Mary came back and laid it in Katie's lap. Katie sat staring at it for several moments.

"Blimey, Katie girl, ain't goin' to open itself!"

Katie gently lifted the small package and began tearing away the paper. She uncovered a small box. There was a note attached. Katie opened the note first.

Dear Katie,

Merry Christmas! I know we can't spend it together, but please know that you are in my heart as you read this. You will always be in my heart. I want everyone to know that you are my lovely wife, and so I give this ring with all my love. James

Katie's hands trembled as she slowly opened the box. There, wrapped in purple velvet material, was a small gold band. The firelight danced off of it. "Oh my, oh my," was all she could say.

Maggie and Mary giggled as they took pleasure in watching her. "Ain't ya goin' ta put it on, Katie?" Mary asked.

Katie nodded, never taking her eyes off the ring. Holding her hand out, she pushed it on her ring finger. She stared at her hand, flexing her finger. Without warning, she burst into tears. The two women rushed over to Katie. Not quite knowing what to do, Mary grabbed the hanky she had made for Katie and handed it to her. Maggie just stood shifting her weight from one foot to the other. Mary patted Katie on the back, cooing as if comforting a babe. Before too long Katie sniffed, wiped her eyes, and blew her nose. "How in the world did he ever get a ring for me? How did he know it would fit? Did you two have something to do with this?"

Smiling, they both nodded. "Aye, but Lady Wilson was part of it too," Maggie stated.

"'Twas surprised were ya now, Katie?" Mary laughed.

"Surprised isn't the word for it. Isn't it beautiful?" Katie held her hand up to examine the ring once more. "Thank you for this!"

"No need to thank us. James would have done it himself if he was able. We just did his footwork for him," Maggie replied.

"'Tis the truth, Katie girl. 'Twas the first time I e'er be in a fancy store fer such things. Ne'er been in a shop jest for baubles. Didn't know there be such a thing. Should 'ave seen the sparklers. Ne'er saw anythin' like it! Why, there be jewels the size of me big toe, an' some bigger still!"

Maggie stared at Mary as if she had grown another head. "Calm down, Mary. You're starting to sweat; it was only a store. Katie, I wish you could have seen her in there. I almost had to tie her down for all the commotion she was making."

"Hey, 'twas all new ta me. Just lookin' I was," Mary teased back.

"Where in the world did he get the money to pay for it?" Katie thought out loud.

"Don't e'er ask a man such a question. His pride will bruise for it," Maggie quipped.

"'Tis truth she speaks," Mary added. "A man's pride is somethin' fearful. If ya wants to be knowin', ask Lady Wilson and not James."

"Oh, Mary! I dirtied the beautiful hanky you gave me already."

"'Tis a grand thing when it be used fer tears o' joy, an' not sorrow. A grand thing indeed."

The women spent the rest of the morning talking, laughing, and enjoying their time together. It went by fast, and before too long it was time to get ready for their visitors. They set the table with their finest dishes, making sure all was in order. Soon the Wilsons' carriage pulled up. Katie ran to open the door, catching sight of the footman struggling with many gifts. "Goodness, what is all this? It looks like you bought out the stores."

Lady Wilson hugged Katie. "Don't say that. Edward always says I overdo it, but I can't help myself. It's my favorite holiday. I love to shop."

Lord Wilson patted his wife's hand. "I've given up trying to hold you back, my dear. We've been together long enough for me to know that I've lost the battle. I surrender."

They had a grand day. The dinner turned out wonderfully. Maggie, along with Mary, beamed with pleasure at all the compliments given them. Gifts were exchanged along with laughter, and a few tears of joy.

Lady Wilson gasped as she opened the shawl Katie gave her. "It truly is beautiful, dear. It really belonged to your mother, and you want me to have it? I feel honored that you would give me such a wonderful gift. Edward will treasure your father's watch, won't you, dear?"

"I certainly will. Your father meant a great deal to me. He was more than a worker to me. He was my friend. Thank you, Katie, for such a heart-given gift. I don't think anyone, except my dear wife, has ever given me such a thoughtful gift."

Katie, Mary, and Maggie were heaped with gifts from the Wilsons. Katie noticed that all the gifts for her were practical things. She was given warm clothing, blankets, bedding, and such. One thing stood out for Katie, a beautiful picture with their sweet faces smiling at her. The frame was exquisite. She would treasure it forever.

"I see you received a very special gift from your husband," Lady Wilson said.

"Isn't it beautiful? I was so surprised to get it. I know you had a lot to do with my receiving it. Thank you both for all you've done, and for your love and support."

Mary broke in, "If ya ever need to shop in one of them fancy sparkler stores again, Lady Wilson, jest let me know. Ol' Mary will be happy ta help."

Katie turned towards Lady Wilson. "How is it going with your Christmas ball?"

"Fine, just fine. I haven't had a chance to tell you that it's more an engagement party for Tess than a Christmas ball."

Katie flinched at the mention of Tess. Her stomach flip-flopped, but she held her composure. "Oh, how interesting," was all she could say.

"Yes, what a shock it was for me when Edward and Tess told me about her engagement. I used to think a mother was the first to know, but I guess they wanted to surprise me. They certainly did. David, Tess's fiancé, and his father arrived a few days ago. We've had a splendid time getting to know each other."

Katie only acknowledged with a nod.

Lady Wilson shared some of her plans for the party, which was to be held the night after Christmas. "We have wreaths hanging in every window and next to the orchestra will stand a fifteen-foot tree."

Mary exclaimed. "A fifteen-footer? Yas can be fittin' such a tree in your room?"

"Yes, it happened to be a Christmas surprise. David had it shipped in and it arrived the same day as they did. He talked to Edward and planned to surprise Tess and myself with it. It is breathtaking! I wondered why Edward fought me so when I wanted to get a tree ready for their arrival. Now I know. David is such a thoughtful young man. He and his father have some relatives here in London, and they wanted to spend the day with them. It worked out so nice since that gave us a chance to be here with all of you. Tess went with them. They seemed so happy. I've asked Tess how she met him, and how they could have had a courtship without me knowing about it. She just laughs, saying she'll explain later. I'll never know how she kept this from me. Between being surprised with the engagement and the tree, I wonder how many more secrets my husband is keeping from me." Lady Wilson laughed.

Her husband cleared his throat nervously, taking a drink offered him. How he wished she would stop talking about Tess. He knew it made Kathryn uncomfortable. His wife was always sensitive to other's feelings, but she was just overexcited. It was a dream-come-true for her daughter to be engaged.

Soon it was time for church. Mary flounced about, showing off her new dress. Everyone ooooed and aaahed, making her feel special. Maggie wore the crocheted hat Mary had made for her.

They all loaded up in the carriage and were off. The team of horses wore sleigh bells, although they pulled a coach instead of a sleigh. Still, it added to the magic of Christmas. The Cathedral was filled to capacity, but Lord and Lady Wilson led the others to their private booth. The music filled the ornately built structure with beauty, and the feeling of goodwill. Mary couldn't keep the wonder of the place to herself. Pointing and declaring appreciation at the sight of the statues and stainglass windows, she caused many a smile. As Katie looked around, she sadly thought of those who didn't have a warm cottage, food to fill their bellies, or family. Guilt tugged at her. No, she would not feel guilty, but would enjoy her Christmas. It could be the only one she would ever spend with those dear ones around her.

⨯⟐⨯

The music spilled out of the Cathedral onto the streets, where two children stood and listened. They had stopped picking up loose coal that had fallen from the wagon that was heading down the street.

"Listen 'ter that, Sadie! Sounds like angels singin'!" the young boy said to his smaller sister.

"Real angels? Do you think so, Tommy? What a wondrous thing it would be to hear angels sing!"

The two began running after the coal wagon once more. "Mum will be 'appy fer sure with all the coal we got! She be cookin' up a fine hen fer dinner. What a Christmas we will 'ave. Let's go home."

And the two skipped off with their wealth of coal and hearts full of all that Christmas held.

⨯⟐⨯

Finally, the day of the ball had arrived. Only three days after Christmas, it was an exciting time for all. Tess stood gazing at her image in the mirror. The gown she wore was a beautiful emerald green with puffy sleeves. Filmy red material was ornately tucked in at the bodice. Her hair was pulled back with curls cascading down her back. Holly sprigs were pinned amongst the curls. She knew she looked beautiful. She tried to think of the evening ahead, but her mind kept drifting to Peter. He would be there tonight, since he had responded to her personal invitation. The guests did not know it was going to be an engagement party, including him. She was afraid to tell him; afraid he wouldn't come if he knew. The announcement would come during dinner.

Looking out her window, she watched as carriages of all shapes and sizes pulled onto their road. Tess tried to ignore the nagging feeling of fear in the pit of her stomach. Of late she had enjoyed her fiancé, his father, and the new attitude her parents had towards her. They treated her like a mature adult instead of a child.

Her feelings toward Peter had also begun to change as of late. He wasn't as attentive as he had been. She wanted to see his reaction to the news of her engagement. Would he get angry or be relieved? Would there be a confrontation between Peter, David, or her father? If so, she knew her parents would be mortified. Still, it would be interesting to watch his reaction. Secretly she wanted men to quarrel over her in front of all the guests. It would serve some of those snooty women right. She smiled to herself. She would be the talk of the season.

Tess turned as her mother knocked on her door. "Oh Tess, you look beautiful! Isn't this the most exciting Christmas we've ever had? Everything is happening so fast! Since David has been here, I can see how much he truly cares for you. Oh honey, you look gorgeous!" she repeated. Lady Wilson was simply gushing with excitement.

The young woman smiled at her mother, saying nothing. Tess was struggling with her feelings. She felt trepidation about her upcoming marriage mixed with some degree of excitement. Then there was the shame she felt, knowing her father knew about her liaisons with Peter. She was angry with him for his interference and for how easily he cast her off on to another man.

Lady Wilson went on, "You seem happy with David. What do you think of his father? He seems honorable and pleasant. He is taken with you, but how could he not be? Look at what a beautiful daughter-in-law he is getting. Just think, Tess, by next Christmas I could be a

142

grandmother! What a wonderful present that would be! We should go downstairs. David is waiting for you and our guests have been arriving."

"I'll be down shortly, Mother." Tess kissed her mother's cheek. Once alone, again she sat in front of the fireplace trying to compose herself. That was just like her mother. To make her feel pressured to have a child right away. She was trapped into this and didn't like it. She had no choice. Peter never promised her anything. Then there was his wife. Tess heard the woman could be ruthless. She didn't want to explain to Victoria why she was taking up a lot of her husband's time of late.

Her thoughts then turned to David. He was very handsome and seemed kind. He was also intelligent. She remembered their first meeting when she was much younger. It was at the theater. She remembered flirting with him, but he hardly took notice of her. She was as surprised as anyone that he had made a bid for her hand.

A horrifying thought entered her mind. Did her father offer money to David to marry her? Tess's face burned with humiliation. *How can I ever face David again if my father has paid him?* She had to know the truth before she went through with it. She would not start her marriage like this, even if it meant losing her father's support. She pulled the cord to summon her maid.

When Betsy knocked, Tess drew her in. "Go downstairs and tell my father I need to speak to him right away. Tell him it's very important, and hurry!"

Soon her father knocked. "Tess?"

Tess opened her door to let him in. "I need to know one thing, Father, before I go through with this. Did you pay David to marry me? Did you tell him I had to get married, and then offer him money?"

For the first time since he had planned all of this, Lord Wilson felt compassion for his daughter. Wrapping his arms around her, he held her close. "Oh Tess, don't you know that I have done this because of my concern for you?"

"And Mother," she simply stated.

"Yes, that's true, but I do love you, and I have been gravely worried about you. The answer to your question is no. I did not bribe him into it. I had a business meeting with his father, and he mentioned that David had asked about you. He said his son was seeking out a suitable wife and had been struck by your beauty, good humor, and family. I lied and told him you had mentioned his son from time to time as well. One thing led to another, and here we are. I'm sorry I had to do this against your wishes. I would not have embarrassed you by paying someone to take you. You are a worthy wife. David is honored that you have consented. He believes this is all his idea. Of course he doesn't know it was me who consented for you. Tess, this is an extraordinary chance for you to be happy in the way God meant women to be...married and, hopefully, a mother. People have been arranging marriages since the dawn of time. You know my marriage with your mother was arranged, and look how much we love each other. You need to give it a chance. By the way, you look lovely."

Tess could hear her father's heart beating as she kept her head on his chest. "I thought you didn't love me anymore."

Gently pushing her away from his chest, he looked down at his only child. "How could I not love you? You are my daughter. Besides, I can only stay angry with you for a short time. You must understand what a great marriage you are entering into. David is a young suitable man with a good family name...and money. Most women would give anything for a marriage such as this. Please promise me you will work hard to make this marriage work. Will you make me proud?"

Tess felt irritation at her father's words. This wasn't about him. It was about her life, but she knew she was stuck. Why alienate him from her by getting angry? Instead of expressing her true feelings, she looked up, trying to give her most innocent gaze. With a pout she nodded. "Yes, Father, I will work hard and make you proud."

Lord Wilson beamed down at her. "Come now, Tess, let's greet your guests who have already begun to arrive." Tess held tightly to her father's arm as she descended the staircase. Holding her head high, she made quite the entrance. She only hesitated for a second when she saw David and Peter standing together at the bottom of the staircase...waiting for her.

144

It was Katie's second visit to her husband after the holidays. James held his wife tenderly. As they embraced he prayed silently, *Thank you, Father, for Katie. Bless her, and help me to be the kind of husband you want me to be, amen.*

"So, have you given your Christmas presents away yet?" Katie teased.

Smiling, James shook his head. "I couldn't after all the hard work you put into them. I've been enjoying them myself."

Katie giggled. "I still can't believe you got me a ring. I'll have to remember that you are quite the schemer." She laughed.

"So are you still meeting with the women's group? What dragons are they fighting now?" James asked.

"Aye, and don't tease about it, James. We have done much to help prisoners in various gaols. It's important what we do. Especially to you, who are still locked in this place. You know Newgate and Kirkdale are the worse prisons, but the others are not much better. Think of those who don't have families to comfort them, or bring them extra food and clothes."

"Scolding me, are ya? Don't forget that I know exactly how it feels to be alone as you do. I thank God every day for you, and the blessings He gives. I don't take your work for the prisoners for granted one bit."

Katie relaxed. "I'm sorry, James. I guess I have been fighting so long for the prisoners, and arguing against the wrongs done them. I get a bit touchy when talking about it."

Smiling, James told his wife how happy he was to have her on his side. "I wouldn't want you against me, Katie Murphy."

Katie went on to tell of the blankets and Bibles that her group had passed out. "We have been able to successfully argue for better conditions on the prison ships. The prisoners are getting more exercise time, and surgeons to help with their ailments. Now we're working on getting them more blankets and food. More matrons are needed for the women as well. Most of them are attacked within days of arriving. With matrons on board, it keeps everyone in their place, if you know what I mean. We don't have time to rejoice in our winning small battles. There is so much more needed. "

James nodded in understanding, then turned the subject. "I believe when spring comes we will sail out. I could be wrong, but I know a man on one of the harbor crews who knows they like to pull out in spring."

It was Katie's turn to nod in agreement. "Aye, I think you may be right. When I think about it, I get such mixed feelings. I think I'll have myself worked up into a tizzy when the time comes to set sail."

Like so many times before, they made small talk, got to know each other better, and became closer. In one way this time was different, for they began to share together the importance of God in their lives. They laughed, held hands, and shyly kissed good-bye. As always, Katie walked out alone. Loneliness covered them both each time they had to separate, but they were thankful for having each other. They knew it wouldn't be long before they could be together...in every way. Yes, a time of change was coming for them.

15

Conversion

Lord Wilson leaned back in his chair and smoked his cigar, content to listen to the four men telling of the prison hulks. Grimes was there as well. Lord Wilson wanted to hear more. If he was to help, he would need more information. Some of what they said he already knew from the men who had talked to Katie, but some information was new. He didn't like the fact that they were in his office where his dear wife could come knocking at his door at any moment. There was much of what was being said that he didn't want her to overhear.

"The hulks are necessary, Lord Wilson. What with the war ending and the population doubling, crime increases. There's been an increase in transports over the last five years with no end in sight," a man named Trace informed the others. "I can tell you stories well into the night about when I was quartermaster on the Liberty. Fine name for a prison hulk wouldn't you say? Liberty, ha!"

Lord Wilson detested this brass braggart of a man, but he had a wealth of knowledge when it came to this subject. Lord Wilson told Grimes to find him a man who lived in the thick of it, and he did.

Trace went on, "These people aren't any better than dogs on the streets, maggots one and all. If they make it alive, fine. If not, there are more to replace them."

Brice interrupted, "It has gotten much better than it was, but it's still a hard journey for sure. Takes from four to six months before dropping anchor off of New South Wales. Most of the prisoners are half dead before they even leave Langston, Portsmouth, Deptford, or Woolwich Harbor. Don't make any difference what hulk they're on, they are all treated pretty much the same. If the lot is lucky, they'll work ten hours a day on the docks while they wait to sail. If they aren't lucky, they are left on board chained up, starved, beaten, and sick of heart and body."

"What do you expect? You think we should pat them on the wrists, and feed them good beef? It be best for everyone to be rid of them. They deserve to be punished. That is my job," Trace bragged.

"And I hear you do it well." Grayson narrowed his eyes at the man.

"I assure you, sir, I do the job I'm hired for. After a week in that hell's pot, you'd not fair any different."

Lord Wilson jumped in before an argument erupted. "What about the families left behind? Can they be transported with their husbands or wives?"

"Not often," came the answer from Brice. "There have been thousands of letters written by families. They often ask to sail along with their mates, but unless they have a ticket-of-leave, chances are they stay behind."

"What's a ticket-of-leave?"

"It would show that the convict could somehow support his family once transported. If a person had money to do that, he probably wouldn't be in a gaol in the first place. Usually it's all they can do to survive, let alone bring a wife and brats in tow. Sometimes letters are written, beseeching the authorities on behalf of the convict. If funds follow, they may let the family go then, but that is a rare thing indeed. Once in a while a husband and wife are convicted together, and transported out, but not always to the same place. The brats are shipped out with the mothers, though. We have no need to keep them. The foundling homes bulge now."

"And it only gets worse," replied Grayson. "Any time a new prisoner comes on board one of the hulks, the 'old-timers' steal from him. They take whatever is of value after one of the marines attaches a fourteen-pound iron to his right ankle. They aren't likely to try to swim away with that on their leg. Once the irons are removed, their legs jerk up uncontrollably when the prisoner tries to walk. It depends on how long the iron is left on. It takes a long time to get over that, if they ever do."

148

"Tell me about the food on these prison ships. Why did you say they were starved?" Lord Wilson asked, sitting forward.

It was Knotts' turn to share his knowledge. "The Naval agent assigned to the transports mostly determines whether prisoners see the food they're supposed to get. They're usually issued an 'institutional pound' of raw meat but..."

"Institutional pound? What's that?"

"About fourteen ounces, but before the prisoners get it, it gets picked off. The agents, cooks, inspectors, and boat crew help themselves first. They're lucky to get six ounces. Salt horse is a staple. It's brined beef. Then they usually get rice, plum pudding with suet, pork with peas, and the like. Of course, scurvy was a problem a while back, but they have a handle on it now. At times they are given small beer, which is a brewery byproduct. Ale and real beer are never allowed. Poorly filtered river water caused dysentery and typhus, but there aren't as many outbreaks now that the cause has been discovered."

"That's exaggerated," Trace quipped. "You sound like you favor the convicts over authority."

"Just stating the truth as I found it to be," Knotts said.

"What about the trip itself? How bad is it?" was Lord Wilson's next question.

"It's a hardship for sure. Hard for the captain, crew, and their families that go, but hell for the prisoners. They're chained below; don't see the light of day sometimes through the whole voyage. Sick, and laying in their puke. They get bloated and suffer starvation. If the bloke next to you kicks, you hope nobody finds out until the body begins to swell and stink. That way you can have his ration of slop along with your own. It's bad. You sail from Portsmouth to the Canary Islands, where you pick up supplies and water. Then they head to the Cape Verde Islands. After that it's the long haul to Rio de Janeiro, then Cape Town, which is 3,300 miles itself. From there you travel 6,500 miles to Botany Bay. Once there, it's a whole different story. Surviving there in the past made the trip look like an outing on the pond, but things are better like I said."

Throughout the afternoon the men shared what they knew. Much of it was not encouraging. The conditions weren't as bad as in the past but were far from good. There had been vast numbers of prisoners lost on the prison hulks and on the journey. Even though all the information shared by Trace was one sided, he did give some insight to the horror faced by the poor, wretched souls.

All this tragic talk was taking its toll on Lord Wilson. Certainly he had seen the poor on the streets his whole life…the beggars, prostitutes, orphans, but he never gave them any serious thought. They were a part of the scenery…castoffs of society who were given as little notice as possible. At Christmas time he would give to the workhouses and hospitals…enough to ease his conscience for another year.

Lord Wilson abruptly stood up. "Gentlemen, I just realized the time. I fear I need to end this. Thank you for coming to share your insights and knowledge."

After everyone but the detective had left, Lord Wilson sat back in his chair. "Grimes, how can I allow Mrs. Murphy to go on such a terrible voyage? How would she ever survive? I never realized the horror going on outside my door."

"How could you, sir? If something hasn't touched your life, then how would you know of it?"

"I don't think that's any excuse. How will I ever be able to, in good conscience, allow Mrs. Murphy to walk innocently into such a horrible situation? She's going because her husband is being transported, and she's only married to him because she was forced to. It was my daughter who lied having her locked up. Tell me I'm not responsible? And yet aren't we responsible even if we don't know these people? Who is responsible for those who can't help themselves? Do you really want to live in a world where no one looks out for anybody but themselves? What hope is there then?"

Grimes was surprised by his employer's words. Wilson was a shrewd businessman, a caring family man, but not given to sentiment. For him to show such emotion meant he must have been touched deeply by what he had heard. Nonetheless, this conversation was getting to be a little uncomfortable for Grimes.

"Grimes, get me a list of the prison ships, and all the prisoner's names, then find out what transports are listed to leave for Botany Bay. When you've done that, get me the names of the captains, and who they are contracted with to sail. I want to know if they are private or government contracted. I want to know everything about these men. How many times they've sailed, their past records, what their crews think of them. That's important, you know, and if they are family men. Give me the names of any agencies that help these prisoners and their families. Please do this as soon as possible. I'll write the governor of Botany Bay, letting him know that I am interested in helping the colonies over there. I'll tell him that I realize there is much to do, so I'll ask him to prioritize the needs. I need to be realistic. Perhaps there is some good that can come out of all this."

Grimes thought about the gargantuan task setting before him, but also about the money he was about to make. One thing was sure, Wilson kept him busy, and in money. He extended his hand to the older man as he got up to leave. "You've got it. I'll contact you as soon as I have any information."

After Grimes left Lord Wilson needed to decide how much he would tell his wife. Protecting her from the truth was tricky at times, but necessary. He would have her help him plan what they could do for the prisoners. She would need something to occupy her time after Tess was married. He didn't feel any better even after making his decision to help others. He had a nagging feeling as if someone was pointing a finger at him; blaming him for all the misery in the world. He decided he would give a lot of time, and money to his new cause. That would ease any guilt he may have for not "acting sooner" to help others. He knew it would. It had eased his guilt before…many times.

"We're leaving, Katie. We're leaving soon," Red told his wife.

Katie's heart skipped at his words. "Are you sure, James? Lord Wilson didn't tell me anything."

"I got the news from Flores. He's one of the gaolers here. He was on the docks the day before last. The ships are here and being loaded up with provisions."

"But are you sure one of them is 'our' ship?"

"Best as I can tell, yes. We've been waiting all winter long. Now a fleet has arrived and anchored in. Why wouldn't it be for us?"

Katie was torn between excitement and dread. They had waited for so long that she often forgot they would be leaving at all.

James interrupted her thoughts. "Flores also said that there are two naval vessels set to sail with the transports. He said they are fine-looking ships, sturdy too. He is going to try to find out if we're being shipped out. He said he would let me know by tomorrow, if possible."

"James, I'm afraid. Knowing we would leave at some point in the future is so much different than knowing we're going to be leaving soon."

"I know, Katie, but God knows all about it. He is our refuge and strength. We need to put our trust in him. Remember what I told you? In Jeremiah 29:11 it says; 'For I know the thoughts that I think toward you,' saith the Lord. 'Thoughts of peace, and not of evil, to give you an expected end.' As long as we trust Him, whatever happens to us will be for our good."

"James, you know I believe in God, but I've never felt the assurance you talk about. Many of the other women in my women's group have that same assurance, but I'm not sure how to get it."

"Katie, I've told you that you only need to accept Jesus Christ as your Savior. Confess that you are a sinner; that only through Him is there hope for our salvation. We've talked about this many times."

"Yes I know, James, but I don't feel any different."

"Feelings have nothing to do with salvation, Katie. Do you believe that Jesus Christ is the Son of God, and that He died on the cross for you? Do you believe He rose again, and lives?"

"I guess so."

"Pray, Katie, that He will reveal himself to you. I cannot convince you, and your friends cannot talk you into salvation. It has to be between you and the Lord. He loves you so much that He died for you, so I know if you ask Him to reveal himself to you in a very real way, He will."

"All right, James. I'll start to pray that He speaks to me, and that I will know it is Him."

Soon it was time for Katie to once again leave her husband behind.

Before heading home, there was one more stop to make. Katie instructed her driver to go to the Cathedral. As she stepped through the door the quietness of the place wrapped itself around her. It was nothing like Christmas when it had been filled with people singing. The echo of her steps vibrated off the walls. Easing into one of the pews Katie knelt down, and bent her head in prayer.

Lord, I've been talking to you more and more, but I don't feel like you are there or that you hear me. James says I can't go on feelings, but I need to know you are there. I never felt close to you like Gran and James. I want to, but I don't. I don't know what to do. James said I should ask you to reveal yourself to me. Part of me is afraid you won't, and part of me is afraid you will. I'm afraid, Lord. Afraid of the unknown, afraid of my future in the far away place, and afraid of you. How can you love me enough to have died for me? Everyone says you love me, but Lord, I want you to tell me that you love me. If you are real, and I do believe you are, then you tell me yourself that you love me. I need to know, I need to hear. I need you. I know I'm a sinner, and only you can save me. Please, Lord.

Before Katie could lift her head, a warm comforting sensation began running from the top of her head to her feet. It felt like warm oil being poured over her. Every fiber of her being knew, really knew that God loved her. He loved her! He knew her, and loved her! Katie couldn't move. The beating of her heart sounded in her ears. She took a deep breath when she realized she had been holding it. Katie began to laugh and cry at the same time. Her heart spilled over with joy, causing her to laugh out loud.

A man standing off to the side stared at her. By his robes she could tell he was a priest. Wiping her eyes she smiled at him. A look of uncertainty crossed his face, but he stepped closer to her. "Are you all right, miss?"

Katie laughed again. "Oh yes, yes, I'm fine! I was praying, asking God to tell me if He really loved me, and He did! He did! He loves me! Isn't that amazing?"

The priest nodded in bewilderment while backing up a little. "Yes, He does love us. He loves us all."

"I know, but He told me himself! He loves me!" Laughing again

Katie couldn't help but jump around in her excitement. The man stepped back even further. After a few moments, Katie turned to pick up her cloak. She needed to go home to tell Mary and Maggie. They had to know, to find out the truth. He loved them too, and she needed to tell them. "Thank you, Father," Katie called back to the priest as she ran down the aisle. "Thank you so much!"

The priest scratched his head wondering whether it was rum, or did the Lord truly speak to the young woman? He decided it must be rum for he was a priest, and God never told him. He knew that God loved him, but still he wondered why he never felt the excitement of it as the woman did. *Surely must be the drink,* he thought. He turned back towards the altar. He had work to do.

Tess yawned, stretching out her long legs. It was late morning, time to get up. She rang for the maid. Once she arrived, Tess instructed her to ready a bath and bring breakfast. She then set about the most arduous task of the day, picking out what she would wear. Once she finished eating she stepped into the hot tub, sank back, and let her mind wander. Of late she found herself thinking more and more of her husband-to-be instead of Peter.

She smiled as she remembered back to her engagement party, and the moment when she was descending the staircase with her father. Her eyes had found Peter and David standing next to each other. Peter had stepped forward to claim her hand from her father's, but David cut him off, taking it instead. Peter looked at him with surprise, and at her with question. She had liked David's aggressiveness claiming her hand from Peter. It was her father who had stepped in, guiding Peter away from them. She was curious as to what her father had said to Peter, for shortly afterwards he left the ball.

What an enchanting evening it was in that beautiful setting. She had been the center of attention, having David hang on her every word. She could tell that he did his best to please her. She had seen envy on many of the young women's faces, but best of all was the way her parents acted. They were so puffed up with pride, her father strutting around like a Banty rooster. Her mother seemed like a young girl herself. She laughed and danced the evening away. Tess let a giggle escape as she remembered the stolen kiss she shared with David out in the garden. He was so charming and handsome. She hadn't felt this happy in a long time. It was almost like her very first love. Could it possibly be that she was falling in love with him? It had been a long time since she felt like this. Tess was jarred out of her daydream by a knock at her door. "Who is it?"

"'Tis Betsy, miss. I 'ave a letter for ya."

"Bring it to me, then hurry and fetch me that towel. I may as well get out since you're here to help me."

"Aye, miss."

Sitting by the fireplace in her warmest robe and slippers, Tess ordered Betsy to get her fresh tea. After Betsy left, she started to read, but stopped to see who signed it. In delicate script, Kathryn Brady Murphy appeared at the bottom of the page. She stared at the signature, trying to figure out who the name belonged to. It escaped her for the moment. When it finally dawned on Tess who Kathryn Brady was, she was dumbstruck. *Why in the world would she write a letter to me? Why is her last name Murphy now? Don't tell me she got married!*

Tess knew nothing that had happened to the servant girl except she had been released from prison. Tess knew her parents had something to do with it. She knew she was being "punished" when she was sent off to her Aunt Marilyn's. Everyone, including Tess, was very careful not to mention the Brady girl's name. She turned the letter over and began reading.

Dear Miss Wilson,

I'm sure you are surprised to hear from me, but I feel that I must write to you. I would like to meet with you. There is something important I need to speak to you about. I could come there, or we could meet somewhere else if you wish.

Please say that you will come. I feel it would benefit us both if we spoke together.

Sincerely, Kathryn Brady-Murphy

Tess' first instinct was to tear the letter up, but something held her back. She re-read it several times. *Why would she want to talk to me now? So much time has passed since she was in prison. Does she still hold me responsible? Is she out for revenge? Wouldn't she have done something before now?* Tess rang for Betsy. "Who brought this letter?"

"It came by coach, miss."

"Do you know where to send a response?"

"I was told by Graines that he was given instructions on where to take any reply."

"Then go down to the kitchen and ask the butler what instructions he was given. Come back and tell me."

"Aye, miss."

Tess felt impatient waiting for the maid's return. Soon Betsy came back with the answer. "Graines said he was told to either have a reply mailed or brought to 750 Courtney Road here in London."

"Stay here while I write a response, then take it to Graines." Tess quickly penned a note, sealed it, and handed it to Betsy. "Give it to Graines, and be sure he has it taken to that address immediately! Come back to help me dress afterwards."

"Aye miss."

Kathryn read the note that had just arrived.

I received your letter and must say that you were right: I was very surprised to hear from you. You have aroused my curiosity, so I will meet you at the Hill Café for tea on Grignon Street. I'll be there tomorrow at noon. If that doesn't work out for you, please reply. Otherwise I will see you then.
Tess Wilson

So there it was. She would finally see Tess...the Princess. Katie's heart raced at the thought of it. She still wasn't sure what she would say to her when she saw her. The last few weeks had been a blur of joy and blessings. She never before felt such happiness. It was a freedom that she had never experienced before. She felt like she had been drowning, and a strong hand lifted her out of the water. Except she didn't know she was drowning.

She made several attempts in the past week to explain how she felt to Mary and Maggie. Poor Mary just watched her closely as if she had lost her mind. Katie shared what had happened in the Cathedral with them. They said they understood, but how could they? She still didn't understand it all herself.

The most wonderful thing of all was seeing James the next day, and telling him. He laughed and cried with her. She knew that he truly understood. He shared how he felt when he realized that God loved him, and forgave his sins. They rejoiced together, then James prayed a thankful prayer for his "new" wife.

The only thing that hindered her happiness was the knowledge that God wanted her to forgive Tess. She wasn't even sure when God had laid it on her heart, but He had. Oh how she struggled with that. She felt angry, for her newfound joy was tainted now with the knowledge of what was required of her.

A spiritual battle raged on within her soul one night. Alone in her bedchamber, the Lord gently spoke to her. She knew what she had to do but simply couldn't or didn't want to.

How can you ask me this, Lord? Katie prayed. *You know all she did to me. She lied, and had me imprisoned. She treated me worse than dirt when I only tried to serve her well. She talked awful about Papa and Gran. She teased me about who I was, and where I came from. Every chance she got she made my life miserable. That wasn't enough for her! She had to steal those years away from me when I was locked up!* She repeated her prayer, *Lord, how can you ask me to do this?*

Hour upon hour she wrestled in prayer. She decided to give up and went to lie down. She wasn't going to forgive Tess; she couldn't. God must understand that. She was miserable tossing and turning throughout the night. Getting up, she stoked the fire, then picked up her new Bible. Opening it she read a few verses. They didn't mean anything to her. She had a hard time understanding some of what she read. She laid her head back on her chair.

Everything was fine, Lord, until you asked me to forgive Tess. You must know I simply can't. I don't want to. I hate her, Lord. She's evil and mean. I don't plan on revenge; isn't that enough?

Nothing...only silence.

How come I heard you speak to my heart to forgive Tess just fine, but I can't hear you now? I need you!

Katie fought hard for *her* will to be done. The hatred she felt for Tess was entangled around her very soul, and she wouldn't let it go. It was all impossible. She could never...no, she didn't want to forgive her. She didn't want the Lord to forgive Tess either. The Lord was hers and not Tess's. Katie began to cry in frustration. The battle of wills continued on through the night, lasting until the early morning hours. A fight for her very soul was fought that night. Yes, she had accepted Jesus Christ as her Savior, but there was more required of her. Her hate for Tess had no room in her heart now that He abided within it.

Katie felt compelled to open her Bible once more. She began to read Matthew 5:44: "But I say unto you; love your enemies, bless those who curse you, do good to them that hate you, and pray for them which despitefully use you, and persecute you." Her eyes then fell on Matthew 6:14: "If ye forgive men their trespasses, your heavenly Father will also forgive you." Katie flipped back to Proverbs 16:7: "When a man's ways please the Lord, he maketh even his enemies to be at peace with him."

Katie knew the Lord was speaking to her through His Word. She knew He was instructing her. Eagerly she continued reading even though she was not familiar with her Bible. She knew He was leading her on to His Truth. She read of the account of Jesus' trial and crucifixion. Who knew better than He of being unjustly and cruelly treated? She then turned to the book of John.

John 15:10: "If ye keep my commandments, ye shall abide in my love; even as I have kept my Father's commandments, and abide in his love."

John 14:21: "He that hath my commandments, and keepth them, he it is that loveth me and he that loveth me shall be loved by my Father, and I will love him, and will manifest myself to him."

Katie read on and on. Scriptures seemed to "jump" out at her, and she drank deeply of the Living Water. The hatred she held in her heart seemed to melt away, and she made her choice. Just like the choices Gran had told her about, she made the choice to obey, to allow Jesus to cleanse her from all unrighteousness. It was as if she could float. She never realized how her hatred of Tess had weighed her down. As she rejoiced in her newfound freedom, she heard a soft whisper inside her heart. *Go and tell of your love for her...and mine.*

Lord? You want me to tell her I love her! Isn't it enough I forgave her? You see my heart! You know I have forgiven her. Isn't it enough?

Go...

I'm afraid! What will she say? What will I say? She'll probably laugh at me!

Hebrews 13:6: "That is why we can say without any doubt or fear, 'The Lord is my Helper and I am not afraid of anything that mere man can do to me.'"

Again and again her eyes fell on His promises. "Fear is not of the Lord....I will never leave nor forsake you." With great joy, Katie finally relented. *Okay, okay...I get it. Thank you for loving me, and speaking to me! I will trust you, Lord!*

Katie went to lie down. She was exhausted but full of joy. Katie was awestruck. Almighty God, Creator of heaven and earth had just spoken to her...to her! He knew *her* name, and He loved *her*! A tear of gratitude slipped down her cheek as she slipped into slumber.

❧❧

A couple of times Tess had almost changed her mind. Why should she meet with Brady? She didn't owe anything to this girl. Why should she even bother? But her curiosity got the better of her. That's why Tess arrived at the Café early. She would have the advantage if she were the first one there. Requesting a table by the large window, she watched for the girl. Sipping her tea she saw a carriage pull up. The driver helped a young woman as she stepped down from the coach. Tess did a double-take leaning closer to the window. *Is that really her? Where did she get such a fine rig and horses?* The young woman carried herself with ease and grace. Gone was the scrawny girl with the big doe eyes. Jealousy gripped Tess as two gentlemen tipped their hats and held the door for her.

Katie looked around the crowded room until she saw Tess. Smiling hesitantly she walked over. Her heart pounded in her ears while her knees threatened to buckle. This was harder than she thought it would be. Reaching the table, Katie smiled again. As she reached to pull out one of the empty chairs, a waiter pulled it out for her. Thanking him, she turned her attention back to Tess.

Tess coolly tilted her head to the side. "You're looking well. It's been a long time."

"Hello, Tess. Yes, it has been a long time. You haven't changed."

The waiter walked up to their table to take their orders, "Tea, miss?"

Katie declined. "No, I prefer coffee if you have it."

"Certainly."

Once their order was taken, the two women looked at each other, waiting to see who would speak first.

Clearing her throat, Katie started, "Thank you for coming. I wasn't sure you would." When there was no response, she continued. "I'm sure you are wondering what this is all about. I'm not sure how to say this so I will come right out with it. Will you please...forgive me?"

Tess had steeled herself for any words Katie had to say, except for those. In her mind she had played out every scenario, but this one. The look on her face was of pure shock. Not too often did she feel unsure of herself, but this was one of those rare moments. Tess blinked a couple of times, then focused on her lap. She looked back up at Katie, then down again. She wasn't sure how to respond.

Katie went on. "I have had bad feelings towards you in the past. I no longer feel that way. I'm asking your forgiveness for how I've felt about you in my heart. I'm truly sorry. A lot has passed between us. Even when you were not near me, I sensed your presence. We have been a part of each other's lives for some time now. Years ago, when we first met, I was hoping we could be friends. I don't know if it's too late for that, but I would like to try to be friends now."

Tess searched her mind for words, but none came. She had never been in a situation such as this. She had never asked forgiveness from anyone, and no one had ever offered it to her...until now.

Katie placed her hand gently on Tess's arm. "Do you think that could be possible? Can we be friends, Tess? Can you forgive me?"

Tess reacted on raw instinct. She pulled away. "What...friends? Are you jesting? I have friends. I don't need any more!"

Katie sent up a quick prayer for help. "I know you have many friends. I just thought you could use another one. I know we have never liked each other, but I want you to know that I feel differently now."

"So what's changed?" Tess said suspiciously.

Katie went on to tell Tess about her new life in the Lord. To her amazement, Tess sat quietly and listened. Katie spoke with a boldness that surprised her. She told of her experiences in the gaol, of James and her marriage. She told of Brady's Brick, and how her papa had left it for her. Katie spoke of the love she felt in her heart since she had become a Christian, and of the love she felt for Tess.

At that moment something stirred Tess's heart. She looked into Katie's eyes and saw just how sincere she truly was. Her hard heart cracked. Tess had lied; she never had a true friend, and she longed for that. Other women were to be avoided. She needed to protect herself from them. They could be so hateful, but at that moment her eyes were opened. She realized how hateful she was...and how much she longed for acceptance from others. She had no one except her mother and father to share things with, and David. Now she was being offered a true friendship, for the very first time in her life. Any friendships in the past had been shallow and used for gain. She had paid dearly for her folly. Having no one close to share her life with meant loneliness. Maybe that was why she felt so drawn to David. He would be someone to share her lonely life with. It came as a shock to realize how lonely she truly was. Her face burned; she had to fight back tears.

"Are you all right?" Katie asked with concern.

Tess wiped the corners of her eyes, sniffed, and smiled at Katie. "There's not much that surprises me anymore, but you about knocked me off my chair. I thought you came to rail on me. I thought you were going to tell me what a horrible person you think I am, but instead..."

Tess tried to swallow the big lump in her throat. These new feelings overwhelmed her. Her heart had been hard for so long that once it cracked, there was no stopping it from crumbling.

"Does this mean you forgive me?" Katie whispered.

"I…guess so, but I'm not sure what I'm forgiving. Shouldn't I be the one to ask forgiveness from you?"

Katie smiled. "I have forgiven you, and that's what I wanted to tell you. It must be overwhelming for you right now. Are you sure you're feeling all right? You look a little pale."

"I don't know what I'm feeling. I feel strange. Can I ask you something? You became a Christian and felt you needed to see me?"

Katie explained what had happened the night the Lord had spoken to her about Tess.

Tess wasn't sure what to make of it. "Are you telling me that God Almighty told you to forgive me, and then come and tell me?"

"That's exactly what I'm saying. I know it sounds strange. I wouldn't have believed it either, but it happened!"

"I'm not sure I could ever forgive you, if things were reversed," Tess said hesitantly.

"I understand, but it doesn't matter now."

Tess began to pour her heart out to Katie. She told how she resented the relationship Katie had with her parents. Her jealousy in knowing they cared for her. She felt so insecure and vulnerable growing up.

"You were jealous of me?" Katie was astounded. "I thought you had everything. I even thought you were the prettiest girl I had ever seen when I first saw you. I believed you to be a princess."

"I've been called a lot of things, but never a princess."

Both laughed at that.

The two young women talked as equals, sharing what was happening in their lives. Old hurts and scars melted away. Tess was greatly surprised to hear about the circumstances surrounding Katie's marriage to James. Katie also shared how she and James would be leaving soon…on a prison ship!

Guilt washed over Tess. "It's because of me you are leaving."

"No, you're wrong, Tess. God had a plan for James and for me, and

He used you as one of his instruments to accomplish that plan."

Tess wasn't sure she understood all of what Katie was saying. "I don't know what to say to you. I can't believe we are here talking like this; as if we are old friends. For the first time in my life, I feel sorry for my actions. I always felt justified in what I did, until now. Oh, Katie, please forgive *me!*"

Katie was quick to assure Tess that all that had happened was in the past. "Let's begin anew, as if none of this ever happened."

"How can you do that?"

"With God's help, and knowing that I am not without guilt myself. We all sin, Tess. No one is better or worse."

Overwhelmed with gratitude, Tess felt heady from what was transpiring. She never thought this could happen. "Yes, let's begin anew, like you said. Thank you, Katie."

The two young women hugged and laughed in their joy. They spent another hour listening to one another and the stories they had to tell. Katie listened intently as Tess talked about her upcoming wedding. To anyone sitting close to their table it would seem as if two old friends were simply catching up on each other's news, and by the grace of God, they were.

"Look at the time!" Tess shouted. "My mother will think I've been kidnapped, or worse! She's such a worry wart."

Getting up to leave, she found that she genuinely did not want to leave. The two young women made plans to meet again soon. Shyly they took each other's hand and squeezed.

As her coach moved away, Tess pinched herself to see if she was awake. Did all of that really happen? Exhausted, she longed for sleep. Her mind was so befuddled she couldn't think anymore. She felt different, and it frightened her a little. *I'll go home, sleep, and figure it all out later.*

Katie smiled from ear to ear. Only God could have made their meeting as perfect as it was. Never had she dared believe that she and Tess could forgive each other. Katie caught her breath as she remembered the passage of Scripture where it said God would give her the desires of her heart. Even before she had met Tess, she had hoped they would be friends. *Oh Lord, only you could do this.* Katie was just grateful that she had obeyed and gone to see Tess. *Help me to always be obedient, Lord.*

⁋☙⁊

"What do you think, Mary? Is she losing it? After all the poor wee girl has been through?"

"Do not know, Maggie. Would seem the girl's got Jesus all right. I knew of a man who got holy and goofy in the 'ead. 'Is poor wife didn't know what ta think, what with 'im prayin' all the time instead of workin' for 'is family and her 'avin' to work so 'er little ones could eat."

Maggie went on, "I just can't believe the change in her. She has always been a happy person, but she seems downright giddy. Don't seem normal. I can remember when her father first brought her to the Brick House. She was such a shy little thing, but once she got to know a person she wouldn't stop smiling. Except for when Tess was around of course, and to find out she actually went to see the snit today! I don't know that any good can come from it, Mary."

"Aye, 'tis a strange thing all right. I don't trust that Tess anymore than I trust the devil hisself. Got a shifty look 'bout 'er. I saw 'er one day while at the Brick 'ouse visitin' Lady Wilson. Made me blood run cold knowin' what she 'ad done to Katie girl. I 'twas surprised when Katie girl told of wantin' to go see the she-devil."

"I know. You could have knocked me over with a feather when she told me too!" Maggie added.

The two women talked about the changes in Katie. They didn't know what to make of it all. "We need to keep an eye on her. If she gets out of hand, we'll need to speak to someone," Maggie stated matter-of-factly.

"Who?"

"Don't know, but someone."

That was all that was decided before Katie returned home. She only confirmed their suspicions with her humming and light step. She hugged them both, exclaiming how good God was. She proceeded to make their supper, telling them "to rest themselves." It was a tough time for the older ladies…they didn't like change.

16

Sally Mae

"What do you mean you already belong to the Prison Reform League?" Lord Wilson was incredulous.

"What's the matter, Edward? I told you of it a while ago. Mary, Maggie, Kathryn, and I all joined to help James and the other prisoners."

Lord Wilson stared at his wife as if she had just grown a second head. He thought the idea of helping prisoners was his alone.

"Honestly, Edward, I've told you and told you that you don't listen to me."

He had to admit she was right. He never took interest in his wife's activities. He just went along with what she was doing as long as it made her happy.

"Why do you ask about it now?" his wife questioned.

"I want to help in some way and thought we could do it together is all."

Barbara Wilson was touched by her husband's words. Putting her arms around his neck in a rare show of playful affection, she nuzzled him. "Why, dear Edward, has your heart been moved by those poor wretched souls in the gaols?" She smiled up at him.

He looked down at the only woman he had ever truly loved. "I must say it has shocked me how so many people just trying to take care of themselves and their families have been caught up in such hardship. Taking clothing or food to survive and being sentenced to hell is quite sobering. I have come to realize how blessed I am. I cannot imagine being pulled away from my family to another part of the world, never seeing them again." He held his wife close. He buried his face in her neck. "I love you, Barbara. I have loved you my whole life." They held onto one another for some time, thanking God for each other.

Captain Miles Warwick stood watching as provisions and livestock were brought on board. He was an impressive man in his forties with fine features and a solid build. He could be a hard taskmaster when needed, but most of the men had been with him for a long time. They had learned to respect his fairness and his knowledge of the sea. It was not beneath him to work alongside his men, and because of it his men held him in high regard. "Get that cargo below! I want this ship ready by the end of the week!" Above the shouts of men working, and the terrified bawling of cattle and sheep, the man's deep voice rang out. Men scurried about the deck as if their lives depended on it. When their captain gave an order they obeyed.

Addressing the Naval agent, the captain gave a slight smile. "Richards, make sure that the food, water, and especially the port are under lock and key. Remember, I know how much port we are loading."

"Yes, sir!" The man saluted and grinned.

The two men were old friends. The captain counted it fortunate to have this Naval agent on his ship. Lieutenant Gaylord Richards was diligent, caring, knowledgeable, and experienced in transporting large numbers of prisoners. It was his job to outfit the transport ships with provisions of water, clothing, and other materials. He then supervised the loading, which was no small task. Each ship carried 160 gallons of water, huge barrels of rice, wheat, salt pork, beef, butter, raisins, suet, sugar, flour, and other foodstuff. Live animals, clothing, material, medicines, along with tools, cooking utensils, and bedding were also brought aboard. The supplies were endless. He had to check every bale, barrel, and flask on all three ships. It was imperative for him to keep careful records.

At least they did not have to carry a vast amount of extra supplies to the colonies since they were well established and self-sufficient.

Trade ships sailed on a routine basis, lightening the load considerably for the transports.

Richards was also in charge of overseeing the prisoners taken from the gaols and prison hulks to the transport ships. He inspected the tween decks. They needed to be fumigated since that was where the prisoners were housed on arrival. He issued each male prisoner new clothes, consisting of a jacket, waistcoat of blue, duck trousers, a coarse linen shirt, yarn stockings, one woolen cap, and one pair of shoes. The women were given a brown "serve" jacket, one petticoat, two linen shifts, a linen cap, one neck handkerchief, one pair of worsted stockings, and one pair of shoes.

Although Richards was in charge of supplying and loading the full fleet, he could only sail on one ship. He chose the *Sally Mae* whenever he could. Warwick ran a tight ship when most did not. Once sails were hoisted the fleet of ships rarely sailed together. The weather saw to that. At times the ships were left to the wind while the provisions and prisoners were at the mercy of the ship's captain.

In all the chaos Jules Crane, the Surgeon-Superintendent, came aboard. His knowledge and aggressive care of the prisoners made a vast difference in the number of healthy convicts at the end of the journey. Captain Warwick smiled after spotting Crane. Having Richards and Crane on board helped him sail successfully time and time again. That was why the British government eagerly contracted the *Sally Mae*.

Warwick turned once more to eye his ship. With pride he had made her into one of the most successful convict transports. No ship had ever been built for the express purpose of transporting prisoners, and the *Sally Mae* was no exception. She was all of 672 tons. She was one of the larger convict ships running. Being built in India made her a solid ship…a prize indeed.

The ship was divided into three decks with part of all of them used for holding the prisoners. The men were kept down in the orlop—the very bottom of the ship. It held eighteen secure bays, nine on each side of the ship. A corridor ran down the center of the deck with iron bars separating it from the bays. The two end bays housed the livestock, leaving the air pungent. The light was dim at best. The sway of the ship was the only real difference between the lower bays and a dungeon in

Newgate.

Of course, Captain Warwick didn't see it that way. His job was to get as many prisoners as he could safely to Botany Bay. Warwick was a fair and compassionate man, but in his business life was hard. He treated the convicts and his crew with a lighter hand, and some humor. He found it made a vast difference to morale, but he was tough when he needed to be. He did all he could to make the voyage just as safe for his prisoners as the marines, their families, and his crew.

The transport was almost ready to sail. Along with the *Sally Mae* were two other transport ships and two naval vessels. They were set to sail together if the weather held.

Warwick, Richards, and Crane fought and won to keep the number of convicts transported on the *Sally Mae* to a manageable number. Many fleets were overloaded with convicts, but the *Sally Mae* was able to ask for special favors because of her record.

The other convict ships of the transport were called the *Greystone* and *The Clip*. They also tried to keep the number of prisoners down to 624, which averaged out to 208 convicts per ship. Less crowding meant less disease and discomfort for everyone. The sad truth was that no matter how much effort was taken, hardships were had by all. It was such a long and arduous voyage. Most times overcrowding was a fact of life, and few ships were given special attention.

Warwick also made it a habit to meet with the commander of the guards, his officers, warders, along with the matrons to head off any trouble. Communication was vital and welcomed between the captain and service personnel. Since the warders and matrons were in charge of the prisoners, Warwick felt it was important to keep communications open with them.

It was one such meeting that Kathryn Murphy's name was first spoken. It was with great interest that Captain Warwick listened to his First Officer, Marks, read a letter regarding Mrs. Murphy. It was a common occurrence that a free woman would ask to follow her convict husband. Most were turned down. This letter was not a request, but more of an order given by top government officials. That was the reason for such interest. An Irish woman given any thought at all was a rare thing. To be given special favor was unheard of.

"What do you think, Captain?" Marks asked.

"I think it's strange that we would get a letter like this in the first place. We will do as the letter says. One more woman on board will make little difference. If the British government wants her on this ship, then on this ship she'll be."

"Aye, sir."

The cabin boy entered after knocking on the captain's door. He stood silent until Warwick acknowledged him. "Yes, Fred, what is it?"

"A man named Smith is asking for you. Says you needed to talk to him about the marines and their family's quarters."

"Yes, yes, send him in, Fred. Bring some port." Warwick reached for his pipe to light it. He continued his instructions to his men. "Well, everything is pretty much ready to set sail. Remember, I still want the rest of that information on the convicts. Make sure there are enough matrons on board to help the females."

"Aye, sir." The men left their captain to finish their tasks.

Warwick had a moment alone before his visitor arrived. He stretched his heavily muscled legs yawning. He felt good about the progress made; he was sure all would be ready to set sail in time. The more trips he made the more was learned, and the easier it was to ready his ship. The hard times were coming once they left the harbor.

A knock was heard, and Warwick acknowledged. One more person to deal with, and his day would be done. "Smith, good to see you. Let me get you some port." The door closed behind the two men, and business was taken care of.

"Oh Edward, isn't that the most exciting news!" Lady Wilson beamed at her husband. "Who would have ever thought that Tess and Kathryn could become great friends, after all that has happened?"

"Are you sure you heard Tess right, my dear? Maybe you misunderstood her."

"No, she even sent a dinner invitation for tomorrow night to Kathryn."

"Well, I must agree this is exciting news. Too bad it couldn't have happened years ago. What brought all of this on in the first place?"

Lady Wilson repeated everything to her husband as it was told to her. "Haven't you noticed a...softening in Tess since she's been engaged to David? She genuinely seems to love him."

They spent a long time talking, expressing their hope in the changes in their daughter. Lord Wilson took his wife's hand tenderly, holding it. He didn't want to spoil her happy moment, but he needed to give her the news. He waited until the last possible moment to tell her. "I have some news that may upset you, Barbara. Kathryn and James will be leaving very soon. The fleet is being loaded up as we speak."

Surprise and then sadness crept across Lady Wilson's face. Tears formed as her husband pulled her to his chest. "There, there, we knew it was coming. I want you to know that I have had the captain investigated, and he runs a tight ship. He is a fair man, and his crew respects him. I've written letters, and even bought extra provisions for the voyage. All that can be done for Kathryn is being done."

Wiping her eyes, Lady Wilson lifted her head. "I know you are doing everything in your power to help her, Edward. I just wish she wasn't going. What a horrible, dangerous journey it is going to be for her. I can't even imagine all she will face."

"Just remember dear, there are other women on board—marines' wives and families, along with matrons for female prisoners. The ship is sound, and like I said, the captain and crew are experienced."

"What about when they get there? Where are they going to live? How in the world will there be enough food? Oh, Edward, I feel so helpless. What if Tess and Kathryn had become friends long ago? We wouldn't be having this discussion now. What if she wasn't forced to marry James?" Tears spilt down her cheeks.

"Don't do this to yourself, Barbara," Lord Wilson said gently. "It won't help anything. We've been through this. Kathryn could have backed out of her marriage but chose not to. I've been corresponding with the governor of Botany Bay. That's where Kathryn and James are sailing to. The colony is established and strong. I told the governor about James being a farmer. He said they have great need for men who know how to take care of land. If he does well, he can farm his own place in no time. Life is hard there, but after what these two have been through, I think they will be fine." He held his wife a little longer.

The couple talked until they came to the conclusion that God would have to watch over Kathryn and James. After all, James was a hard-working, capable man. He would take good care of their girl. There were many things in the world they couldn't control, and this was one of them.

It was late as they climbed the staircase. They both turned towards their separate bedchambers. Ever since Barbara had given birth to Tess, she thought it best to have her own rooms so as not to disturb her husband. After all these years, they still kept separate rooms. Tomorrow was going to be a hard one, and they needed to be strong, strong for Kathryn, and for each other. Hesitating at the top of the stairs, Edward turned towards his wife. He decided to stay the night with her. She looked so vulnerable...how he hated to see her suffer. After climbing in her bed he held her in his arms until she slept. Looking into her sweet face, he drew her closer, to ward off any evil.

Katie left early with Lord Wilson to go to the harbor. Lord Wilson was concerned for her but kept it to himself. He stayed close to answer all of her questions. Katie could not help but think the ships seemed small for transporting so many, yet they did look sturdy. The docks were buzzing with activity. Men were loading and unloading, others were barking orders. Katie saw prisoners in their telltale filthy rags. They were working on the docks and in long boats heading out to the harbor. They all looked so thin and sickly. Nothing at all like James...thank God! She was surprised James had not been brought to work on the docks.

Katie turned her attention to the prison hulks anchored out further in the harbor. They were a far cry from the transport ships. They reminded her of the filthy tenements of London. What looked like bedding hung on makeshift lines. The hulks were in great disrepair. Lean-tos stuck out at all angles from the original hull. Waves slapped the hulks, heaving them to and fro in the water. A few of them looked as if they would sink at any moment. Lord Wilson explained to her that some were French war ships captured in battle, and some were obsolete first-raters. Rusty chains and rotted wood were all that was left of their glorious service to England.

Lord Wilson caught her watching the prisoners working the docks. He wanted to shield her from the harsh realities in the world, but he couldn't...and she wouldn't let him. "I've made arrangements to visit your husband this afternoon. I thought he would like to hear the news on the fleet. Would you like to come too?" he asked.

"Yes, thank you, Lord Wilson. What would we have done without you?"

They walked along the harbor, taking in all the sights and sounds. "I'm not afraid anymore," Katie stated bluntly. "I used to be, but I'm not anymore...not right now anyway. I know God is going to take care of us. I have to remind myself of that from time to time, but just because I falter in my faith doesn't mean He falters."

Lord Wilson wished he could feel so assured. This newfound faith of hers seemed to give her strength, and she would need it.

"You really don't have to worry," Katie went on. "We will be fine. It may be hard, but life is hard all over, isn't it?"

Lord Wilson couldn't help but marvel at this girl. Her concern had always been for others. Here she was leaving soon, yet she was trying to comfort him. "Yes, life is hard, but when you came into our lives, you made things easier for us. We will miss you dreadfully."

Katie placed her hand on his arm and squeezed. She would miss them too. She fought hard to keep that feeling of excitement about leaving, but right now it was anything but exciting. Reality shouted at her: that her husband was a prisoner with no rights or say in their future. Their lives were in the hands of strangers.

No! Our lives are in your hands, Father! Katie silently and stubbornly declared. Harder still was leaving these people, her family. Just thinking of it tore at her heart. She prayed again. *Lord, help me to remember that you know all things, and we are in YOUR hands. Fear is not of you, Lord. Ease our grief and help us to trust you in everything.*

Katie and Lord Wilson kept walking along the docks, lost in their own thoughts. Her thoughts turned to God's Word and promises for the future; his turned towards all the horrors and danger this young woman would be facing.

❧ ☙

Mary wailed uncontrollably while Maggie patted her shoulder. "I can't bear that Katie girl be leavin'! I be knowin' she was to leave, but not now."

Maggie nodded, wiping a tear of her own. The time seemed to come far too quickly.

"We ne'er see 'er again," Mary howled, burying her face in her apron.

Maggie could only nod and pat her friend's shoulder.

"What 'appens if she sinks in the sea or is killed in the jungle where she be goin'?" Mary asked between sniffles. "What if she gets eat up alive from those black heathens I 'ear 'bout there? What if?"

Maggie couldn't listen to any more. "Don't be thinkin' like that, Mary! It will only cause her leaving to be harder. It was Katie's decision to go. There are others there to help, and James will take care of her. Now stop the cryin' before she comes home. We don't have much time to spend with her, so let's not fill it with tears."

Mary was truly worried about Katie, but something else held her back from sleep at night. She expressed it to Maggie. "What will 'appen to ol' Mary when my Katie is gone?"

"You will stay with me. I've gotten used to your sour old puss."

Mary smiled weakly at her friend, then blew her nose. "Ya be right. Time ta stop wailin' 'bout it. Cannot be doin' anythin' 'bout it 'tis true. Needs to be strong for Katie girl. 'Tis feelin' better I am. Aye, a good hard cry 'tis good fer the soul."

A knock sounded, and Henry stepped inside the door. Before he knew what hit him, Mary flew into his arms, letting out a howl. She held onto him with all her might, burying her face in his shirt. Poor Henry looked bleakly at Maggie. His eyes begged for help. There was none. Maggie simply shook her head and went into the kitchen...so much for being strong.

Lord Wilson had never met Kathryn's husband. He'd heard about him being a big man in size but was caught off guard nevertheless. Kathryn walked around the table to give her husband a hug, then turned to introduce the two men. "Lord Wilson, this is my husband, James."

Red offered his hand to Lord Wilson even though it was chained. "Sir, I'm glad to finally meet you. Katie has told me all that you have done for her, for us. Now I can thank you in person."

Lord Wilson shook the big man's hand. He did not usually feel awkward, but he did now. Standing with this stranger who just happened to be a prisoner and was bigger than a mountain made him feel uneasy. Lord Wilson pulled out a chair for Katie, then spoke, "I've wanted to meet you, Mr. Murphy."

"You can call me James, or Red. That's what most call me."

"James then; news has come down of a voyage. Kathryn and I thought you would like to hear it."

"I've wanted to meet you too. What of the ships in the harbor? I've heard rumors, but there's always rumors flying here. I know there is a fleet anchored in the harbor. Several have come and gone, yet here we are. It was said we were leaving, but I don't know. I was beginning to believe that I would spend my seven years here at Newgate. Since it is late May, I thought I would be here at least another year."

"Actually you could have left two weeks ago on another fleet, but I requested that you be held back."

Katie hadn't known this, so it surprised her as well as her husband. They looked at each other then quietly waited for his explanation.

"The fact is, I had both captains and fleets investigated. I found Captain Miles Warwick to be outstanding. He's one of the best, as far as a transport captain is concerned. The first fleet was questionable, but Captain Warwick's record is impeccable. It would seem that he has over twenty successful voyages credited to him. His crew respects him, and he treats his prisoners humanely. I hope you don't feel I was overstepping. I know you were not able to do any investigating yourself so I took it upon myself. My family cares deeply for your wife, and my wife would not be able to rest if Kathryn was put into more danger than necessary. If my wife doesn't rest, I don't rest."

James smiled at that. "Sir, I would not ever question any of the decisions you make regarding my wife. I know you have only her best interest in mind. That is all I need to know."

Lord Wilson was rather surprised. He didn't expect to find him an educated man. Oh, he knew the man could read and write, but Murphy held himself with confidence. Where most men would have balked at the thought of someone else making decisions for his family, this man understood. Yes, Lord Wilson was surprised indeed. Grimes said this man gained respect from everyone he fell in contact with. Now he understood what was meant when he heard Grimes say, "It seems he's not just big in stature."

After a few minutes Lord Wilson continued, "I have a few details you may want to know. There are five ships in the fleet—three transports, and two naval vessels. The entire transport can hold 1,730 prisoners, but they are loading fewer than that. It's one of the stipulations of Captain Warwick. He'll hold the number of prisoners to just fewer than 300 per ship. The ships are stout, and I heard they are fast as well. Life on board is going to be very difficult. The ships were loaded a couple of weeks ago and are now anchored, waiting for the prisoners to arrive. If the weather holds, you should leave at the scheduled time."

"I'm sure we'll be fine," James said, looking at his wife. "Our trust is in the Lord."

"Of course," answered the older man.

They continued to talk about the voyage ahead—what to expect and how long it was going to take to reach their destination. Lord Wilson explained that Kathryn would share a cabin with several of the matrons. He explained that matrons helped with the women prisoners. He surprised James by telling him of his request to have James part of the crew instead of a prisoner. It wasn't to be. James would be transported same as the others. There would be no privileges there.

"I was able, however, to keep you off one of the prison hulks, or forced to do any dock work while waiting to be transported out."

"I was wondering why I wasn't taken out. Most of the men who

176

work with me have been kept here as well. Again I see that I need to thank you, sir."

Lord Wilson cleared his throat. "No need to thank me, young man. I personally think it's a crime to sentence a man to seven years for being hungry. Whoever made that law should be the one locked in here. I must admit, I had you investigated. If I was to help you; I wanted to know what kind of man I would be dealing with."

Katie broke in. "I told you that James is an honorable man."

"Yes, I know, but love is blind sometimes."

Katie blushed.

James spoke up, "He was right to question, Katie. I would have done the same thing." Turning to Lord Wilson he continued, "So when do we leave?"

"If the weather holds, and all goes well, the end of next week."

Katie and James looked at each other. "That soon?" they said in unison.

Katie jumped up. "I didn't realize there was so little time left. I've waited and waited, and now...well, I don't know what to do first! I must go, James. There's so much I need to do."

Lord Wilson and James stood watching her as she began to pace the room, talking to herself.

"I have to decide exactly what I need to take, and I have to sign those papers at the lawyers, and I have to..."

"Katie," James said, as he caught her arm, "there is plenty of time. Don't worry, everything will get done."

"Oh, James, next week! We're leaving next week!"

James turned to the older man. "Would you mind if I speak to my wife a moment? Thank you again for all you have done for us. I'll never be able to repay you. I give you my word that I, along with the Lord, will take good care of Katie."

Lord Wilson shook James's hand once more. Smiling, he leaned forward. "Don't worry, my boy; women always panic at any news they get. I will see you before you leave. Now that I have met you, I know she'll be fine. Kathryn, I'll wait outside."

Katie nodded. "Thank you, Lord Wilson. I'll be out shortly."

James took Katie's hands. Looking deep into her eyes he said,

"Katie, are you positive you want to do this? It's not too late to change your mind." Katie began to speak, but James rushed on, "I know we talked about this before, but that was when the voyage was somewhere in the future."

A doubt crossed Katie's mind, but it went away as fast as it came. "No, absolutely not, we are going together. God will be with us whether we sail or stay. I thought we decided to trust Him and each other."

"Yes we did, and I do but if…"

"James, you're wasting time and words."

James hugged his wife. "Well then, you best go so you can get ready. It will be hard for me to sit here waiting to go when I feel I should be helping somehow."

Katie wrapped her arms around her husband. "I love you, James. I know we will be fine." Katie kissed him good-bye.

Once outside she mouthed a quick prayer. *Father, give us strength, and help our faith grow. Give me wisdom to know what things I need to do to prepare for the voyage. Help me to say good-bye to all the people I love.*

Lord Wilson stepped down to help Katie into the coach. "Are you all right, Kathryn?"

"I'm fine. I knew we would be going soon, but I didn't think it would be next week. I guess I wasn't sure what soon really meant."

"He seems to be a fine man, Kathryn. I've always wondered what attracted you to him. Now I understand. I'm a pretty good judge of character. The little I've talked to him I can see he is a man of integrity and strength. You will be just fine."

Katie smiled. "I wish we could have met under different circumstances, but the Lord works in mysterious ways."

The rest of the ride home was spent in deep thought. It would not be long before they would be saying good-bye. It would be a difficult thing to do, for it would likely be good-bye forever. Katie smiled when Lord Wilson took her hand in his. He didn't say a word, just held her hand gently in his own. They rode home in silence. How he would miss this gentle, sweet-natured young woman.

17

Good-byes

The chandelier in the dining hall cast soft light over the room. Servants walked around the massive table while Lord and Lady Wilson engaged their guests in conversation. Lady Wilson planned a very special evening since there was precious little time left. She was intent on making it perfect, but the mood was still subdued in spite of all her efforts.

Tess, and her fiancé, David, sat next to each other with Kathryn across from them. Great care was taken on everyone's part to keep the conversation light and interesting. It was difficult to say the least.

After dinner everyone strolled into the parlor, each finding a seat in front of the fire. Shortly, the men excused themselves, going into the den for brandy and cigars. The ladies stayed to talk about the upcoming wedding and sip their tea. Lady Wilson marveled as she watched her daughter. It was if someone else who looked like Tess sat across from her. In a short time Tess had turned into a new person. Her daughter had even gone so far as to ask forgiveness from her parents. What a wondrous time it was for this small family.

Tess addressed Katie. "I wish you could be here for my wedding. I was going to ask you to stand up with me. I'm just being selfish, I know, but I don't want anyone else. I want you to share in the biggest day of my life. Then again it is my fault you're leaving in the first place."

"Tess, that's all over and done with. The decision to leave was mine. It had nothing to do with what happened. I could have chosen to stay here. It's all water under the bridge so please, don't mention it again," Katie stated firmly.

A sigh escaped from Tess, "I feel free and happy for the first time in my life since I'm not the center of my own universe. Yet my heart is breaking at the thought of losing you. When I think of all the years I've wasted…"

"Now stop; didn't you hear anything I just said? You need to forgive yourself. That's the only thing holding you back. Everyone has regrets. We can't change that. As far as wasted years, they weren't wasted. It took all that happened to bring us to the Lord, and our friendship. We will always be close friends. Distance can't change that, nor can time. I still can't believe the changes in our lives. How grateful I am for new beginnings." Tess nodded, then bent forward to hug Katie. The two women clung to each other. Just then a maid entered to announce there were more guests waiting in the great hall.

"Show them in, Esther." Just as Lady Wilson stood up, Maggie and Mary came in. "Ladies, I'm so glad you could make it. I was sorry you couldn't make dinner, but at least you are here now." Katie was pleasantly surprised. Neither of them had mentioned that they were going to be coming. In fact, Katie was a little disappointed when she thought they had not been invited. She noticed Maggie carrying a package.

"Here's the package you wanted, Lady Wilson."

"Thank you, Maggie. I'm glad it came in time."

"What's this?" Katie questioned.

"Well, dear Kathryn, we all have a going-away gift for you." Lady Wilson handed the wrapped package to Katie.

Again Katie asked, "What is it?"

"Blimey, Katie girl!" Mary laughed. "Open it up. I can't wait 'til ya sees it!"

Maggie placed her hand on Mary's shoulder. "Easy, ol' girl."

Everyone laughed at Mary's excitement.

Katie slowly unwrapped the package, then drew in her breath. "Oh, they are beautiful!" Katie lifted three pewter framed mini-portraits out from the wrapping. One was of Lady and Lord Wilson, one of Tess and David, and one was Mary and Maggie.

Mary tittered, "Yas like 'em, Katie girl? See me? I ne'er 'ad a picture of me drawn afore. They be tellin' me ta smile so I tried ta make it a good one." Mary beamed with pleasure.

"Oh how beautiful," Katie repeated. "I don't think I could ever treasure anything so dearly as these. Thank you so much." Katie choked back a tear.

Mary broke in. "Cannot be cryin'! Won't be havin' it! Ya start an' we be startin' right behind ya."

Lady Wilson explained to Katie they thought small portraits would be easier for her to take. She continued, "We have a friend whose cousin is Randolph Case. He's an accomplished artist, and just happened to be in London a few months ago for a show. We were so lucky to get him to do these for us. He did some quick sketches of all of us, and just finished the portraits a day ago. Randolph sent them to his cousin's house, and we sent a coach with Mary and Maggie to pick them up."

Mary added, "'Twasn't goin' to let nobody else pick 'em up. Sure didn't want 'em to get lost."

"Katie, I've never seen anyone as excited as Mary over these portraits. I wish you could have seen her." Maggie laughed.

"'Tis important is all I be sayin'," Mary broke in. "Whene'er ya look at me picture, ya won' ferget ol' Mary."

Katie got up from the couch and walked over to her. Putting her arm around Mary's shoulders, she gave her a quick squeeze. "I would forget to breathe before I would forget you, any of you."

"When David and I have our wedding portraits finished, I'll send you one," Tess promised.

"I would love that!"

The evening went all too quickly, and soon Katie, Mary, and Maggie had to leave for home. The women planned to gather at her cottage the next day to help pack. After saying good night, the ladies climbed into their coach. Sadness fell on them, thinking of the short time they had left. Katie thought of the days of Gran and Papa. She had believed her whole life would be lived with those two special people. It had all been so simple back then, before her life had taken on so many twists and turns. What would Gran think if she knew all that was going on in her life now? Maybe she did.

Katie's thoughts turned to Maggie and Mary. After discussing Maggie's future with the Wilsons, she'd had papers drawn up to give Maggie and Mary co-ownership of the cottage. It would belong to them, along with her and James. She knew they would be happy there. It did her heart good to know that if she and James did ever come back they would have something, and someone, to come back to.

Soon the coach pulled up in front of Brady's Brick. The driver jumped down to help them out. Katie hesitated on the front walk, looking at the cozy cottage. Smoke from the fireplace gently rolled from the chimney, leaving a curly line reaching for the sky. Buds on the few trees in front promised to open soon, and flowers peeked out from the Earth. She wanted to remember the warmth, love, and promise this little cottage held for her. It was her father's dream, passed on to her. In turn she would pass it on to her family.

"Ya be comin' in, Katie girl?" Mary asked as she passed Katie on the walk.

"I'm coming. I was just thinking how pretty the cottage looks from the outside at night. All cozy and warm. I'll surely miss it."

The three women promised each other that there was not going to be another crying session. They all made a valiant effort, but tears still fell. They talked long into the night, pledging to always write and pray for one another.

❧ ❧

James ran his fingers through his hair in frustration. Pacing up and down his cell, his forehead creased in thought.

"Sit down, boy, or there will be a rut in the floor where ya be walking," Ben stated.

"I can't sit down. Now that I know we're leaving, I want to do something to get ready, but what?"

Ben, much older than Red, stepped up, placing his hand on the big man's shoulder. Red turned at his touch.

Ben gently reminded him, "Be careful for nothing; but in everything, by prayer and supplication with thanksgiving, let your requests be made known unto God. And the peace of God, which passeth all understanding, shall keep your hearts and minds through Christ Jesus."

"You're right as usual, Ben. It seems I need a daily reminder of those things."

"We all do," Ben assured Red. "I have some good news too. I will be transported on the same fleet as you."

"How do you know?"

"I just talked to my sister today. She had a list of prisoners leaving, and both our names are on it. So are Hayes, Thomason, O'Hare, and Jameston."

"That is good news!" Red said, slapping Ben on the back. "How did she get that list?"

"Her husband knows someone who had access to it."

"Hey men, we're all sailing on the same ship to Botany Bay!" Red announced to the others. All the men who had been a part of the work crew with Red gathered to discuss the voyage. Their talk became more excited by the minute until the cell was full of men's voices lifted in excitement over their departure.

One man sitting watching the group couldn't stand it anymore. "Blimey, ya bunch of patties. Don't ya knows yer all gonna die? Yas talk as if yas goin' on a trip 'ter Paris or somethin', but it be hell yas goin' to. Don't yas realize it, or is the whole bunch of yas daft in the head?"

"Ya! Yer all be nuts, ya are!" added someone else.

The group of men stood silently for a few minutes, then all eyes turned to Red. Since they all seemed to expect him to say something, he did. "You are right! We're daft all right, but at least we have enough brains to know we want out of here."

The other men laughed and began talking again. Now that they knew they were leaving, a feeling of expectancy filled them. The men separated and settled down, losing themselves in their own thoughts. They were not fools. They knew dangers were coming, but these men had known danger all their lives. Hardship and hunger had been companion to most of them since they were lads. If anything frightened them it was the sea...the sea with its black water and monsters just under the surface. Not hunger or hardship, but the unknown was the enemy, the fear-giver. Hope was lost to them early in life, and they had learned to live without it.

Then this large man with the large heart had told them of a new hope. In the beginning many wanted to believe, but some felt foolish, and some were doubtful. As the days, weeks, and months went by they watched Red and Ben walk in faith. That was why most of the men turned to Red in the first place. He replaced their fear of the unknown with hope in the absolute…God's Son.

Ben and Red prayed by themselves, but one by one the others joined them. The rest of the afternoon was spent talking about God's promises and of the hope only He could give. Some of the men expressed a longing to know that kind of hope, and they asked the Lord into their hearts. Several men on the other side of the room scoffed, making coarse jokes, but some sat quietly watching. The men cracking jokes fell silent. Red and the others could feel the presence of the Holy Spirit. It was so sweet, and there was a wonderful fragrance about the cell. Men began to loudly praise God with tears streaming down their faces. The men across from them became fearful, knowing that something was happening but not understanding what. They knew something powerful was taking place, and that inspired awe in the most wretched of them.

The afternoon was spent in fellowship. Ben shared many Bible verses that he had memorized over the years. Several others came to listen and accept Jesus as their Savior. In that filthy, cold, and damp cell men's lives were transformed. Hearts were broken, only to be healed anew. Spirits rose along with voices of praise, and the sweetness of it was powerful.

Red looked over at the men who remained on the other side of the cell. "Men, would you like to join us?"

"Ya mean fer yer little girly tea party?" one man scoffed. The others laughed.

"This journey is going to be difficult. God will care for you and protect you if you let Him," Red said.

"Ahhh, I'll give ya a week an' ya be at each other's throats. Ya be scrappin' fer bread and blanket 'fore ya even leave the harbor in that hell hulk. Yas talkin' freedom, but yas ne'er have freedom. The rest of you men listenin' to him will be hatin' him afore the week is out."

"God don't love us!" another spoke up. "He only loves the rich an' stupid. Blimey, He may love yas after all!" Laughter once again rang throughout the cell.

Red could see it wouldn't do any good to talk to them. Maybe once they were on their way, and it became harder they would be more open to listening. For now he was going to concentrate on the others. He leaned against the wall closing his eyes. He felt refreshed and strengthened by the Holy Spirit. It seemed as if a new chapter was opening up in his life while the old one was being closed. How would this chapter read? Would it be success or failure, happiness or grief? Whatever the future held, Red knew he would not face it alone. He had the Lord and Katie. He felt bad for the others who were leaving loved ones behind. Many had children they would probably never see again. He just couldn't understand how they could face all that without the Lord. He felt gratitude to the Lord for his salvation, his wife, and yes, for the difficult journey ahead.

One day at a time, Lord. Help me to live just one day at a time.

Katie went through her bag for what seemed the thousandth time. Space was limited, and she had to leave a lot behind. She had to decide what would be more important to her and James in the future. Two trunks filled with her belongings were allowed to go with her. There was so much, and only the most important would need to go, but what was the most important? Katie didn't know what would be available to buy once they reached Botany Bay. She had brought material, needles, thread, medicines, garden tools, and even some seeds for planting. For the household she packed blankets, soap, candles, wicks, pots for cooking, and extra clothes. Along with Mary and Maggie, she had made extra socks, pants, and shirts for James. For her there were dresses, aprons, under things, shawls, and bonnets. She purchased an extra pair of shoes and boots for both her and James along with warm coats, hats, and gloves for the cold. Her trunks were filled. The bag she now packed bulged, threatening to tear. Katie had her most prized possessions in the center of her bag with the clothing around to protect them—her Bible and the small portraits of her "family."

She and James had gone over a list of items to bring, but she was afraid of forgetting something. She had packed and repacked many times. A soft knock sounded at her door. "Come in."

Maggie opened the door, followed by Mary, carrying a tray of tea and coffee. "Thought you would like a break," Maggie said as Mary set the tray down.

"Oh that sounds good. I need to stop for a while."

The women talked over any possible items that might be forgotten, but each item was accounted for. Katie decided her packing was done. Lady Wilson and Tess planned on coming over later in the day to take all of them out to dinner. Lord Wilson would meet them after work. The ladies finished their hot drinks then proceeded to get themselves ready for dinner. Once the other two left Katie washed up, putting on a clean dress, and fixed her hair. She wondered if she should chance taking a mirror on her journey but decided against it. Hopefully there would be one available to buy. She had a feeling she wouldn't be caring that much about her hair once there. When she was ready she pulled Gran's shawl out of her bag, placing it around her shoulders. It had seen better days, but it gave her comfort.

"Ya be ready, Katie girl?" Mary shouted. "Lady Wilson and Tess be 'ere with the coach."

"Aye, I'll be right out." After checking her reflection in the mirror once more, she dabbed a little cologne. The women all loaded up in the coach and were off. They all spoke in excitement of the evening.

"'Ere we are," Mary murmured as the coach pulled up.

Lady Wilson led the procession to a large table in the dining hall. It was only a few minutes before Lord Wilson arrived, and their orders were taken. It was a lovely evening of good food, and friends, but Katie longed to have James there.

The talk around the table was light until Katie broke in, "Lord Wilson, do you think James will be able to get a homestead once we get there?"

He looked at her with surprise. "Well, I wrote to the governor. He said they needed men who knew their way around a farm. He also said it was hard work, and many just gave up. I can't guarantee anything, but by the sounds of it there's more than a chance of it."

"James knows everything about farming. His dream has been to own land, and farm it. I know that this may be a strange way to obtain it, but like I said before, God works in mysterious ways. Well, I keep saying I'm going to trust in the Lord so I need to trust Him in everything, right?"

Through the rest of the dinner, conversation was kept light. All too soon it was time to leave.

Lord Wilson spoke up, "The captain wants everyone on board early, so I better get everyone home. We leave at dawn for the harbor. It's drizzling rain now, but hopefully it will clear by morning," Soon everyone was in their own carriages, heading for Brady's Brick.

"It is getting late, but I don't want to go to bed as soon as we get home. We have such little time left," Katie said to Mary and Maggie.

It wasn't long before they arrived at Brady's Brick and everyone sat in front of the fireplace talking. All too soon it was time for Lady and Lord Wilson and Tess to be leaving. Lady Wilson would not be accompanying them to the ship in the morning. It was too painful, so she said her good-byes to her sweet Kathryn.

"As long as you live, remember that you have many people who love you. If ever you get a chance to come back to either stay or visit, please do so. I love you for your good heart and your sweetness."

Katie hugged the older woman. "I promise that as soon as possible, I will do my best to come back and see you. Thank you for being the mother I needed all this time. I love you."

Tess and Katie walked outside arm in arm. They planned on saying their good-byes in the morning. Tess wasn't about to miss out seeing her one more time. Lord Wilson gave Kathryn a hug, telling her he would be there bright and early.

So here it was; her last night in the cottage. It had threatened to come all too quickly, and it did. Mary, Maggie, and Katie stayed up a little longer, but all too soon it was time for bed. As Katie lay in her room, she went over the contents of her baggage once more in her mind. She tried to think of anything she may have forgotten. Finally she decided she had done all she could, and would trust the Lord in the rest.

Sleep came quickly, along with disturbing dreams. Dark waters swirled around her, people were screaming, wood splintered as she frantically looked for James. She saw him sink under the depths of the sea. She tried to scream, but nothing came out. Katie swam as fast as she could to grab onto James before he sunk further down into the waters. Suddenly she was pulled away from James by a horrible sea monster. Just as the monster was about to devour her, she awoke.

Mary stood over her with concern on her face. "Katie girl, are ya all right? It be dreamin' ya be doin'. Wake up now, wake up."

Katie slowly sat up in her bed, wiping the tears from her eyes. "It was awful, Mary. The ship was sinking, and James was drowning. I went to grab him, and a monster came up from the depths and..."

"Hush now, jest be a dream, Katie girl. Jest be a dream." Mary sat with Katie until late into the night. They talked about the dream, the voyage to come, and what it all meant. Katie finally lay back on her pillow, closing her eyes as Mary watched over her.

Soon Mary could hear Katie's deep breathing. "Keep 'er safe, God. Let 'er be 'appy and blessed," Mary whispered.

She quietly slipped out of Katie's room. Sadness filled her as she shuffled off to bed. *'Tis the last day afore she be gone,* Mary thought to herself. *May be the last I e'er see 'er again.* Mary got into bed, but sleep didn't come. She was afraid to sleep. She didn't want to miss any time remaining with Katie. She just waited to hear the first stir of someone in the kitchen. She didn't have to wait long.

⸺✦⸺

Katie lay awake, determined not to cry. Mary had just tiptoed out of her room thinking she was asleep, but she wasn't. They all would have a hard enough time at her leaving. Katie determined she would not break down again, but that dream had left her shaken. For the thousandth time Katie set her mind and heart in trusting the Lord. He was leading the way for her and James, so she would trust. At least she would keep trying. Excitement, along with dread, swept back and forth within her. A spiritual battle raged throughout the night.

By early morning Katie felt the wounds of that battle in her numbness. She was exhausted. Trust was an easy word on the tongue, but the heart was a different matter. Trust would have to be a choice she would make minute by minute, if necessary.

Katie gave up on any notion of sleep. This was to be the first day of her new life. She got up and knelt beside her bed.

Well, Lord, you see my heart. I want to walk boldly in faith, and sometimes I do, but many times I stumble. Forgive my lack of faith, and help me to be strong. I know you will take care of us. It's just I'm afraid of the unknown, and of the sea. I've heard such awful things, Lord. Help me not to be afraid. Give me strength to help others on the voyage. Help me to keep my eyes on you.

Katie continued to kneel when she felt His words in her heart.

I will never leave you or forsake you. The sea is my creation, as are you.

Katie barely breathed as she let His words wash over her. Tears glistened in her eyes as she thought of His love for her. She would never stop being amazed when Almighty God, Creator of Heaven and Earth, the living, sovereign God of the universe, spoke to her! His love astounded her, and His words gave her strength. She felt revived. There were no words to express her love and gratitude so she simply whispered, "Thank you, Father."

❦❧

Maggie stumbled into the main room to see the clock sitting on the mantle. It was just about to chime 4 a.m. She returned to her room to get dressed, hoping she would get more time with Katie. Lord Wilson would arrive before too long. As Maggie returned from getting dressed, she ran into Mary coming out of her room. Whispering as not to wake Katie, Mary leaned over to Maggie, "'Tis she up yet?"

"Don't think so. I want her to get her rest, and yet I want to wake her."

"Aye, it won't be long afore Katie girl be gone." Mary sniffed.

"Now, don't you start your howling. You know once you start, there's no stopping you," Maggie warned.

As the two women went into the cook's room they were surprised to see Katie already sitting at the small table.

"About time you two showed up," Katie teased. "Come sit down while I pour your tea. There's something that I need to talk to you about. I put it off to the last minute because I didn't want any arguments from you."

The two older ladies looked at each other, then back at Katie.

"I have some papers for you. They are co-ownership of the cottage and lands. I had them made out in both your names, along with James and mine."

Maggie was shocked. She would not have been surprised to learn the cottage was given to Mary, but why her too? She was here as a servant, though Katie never treated her as such.

"Blimey," Mary sputtered. "Ya be given me an' Maggie the cottage? Yer father gave it ter ya, Katie girl. What do ya think 'e would say 'bout that if 'e knew 'bout it?"

"Mary, my father isn't here, but he would agree with me. This decision is mine and James'. You and Maggie are my family, so it will stay with my family. If and when James and I return, we want a home and family to come back to. This is selfishness on my part."

It was Maggie's turn to question Katie. "Why me, Katie? I was brought here to work for you. Mary is more family than I."

"You are both family to me, and will always be." She then handed another envelope over to the women. "This is an account that has been set up at the bank for you. Each month there will be monies in there for you to live on, and for the maintenance of the cottage. Lord Wilson's lawyer will help to oversee the account. If there is anything you need, just go to him. If there are repairs that need to be done, just contact him, and he will arrange for the workers to come. The land will be rented out to other farmers, and money will come in from that, along with some produce." Pausing for only a second, Katie continued, "I know that in a few hours we will be saying good-bye. I really don't want to discuss business, so please accept this with no arguments. Like I said before, I'm really being quite selfish because I could never leave if I had to worry about the two of you. This way I know you have each other to look after, and the cottage will be loved and cared for."

Any arguments the women had dissolved with Katie's words. Wiping tears they thanked her and tried to enjoy the remaining time they had together.

Lord Wilson arrived and had Katie's trunks loaded. "Lord Wilson," Katie asked, "when will the ship be leaving?"

"I was told this very morning. Everyone is to be boarded by 7 a.m., so we don't have much time."

"Do you think I'll be able to see James?"

"I doubt it. There are no women allowed near the men prisoners the entire trip. The captain makes sure that even his crew stays away from the women prisoners. There are no exceptions according to Captain Warwick." Lord Wilson left shortly after that. He intended to make sure Kathryn's luggage was delivered safe and sound.

Soon Tess arrived with her mother in tow. Lady Wilson had planned to stay away, but could not. The woman treasured the remaining time they had.

18

Awestruck

It was still black as pitch when James and seven other men were transported to the harbor. They were manacled together, then placed in an open cart. James had talked to Katie the evening before but had not known then that he was being brought aboard ship today. He hoped she wouldn't worry once she found out. Although still dark, a swarm of activity was everywhere. People scurried to and fro.

James turned when he heard a scuffle a few feet from him. In another group one of the men tripped, causing four others to fall. One of the turnkeys kicked them and swore. "Git up, yer piece of filth! Git up now!" The men struggled to stay on their feet.

James could see in the dim light of glowing torches women being loaded up into open carts as well. Their heads were shaved, and they looked half starved. A few of them had children holding on to their skirts. All were in rags, and many had no shoes. The children whimpered as they clung desperately to their mothers. A cold mist began wetting everyone down, adding to their misery. By the time all the carts were loaded the prisoners were soaked and shivering.

Ben whispered to James, "Seems a tough beginning."

Another man added, "Told yas, I did, that it were no holiday yas were goin on. Don't see yas laughin' and praisin' the Almighty now. Yas think cause yas say so God will make it easy fer ya?" He ended his tirade once he got switched across the mouth by one of the guards.

"Shut up! No talking!"

It took longer for the carts to arrive at the harbor than expected. The gaolers were anxious to get out of the rain. People were being pushed and pulled as they were led to the long boats. The waters were rough, causing the loading of shackled prisoners to be treacherous. One of the small children nearly fell in when he tripped on his mother's skirt. Chaos ruled, and the mood was foul. The gaolers took their discomfort out on the prisoners. Fortunately for all, the long boats were finally loaded and heading out to the transport ships.

James noticed many boats. Some prisoners were being loaded off the prison hulks. It looked as if they fared worst of all. The rags that they were wearing barely covered them. They were so thin; a good wind could have knocked them into the water. Once they reached the transport ships they were hauled aboard and made to stand on the deck.

James saw a man standing off from the rest. By the looks of him, James figured it was the captain. Another man pushed a prisoner down, kicking him for not getting out of his way fast enough.

"Barrett!" the captain yelled.

"Yes, sir!" The crew member snapped to attention.

"What did I tell you about mistreating the prisoners? See that it doesn't happen again!"

"Yes, sir!"

"Get these prisoners below, starting with the females and children. Make sure you hand out proper clothing, and everyone gets a blanket once they are deloused!"

"All right, women, down the hulk with yas! Git a move on. Ain't got all day," one of the sailors barked. Two matrons came forward to lead them down.

It took some time for the women to get settled before the men were led to their bays. The warder, in charge of the orlop, designated eight men per bay. He had their shackles replaced with leg irons that were attached to rings in the bay. Each man was severely restricted in movement, having to mostly sit or lay on his wooden berth. It was not much more than a plank of wood.

The sound of frightened animals at the end of the bays filled the air. So did the smell of them. James noted the lack of fresh air. With all the bodies coming in, he knew it would soon be unbearable. He had no way of knowing that iron bars were put in to replace solid wooden doors throughout the corridors. This gave them more air, but "fresh" air was another matter. Between all the humans and animals alike, there was none to be had. The deck above the orlop, also called the lower deck, was set up similar to the orlop. The only difference was a few cabin rooms for marines and their families were added between bays. Between those rooms and a chapel, which occupied a great deal of the space, there was room for only fourteen bays. The upper deck had twelve bays, and storerooms at the aft. It also held the captain's quarters, the surgeon's quarters, and a few other cabins at the forefront.

The captain's quarters held a bedchamber, a pantry, and an open living area. A huge table in the center of the room took a lot of the space. The captain's massive desk was placed near the windows. Cook rooms and wash rooms were in the forecastle, along with one large cabin used as the sick room, or "hospital."

The women were held on the upper deck located at midship. The head matron, Annie Hill, gave orders. She was a tall, thin woman who appeared hard but had a big heart. As she directed the women to their bays, she unlocked their manacles and placed the chains through heavy rings bolted in their bays. After being deloused, given clothes, and blankets, the women settled down. They were grateful to be out of the cold, damp weather. The children cuddled close to their mothers for warmth. It was hard to sleep, but exhaustion claimed many of them.

Once all the men were in place they were given a blanket to ward off the chill. In each bay were several slop jars for personal use, and nothing else. It was sparse, dark, and stuffy. The pitch of the ship in the rough waters didn't help. It felt as if they were already on the high seas instead of anchored in the harbor. Before the day was out, a few people used the slop jars frequently.

James and the seven others in the bay sat on their wooden berths watching the warder. Several marines were there to help get the other bays settled. At one point the warder came back to one of the bays and had a young boy removed.

"What is he doing here?" the warder yelled at another. "You know we got the young ones on the upper deck. Take him out, and bring a man back here."

Once everyone was settled, the warder and marines left. It didn't take the prisoners long to realize they had long days ahead of them. Many sat upright, trying to sleep, while others quarreled and swapped stories. It would be a few more days before they were to set sail. They sat in the dim light, fighting off panic, nausea, and anger. This was it; no turning back for them even if they could. Some of them hoped for a last-minute reprieve or pardon, but it was not to be. Some were in shock while others were in denial, but all were now on board the ship that would take them from their homeland. Most would never see it again.

James felt peace. He knew without a doubt that God was using this for His purpose and plan. He was determined to be open to God and His direction. He had to smile at that. To see him chained up one would think God wasn't any part of his life, but they would be wrong. Yes, he had gotten himself here, but God would use it for His glory. James looked around. He saw the suffering and the hopelessness in men's faces. *Oh Lord, help me to help them. Give me words, and let your Spirit fall on us to comfort us. Lord, let us sense your joy. Open these men's hearts to take your Holy Spirit in. Give me wisdom, Lord, to know when to speak, and when not to. In Jesus' name, amen.*

❧❧

Kathryn waved to her "family" standing on the dock. Mary was jumping up and down like a little girl. "Bye, Katie, girl! Ol' Mary be a prayin' fer ya! Love ya, I do!"

Lady Wilson and Tess could be seen wiping their tears. Lord Wilson looked concerned as he waved. Katie waved and blew kisses as tears streamed down her cheeks.

The women standing on the deck of the ship were shooed off. "All right, ye women, git in yer cabins where ye belong!" a scruffy looking man barked.

Katie looked around her. There were about twenty women scattered along the deck. They all looked lost, except for one woman who stepped forward, barking right back at the crewman. "You are not speaking to prisoners, but ladies, sir. You will not use that tone with us!"

The man spit on the deck, scowled, and began muttering

something about women not belonging on ships in the first place. It was bad luck. He disappeared around some scaffolding.

The woman holding some papers called out, "Ladies, come together. My name is Annie Hill. "Please follow me, and watch your step."

Stepping around rope and canvas, the women followed in obedience. Katie turned once more to catch a glimpse of her family. She waved again before joining the others. It didn't seem like much of a glorious departure. Not like she had imagined it would be. Of course, what did she expect? She was to get on the ship, wave, and leave.

"Our cabins are this way. Matrons will be sharing cabins." Holding out a piece of paper, she continued, "Is there a Mrs. James Murphy here?"

Katie stepped forward. "Aye."

"Mrs. Murphy, you will share a cabin with matrons Bess Tills, Jenna Knolls, and Grace Key."

Annie led all the women to their perspective cabins. Katie, along with the other three, stepped into a small, dark cabin. On each side of the room were two wooden planks. One was above the other. They were covered with thin mattresses and blankets. Katie saw several trunks and one chair next to a table on one side. Another small table with a lantern sitting alongside a dry sink was on the other side. A chamber pot sat in the corner with a curtain hanging from the ceiling. A tiny window eked out a miniscule portion of light.

"Ladies, we need to settle the other women, so please drop off your bags and follow me."

"May we return to the deck once more to say good-bye to our loved ones?" Katie inquired.

"Captain Warwick prefers you stay in your cabin once you are assigned. His crew has much to do, and they don't appreciate women in their way, as you witnessed earlier."

Closing the cabin door the four matrons left Katie alone. She walked over to light the lantern, then sat on one of the beds. Looking around, Katie decided to read until the others came back. She pulled her trunks near her bed and opened one to find a book. She would offer to help with female prisoners once things were settled.

Soon the other women were back. Bess Tills offered the first bit of information about herself. "Well, here we are at last. I didn't think we would ever get aboard. In case you don't remember, my name is Bess, Bess Tills." Katie warmed to the young woman's smile and easy manner. "I'm a matron to the women prisoners. My husband is a Marine in the Royal Navy. He's in Botany Bay as we speak. That's why I signed on. It's been two years, and I don't mind saying, this ship isn't moving fast enough for me. Oh, and one more thing. I tend to chatter on and on."

The other ladies smiled, helping to break the ice. Soon they were all chattering away. Jenna Knolls and Grace Key were not new to sailing to Botany Bay. They had served as matrons for some time. Katie and Bess were anxious to hear all about it.

It was Katie's turn to tell of herself. She told how she came to marry and how her husband was in one of the bays. She told how she was released after being imprisoned for some time. She even shared a little of her faith.

"You mean to tell me you spent time in Newgate, and you were found to be innocent? You poor girl! Then forced to marry, and now because of him you have to sail from your home? Why didn't you leave him?" The other women were incredulous.

Katie went on to share how she had come to love James, and what an honorable man he was. How he struggled for many years to survive. How he ended up at Newgate by stealing food. She had not intended to share so much about herself, but everything just poured out of her once she got started.

"Bless yer soul," Jenna quipped. "I don't think you know what you're in for, but you seem to have a good head on your shoulders, and a healthy body. You'll do fine." The other women liked Katie's openness. They sensed her sweet spirit.

Katie smiled, feeling more at ease. Although she had just met all three women, she liked them. She also felt drawn to Jenna Knolls for her matronly concern for the others. Grace Key seemed quiet, but not at all timid. She seemed self-assured and intelligent.

Soon they all claimed a bed and began setting up housekeeping. It didn't take long with their meager belongings. The chattering stopped as the women lay on their beds, lost in their own thoughts. Katie couldn't believe she was on board the ship. It had seemed like the time for her and James to leave was far away, and now here she was.

Turning towards the wall, she let her tears fall and began praying. Lord, *I hope you know that if I cry it's not because I don't trust you. I feel a little overwhelmed even though we haven't left the harbor yet. Please take care of Mary and Maggie. Make sure that Lord and Lady Wilson come to know you. I've told them about you. They listened out of love for me, but I don't think any of them really understood what I was saying. Help them all to find you, and love you.*

The ship tossed and turned in the choppy waters of the harbor, causing Katie's stomach to lurch. She fought hard not to be sick. It didn't work. Before she knew it, she had to lunge for the chamber pot.

"Ah, you poor girl!" Jenna jumped up to pour some water onto a towel for her. Dabbing Katie's forehead, she helped her to her cot.

"Some get sick and some don't," Grace said. "I used to, but not no more. Guess I got my sea legs now."

Katie would have been horribly embarrassed any other time, but feeling the way she did, she didn't care. She hadn't felt this sick ever. If she was this ill anchored off shore, what in the world was it going to be like out in the open sea? She asked the Lord for help. She thought of the story in the Bible where Jesus walked on the water, and held out his hands to Peter. In her mind she held her hands out to Jesus, and the waters seemed to calm. Soon she was sleeping.

−−−

"Come with me!" the man barked, yanking on James' chains.

Once his leggings were thrown off, James was led outside of the bay. He gave Ben a look of question but said nothing. The man led James up the steep steps to each deck until they were on the top. Men scurried about, giving the feeling of total chaos when actually they were time-tested sailors. They were simply doing the work they had to do to get *Sally Mae* ready for sail.

James was being led to the man he assumed to be the captain. James towered over him, but the man had an air of confidence. The man gave orders, and the men responded quickly without question.

"Here 'e is, sir!" the man leading James, stated.

"Thank you, Pratt. You may leave us."

"Yes, sir!"

James' mind raced, wondering why he had been summoned. He stood for a few minutes before the man turned to speak to him.

"Murphy is your name, correct?"

"Yes, sir."

"I've been told you can read and write. Is that correct?"

James repeated, "Yes, sir."

"While in the gaol, you led a team of men in work who are now aboard this ship with you. Is that also correct?"

"Yes, sir."

"Good, then follow me."

James was surprised that the man would have him walk behind him. He could easily lay the metal of his chains around the man's neck if he had the mind to. Along the way to his cabin Captain Warwick gave a few more orders. Walking up to a young lad, he placed his hand on the cabin boy's head as he spoke. "Fred, I'm going to my cabin. Bring tea, enough for two, and make sure it's piping hot."

"Aye, sir."

Shortly after entering his cabin he ordered one of the marines to take the chains off of James. Shortly Fred came in, and served tea.

Only when they were left alone did the captain speak. "I guess by now you know I'm the captain, Captain Warwick."

James nodded, saying nothing.

"I've heard many things about you. Quite frankly, next to the Pope himself, I don't think I've heard men praise a man as much. I know the reason for your sentence, and that your wife is aboard. I also know that she is a free woman. What I don't know is whether you have any plans, sir, to rile your men once at sea and try to take my ship over."

James was stunned. That had never entered his mind. He wasn't sure what this man wanted but didn't expect this. He simply stated, "I would never do that."

"I thought not, but I wanted to see your reaction to the question. I need a clerk, and since you can read and write I called on you. I don't trust you. I want to say that up front, but high words have been spoken on your behalf. I trust the men who told me of you, and they have earned my trust. You have not. If you fail me one time, it will go hard on you, understood?"

"Is that why you had me walk behind you? To see if you could trust me?"

"I heard you were intelligent. That was the first test. There will be others. I keep duplicates of my log. One is given to the governor of New South Wales when we arrive. The surgeon superintendent, Crane, also needs a duplicate of his records. He will speak to you regarding what he needs. I expect you to write word for word my instructions, or any information I give you. It needs to be legible. Is that understood?" James nodded, standing silent. "Well, do you want the job?"

James nodded again, but this time voiced his thanks. "I appreciate your trust in me to do the job, sir."

"I didn't say I trusted you yet. I do not, but I will give you a chance. Because you have agreed to be my clerk, you will receive special compensations. You will have your own cabin, and your wife may join you there. It is quite small, but private."

The big man's heart leapt at his words. "Alone…with my wife?" He looked like he was about to be attacked by wild dogs.

"Is she so hard to look at, man?"

James didn't know what to say. Stammering a bit he tried to explain. "Captain, my wife and I were married after we were both sentenced, and…we never ah…well, we've never been alone except to visit in the gaol, and well…"

"I understand, man! No need to explain. I don't think I've ever seen a man with a more panicked look." Warwick's laughter filled the cabin. "Actually, I know all about your situation. It was made known to me when a letter arrived, requesting me to take your wife on board. It was more of an order than a request. It would seem life has handed you some surprises. You are a prisoner, yet I get letters from important people requesting special attention and favors."

"I'm not looking for any special favors for myself, sir."

"Don't get your hackles up, man. I owe you no favors and don't intend to give you any. It just happens that I need a man who can read and write. My clerk decided to stay landlocked while his missus has her belly full of babe. The cabin is usually his, and near to mine. I need to have you close in case I need you. I know you have a motley crew of men who have worked with you in the gaol. Heard they do fine work at whatever is given them. I can use them as well. There may be times I call for you, and your men for work. If they do a fitting job, they will get extra rations. Is this acceptable to you, sir?"

James was thanking his Almighty God as the man spoke. He was awestruck how the Lord worked everything out so he and Katie could be together. He wouldn't have to sail in that bay all the while! There was a sense of guilt at the thought. His friends were stuck there when he was not, but maybe he could help them more in this position.

"Well, I know you can talk. What will it be: cabin or back to the bay?"

"Cabin, sir."

"You are indeed a smart man. Now pour me some more tea. I cannot express how important it is to keep concise records. We will keep records of the weather, the ship's position, my steering orders, sickness, deaths, births, and any other out-of-the-ordinary occurrences. Right now I need to go over the Indent Papers. There should be a listing with all of the prisoner's names, where they come from, and the crime they committed. Let us begin."

James stood until summoned to sit and, with that, became the Captain's clerk.

Mary, sniffling and blowing her nose, headed for her room to lie down. She was overwhelmed with grief.

After the Wilsons left, Maggie stoked the fire and sat on the settee, staring at the flames. The cottage felt empty without the young woman. It even seemed colder, though the fire roared. Maggie was concerned for Mary. She had thought the old girl might even collapse before getting home from the ship. She decided to give Mary a few days to grieve, but then she would have to do her best to snap her out of it. If

Mary didn't, then Maggie was afraid she would not be able to physically bounce back from it.

Sighing, Maggie walked to Katie's room. Standing quietly, she closed her eyes, picturing the young woman's smile, her laughter. Covering her face with her hands she began to weep. How lost she felt without Katie there. Sinking to the floor, Maggie's weeping turned to sobbing. Her shoulders shook as her heart broke. She only looked up when Mary sat next to her. On Katie's bedroom floor they put their arms around each other. The two women clung to each other and cried until there were no more tears. Then they got up, wiped their eyes, and helped each other into the kitchen. They proceeded to make tea. Many were the days and nights to come that they would reminisce about their lives with Katie. Many would be the days to come that they would be thankful they had each other.

The Wilsons sat in their parlor, staring at the fire. Lady Wilson had stopped crying a while ago but was left with a headache. Rising, she walked over to her husband to give him a peck on the cheek. "I need to lie down. I hope you don't mind if tonight we have dinner in our room?"

"Not at all. In fact, I'll inform Tess that we will be spending the rest of the evening there." After giving Graines instructions for dinner the couple climbed the staircase. It would take time to get over their grief of losing Katie, but they had their daughter's wedding to arrange. Holding hands, they climbed the staircase and softly closed the door to Lady Wilson's bedchamber. They didn't want to be alone in their own beds tonight. In fact, they made the decision never to sleep apart again. Life was too short.

19

Voyage

The month of May was the "birth" of their voyage—the beginning of a new life for James and Katie. The anchor was pulled, and the ships headed for the open, endless waters. Excitement filled the men on the upper deck while fear and trepidation held them in the lower.

James sat in his newly acquired cabin, impatiently waiting for the arrival of Katie. When a knock sounded on the door he expected to see her, but instead it was the same little man who had led him earlier to the captain.

"Yes?" James stated.

"I'm Pratt. Captain sent me to fetch ya, but I want to tell you something first. Don't think just because the captain made you 'is clerk that I won't be a-watching ya! One wrong move, and the whole ship will have yer head." Pratt emphasized his words by hitting the wall while glaring at the big man.

When Pratt left, James wondered if he had really been there. If anyone else were standing there, they might have found the whole scene funny. There was Pratt, bent over by years and maybe all of 150 pounds verbally protecting his captain. James thought Pratt looked like one of those leprechauns Katie had told him about—mystical, tiny men with upturned noses and twinkling eyes, except that Pratt's eyes were dark with warning. Instead of feeling threatened by the man's words, though, James felt hope. Surely to earn such loyalty from such a rowdy bunch that worked this ship, the captain had to be honorable and fair.

A few minutes later James was summoned to the captain's quarters. The little time spent with the captain proved to be valuable. James saw that the man was kind in the way he treated Fred, the cabin boy. Captain Warwick summoned one of his crew to show James around the *Sally Mae*. Then James was introduced to Crane and Richards. Soon he was back in the small cabin, still awaiting Katie.

James looked around. The room seemed even smaller because of his size, but it was more room than he had in the bay. He wasn't sure when Katie would be brought to him, but the captain said he would arrange it. His hands were sweating so bad he had to wipe them on his pants. *Easy, Red. You faced your time in the gaol and the idea of being transported with less nervousness than the thought of being alone with your wife.* He smiled to himself.

The berth was made for a single person. James couldn't imagine how in the world two people could fit. He doubted he could fit on it by himself, let alone with Katie. When he realized his thoughts, his heart fluttered. He wiped his hands on his pants once more. *Husband and wife at last.* He never thought they would be together until they reached their destination. James looked around, trying to think of some way to make it seem a little less bare. It was next to impossible to make a bare cabin into a "home" when there was nothing to work with. There was a small table with one chair, and a water pitcher sitting on the top. A slop jar sat in the far corner with a curtain. A tiny window was all there was on one wall, and one blanket covered the bed. That was it.

A knock sounded on the door, causing James to jump. A man stood on the stoop. "Lieutenant Richards wants to see you on top!"

The man quickly disappeared before James could follow him. James was left standing, looking out his cabin door. At this rate he would never be with Katie. He was not used to roaming around on his own. It had been a long time since he could walk around freely. He wondered if this was another one of the captain's tests. Once on the top deck, he looked around until he spotted Richards. Standing quietly, James waited until the man turned towards him and spoke.

"Murphy, come with me. We need to go over supplies. Once we land in the Canary Islands we will need to restock. I want to recheck my list as to what we have then on a weekly basis, check to see how low we are. Rationing is a must, and you will help me with that as well."

Richards took James to one of the supply bays. Unlocking the door, the lieutenant lit two hanging lamps, giving James vague instructions. Richards told him to stay in the bay until someone came to get him. Turning toward the doorway, Richards stopped suddenly. "By the way," he added, "I am to inform you that your wife is on her way to your cabin." Richards left the door wide open as he exited.

So she would be waiting for him when he was finished! James felt jubilant while his heart fluttered at the thought. He fought the urge to tear into the supplies, to finish the work hurriedly. The bay was in such disarray. Different food stuffs had been thrown around, and many bags, barrels, and boxes lay in no particular order. He knew nothing about sailing or how ships were run, but he had a hard time believing they didn't have a list somewhere of all the supplies. What capable captain would go on such an arduous journey without knowing what he carried? The captain had sailed many successful voyages. Isn't that what Lord Wilson had told him?

Warwick was intelligent and seemed to be an orderly man so James knew there was more behind this. After all, it was the captain who stressed the need for proper records to be kept. He was given a lot of freedom all of a sudden, and to what purpose? This seemed to be another arrangement made by the captain to test him, but for more than just a job as a clerk. Clerks did bookwork, not cleaning and straightening supplies. The captain had more than enough crew to clean the bays out if need be. This was just another example of trusting in the Lord. Men had many motives. Mind reading wasn't a talent James had acquired so trusting in the Lord was far better than guessing. James rolled up his sleeves as he began working and praying that he would do a good job...for God's glory. He didn't know what the captain was up to, but God did.

Katie woke, feeling much better. The others must have felt she needed the rest for they let her sleep. She was grateful. Since she was alone, she looked out the window. She saw it was still daylight, but gloomy. Relighting a lamp she sat back on her bunk and began to pray. Afterwards she wrote in a book that Lady Wilson had given her. She described all the events that had happened since she came aboard. It wasn't long before the others came back. Now it was their turn to eat. They brought plates of gruel and some dried fruit back to the cabin for themselves. Bess carried one for Katie, who ate sparingly. She was afraid of becoming ill again. She smiled at Bess. "I'm feeling much better, but I'm afraid to eat too much. My stomach is sore from being sick, but thank you."

A knock sounded, and Annie Hill stepped into their room. "Mrs. Murphy, I need to talk to you alone. Do you mind coming with me?" Katie followed her out into the corridor.

"Mrs. Murphy, I have just been given some news."

"Please call me Katie."

"You can call me Annie. The captain summoned me to his cabin to discuss your husband."

"James, why?"

"It would seem that because your husband can read and write, he has been made captain's clerk. It's not all that unusual to have a prisoner given that position when his regular clerk is not on board. The good news is that you, and your husband, have been given the clerk's cabin. I'm to help you settle into it."

Katie didn't know what to say. Her heart felt like it was about to tear out of her chest. This meant so much more than just having a cabin to herself.

"I know your husband is working right now, so I peeked in. I'm afraid there are no frills at all about the place, but who would expect frills on a prisoner transport, right?" Annie gave Katie a sheepish look. "I also heard this is your honeymoon." Even in the dim light, Annie could see Katie blush. "Oh Katie, I didn't mean to embarrass you. Please don't worry. No one else has to know it's such a special night. Now let's go see what we can do to make it a little cozier before your husband gets back."

206

Captain Warwick finished what he was doing, then sat back in his chair lighting his pipe. Putting his feet on his desk, he let his mind wander until it settled on Murphy and his wife. He couldn't help but smile as he thought of the reaction he got out of the big man when he told him of his cabin. Warwick thought for sure the man was going to try and bolt at the news. Laughing softly to himself, he thought back to a time, long ago, when he was as naïve about women. Murphy would have to wait to see his wife until his job in the bay was finished, then the captain would know what kind of man Murphy was. Would he do the job that was asked of him or would he leave the bay to go to his wife? He drew on his pipe, then watched as smoke circled his head. Once again he smiled to himself. What he would give to have his own wife there with him. As much as he loved sailing, and having his own ship, he hated being separated from his Elizabeth. She was the most important person in his life. It was times like this he missed her most...at the beginning of the sail.

A knock came at the door, pulling his thoughts away. "Enter."

"Captain, I checked on Murphy without him seeing me. Seems to be working all right, and it looks like he'll be finished soon."

"Thank you, Richards. What about his wife? Is she settled into the cabin yet?"

"The women are all fluttering about the cabin. Sounds like a bunch of hens nesting in there." They both laughed.

Dragging on his pipe once again Warwick made a face, discovering it had gone out. He rose from his chair and headed out of his cabin to check on his crew, ship, and prisoners. He was determined to keep busy. It would help keep his mind off his wife. Richards followed closely behind, wondering what was on the captain's mind that he needed to check on things now.

James worked all afternoon; still no one had come to get him. He had made an accurate count, for he counted twice out of sheer boredom. Did they forget about him? He thought about locking the door and going to his cabin, but Marks told him to stay there until someone came to get him. So that is what he would do. Why was time so slothful when you watched it?

He was anxious to see his Katie. It seemed like a lifetime since their last visit. He thought of her, but mostly he spent time with the Lord. He would have his own cabin, his wife with him, and work to do to lessen the strain of the voyage. How good God was to him. Looking about he decided to make a bed in one of the corners until someone came for him. He pushed some heavy bails up against the wall, then placing a blanket on top, reclined on them. He was exhausted from lifting all the heavy barrels and sorting through everything. The rocking motion of the ship had him dozing in no time, and soon he was with Katie in his dreams. That was a fine thing indeed.

A few matrons and marine's wives flocked around Katie with suggestions to add comfort of the cabin. Katie was amazed by their friendliness. They seemed genuinely excited for her. Katie wondered how many knew it was to be her honeymoon cabin. The ladies had men bring in a double plank to replace the single bunk. When Annie had the men brace it for strength, Katie blushed scarlet. Next a thick, feathered mattress was placed on the plank. Katie asked Annie where it came from.

Annie whispered, "It's a wedding present."

One woman sat on the only chair in the room sewing curtains for the small window while other ladies went in and out, sprucing up the room. It didn't take long before the little cabin was cozy and inviting. The curtains were hung, a couple of rag rugs lay on the floor, and candles were lit. Soft pillows lay on the heavy coverlet on the big bed. Even a crocheted doily lay on the table. The women soon left. Katie stood alone in her new "home." She felt such joy. She had prayed the

Lord would help her bring joy to these women, and look what they had done for her and James instead.

A knock sounded. Thinking it was James, Katie rushed to open the door. Annie stepped in, carrying a pot of steaming water. "Here's some hot water for you to wash with. I'll be bringing you supper tonight. Isn't much to eat, but since this is a special night for you we'll bring it to you this one time."

"No need! You've done enough!"

"Let me do this, Katie. On these voyages we have little to bring us joy or celebration. I haven't seen these ladies laugh and work together like this in a long time. We all needed it."

"I just don't know what to say. I can't believe how hard everyone worked to fix our room up. It's lovely. All of you have been so kind."

"You can count your lucky stars you got on Captain Warwick's ship. He's a decent and honest man. He watches out for his crew and prisoners."

"I am blessed, I know," Katie stated. "I would like to help some way if I can...with the women prisoners, I mean."

"Can you sew?" Annie questioned.

"Aye, and I can cook too."

"Well, tomorrow is soon enough for you to begin, but tonight you relax. I best be going. I don't want to be here when your husband gets back. I'll be back in about an hour with supper."

"Good night, Annie, and thank you again for everything." Katie looked around once more at her cabin. She straightened an imaginary wrinkle in the coverlet, and wiped dust off the furniture that wasn't there. She decided to wash up and put on a clean night gown. She wrote in her book until she began to nod off. It was funny that James wasn't back yet. It must be very late. She wasn't sure what James' duties as a clerk were, so she had no idea when he would get back.

Katie retrieved another book from one of her trunks, along with her watch bobble. She had forgotten to wind it, so it had stopped. She sat at the table and read in the dim light until her eyes started to blur.

A soft knock had Katie's attention. She bolted towards the door, hoping for James to be standing there. Annie stood with a tray of food and stepped over the threshold once the door was opened. She proceeded to set it on the small table. Just a quickly as she had come, Annie left. Katie wasn't sure whether to wait for James or not. Her stomach was empty and her will weak, so she ate. Covering the remaining food for James, she glanced at the bed. The soft mattress and warm covers beckoned to her. She couldn't resist any longer. She didn't want to mess the bed up before James came in, but her weary body won out. Lying in the middle of it, she soon fell asleep. It was good she didn't wait up any longer for James, for he was sound asleep.

⇛⇝

Fred knocked on his captain's cabin door. After hearing the captain's bidding, he stepped in. He was balancing a tray of food, and hot tea.

"Fred, get me Richards as soon as you're finished serving me, and I need Dr. Crane here as well."

"Yes, sir."

Once the men arrived and were seated Captain Warwick lit his pipe, then ordered more tea from Fred. "Richards, is Murphy still in the bay?"

"Yes, it seems he made a bed and stayed all night."

"Send one of the crew down to release him to his cabin. I want you to check the supplies. See if there's anything missing, or if he arranged the foodstuff in wrong containers."

"Yes sir, but I didn't tell him certain foods need certain containers."

"I understand," Warwick answered, "but I want to see if he has common sense and uses it."

⇛⇝

James quietly opened the door to his cabin, stopping in midstep. He backed out, shutting the door, and looked around in confusion. He could have sworn this was his cabin. Standing there for a minute he tried to get his bearings. Maybe he was on the wrong deck. He looked around again, only to see that he was on the right one. He took a couple of steps back to see if maybe he had gone too far down the corridor. No, this had to be his cabin.

Katie stirred, sensing a presence, but just as she lifted herself up from her pillow she saw the door close. Frightened, she quickly climbed out of bed and grabbed her robe. She looked around for a weapon. Maybe the lamp? No, it could start a fire. Bending down she picked up one of her shoes. That would have to do. A soft knock sounded. "Who is it?" Katie gasped.

"James."

"James?" Katie ran to the door, flinging it open. "What in the world are you doing? Why didn't you just come in?"

James looked around at the once-bare cabin. "I did, but I thought it was the wrong one. I saw someone lying on the bed, but didn't know it was you. What in the world? Where did you get all these things, and why are you holding up your shoe?"

Katie giggled. "I was going to use it to protect myself. I awoke to see the door close and didn't know who was outside."

"So you were going to have someone sniff your shoe, hoping they would pass out or what?" It was James's turn to laugh.

"Oh, aren't we the funny one. Where have you been? Did the captain have you working all night?"

James explained to Katie what had been going on and where he had been. "I suspect the captain was testing me to see if I would do as I was told, or come to you."

"You mean that a bunch of barrels won out over me?" Katie teased.

"Some of those barrels held port!"

"James!" They both broke out in laughter.

Katie told James of all the ladies and what they did to get the cabin ready for them.

"You mean perfect strangers did this for us?"

"Aye, but they are friends now."

"Yes," was all James said.

Katie left to find Annie to get hot water for James. He was hoping to wash, and have some hot tea. He said he hadn't eaten last night so the food left on the tray was a welcome sight.

James looked around the cabin while he ate. He stared at the big bed, which took up most of the width of the cabin. There was just enough room to climb in, and that was all. When he finished eating he stretched, yawned, and lay on the bed. Soon Katie was back with a tea kettle of hot water. After James washed, they both had a cup of hot tea.

"I bet you are missing your coffee, eh Katie?"

"I'm thankful for everything. How could I miss coffee when God has blessed us so abundantly?" Suddenly Katie felt shy as she looked at her husband. It was the first time they had ever truly been alone together.

A knock sounded and the man named Pratt entered when invited it. "Captain wants to see ya," was all he said before leaving.

"Is everything all right, James?" Katie was worried.

"I'm sure it is. I did what I was told so there is nothing to be frightened of. Just say a prayer, and I'll be back as soon as I can." James bent down to kiss Katie, leaving her again.

James stood in front of the captain's desk waiting for him to look up from his log. "So Murphy, I had Richards go over your work. You did a fine job organizing and logging all the supplies. I needed to see if you would follow orders and if you were a man of your word. I'm glad to see that you are. How do you like your new quarters?"

"They are fine. Thank you, sir."

"Tomorrow I have a job for you and some of your men, but today you rest. Spend time with your wife. You will find that I reward good work. You and your wife may join the marines and their wives in the quarter's dining hall at dinner hour. That's all."

After thanking the captain once more, James quickly returned to Katie. They had the whole day! His heart beat double-time at that thought of it. He knocked on the cabin door so as not to frighten his wife. Katie had been reading but put her book down when she saw him. Once he explained what the captain wanted, James shyly placed his arms around "his" Katie, whispering in her ear, "I've missed you terribly."

Katie responded by pressing her body against James. "I've missed you too."

James wondered if she knew what effect she had on him. "Katie, I want you to know I love you more than I thought possible. I know this is awkward as far as a honeymoon goes. I, well I mean, well..."

A large smile broke out across the young woman's face. "James, it's all right. I love you too, and you are my husband. I guess all newlyweds are a bit nervous about...things."

They both had waited so long for this moment. James took Katie in his arms, gently kissing all her doubts away. He had, in his gentleness, replaced the fear with longing. Finally they could be complete as God had intended, and they had longed for.

☙

Waking up with a start, Katie looked up into the face of her husband. Tenderness filled her. Her heart skipped a beat as she thought of what they had just shared. She quickly dressed, then ran to get more hot water for tea. It was still early afternoon so once James woke, they sipped their tea and snuggled. Afterwards they strolled along the top deck. It was getting hot, so they decided to go back to their cabin. They lay in each other's arms until, once again, passions were stirred.

☙

It was dusk before they decided to see about dinner. They entered the marine's dining quarters just as most of them were finishing up.

One of the men came over to James. "My name is Brandon Rogers, and this is my wife, Doris. Come join us."

James and Katie introduced themselves as they walked over to a plank that held food. Gruel, the staple, was cold, but there were some vegetables, dried fruit, and potatoes...a feast. Once their plates were full, they sat across the table from their new acquaintances.

"I thought your name was Red. Did your wife call you James?" Rogers questioned.

"Many call me that. In fact until Katie and I were married, no one called me James. How did you know I was called Red?"

"Well, let's just say, there is little that is unknown aboard a ship."

Katie wondered if that meant everyone knew it was their honeymoon. She looked down at her plate, trying to hide the fact that once again she was blushing.

A man jumped up from the same table, wiping his mouth on his sleeve. "'Tis a sorry day when good, honest men got to sit and eat with the likes of prisoners," he hissed in the direction of James.

"Ah, don't start up, Lark," another man retorted.

"Ya can eat with 'im if ya wants, but don't be telling me what ter do."

After the man left, the others turned to James and Katie to apologize. James eased the tension by joking, "I don't blame him. I've seen the way some of the prisoners eat."

Laughter rang out.

"So the captain made you his clerk, I hear, Murphy," Rogers stated.

"Yes, to my surprise."

"Why would you be surprised? The captain is a smart man. He uses everything, and everyone to the best advantage to ensure a safe and smooth voyage."

"I was just surprised that he knew I could read and write; that he knew anything about me at all. There are hundreds of prisoners. For him to know about me was surprising."

"I can assure you that the captain knows about everyone or most everyone aboard his ship. He prepares months before the sail to know who he is dealing with. It's important to him for the safety of his crew, and ship."

"I can understand that. He seems like a fair man."

"He is, but don't ever cross him. I saw what happened to a man who did. Let's just say that the sharks didn't go hungry that day."

Katie swallowed, putting her fork down.

"Now see what you've done, Brandon?" Doris Rogers scolded. "I'm sorry, Mrs. Murphy. My husband forgets his manners from all the years around sailors."

Katie smiled. "No, please don't apologize. I'm all right, and please call me Katie."

"I do need to apologize Mrs. er, I mean Katie. My wife is right. I tend to forget my manners in front of ladies. I apologize to you as well, my dear." Rogers smiled at his wife. She tenderly touched her husband's arm to let him know all was forgiven.

Doris turned to Katie. "Would you both like to join us for a night stroll on deck? It's beautiful tonight."

The evening was beautiful, but a little chilly. James went to retrieve Katie's shawl, leaving her with the Rogers. Once back, the foursome began strolling along the deck, admiring the moonlight on the water. All stopped by the rail to look at the beauty of the sea.

"It's beautiful and so calm," Katie whispered.

"I've sailed twice before with Brandon," Doris said. "The sea is treacherous. One minute it can be beautiful, then the next…well, thank God, we are safe aboard a sturdy ship."

"I don't think I've ever seen the moon so large or so many stars. It's breathtaking." Katie stood with her hands on the rail, looking up into the night sky.

James caught his breath at the sight of her. Her long hair trailed down her back blowing in the soft breeze. She held a sweet expression of awe on her lovely face.

Rogers cleared his throat, taking his wife's arm. "Come dear, I think we need to leave these two alone for a time. Good night, James, Katie."

"Good night," was said in unison.

James and Katie stood by the rail in silence. The creaking of the ship along with the gentle roll of the waves was calming. James took his eyes off of Katie long enough to see a couple of sailors eyeing them up. James took Katie by the arm, leading her back to their cabin. "It is getting late. I think it's time to go."

"All right, James."

James entered the cabin first so he could light the lamp, then closed and locked the door behind his wife. They stood looking at each other shyly for a few moments. Katie went across the room by the bed to disrobe. James turned his back, doing the same. Blowing out the lantern he climbed into bed with his bride. James reached for her, and she eagerly went to him. Laying her head on his massive chest she could hear his heart beating fast and furious. Katie shivered, causing

James to hold her closer, but she hadn't shivered from the cold. James gently lifted Katie off his chest. Leaning over, he kissed her deeply. Something else besides nervousness stirred within her....

20

Murder

Tess rolled over to snuggle with her husband. He was still sleeping but stirred to hold her as she pressed in on him. She lay there content and thankful for him. Where had he been all her life? She thought she would never fall in love, not real love anyway. She had been determined never to be forced into marrying anyone. She would be forever grateful for her father's bullheadedness in this matter.

Tess closed her eyes, reliving the beautiful wedding. Her parents spared no expense. She had the best of everything. The long, cream-colored gown shimmered with pearls in the soft candlelight that filled the Cathedral. Her full skirt was covered with several different lengths of lace. She wore a long, matching veil held on her head by a diamond tiara. Her bouquet of flowers consisted of cream-colored roses mixed with tiny pink rosebuds. Silken ribbon and lace fell from under the flowers in a long train. The altar was filled with cream colored roses and candles. Her father marched her down the aisle with his chest puffed out. She heard her mother crying even before she could see her. David looked so regal waiting for her at the altar. He was so handsome! It had been a wonderful day, and even more wonderful was their honeymoon.

Yawning, Tess extended her fingers, admiring her wedding ring once more. She smiled as the diamond caught the early morning light. Tess remembered when Kathryn received her wedding ring. She had been so excited. Their rings were vastly different, but the importance was the same to both women. She wished she could share her happiness with Kathryn right now. *How I miss her,* she thought letting out a long sigh. It was amazing to Tess that she and Katie were now friends. She didn't understand exactly how it happened, but was thankful that it *did* happen.

"Are you bored with me already, dear wife?" David smiled down at her.

"Never! I'll never get bored with you. I was just thinking of Kathryn, and wondering how she is doing."

David continued, "What do you want to do today now that we are back from Venice? I have to think about going back to work. My father will disown me if I let you keep me away from the business much longer."

Tess laughed. "I think you are the one bored. Actually I want to go over to my parents. I've missed them. Since we arrived home late last night, they don't have any way of knowing we're back. I would like to take them the gifts that we brought them."

"Why don't I drop you off there, and go to the office so I can get some work done in time to come home for dinner? In fact, why don't you invite them over for dinner tonight? Just tell the cook, and she'll have everything ready for you."

"That would be wonderful! What do you want me to serve?"

"It's time you make those decisions yourself since you're the mistress of the house."

Tess watched as David got up to stoke the fire. She reached over to ring for Betsy to bring them tea. Tess had brought Betsy along to her new home. Tess had sat the young girl down one evening before the wedding. She asked her forgiveness for treating her so badly. The girl was speechless at first, then broke out into a big smile. She informed Tess that she was more than happy to come along. Tess was relieved. Somehow knowing that Betsy was there made her new home seem more "her home." Tess couldn't believe the change in Betsy. She seemed to know what Tess wanted before she asked. It never occurred to Tess that it was she who had done the changing.

Waiting for the young servant, Tess quickly jotted a note to her parents, letting them know she would be coming to visit that morning. Just as she sealed it, a knock sounded. Sure enough Betsy came in with a tray of tea, biscuits, and jam. She then set about preparing the bathtub and informed Tess that water was already being warmed.

"Betsy, please send someone over to Brick House with this note as soon as possible."

"Aye miss, I mean mistress." Betsy smiled shyly when the handsome master looked at her. She curtsied, then left the room.

Tess sat up against her pillows, sipping tea and smiling. She dreamily thought of her future. How wonderful everything was. She felt a stab of fear at the thought that all was too perfect. Something was bound to go wrong. Things didn't last forever.

"Darling, you're scowling. What's wrong?" David said as he poured himself a cup.

"Oh, I was just thinking how happy I am, and how wonderful our lives are."

"So you're scowling?"

"It's too perfect! Something will change and ruin it."

David gave his wife a blank look before breaking into laughter. "I've never heard of someone worrying before about having nothing to worry about."

"I know I sound silly, but I'm so happy, David. I can't help feeling something is bound to go wrong."

Sitting on the edge of the bed David set his cup and saucer down. He reached over to place his hand on her arm. "Things will change, and they need to. We can't stay in this room for the rest of our lives worrying about changes. We need to have faith that whatever changes come, we will face them together."

"Tell me that you will always love me. Promise me that will never change."

David took his wife's cup, then set it down to reach for her. She let him draw her close. "I already promised you that when I stood in front of God, and all those people in the Cathedral."

They kissed, then talked about their plans, hopes, and dreams.

It took less than a month to reach the Canary Islands. By that time there was a routine about the days for Katie. She kept the prisoners'

welfare utmost on her mind. Guilt seeped into her happiness with James. She had a cozy cabin while many suffered the heat and confinement of a small bay. She and James had a varied diet while the prisoners were fed exact portions consisting mostly of gruel. Adding to her guilt was the knowledge that she had her husband. Many of the women prisoners, and men as well, were forced to leave their mates behind. Katie thanked the Lord often for her many blessings, and prayed continually for the prisoners. She worked hard to do what she could for them. She prayed that her heart was motivated for the right reason, for the love of God, and not out of guilt.

James was kept busy writing logs and ledgers of numbers for the captain. He helped Richards keep track of the rations and worked with the other men on repairs. It was a much needed reprieve from the dark, dank bay for the men. They were happy to do any and all work, and the ship's crew was happy to oblige them.

The suffering of prisoners was great in spite of all considerations. Seasickness and lack of sun seemed to take their toll. Many of the men and women became lethargic and weak. It was apparent that all were losing weight. It was easier to shave heads to get rid of the "hair bugs." The prisoners were a sorry sight indeed.

Supplies were bought at the islands, and fresh water was brought aboard. There still wasn't an overabundance of fresh water since it was worth gold on board ship, but with rationing, it would be enough. The layover allowed the prisoners to be taken on shore and housed in a large storehouse where they could have more room. They enjoyed fresh air, sunshine, and exercise. The bays on ship were fumigated and scrubbed down once again. But the day quickly came when the prisoners were brought back on board.

Katie was just as busy as James with helping the woman prisoners. She obtained permission from the captain to teach reading and writing. It helped keep the women out of trouble. A few of them proved difficult, but nevertheless they touched Katie's heart. She knew their exterior was hard but suspected they were only protecting a tender heart. When she looked at them, she thought of Mary. Oh how she missed her friend.

After leaving the Canary Islands they headed towards the Cape

Verde Islands. Hot breezes filled the sails, pushing the ship along. Down below the prisoners lay on their hard plank beds sweating and longing for more water than they were given. It was better to be a little thirsty than completely out of water in the long run. Even the captain and crew were given rations of water. For a time tea was not allowed to be brewed. Finally they anchored off Cape Verde, and again they loaded up with fresh supplies. This was the time of plenty. There was water to wash with and to drink. It was especially important for them to stock up since they were in for one of the hardest and longest parts of their voyage. They would not stop again until Rio de Janeiro. That would take them another couple of months to reach, and it was indeed a treacherous stretch. There was still a lot of ocean to cross.

Once again the ship hoisted anchor, and soon Cape Verde was behind them. After leaving, the weather took a turn for the worse. High winds and rain kept the prisoners below. Many prisoners found themselves unable to eat with the pitch of the ship. In good weather prisoners were brought up in small groups to take in the fresh air and exercise. If the weather was bad, the wait for exercise and sunshine could be weeks. It was during these times that arguments broke out, and a few prisoners had to be separated. The prisoners lost even more weight and suffered terribly in their closed, cramped quarters. Despair fell heavily on many of them, to the point that several men and women tried suicide. After a full week of bad weather the sun finally broke through the clouds, leaving a brilliant rainbow across the sky.

Katie and some other women took advantage of the good weather by hanging wet clothes on the ropes. Laundry had piled up, and trying to hang them to dry below was useless. Laundry was a daily chore and a difficult one to be sure. Seawater was hard on the skin and cloth. It tended to take away any moisture from the hands, and strength from the material. During the day the women washed, hung, and folded clothing and bedding while in the evening they mended.

Between that and teaching the women their letters, Katie had busy days. She helped them wash their hair once it grew out. With the doctor's help they worked hard to clear up any "head bugs." If it proved too difficult to get rid of them, the prisoners' and children's heads were once again shaved. Katie enjoyed her time with the women convicts.

How misjudged they were. Very few turned out to be violent or guilty of a crime worthy of this punishment. They were women with hopes and dreams similar to her own, who had found themselves in difficult circumstances that landed them aboard a convict ship.

Katie would listen to their stories, nurse the sick, and many times care for some of their children. The children were allowed a small section of the deck in which to play. They played in the sunshine and fresh air they so badly needed as long as they never got in the way. It was especially important to keep them away from the crew. It was not unheard of for a crew member to throw a wee one overboard if underfoot. So far that hadn't happened, but it wasn't a promise that it wouldn't.

Sometimes the mothers could accompany their children, but most times not, so Katie stayed with them. The mothers were indeed appreciative and found themselves drawn to the caring, young woman.

It was still horribly hot and humid, but Katie tried not to complain. She knew how awful it was in the bays. The water was rationed, and although it was warm and close to becoming stagnant, it was appreciated.

In the third month of the voyage another storm hit. It was amazing how quickly the blue sky could turn black. Clouds swirled, and the wind blew so hard it sent waves crashing over the deck, threatening to spill men into the ocean. Sails were lowered, and the crew rushed to latch everything down.

Katie was teaching several women their lessons when it became impossible to concentrate. The gentle rocking motion of the ship disappeared and was replaced with great lifts, then a deep thunderous drop that threatened to break the ship apart. Thunder crashed while lightning lit up the sky. Fearing the lanterns would swing and break, Katie blew them out, leaving everyone in the darkness. One woman began vomiting from the rough-and-tumble pitch of the ship. Wood creaked, threatening to break apart. Children cried in fear, clinging to their mothers. Thoughts of drowning frightened most, but the unknown mysteries in the black waters terrified them more. Mental pictures of being cast into the vast, swirling waters filled their heads. They knew they were about to be dragged down by some slimy, scaly monster.

Katie began to pray softly. One by one the women encircled her and listened. Her soft and barely audible prayer changed into a more powerful, faith-filled talk with her Savior. Some weren't sure how to pray, but they found that the young woman spoke to God Almighty as if He were there with her.

"Father," Katie was saying, "protect us and help us not to be afraid. Help the crew know what to do and protect them from falling overboard. Let these women, all of us on board, know that you hold us in your hand. Heavenly Father, you are our Creator and the Creator of the seas and the wind and rain. I know you love us and care about us. I ask that you would place your hand upon us and this ship along with the other vessels as well. Calm our fears, Lord, and help us to know in our hearts the peace and joy that only you can give. In Jesus' name, amen."

The women seemed calmer, but still they huddled close together, waiting for the storm to subside. A few more hours went by before the storm lost some of its intensity. Except for some of the children, all crying ceased. Katie turned to help the sick woman and began cleaning up after her as best she could. She stayed with the women until late.

James wasn't in their cabin when she entered, so she took the time to pray. She then lay on the bed, turning her thoughts to her dear old friends in London: Mary, Maggie, and the others. What were they doing right now? Were they well? Had they by now given their hearts and lives to the Lord? She felt homesick for her cozy cottage and friends. Curling up on her bed she let her tears wet the pillow. She missed their smiling faces. When her thoughts turned to James, it dawned on her that he should have returned by now. Was he all right, or had something happened to him during the storm? Just as Katie swung her legs off the bed to go check on him, James entered the cabin. He could tell she had been crying. Concern creased his brow.

"Katie, darling, what's the matter? Is it the storm? It's almost over now. We're safe and sound. No worse off from it."

"Oh James, I was about to come looking for you. I was just feeling a little homesick. I've been wondering how everyone back home is doing."

James put his arms around his wife. "I understand; you are very close to them. An ocean can't change that. Of course you miss them."

Sniffling, Katie told James about the woman prisoners. "You're right, James, God is blessing us every day, and here I am crying."

And so the days and nights went on and on. It took longer for them to reach Rio de Janeiro since the storm had blown them off course, but they did arrive…safely. Some major repairs had to be done, which held them up even longer.

Captain Warwick informed everyone that *Sally Mae* wasn't in a race. They had made good time in the beginning of the voyage, and time was not as important as safety. They did what they needed to do to make the ship safe and secure once more. *Sally Mae* was anchored for three full weeks before leaving to sail to Cape Town. It was now mid-October. They pressed on and so did the days.

⋘⋙

Magistrate Peter Reeves was dead. He had been dead for days before anyone was notified. His body was stuffed in some alley doorway in the seedy side of London. Many probably saw it there, but what did it matter? It was a common occurrence to find bodies. If any notice was taken at all it was the richness of his clothes and whatever else could be picked off the body.

Some were shocked at the news, and some were not. Peter had quite the reputation with women, causing many a jealous man to seethe with anger when his name was mentioned. But all wondered who had been brave enough or stupid enough to kill him. He had been a powerful man.

Victoria made a beautiful grieving widow. She had several bereavement gowns made. It had taken a lot of planning and arrangements to have him killed. She had entrusted Justin, her lover, to find someone to do the deed. Even more good news, Justin informed her that the man he had hired was found a few days later beaten to death. No one knew but them. How perfect.

Sitting by the window in her room she let her mind wander back to when she and Peter were first married. Oh, she knew he didn't intend to marry her at first. She was just another one of his conquests, but she had loved him in the beginning. Knowing that a high position would come along with her hand in the marriage tipped the scales. She and Peter were wed with great fanfare. It wasn't long before she discovered that Peter was not content with just one woman. She had threatened him for years to stop his late-night rendezvous with his trollops. He thought he was clever enough that she wouldn't find out. She certainly wasn't one of those women who simply turned and looked the other way. He had rubbed her face in his infidelity long enough. Yes, he had made her look the fool for too long. But what had pushed her over the edge was when he openly pined for that Wilson snit.

They fought violently, and he said some unforgivable things to her. How she and her father ran his life. How her father "paid" him to marry her, then kept his position as a magistrate over his head to keep him married to her. How hateful he had been and even confessed his love for the Wilson girl. He planned to have her as his own. What did that...that female have that could ever compare to her?

When Victoria saw Peter with the girl the day she left for Paris, she hired the usual men to have him investigated. She might have even forgiven him one more time if he had not voiced his love for the girl. It was too much to bear. That's when the idea was conceived in her mind. She would make Peter pay...the girl too. When she heard that he was found dead, it was a relief. The stress of not knowing when it would happen was unbearable, but now only half her plan was accomplished. She needed to set things in motion to throw suspicion on the Wilson girl. Oh, it wasn't Wilson anymore. What was her last name...Day? Yes, that was it, Tess Day. That was her married name, but Victoria knew her by only one name...whore.

"The captain will 'ave yer liver if yas get caught."

"How will I get caught unless you tell someone?"

"Ain't sayin a word to nobody, but I ain't goin' in on it neither. I've been flogged once. Ain't goin' ter git it again."

The two men whispered in the dark as they slithered along the rail. Making sure there were no warders or matrons patrolling the women's bays, the men snuck down to the last bay.

The man leading the way pointed at a woman asleep and whispered, "She's the one; 'er name is Betty. Don't unlock 'er until I be gone. If someone 'ears ya, I don't want to be 'ere."

Leaving his partner, the man tiptoed out. Shaking his head, he went back to lie down, covering his head. If hell was going to be let loose, he didn't want to be a part of it.

The remaining man unlocked the bay and stepped in. Some of the women snored softly, but one leaned up on one elbow and stared at the man. "What ya want 'ere?" she spat.

"Looking for Betty," is all he said.

The woman leaned over to push a finger into the side of the woman across from her.

"What? What's the matter?"

"Seems there's a man fer ya here."

Betty turned and peered into the darkness. "What ya want?"

"Heard ya is willing to give a man a little fun fer some extra considerations."

"Ya," was all she said.

Another woman whispered, "You're going to get all of us into trouble."

"Shut up, ya old hag," Betty hissed. "Yer mad cause ya can't get a man of yer own."

The woman only shook her head and turned away.

After they both crept out, he relocked the bay door. "Keep your head down now or we both get caught," the man instructed.

"Don't worry. I can be as quiet as a mouse when I needs be."

Sneaking into one of the proper boats the two felt safe and secluded, but they should have known better. Very little went unnoticed on board a ship. It was only a matter of time before "all hell" broke loose.

Katie flew out from under the bed covers and tried to dive over James to get to the chamber pot, but she didn't quite make it. Instead she landed on his stomach, startling the man out of a sound sleep. He grabbed her, not realizing what was going on.

"James, let me go!" She made it just in time before she vomited.

Setting his feet on the cold floor he grabbed a blanket draping it around her shoulders. Concern creased his brow as he wet a towel for her. Katie let James lead her back to bed.

"Are you seasick again?"

"I don't think so. It's been a long time since I was seasick. Maybe it's something I ate."

"Maybe I should get Dr. Crane."

"Not yet, James. Let's see how I feel later on. It's so early I don't want to disturb him."

"Fine, but you stay put in bed today. Don't even think of heading out to do laundry. I told you that you've been overdoing it. You're overworking yourself."

"James, I'm not working any harder than the others."

"The others don't do laundry, mending, and then teach the women. If that's not enough, you help them with their children. You need rest. Now I'm telling you to stay put. I'm going to go get you some tea, and hopefully that will help your stomach."

"Yes, sir!" Katie smiled up at her husband.

"Huh," was all he said as he got dressed. "When I come back, you better still be in that bed." Then he was gone.

Katie felt her stomach lurch again. She hit the floor running. This wasn't seasickness. She didn't feel dizzy or lightheaded, just sick to her stomach. Snuggling down into bed, Katie yielded to the fact that she would be there for awhile.

James brought her tea before leaving to answer a call from the captain. He admonished her once again to stay in bed. She did feel tired so she didn't argue with him at all. Lying in a soft bed was more tempting at the moment than facing the day. Soon she was fast asleep.

Annie knocked on the cabin door, then opened it slowly when she didn't get an answer. James had asked her to peek in on Katie. Seeing her sleeping, Annie crept over and placed her hand on the young woman's forehead. No fever, her color was good. The girl took deep breaths in her sleep. Maybe she should get Dr. Crane like James suggested. She had a hunch of what was going on, but thought it best to talk to the doctor first. Annie was able to leave without waking Katie. She found the good doctor putting salve on one of the men's ankles.

"Damn shackles rub a man's skin raw; then it gets infected. Where do they expect these men to run to?"

"Doctor," Annie began, "Mrs. Murphy is sick and throwing up. She's sleeping sound right now. She doesn't have a fever, but I would feel better if you were to look in on her."

"How's her color?"

"Looks good; there's no telltale signs of sickness, just the vomiting."

"I'll see her when I finish with this man."

"Thank you, Doctor."

It wasn't long before Dr. Crane knocked on the cabin door. Katie had just gotten up. After asking who it was, she invited him in. He noted Katie wrapped in a blanket sitting at her small table.

"Mrs. Murphy, I've heard you aren't well."

"I don't know what's wrong with me, Doctor. I was quite sick this morning but feel much better now. I wonder if it was something I ate?"

"I'll be able to tell more after I examine you." Dr. Crane touched Katie's cheek for fever. There was none. He checked her throat for redness and listened to her heart and lungs for any telltale rattling. No, her lungs were clear, and her heart beat steady and strong. It wasn't long before he had completed his examination.

"Doctor?"

"Mrs. Murphy, have you noticed any changes in your body of late?"

"Changes?"

"Yes, when was your last monthly?"

Katie blushed at the question. "A few months ago, but I thought it was stress. Is everything all right?" Worry creased her young brow until realization hit her. "You mean...I could be expecting? I'm going to have a wee bairn?"

"I think it's safe to say that you will have a summer baby. July is my guess."

"It's so soon. I must of… I've, we've…I must be just pregnant. I didn't think women knew so soon."

"Every pregnancy is different. Some women can tell sooner than others."

Katie sat on the bed in shock. She always wanted children but didn't expect to have a child so soon. What would James say? Would he be happy about the bairn or disappointed in the timing?

"Mrs. Murphy, I've noticed you are an industrious person. I hear from others of your involvement in the female prisoners' lives. I see you always washing clothes or helping with children. All of that is fine, but I feel you should confine yourself to bedrest for the time being."

"You sound like my husband, Doctor. For how long?"

"No, I sound like your doctor. A week for now. I will see how you're faring after that, but for now you need your rest. I will also speak to the cook and the captain. You need extra food."

"Please don't tell my husband about our wee bairn, Dr. Crane. I would like to tell him myself."

"Of course. I wouldn't want to spoil your surprise for him."

Crane left to speak to the cook and the captain. He felt sad for the young woman. She had enough hardship to face, but to be pregnant now would be doubly hard on her. The chance of her baby surviving was questionable. Over half the babies born on board a ship died, but of course they would be at their destination by the time she gave birth. Still, with the dankness and the close confinement of humans, it wasn't hard to catch something. Three of the women prisoners and one wife of a marine had already miscarried. Chances were Mrs. Murphy would do the same. Of course, having her own cabin might help. Well, time would tell. Such was life on ship. No one knew that better than he.

Katie sat in quiet shock for a time before lying down. How was she to tell James? Did he suspect? Why hadn't she known herself? Strange, but it had never crossed her mind that she was going to have a baby! Excitement and dread consumed her at once. Her heart beat faster as she gently lay her hand on her stomach. Staying as still as possible she tried to "feel" the life within her. There was nothing, no movement or any indication of a body growing inside her own. It was early after all. She was not bound to feel the bairn yet. A boy, a girl, names, clothes? Oh, she felt overwhelmed. She wasn't ready for a wee one, but how did you make yourself ready for that? Her mind swirled with thoughts and emotions until she felt exhausted. Suddenly, as if a feather brushed against her a thought touched her mind: *The Lord is my fortress.* Katie concentrated on remembering part of a Psalm that she had read.

My soul finds rest in God alone;
My salvation comes from him.
He alone is my rock and my salvation.
He is my fortress; I will never be shaken,

Excitement flooded her. Of course, that's right! God knew all about this wee one. He knew she was pregnant! He had a perfect plan for her. He would take care of her. Why was she always panicking every time something happened? It was as if she forgot the Lord in her day-to-day life until something happened to turn her back to Him. Katie closed her eyes, lifting her heart towards heaven. *Lord, forgive me for being so afraid. I keep fighting fear over the future when I know my future is in your hands. Build my faith, Lord, and thank you, thank you, thank you, for this new life. Help James to be happy about the news too, Lord. Amen.*

The man's screams filled the air. He pulled at the leather binds around his wrists. He was to be given forty lashes. After less than half, he could stand no more. Blood dripped from the open wounds on his back. His mangled flesh hung in strips.

Many were there to witness the flogging. Some of the men looked down at the deck, remembering the searing, flashing pain they experienced when it was their misfortune to be flogged.

Captain Warwick stood stiffly watching the proceedings. He hated it. This was one of the few things he hated about being captain. He had no choice. Any orders given to his crew that were not enforced threatened the voyage; it also threatened lives. But more than that, it threatened his authority. He could have ordered different punishment. He considered doing so, but he'd had trouble with these two before. The flogging would cause them to think twice before giving any trouble again.

The crewman began begging for mercy. The woman standing off to the side cried and had to be held up, for she was to be next. Fear took all strength away from her legs.

Warwick once again thought about changing the punishment for the woman, but it was too late. He couldn't show any kind of weakness. Besides, the woman had been trouble from the start. She was caught trying to steal rations from other prisoners and fought with the matrons. Now she had been found with one of his crew. It was almost impossible to keep the crew from the females, but he had to try. His crew knew before signing on that it was a stipulation of his. No "chasing" the female prisoners. Free women were different. If one of his men wanted to meet one of the matrons, that was up to them, but female prisoners were off limits.

As the lash bit into the man's flesh for the last time, Betty was brought forward. She wailed, fighting against the two men who were trying to bind her. She glanced over at poor Jake. He had mercifully blacked out, hanging from his wrists. Men cut the ties to free him. Betty felt a tugging, then heard the ripping of her shirt being torn from top to bottom in the back. Only the collar helped to keep the material together covering her.

"We didn't do nothin' wrong! We jest 'ad a little fun was all!"

Her words fell on deaf ears. A marine stood at attention until Betty was bound tightly. A slow rhythmic beating of the drum began. Captain Warwick nodded to the commander, who stepped forward to read off the charges.

James swallowed hard. He stood off to the side, wishing he didn't have to witness this torture. He had tried to speak to the captain on the woman's behalf but was rebuked soundly. It came as a surprise to James that Warwick would order such a punishment. The captain had only shown great care and compassion towards the prisoners up to now. James had prayed for the man and now began to silently pray for the woman.

"Betty Johnston, you are charged with mischievous and criminal behavior."

"Criminal? What? What is criminal 'bout lovin' a man? What is criminal 'bout not wantin' ta be alone?" she shouted.

The commander continued. "You will be given fifteen lashes for your crime." He then stepped back, which was indication for the man to begin.

"NOOO!" Betty screamed, throwing herself backwards trying to release herself from the post. Blood ran from her wrists as she fought the ties.

The man stood, waiting for the captain's consent to continue. After hesitating for a moment, Captain Warwick nodded, and so it began.

Screams and cursing filled the air. Tears ran down her face as the lash bit her tender flesh on her side. It would have been better had she held as still as possible, letting her back take the blows, but she found it impossible to do so. Her body writhed in pain, twisting away as if it had a mind of its own. Betty had never felt such pain, even in giving birth to the lifeless body of her babe months ago.

The man lifted his arm to strike again. He had only flogged one man in his life before today, never a woman. He only volunteered to be the one to use the lash on this voyage for the extra money the job offered. He had hoped he would not have to actually do the job he was hired for. He heard many in his position enjoyed their labor, but he did not. Sweat glistened on the man's face as his body labored in his task. He tried to lessen the blows, but it was impossible. There was no such thing as a soft whip. Another blow resounded, along with another scream. It seemed endless, but finally it was over. Whimpering, Betty hung by her wrists. Her eyes were rolled back in her head, and she had soiled herself. Men came forward to untie her. They carried her back to her bay. Thankfully, she blacked out.

James stood there, fighting not to cry. Every blow of the lash cut his heart. He was furious with himself, and with the man who ordered such inhumane treatment. He should have stepped in, but what good would that have done? He imagined Christ being whipped and beaten. If he had been there would he have stood watching? The tears he fought sprung to his eyes as he conceded that he probably would have watched then too. Disappointment, rage, and shame filled him. He needed to leave the deck for his tears threatened to fall. Pride added to his already heavy heart. What would everyone think of him if they saw his tears? James turned and left the deck without the captain's permission.

Warwick watched the big man walk with purpose towards the steps leading to the lower decks. He let him go, for the man's body language spoke loudly. The captain understood only too clearly the anger the man was feeling, for he felt it too. Warwick straightened his spine. He did not have the luxury of giving into his feelings. He was the sole master on this ship, and his decisions could mean life or death. Any other time he would consider reprimanding Murphy for his lack of control, but enough people had been punished this day. He would speak to him later.

Prisoners were brought forward to swab the blood and filth off the deck.

21

Fallen

Katie awoke from a scream that seemed far away, but by the time she was fully awake there was only silence. Probably another dream. More by sensing someone at the door than any noise, Katie walked over and opened it. James stood there. By the look of her husband, she knew something was terribly wrong. "James, what are you doing standing outside the door? What's wrong?"

James hesitated to enter. He didn't want Katie to see how upset he was. He desperately needed to have her gentleness and kindness right now. Anger filled him, anger towards himself and the captain. How could he claim to be a Christian when he stood by and let something like that happen? James stepped in and stood looking at the floor. Before he could stop them, tears streamed down his cheeks. His broad shoulders shook from his sobs as he fell to his knees. He grabbed Katie holding her close. He buried his face in her breasts.

"James, oh James, what's wrong?" she asked again as fear filled her.

It was a few minutes before he could answer. His heart ached, his soul was crushed. With everything else, his pride was hurt from crying in front of Katie.

Katie just held him. He seemed to need that more than anything. Once he released her, she brought him a clean handkerchief.

"I'm going to step out, but I will be back shortly," Katie said. She went to retrieve some hot water and to give James a moment alone.

James was sitting at the small table holding his head in his hands when Katie returned. Carefully Katie poured his tea, then sat on the edge of the bed waiting for him to speak. He didn't right away so she began to silently pray.

After a few moments James turned the chair around to face his wife. He then told her what had happened.

"Why wasn't I made aware of it?" Katie asked. "Neither Annie nor Jenna told me of the lashing."

"I asked them not to. I knew it was going to be ugly. I wanted to protect you from it. Oh Katie, it was horrible. I've seen cruelty in the world, but not like that. And I just stood there. I didn't lift a hand to stop it. I tried to talk to the captain about it when I first learned it was to happen, but he let me know I was to stay out of it. As I stood watching, I kept thinking about Jesus. Of how he was beaten and whipped. I asked myself, if I were there would I have done anything to help Him? I knew in my heart that I would probably have just stood and watched like I did today. How can He ever forgive me or love me? How as a Christian could I have stood by and just watched?"

Katie realized it must have been their screams that woke her. She could see her husband's heart and spirit was broken, but didn't know what to say. She had never seen him so vulnerable. Protectiveness washed over her. She wanted to soothe him. She stood and embraced him, holding his head gently against her breast. Stroking his hair she asked the Lord to give her wisdom and to give James comfort. He held on tight, as if his very life depended on it.

"James, what would have happened if you stepped in to help? Would it have done any good?"

"That's not the point. I didn't even try. I was afraid. How do you feel about your husband now?"

"You did try. You said you had talked to the captain. You did what you could. As for my feelings for you, I love you as much as ever. The Lord's love for you has not changed either. You know that. Remember when you told me that yourself? Nothing that we ever did, or will ever do, will stop Him from loving us. He knows our weaknesses. He also knows how you would have behaved if you were there when He was beaten. You are right. You probably would have acted the same as everyone else. We all would. That's why He came to us in the first place because we are so weak and need Him. There is no hope without Him."

"Yes, but I am a Christian, and I still did nothing!"

"As was Peter when he denied Christ three times. We are all weak, James. You know it is not what we do that earn our salvation, but His grace. We are to rely on His strength, not ours. Yes, having Jesus in our hearts should make a difference in how we live, but we do and will fall short. It is only by grace, James, His grace. How many times have you told me that yourself? Remember when I didn't want to turn to Him in the gaol? I felt guilty about calling on Him only in my time of troubles. You told me that was a lie of Satan's, and that the Lord wants us to call on Him. That is when most people come to recognize their need of Him. Well, you believe in a lie of Satan's right now. Whether you stopped the punishment or not does not decide how God feels about you. He loves you unconditionally. Don't doubt His love for you or mine either because your human nature reacted to a difficult situation. You couldn't do anything about those people getting the lash, but you can do something to help them now."

"What do you mean?" James questioned as he lifted his head.

"This poor man and woman need their backs tended to and probably their spirits as well. You and I can go to them. We can try to ease their pain and suffering as Christ would. Not out of guilt, but out of His love."

James was quiet for a moment. "You're right. I didn't do anything then, but I can do something now. I just pray my motives are right. By the way, how did you get so wise?"

"I don't know about being wise, but He knows we're trusting in Him. I don't know your heart, James, but God does. Pray about it."

James couldn't pray. He still felt shame. He got up and washed his face. They both left to help the two wounded prisoners. They separated to go to the different decks, but not until Katie gave him a quick hug. "I love you, James." She thought of telling him her news, but it wasn't the time. She wanted James to be happy about the baby, and right now there were other things on his mind. He smiled down at his wife, but his heart was still heavy. He nodded, then turned to go. He didn't dare answer. The tightness in his throat threatened to bring more tears.

Betty lay on her berth in excruciating pain. Her nails were dug into the thin mat. It was drenched with tears...tears of anger, hatred, and pain. No one understood why she did what she did, nor did they care. No one had ever loved her. She'd never had a family except for the people she'd worked for. What a laugh—she had slaved and prostituted herself for them. It wasn't of her own choosing, but what difference did it make? She was never given a choice. She was so grateful to have a place to live and food to eat, but the price was high. She slaved for the woman during the day and prostituted herself to the man at night. No wonder they were happy to have her live with them. She hated it. When she ran away, she took a few coins and the babe in her belly with her. She had earned the coins. She was cursed with the babe from the man she hated. Only a few coins were taken. She should have taken more, but it didn't matter since she was caught. Now here she was, beaten and bloody for reaching out to someone for kindness, for security. She had to look after herself. No one else would. She was once again beaten down by so-called "decent people." Whenever she reached out for some human kindness, for love, she ended up hurt.

⧸⟡⧹

Katie found Annie to ask permission to tend the woman.

Annie smiled when she spotted the young woman. "How are you feeling, Katie? Are you still feeling ill?"

Katie didn't want to say anything to anyone about the baby until she had told James. "I'm feeling much better, thank you. I've come to ask if I can tend to that woman that was lashed today."

"You mean Betty? So you heard about it, eh? Why do you want to do that? She would rather spit at you than look at you."

"I just found out from James what had happened, and I want to help."

"I'm surprised you didn't hear their screams. It was horrible. It's never a good sight to see."

"I was resting this afternoon, and I woke when I heard screaming. I thought it was a dream. I'm surprised to hear such punishment is still handed down," Katie stated. "It seems so extreme."

"Captain Warwick doesn't usually use the lash for punishment, and especially on women. I must say I was surprised as well, but he must have had a good reason for it."

"Where is she now?"

"In her bay. The surgeon, Mr. Crane, was going to have her stay in his hospital at the foreport of the ship, but several men are already housed there. There isn't room to separate the men and the women. He felt it best for her to stay here. He already put a plaster on her back."

"I still cannot believe they would do this to a man, let alone a woman."

"Like I said, Captain Warwick usually doesn't. Usually women are placed in the coal hole—that's the darkest part of the ship—for days, or they're made to wear the wooden jacket."

"Wooden jacket? What is that?"

"The top of a heavy flour barrel is cut away, then holes are made for the woman's arms. Her hands are locked in chains together once it is in place. She wears it until she can't stand it no more. She can't sit nor lie down. It proves to be a deterrent in their causing trouble."

"It all sounds terrible, but I think you're right," Katie supposed, "they must have done more than be together to get the lash. Only thing is, I can't think of anything bad enough to have that done to them."

"Well, if you feel you need to help Betty, go ahead. Be warned though, she is a spitfire. She hates everybody, especially decent folks. She seems to hate them most of all. Do you know which bay she's housed in?"

Katie nodded and made her way there after getting the key. Praying as she went, she tried to still her uncertainty. She was afraid, but of what? Rejection from the woman? Being verbally attacked? What? Katie had read that fear was not of the Lord, so she prayed for His peace.

When she saw Betty, Katie's heart went out to her. The other women were up on the deck exercising, leaving Betty alone. She looked like a little girl lost instead of a "supposed" hardened criminal. Her hair was matted and dirty. She was dreadfully thin. She lay on her stomach while the torn shirt still hung around her neck.

"Hello, my name is Katie Murphy." Katie found a stool and sat next to the berth.

"What ya want?" Betty cringed in pain as she turned her head towards Katie.

"I came to see if I could help you." Katie bent down so Betty could see her.

"Help me what? Can ya take me chains off, and set me free? Can ya stop the pain or help me to git 'ome? Wha ya want fer yer 'elp? I ain't got no money."

"No, I can't give you those things you asked, and I'm not looking for payment from you. I thought if you would like I could carefully brush and clean your hair, or maybe feed you some broth."

Betty asked again, "Why ya want ter 'elp me?"

"I just do. Can I brush your hair?"

"Me back's on fire. What I want me 'air brushed fer?"

"I guess you're right. I'm sorry. I wasn't thinking. It's just that I want to ease your pain somehow."

"What fer? Ter make yerself feel better and ease your decent conscience for me gettin' the whip?"

"I do feel terrible about what happened to you. I'm sorry for your pain. Do you think you could eat something, maybe some broth? You need your strength to get better."

"Better...better fer what?"

"I'll get some warm broth. I'll feed it to you and make sure the flies stay off."

"You be doin' that fer me?"

"Aye."

"Cannot think of eatin'. Me back is on fire, like I said. I feel sick ter me stomach. Surely could use a drink o' water though."

"All right, I'll be right back." Katie was surprised at how easily Betty responded to her. *Thank you, Lord,* she breathed. Retrieving some water she headed back. She ran into Dr. Crane. She needed to see if he had any powders to ease Betty's pain.

"I've already given her some for her pain. She can have more later. When I tried to get her to eat something, she refused. Getting her strength up to fight off infection is the most important thing right now.

If you can get her to eat, let her eat her fill," Dr. Crane stated.

"I asked her, but she's in too much pain to eat." The doctor only shook his head in understanding.

Soon Katie was sitting on the floor next to Betty. Holding a cup to her lips, she let Betty drink. Katie sat quietly, chasing any flies away. After a time she placed rags under her so Betty could relieve herself. Katie then gathered the soiled material and began bathing her, avoiding her back. When finished, she then laid a clean sheet over her just up to her waist. Once again she sat next to Betty's berth, making sure no flies landed. Soon the woman breathed deeply in sleep. Compassion and love filled Katie for this woman. Deep down Katie knew the feelings she had were from the Lord. How much He loved Betty. Even when people didn't realize it, God loved them. He sent people to help them in their time of need…if they would only accept it.

❧❦

"What proof do you have that my daughter killed the man?" Lord Wilson bellowed.

"Enough proof to have her put in the gaol, and there she will stay until her trial!" the man bellowed back.

Lord Wilson did not intimidate Joseph Potter. Potter's family was very old and established with many positions within the government. Being Victoria's father and Peter's father-in-law only made him more forceful. "We even found a letter written in your daughter's hand, stating she intended to have him murdered."

"I saw that note, and you must realize it was too convenient. She would have to be crazy to leave something like that lay around her house. It was made to look like she did it."

"She is crazy for what she did, and she'll pay for it. Now I must take care of some business." The man departed, leaving Lord Wilson alone.

Never in his life had he felt so out of control, so beaten down. He had tried everything in his power to have Tess released, but met resistance on every side. Why did this have to happen now? His daughter was truly happy for the first time in her life. She was settled in with her new husband and home. He and Barbara had high hopes for grandchildren, and now this. Barbara was inconsolable with worry and grief. He stood to leave. It was amazing how old he felt. He would go to Grimes to see if he had found out anything yet. Hope flickered in his heart. If there was anyone who could find the truth, it was Grimes.

Tess sat on the bench near the wall. She was in a tiny cell alone. Bringing her shawl closer about her, she leaned her head back. Tears began to run down her cheeks. She believed that she deserved to be there. Oh, she was innocent of the murder, but she was there for what she had done to Kathryn. It must be God paying her back for her wickedness. She had treated Kathryn horribly for many years and then lied. Just because they became friends later, and Kathryn forgave her, didn't mean God did. It had to be Him punishing her now.

Words from Katie came back to her. *"The Bible says that when God forgives our sins, He forgets them. He doesn't remember them."*

So if God forgives me and forgets, why am I being punished? she wondered.

Noise filled the air. She heard crying, swearing, and a low hum of voices that never ceased. *There must be rows of cells full of people,* she thought. *Father must have requested I be placed in a cell alone.* She couldn't see anything from where she was except a plain wall across from the locked door. David and her father had left a few hours ago, promising to get her out. She clung to that, but as time went on, hope began to fade.

Wearily she went to lie on her mat. Sleep eluded her so far, but she would try again. Doing nothing threatened to drive her crazy. If she could only sleep to pass the time it would help. Again she lay down, thinking of Kathryn locked up for over a year. How in the world did she endure? Other troubling thoughts crowded her mind. Who placed that written note in her home, and when? Someone took a lot of time and trouble to make the signature look like her own. Someone planted it, but who?

There seemed to be no answers, no hope, and despair filled her. Was this how Kathryn felt…alone and desperate? At least Tess had family to help, but Kathryn had none at the time. Shame flooded her. She never considered what Kathryn was going through at the time. Yes, she most certainly deserved to be here. God may have forgiven her, but the world "found out" her sin. This was payment for her deceitfulness. This would be her life from now on. If only she could curl up and die.

Victoria basked in the attention. Flowers, notes, and requests for visits came pouring in for the grieving widow. Some gentlemen whom she knew were ready to pursue her had also sent notes. This was working out so well. She never thought she could be so clever. She was able to trick that dimwitted maid Betsy into planting that "confession" note in Tess's room. How did she word it again? Oh yes:

> *Peter has left me to go back to his wife. I could kill him…no, I will kill him. I know someone who will do it for me.*

What looked like scribbling from a rejected, jealous lover made a beautiful confession. Yes, she was clever.

Victoria stretched her long legs. The hard part was having to stay locked up in her house, acting the bereaved widow. It was getting increasingly harder to work up widow's tears. Not able to go to any social functions or outings was difficult. She was not afraid at all of being found out. No one would ever suspect her. Her only fear was she might feel guilty after Peter was dead, but that proved false. With all she'd had to endure with that man, he'd forced her into it. That made it more his fault. And, after all, she didn't actually do the killing. Her hands were not bloodstained.

Victoria sighed heavily at the thought of spending another day closed up in her house with only her parents to keep her company. She thought of walking in the garden but decided against it. Maybe she would play the piano for awhile but decided on reading instead. Maybe a book about high adventure. After that she would go over all the notes she'd received and pen some replies. She was anxious to respond to the gentlemen most of all, but she must be tactful. Oh, how she loved the game of "catch and release" when it came to men.

Smiling, Victoria turned to head downstairs. *Maybe I will plan another trip to Paris.* The world had opened up...now that she was free. Had she realized the benefits of widowhood she might have tried it sooner. Finding a book that looked interesting, Victoria curled up before the fireplace in the parlor. She summoned the maid for tea. Yes, if she could fight the boredom she would be all right. *I wonder how that snit is doing in the gaol right now.* Smiling to herself, she began to read.

⤜⤐

It took two weeks before Betty could sit up. Her wounds had begun to heal nicely during the time Katie had taken care of her. Katie had faithfully cleaned her hair and body and applied plasters. Betty was looking more robust than before from all the good care and food given her.

The other women in the bay also found a change in Betty. Her tough exterior began to crack. She smiled at times. In fact, the mood of all the women was getting better for the presence of Mrs. Murphy. She entertained them with stories and continued teaching them to read and write. To fight off the long hours of idleness they took up sewing shirts. They would be sold for a small profit once they reached their destination.

Betty began to open up to the others and before long friendships blossomed. Katie was able to share God's Word with them, and they listened eagerly to the Bible stories.

"Ya mean to say, God forgived that King David fer sleepin' with that married lady and fer killin' 'er 'usband?" Betty inquired.

"Yes, he did. We're all sinners, Betty, all of us. We are born into sin."

243

"Ya think maybe 'e can forgive somebody like me?"

"Absolutely. He looks at all of us equally. When we ask Jesus Christ into our hearts, we are new creatures, the Bible says. We are clean and whole."

"He sees me and someone like yerself as the same? Yer sure 'e forgives everythin'?"

"Yes, Betty. I'm a sinner like everyone else. Nothing you ever did or thought of doing is bigger than God. Jesus' blood covers it all."

Betty grew very quiet, trying to take it all in. After a moment she had another question. "Is that yer words or the Bible's words?"

Katie opened her Bible to 1 John 1:9 and read it out loud: "If we confess our sins, he is faithful and just to forgive us our sins, and to cleanse us from all unrighteousness."

"What does all that mean?"

"If you talk to God in prayer, and tell Him your sins, he will forgive them."

"Don 'e know 'em already if 'e's God?"

"Yes, He does, but He wants you to tell Him. He wants us to talk to Him, communicate, and spend time with Him. I think too, if we tell Him about what we've done in our lives, it opens us up inside to allow Him to begin to heal us. We all have had things done to us that scar us and cause us a lot of pain."

"Did ya know I 'ad a wee bairn and it died? I didn't want it. I hated it afore it was even born. When it died, I was glad. God will forgive me on that?"

Katie was shocked by Betty's confession but didn't react. "Yes, Betty, He'll forgive that."

Betty went on to tell Katie about her life and the circumstances that surrounded her pregnancy. She told how she ended up on the *Sally Mae*. Katie felt such sadness for all the sorrow Betty had endured in her young life. She felt troubled for the lost bairn, who wasn't at fault.

"What 'appened to yerself to be 'ere? It would seem yer life to be perfect with a 'usband and being a lady and all," Betty asked.

Katie began telling the women of being locked in the gaol for over a year. Of her being a maid, of having been accused of stealing. She shared how she had met and married James, at how he was a prisoner on board. Some of them now remembered seeing her in the gaol, but had forgotten. The very idea that Kathryn could be in the same situation as they gave them hope. In their minds it was "easy" to be religious when you were not hungry, cold, or abused. It was surprising that she had been all of this, yet she loved God. Knowing she had suffered many of the same things as they had helped them see that God could accept them. They came to believe the He would help them, and actually save them as He had done her. God was not the God of the rich, but the God of all.

"Blimey, ne'er thought ya ter be a maid. Thought ya ter be a grand lady and all," one of the women stated.

Katie answered, "Did you know that when we accept Jesus Christ as our Lord and Savior we become princesses? He is King of kings and God is our Father, so that makes us His daughters—princesses!"

Well, the women were speechless. They all looked at each other, then back at Kathryn. All began laughing at such a thought. Katie was able to share more amazing, wonderful things from the Bible. By the time the afternoon was over, there were a few more "princesses" of the Kingdom of God and the angels in heaven rejoiced.

22

Hardship

James was summoned to Captain Warwick's to answer for his behavior on the deck. He told James that he was never to leave his presence again without permission. If he did, he would lose his position and be locked up along with the others. James tried to explain how he felt about the punishment inflicted on the two prisoners. The captain let James know that any decisions he made were law, and he did not need to explain anything to him.

It was unheard of for a prisoner to question a captain and not get the lash himself. Fortunately for James, Captain Warwick liked him and understood him. He knew he was not trying to undermine his authority but was a compassionate, moral man. Men like Murphy were rare. If the man had voiced any objections in front of the others, well then he would have had to be punished. Lucky for him, he had walked away quietly. No matter how the captain felt about the character of the man, he could never let him question or interfere with the running of his ship. It was out of the question.

James walked out of the Captain's cabin with a decision made; he would never stand aside again while another human being was given the lash. He would have to do something. He could not stand to see another person punished like that. He just hoped and prayed it would never happen again. He hoped he would have the strength to do what he knew to be right if it ever happened again.

James kept busy, giving his time and energy to others. It helped him to stay busy. He tended Jake's wounds, helping him recover. He was even able to get the captain to let some of the prisoners work on board the ship doing more repairs.

When the ship's carpenter became ill, James found one of the prisoners to take his place until he recovered. There were a few who could not be trusted, but most of the prisoners, given the chance, wanted to work. James was becoming a trusted liaison between the captain, crew, and the convicts.

Rio de Janeiro took two months to reach. The biggest battle for ship and passengers was the heat. Water, though plentiful, was still rationed out. The wounded, sick, and children were the first consideration when it came to cleanliness. Fresh water could not be wasted on washing clothes or bodies. Rations of salt pork and beef were given out. In the evenings when the temperatures cooled, singing and dancing were encouraged to bring up the spirits and kill the monotony.

When finally the lookout sounded, "Land ahead," it was an exciting time for all. Once anchored and quarantine time was over, the prisoners were loaded into boats and taken ashore. They were placed inside lockhouses, where they were given fresh food and water. Fruit was given out freely, along with more salt pork, beef, and even some nuts.

Though the heat was heavy, fresh water was now readily available, and both men and women took advantage of bathing. Even the prisoners were allowed to wash up.

Dr. Crane kept his eyes open for any signs of fever. It had run rampant a few years back, almost wiping out the *Regal* and her sister ship, *Whirlwind*. The fever was not such a threat of late because of better conditions. The ships were fumigated regularly, and fresh food was supplied. Dr. Crane, however, never took any disease for granted. He always kept a wary eye out for those killer fevers.

Sally Mae was again fumigated and washed down once she was emptied of prisoners. It didn't take long for her to dry out. Fresh supplies were brought on board and repairs were made.

A week before *Sally Mae* was to leave, her sister ship, *The Clip*, arrived and anchored. The late ship was in desperate need of provisions and repairs. Prisoners on board were in worse shape than the ship itself. Eight men and two women prisoners had perished, and it looked like there would be more. It was found that their ship's surgeon-superintendent had also died, leaving no one to tend the sick. The authorities decided to keep *The Clip* under quarantine longer than usual. They had to be sure that no contagious diseases were carried by her occupants.

The *Greystone* had not been sighted nor heard from. Perhaps she was held up on the Islands or blown off course. No one knew for sure. All anyone knew was that *The Clip* needed help fast or more lives would be lost.

"If you go over to her, you will have to stay," Captain Warwick warned Dr. Crane and Richardson.

"I want to know what happened to all the provisions that were loaded," Richardson barked. "If I find the captain sold them to make a profit, I'll have his head!"

"Take it easy; you'll only get yourself shot," Warwick warned.

Dr. Crane voiced his own feelings. "Everything is ready here, and I feel I'm needed on *The Clip.*"

The captain was concerned." I don't want to have to wait until the quarantine is lifted before picking you up and leaving. If you board her, you both may have to stay and sail her." It wasn't a threat, but a fact. Warwick had no intention of holding up because of another captain's blunder or misfortunes. Trouble was, he hated to lose these two men.

"It is my duty to go aboard," Dr. Crane said.

"Mine as well," added Richards.

"So be it. Take one of the longboats and a few crewmen with you. If you need any assistance, signal with the flags."

The two men loaded a few supplies and were soon boarding *The Clip.* She was indeed in dire need of help. Many of the people were quite sick with dysentery and scurvy, but nothing contagious. It didn't matter to the authorities on land. If there was any sickness aboard any vessel, it would be held in quarantine.

When he had a chance, Richards questioned the captain. "Where are the limes I ordered for you?" When the captain didn't answer, Richards knew they had been sold. It was typical of many of the prison hulks' captains to sell provisions to line their own pockets. The all-mighty coin took precedence over the health of the crew and convicts.

Even though Dr. Crane was confident there were no contagious illnesses, he could not be entirely sure. He had the crew signal the *Sally Mae,* who sent some of her crew ashore to buy more supplies. Once on shore they brought their long boat as close as possible, and by rope and pulley brought the supplies on board.

Dr. Crane began to ration everyone an ounce of lemon juice and sugar daily. In addition they were given rice, oatmeal, peas, bread, and a portion of wine and tea to help strengthen them. To many of the wretched souls on board, Richards and Dr. Crane became their saviors. There were some very close to death. Everyone had as much fresh water as they wanted. *The Clip* was cleaned, fumigated, and ventilated. Each bottom board of all the berths were carried on deck, washed with salt water, and thoroughly dried before being replaced. All the bedding was aired on deck or replaced, depending on the condition. Everyone had to have their clothes fumigated with the vapor of burning brimstone and oxygenic gas. Many had their heads shaven.

Much of the extra clothing the women of the *Sally Mae* had made was given to the prisoners of *The Clip*. Materials for repairs were brought on board, and so *The Clip* was made seaworthy once again.

Richards checked each barrel and flask of fresh provisions and carefully logged in every item and amount in his ledger. How he wished he had Murphy there to help him.

Along with Dr. Crane, Richards planned on turning the captain of *The Crane* in for gross misconduct once in New South Wales. Of course he wasn't about to let the captain know this or his throat would be cut before journey's end. Richards ordered the captain of the guard to appoint men to guard the new supplies. These men were not under the captain's authority. They seemed relieved to have someone of competence in charge of the provisions.

After ten days the quarantine was lifted, letting Dr. Crane return to the *Sally Mae,* but repairs were not finished on *The Clip*. Richards had no choice; he had to stay behind. He was disappointed he could not finish the journey with his friends. Three days later *Sally Mae* weighed anchor and left.

By the time all the repairs were done and supplies loaded, *The Clip* was lagging behind two full weeks. Once they began their journey to Cape Town, South Africa, the prisoners were fit to sail. Richards decided he would see they stayed that way. He wasn't a doctor, but all they needed was to be treated like human beings. Dr. Crane gave him a crash course in the everyday ailments before leaving. Hopefully nothing serious would crop up. Any babes born would have to be left to the women. He didn't want to witness that mess. He knew one thing for sure: the "good" captain wouldn't be selling supplies for profit anymore. Richards wondered who the real criminals were sometimes.

⸙⸙

Lady Wilson, Maggie, and Mary all looked at Tess with deep concern. She was pale and becoming quite thin.

"Are you eating all right, dear?" Lady Wilson inquired.

"Yes, Mother, thanks to you. If it weren't for you bringing me food, I wouldn't be. The food here isn't fit for animals. I can't believe people are treated this way. I had no idea."

Lady Wilson sadly shook her head, not knowing how to respond. "I brought the books you wanted. Is there anything else we can do?"

"Just pray, Mother. Pray the truth will come out. Funny, isn't it? That is probably what Kathryn had prayed for when she was locked in here. I bet you never thought you would be visiting your own daughter in this place. Not when you were working in the Ladies' Prison League."

Lady Wilson wrapped her arms around her daughter.

"At least I can testify that there is justice in this world after all. Look at me now." Tess sniffed.

"Don't be goin' over that again, Miss Tess. That be over an' done with. Ye cannot be blamin' yerself anymore fer that, "Mary offered.

"That's right, Tess. What happened with Kathryn is over. You must stop thinking about that and concentrate on getting through this," Lady Wilson added.

"I'll try, but how perfect is the justice of all this? Experiencing this nightmare brings the blackness of my soul in view for doing such a thing. I wonder what Kathryn would say if she knew I was here now."

Maggie spoke up. "She would say the same as your mother, and Mary, 'Tis over and done with.' You aren't being punished by God. You are forgiven by Him and Katie. You are being blamed for something you didn't do by someone who has it out for you. You truly have no idea who that could be?"

"I don't know who would do this. I've thought long and hard, but have no idea. I have many enemies. I've hurt a lot of people, especially my family. Truth be told, I can't blame anyone for putting me here. Now that I'm experiencing the other side, I'm even more ashamed than before." Tess was almost inconsolable. Not because of her situation, but for what she had done to Katie. The three women tried their best to comfort and assure her. All too soon the visit was over, and Tess was once again left alone.

Tess tried to read one of the books left by her mother but couldn't concentrate. It was all too coincidental to be accused falsely as Kathryn had been. She truly felt she was being punished—and deservedly so. She knew God had forgiven her, but she also learned He allowed things to happen for a reason. She would have to trust in Him, and it did not come easy to do. Tess knew consequences for actions were a reality in life. This was the end result of her lies and deceit.

Walking around her small cell, Tess tried to turn her thoughts in another direction. She began to pray, which was still a bit awkward, but she felt comforted.

Tess gazed at a streak of sunshine hitting the floor. She walked over and stood in it. Lifting her head up, she tried her best to "feel" its warmth. Funny how people took things for granted. Sighing, she thought about David, and how hard this was on him too. She knew that her father and husband had been unsuccessful in their efforts to have her released. Too much time had passed. *Better get used to all this, Tess,* she thought. She gave herself the one luxury she had left; she cried and cried.

Lady Wilson had given the others instructions not to tell her daughter that today was Peter Reeves's funeral. Many people came to witness his poor widow burying her murdered husband.

23

Valley of the Shadow of Death

Betsy shook in terror. She knew this man meant what he said he would do to her if she wasn't truthful. He had her arm in a vise-like grip. There was no escape. All she had to do was answer his questions truthfully and he would let her go, or so he said. Why had she let him trick her into coming here?

"'Twas Mrs. Reeves that be a-givin' me the invitation! I swear it!"

"Invitation?"

"Aye."

It was just what Grimes wanted to hear. Walking the young servant over to the divan, he sat her down. Bending over her, he questioned her further, "Tell me what Mrs. Reeves told you."

"She say it be a note fer 'er friend, Miss Wilson. Says it be an invite."

"Don't you usually have one of the coachmen deliver notes?"

"Aye, but she be wantin' to be sure Miss Wilson be gettin' it, and it was ta be a surprise. She told me ta take it meself, and to hide it in Miss Wilson's room."

"How did she contact you?"

"'Er maid Patty, be my friend."

"Why did Mrs. Reeves want you to hide it?"

"It be fer a 'hiding party' and Mrs. Reeves say it be part of the fun. Me and Patty hid it."

"Hiding party? What do you mean by 'hiding party'?"

"Ya know! When you get a bit of paper with things on it and gotta go and find it all."

"You mean a scavenger hunt?"

"Aye, that be it!"

"So Mrs. Reeves wanted you to hide the 'invitation' in Miss Wilson's room, and not say anything to her, hoping she would find it herself?"

"Aye, but she told us ter hide it so's Miss Wilson could find it easy. If she not find it by the week's end, Mrs. Reeves would call on 'er. Then she said she would tell Miss Wilson ta hunt for it. Told us not ta say nothin' so we didn't wreck 'er surprise."

"Didn't you think that was a little strange?"

"Everything they do is strange. I work for rich folk all me life, and none of 'em be normal."

"Oh," was all Grimes could say to that. "Did Miss Wilson tell you she had found the invitation?"

"No, twas Patty that told me."

"So Patty is the maid at the Reeves's house, right?"

"Aye, remember I told you she be Mrs. Reeve's maid? I told ya she be a friend. She be the one ta tell me to come see Mrs. Reeves in the first place. She come o'er one day ta say Miss Wilson found the invitation. She 'ad told Mrs. Reeves, so I didn' 'ave to worry 'bout it."

"So, Mrs. Reeves sent her maid over to tell you specifically that Miss Wilson found it, and you didn't have to think about it again?"

"Aye." Betsy was getting impatient with the man. He kept repeating everything she was saying.

"Didn't you think it strange that Miss Wilson didn't say anything to you about it, and that Mrs. Reeves would bother to contact you?"

"I told ya afore, all they do is strange to me. Why would anyone want'ta go lookin' for lost stuff at a party jest to say ya found it first? I ne'er could figure out the fun in that. Besides, Miss Wilson be mean ta me for a long time. She got nicer lately, but she still don't tell me anythin'."

"I see." Grimes had heard all he needed.

He had spent weeks investigating Peter Reeves's murder, getting nowhere. He knew Victoria Reeves was involved, and any evidence was probably hidden in her bedchamber. He needed to find a way "in."

He had watched the estate almost a week and was about to give up when he noticed Tess's maid, Betsy. She arrived one day at Victoria Reeves's, and a woman let her in the back door. He wondered what she was doing there. He wondered if she had a part in the conspiracy. He couldn't believe his luck when he saw her enter Reeves's house. Betsy was young and could be easily intimidated. Any information she might have would be easy to obtain. He had to wait until she left the house. When she finally did leave, he approached her, saying he had some important papers for her mistress, and would she give them to her? She fell for it. He led her to his office, but now he needed to find a way in the house. Grimes decided to change his tactics by charming the girl into helping him further.

"Betsy, you've been a great help to me. I hope I didn't frighten you. I am going to take a chance and tell you a secret. You know that I work for Lord Wilson and have for a long time. Well, I'm investigating Mr. Reeves's murder. I believe that Miss Wilson didn't kill him."

"Ya know it for sure? Then who? Ya don't think it be me! I ne'er do nothing like that in me life!" Betsy looked panicked.

"No, no, Betsy, not you! I didn't mean to make it sound like I was accusing you." Grimes could see the girl start to breathe again. He had to be careful. She was ready to bolt. "I have an idea, but I can't say in case I'm wrong. However, I'd like you to be my partner if you would. I will even be willing to pay you."

Betsy's eyes nearly bugged out of her head. "Blimey, ya pay me? 'Ow much?"

"It depends on how much information you can get me."

Betsy was suspicious. "Will it be dangerous? I ain't a-goin' ta do anything dangerous!"

"No, I won't let you get hurt. I'll do all the 'dangerous' work myself."

"If that be the case, I'll do it. I'll be yer partner. What ya want me ta do?"

"Just be yourself, but if anything unusual happens, come and tell me. If I'm not here, you can give any information you have to my clerk. The more information you give me, the more money you will make. In fact, I'm so pleased with what you told me today that I'm willing to pay you a pound now."

"A pound! Ne'er 'ad a pound all at once in me life!"

"Just don't tell anyone. Someone may think you stole it, and whatever you do, don't spend it all right away. They'll wonder where you got all the money. If anyone finds out you are helping me, then you won't be able to be my partner any longer."

"What kind of information are ya lookin' to 'ear 'bout?"

"Anything your friend Patty can tell you about Mrs. Reeves. Who she sees, who comes to her parties, where she goes when she leaves the house. Things like that."

"Ya can count on me! Patty don't like the lady, and she be 'appy ta tell anything I want. A pound! I got me a pound in me pocket!" Smiling from ear to ear Betsy took it and hid it in her dress. Thanking him and bowing all the way out the door, she turned to do her errands.

Grimes was excited to bring news, any news to Lord Wilson. They had both suspected Reeves's wife, but proving it was another matter. If Grimes had learned anything in this business, it was two things: people usually slipped up somewhere leaving evidence, and people were willing to talk for a price. He knew Betsy would have been happy with a lot less but knew by giving her more she would dig deeper for information.

Now came the hard task of putting the information he learned today to work in proving Tess Wilson's innocence. How ironic—this was probably the only time in Tess Wilson's life that she was truly innocent. No matter how much time or money it took, he would find the evidence to free the Wilson girl. He smiled to himself as he thought, *Even if it comes down to planting my own evidence against the Reeves woman.* Two could play that game, and he knew he was better at it than she.

Annie and Katie struggled to hold on in the midst of the storm that threatened to capsize the ship. The wind howled, causing great waves to wash over the deck. The crew was forced to close the air-scuttles, leaving the lower decks dark and full of foul, hot air.

"Hold on to her, Katie!" Annie shouted over the noise.

"I will, but we need more towels now!"

Another woman lying on the berth writhed in great pain about to give birth. Jenna held a lantern as steady as possible while Annie went to find more towels.

With wide, frightened eyes the young woman looked at Katie for strength and comfort.

She looks so young, Katie thought. "It'll be all right. The baby will be here soon and..."

Another piercing scream filled the air. Katie looked around for Annie to return. Why didn't she go and get the towels? She didn't know anything about babies. As she witnessed the tremendous pain of birth, Katie's heart filled with fear.

Annie returned with a clean towel for the baby...soon to be born. Kneeling down at the end of the berth, Annie encouraged the young woman, "One more push and you'll be there! I see the baby's head! Push! Push!"

The young woman pushed with all the strength left in her body. Quite suddenly the baby slid out into Annie's hands. Covered in blood and a milky film, the baby lay still. Annie immediately turned the baby over, and began to clear the mucus from its mouth. Once that was done, she gave a good slap on the tiny behind. With that, the baby let out a howl. Relief filled all...followed by laughter. Annie instructed Katie on how to tie off the cord, then proceeded to cut it. Gently Katie laid the baby into a towel. After wrapping the tiny human in it, she began to clean it up. Not ever in her life had Katie held such a tiny bairn. Emotion flooded her as she cleaned the child.

"What is it? What is my baby?" the exhausted mother cried.

"It's a boy," Annie told her. "A beautiful boy with lots of dark hair and a robust cry."

"I want to hold him, please!"

Katie brought the bairn over and settled him in his mother's arms. It was a miracle to see. Katie, of course, had seen animals give birth, but never a woman. Her fears turned to wonder as she watched the tenderness of the mother holding the baby to her breast. Everyone laughed at the hungry, suckling noises of the newborn.

"What are you going to name him?" Annie questioned.

"Stormy William Hughes," was the answer.

"'Tis fitting," Annie answered.

Once mother and baby were comfortable, the other women went about gathering the soiled sheets. The storm seemed to slack off, giving the women steadier steps. Jenna offered to watch over the little family while Annie and Katie took the dirty linen out. After putting it in a barrel full of cold seawater to soak, they made themselves tea.

"I've never witnessed a birth," Katie shared.

"'Tis a wondrous thing, isn't it?"

"Aye, but a bit frightening too."

"'Tis the most natural thing in the world. Do you think women would keep giving birth through the ages if it was so bad?"

"I guess not, but they don't have much choice either."

Annie looked at Katie. "You're going to have a baby, aren't you, Katie?"

"How did you guess?"

"Oh, I've seen the fear in your eyes before. I won't lie to you. The pain is awful as you saw, but you soon forget it after your babe is in your arms. Coming into the world is a hard thing, but so is living in it. If you think on your baby instead of the pain, it helps. You're healthy, Katie, and if you don't mind me saying, you have full hips. You aren't overly large, but you will be fine."

"Thank you, Annie. I watched that woman suffering. It did scare me a little."

"It's only normal to be afraid a little, but God built us to handle it. Now if it were a man pushing out a babe, well, let's just say they would do more than the Irish jig." Both laughed at the thought. "Have you told your husband about the babe yet?"

"No, I didn't mention it to anyone because I thought he should be the first to know. He's had a lot on his mind lately, and there just hasn't been a good time to tell him."

"Don't wait too long. I can see your belly begin to round already. He may not guess it, but others will. He'll wonder why everyone else knew except him."

"Aye, you're right. I'll tell him very soon."

The women finished their tea, then Annie sent Katie to her cabin. "You better rest yourself. It's been a long, tiring night. Thank God that the storm is easing up."

"I am tired. Thank you, Annie, for calming my fears. I must have sounded like a tiny bairn myself."

"Not at all, just a friend who needed some comfort."

Katie made her way to the cabin. James had been there when she was summoned to help with the birth. Maybe it would be a good time to tell him her news. Once she closed and locked their door, she crept over to the bed. Her husband was sleeping soundly. Deciding not to wake him, she quietly got ready for bed. She couldn't sleep. She kept seeing that bairn being born...the wonder of it. The pain kept filling her mind as well. She prayed for the Lord to ease fears of giving birth. Suddenly she recalled the love on the woman's face, erasing the torment and fear that had filled her expression only moments before. Katie remembered what Gran had said about giving birth.

"'Tis as easy as breathing, and as hard as dying."

Katie never understood what she had meant until tonight. Placing her hands over her belly, she tried to feel life, but only her breathing moved her body. Katie fell asleep trying to think of names for her baby. Arthur, like her father, or if it was a girl, Ida, like Gran....

☙ ❧

Grimes watched behind the bushes as the carriage left, carrying Victoria and her parents away. Heading to the back of the house he crept towards the window. Seeing Betsy and Patty waiting, he lightly tapped. Betsy quickly opened the door for him. Patty stood anxiously twisting her apron. Once Grimes entered, she whispered, "Come up the back stairs!"

"Which room is hers?" Grimes loudly whispered.

Patty pointed a shaky finger. "'Tis the door on the right. Don't make no noise! If the other servants 'ears ya, they'll shoot ya, and kick me into the streets."

"Don't worry, Patty, Mr. Grimes knows wha'the is doin'," Betsy assured her friend.

Once he was in Victoria's bedchamber he slipped his shoes off. He wasn't sure where to begin looking. Where would a woman hide her diary? Patty had told him and Betsy that Victoria kept a diary, but she didn't know where. As he scanned the room, he tried to guess the most likely place. Under the mattress? No, that was too obvious. He walked over to a bookcase filled with dainty figurines and books. He then turned to look at the fireplace. Perhaps behind the pictures on the wall? Something told him there had to be a secret panel somewhere.

Betsy stood outside, guarding the door while Patty watched the stairs on the first floor. It was only the promise of money that got Patty to help. Both girls were extremely nervous about the whole thing. If they got caught, they would never work in any house again. It wouldn't take long for the word to get out that they couldn't be trusted. Betsy leaned closer to the door to hear what the man was doing, but there was no sound. How did she get into this? Why did she listen to this man? Life was so much easier when all she had to worry about was taking care of Miss Tess. Then again she did have a pound in her pocket ready to be spent.

Grimes felt along the walls until he noticed a small, almost invisible line running vertically to one of the window panes. Had Grimes not lifted the heavy drape panel he would not have noticed it at all. Running his finger over it, he tried to feel the opening. Whoever built the narrow panel next to the window pane had done a masterful job. Taking out his pocket knife, Grimes placed the end of the blade in the crack causing it to pop open. Inside the narrow opening stood a book and a velvet bag. Grime's heart began pounding. Opening the book, he found it was what he was looking for. Placing it inside his coat pocket he turned to the velvet bag. Inside he found a diamond necklace and matching earbobs. For a second he was tempted to take the bag along with the book, but decided against it. Making sure the secret compartment was closed and the drape pulled over, he turned to leave.

Betsy jumped a full foot in the air, letting out a yelp when Grimes opened the door.

"Is it safe?" he questioned.

"Blimey, ya scared me out of ten years. What took so long?"

"It doesn't matter. I found it."

"Ya found what?"

"The diary you told me about."

"Oh!"

Sneaking out of the house proved easy. After paying the two girls, Grimes was on his way to Brick House to see Lord Wilson. He couldn't seem to get there fast enough. After arriving, he explained what he had found.

"I've had Betsy helping me."

"Betsy? You mean Tess's maid, Betsy?"

"Yes, and it was because of her I was able to get my hands on this diary."

"I'm grateful for that, but I'm not sure I appreciate you involving my staff. Then again I did tell you to use whatever means to find the truth."

"I can assure you, sir, that she was never in any danger. When she told me her friend worked at the Reeves' estate, it was the only way. Once I found out that Victoria Reeves kept a diary, I needed help getting into the house to look for it."

"How did you find out she had a diary? That's personal information."

"Betsy is friends with Victoria Reeves' maid, Patty. She told Betsy about the diary."

"Well, I hired you because you're the best. I've never questioned your methods as long as you got the job done, and I won't start now."

The two men began reading the diary.

"This is better than one of those dime novelettes. You wouldn't have guessed that 'fine' Mrs. Reeves could be no better than one of the bargirls, would you? Not by the looks of her at least," Grimes commented.

"Just goes to show you—fine clothes and jewelry don't make a lady," Edward Wilson agreed.

For nearly an hour they went over the diary. They found it to be very interesting reading. They discovered many familiar names on the pages, including Tess's. The diary read:

260

I found out her name. It's Tess Wilson. I saw that little trollop today. She was coming out of the dress shop. I don't care who her parents are; she has taken up with the wrong man this time. I will not have her and Peter making me the laughingstock of London.

That was all that was said about Tess until ten pages later.

Peter came to me tonight and told me he wants a divorce! I can't believe he wants to marry that little snit. That he would pick her over me after all I've done for him. I won't have it! I won't. Justin said he can help me take care of it. I've decided to do it. It's time to free myself of Peter. Justin is willing to find someone to do the job for a lot less than I was willing to pay. He says he can find someone who would be willing to kill his own mother for the right price. Sounds horrible, but I guess that's the kind of man we're looking for.

"I wonder who Justin is," Grimes stated.

"I can't be sure, but I heard rumors of Lord Reynolds and the Reeves' woman taking up with each other. His first name is Justin."

They read on.

It wasn't easy, trying to figure out how to make it look like the Wilson snit planned the whole thing, but I had a stroke of genius. It's too much to write about, and I don't have time now. Let's just say I have a "party" to plan for. Hopefully I will be a grieving widow within the week.

That was all the men needed to read. They had her! Lord Wilson began pounding Grimes's back in congratulations and shouting, "Hallelujah, man, you did it! Barbara, Barbara!"

Grimes watched Lord Wilson run up the staircase to find his wife. He was surprised at the older man's agility as he took two stairs at a time.

"Barbara! Where in blue blazes are you?"

"Good heavens, Edward, what has come over you? What are you yelling about?"

"I've got it! We can go get Tess! She can come home!"

"Edward, what are you talking about? You've got what?"

After explaining everything, Lord Wilson ordered their carriage to be brought around. All three headed off to their lawyer's office.

Tess's door creaked open, stirring her awake. Irritation at being wakened was replaced with fear when a large man with missing teeth grabbed her arm. He lifted her to her feet as if she weighed nothing. His breath was foul and so was his body.

"Git up with ya now!" the man snarled.

"You're hurting me! Let go!"

"Shut up with ya, and come with me!"

"Where are you taking me?"

"I said ter shut up."

The man led Tess down a long, dank hallway. Rats scurried to and fro, causing Tess to shrink back against the man. It seemed to please him greatly. Before too long they faced a thick wooden door. The man stopped to light a torch left by the door.

"Come with me now, 'urry up."

"Where are you taking me?" Tess questioned again.

The man just grunted, not answering.

Tess found herself being led down a long winding stairway made of stone. It looked as if it hadn't been used in years. The hairs in the back of Tess's neck stood up. She looked behind her, hoping someone would be there to help her. Sensing she was in grave danger she thought of running but didn't have any way of escaping. She was in a mass of black nothingness except for the light the torch threw out. Past the light, Tess couldn't see anything. The stairs wound endlessly until Tess thought they must be close to hell itself. Finally they reached the bottom. Turning to the left, the man led Tess to a small room that had no door.

"Git in 'ere!" he snarled once more as he shoved her into the room.

It was no larger than a small closet. "Go sit on that there bed."

Tess saw a half-rotted plank sticking out of the wall. Did he mean for her to sit there? She walked over to it, sitting on it gingerly to make sure it would hold her. A shiver ran through her as the scurry of something along the wall reached her ears. She shivered from the dampness of the dungeon and peered about in the dim light. The walls appeared to be covered in slime of some sort. The odors of mildew and decay were pungent. Tess let out a squeal when she saw what made the scurrying sound. The man laughed as he stepped out of the room, taking the torch with him. Tess was petrified. Was he going to leave her there?

"I told ya I would bring 'er 'ere."

Tess strained to see who he was talking to.

A calmer, softer male voice spoke, then the burly man asked, "What ya want me ter do with 'er now that I got 'er 'ere?" came the question.

Again, the softer voice spoke in answer. Tess could not make out what he was saying.

Once more the brute spoke, "All right with ya now. Pay me an' I'll be on me way."

Tess heard coins clinking together, then the rough man speaking. "Take the torch. 'Old it fer me to see the stairs."

Tess heard a shuffling noise and noticed the torch light move away from the room.

Should I try to run now? she thought but decided against it. Tess's heart was hammering. *Maybe someone has come to get me out!* The thought soothed her for mere seconds. Why would they bring her to such a dank place as this? Holding her breath she waited to see who would enter.

Footsteps sounded at the doorway. Squinting, she tried to see the man's face. All she could see was a man's torso dressed in a fine velvet jacket, riding pants, and boots. The torch was held low, making it impossible for Tess to see her captor.

"Do you remember me?" The voice was soft and vaguely familiar. "Do you need a hint?"

Tess leaned a little closer, trying her best to see him but could not.

"Who are you?" she asked in a shaky voice.

"So you are frightened, are you?" the man softly stated. "I never thought you were frightened of anything."

"Of course I'm frightened. I'm led to this vile place for whatever reason, I don't know!" Tess was becoming hysterical.

"Calm down, Tess."

"How do you know me?"

"I know you very well. You could almost say…intimately."

"What are these games you're playing? Take me back to my cell at once or my father will…"

The voice chuckled. "Your father will…what? He doesn't know where you are. Besides, you're the last person who should be talking about games. You're the biggest game player of all. You are at my mercy, and mind you, Tess, you had better change your tone. It's beginning to irritate me."

Tess tried to sound brave, but she felt anything but. Once again she asked, only a little calmer, "What do you want of me? Who are you?"

"Just one of your long-lost lovers."

"I refuse to continue like this. If you do not tell me who you are, I will scream."

"Scream away, my lovely. No one can hear you down here. These old rooms were abandoned years ago. They used to be used for storage, and at times for…well, let's say 'special punishment.' Most have forgotten about this part of Newgate. Those who do remember wouldn't come down here for anything."

"So what do you want of me?"

"Much."

"What do you mean?"

"First, let's see if you can remember who I am. A couple of years ago we met at the Spencer's Harvest Ball. We danced, and you led me to believe you enjoyed my company. Do you remember the ball?"

"Yes, but I danced with many gentlemen that night."

"Yes, you do love to play the field, don't you? Anyway, I'll give you another hint. Do you remember the dark corner of the Spencer's garden, the corner with the lovers' bench? We shared some interesting moments there. After that night, we saw each other frequently until you...grew bored."

Tess searched her memory. She had many rendezvous with many different men in her past. Pinpointing one separate night was difficult. She remembered having a spectacular time at that particular ball. There had been many eligible men there that night, including a couple of married men she had danced with. Suddenly a name and a face came to mind. Tess's head snapped up as she remembered who she had shared an intimate moment with in the garden. "Justin Reynolds?"

The man stood quietly for a moment. "Very good, you do remember me."

"Why...why are you doing this to me?" Tess pleaded.

"You know the lovely grieving widow of Peter Reeves, don't you?"

"Of course, but what does she have to do with this?"

"Haven't you wondered who planted that confession letter or pointed the finger at you for Reeves' death?"

"Yes, I've wondered. You mean to tell me it was you and Victoria Reeves?"

"It does take you time to figure things out, doesn't it? Of course I was attracted to your beauty and money, certainly not your brains. It would seem, my dear Tess, that you latched onto the wrong married man with Reeves. Since I am her lover, Victoria contacted me to have him killed. Of course she had no idea that you and I had...a past. This turned out to be the opening I was waiting for."

"Why are you telling me all this? What do you want?"

"Like I said much, but for right now I think you need to hear me out. I've waited a long time for this moment. Don't you remember when I called on you a few months after the ball, and you laughed in my face? You told me not to be ridiculous, that you were just having fun and were tired of me. I poured out my soul to you and offered any and all love I had...you laughed at me. If that wasn't bad enough, you went around telling everyone how I came to lick your boots. You kicked me aside like some dog. Do you remember what I said to you? I told you that I wouldn't be treated like a fool. You would pay. It has taken some time, but now I'm calling your debt."

"You can't be serious! It was just an affair that happened years ago! What are you going to do to me?"

The man held out his hand towards Tess. She cringed backwards against the dank wall.

"I would suggest you take my hand, or it will go worse for you."

Hesitating, she reached her hand out to him. Tess was surprised at his strength.

"I've waited for this a long time."

"I wanted you to call on me again, Justin, but you never did. I thought you knew I was teasing." Tess spoke much too rapidly.

"And I suppose you're about to tell me that you love me?"

Horrifying fear had Tess by the throat. Her mind raced for a way out of this nightmare. *Help me, Lord!* came her plea.

The man laughed loudly, tightening his grip. "Do you really think I'm that stupid? I do realize that Victoria is going to be angry after she hears she had been cheated out of seeing you hang. Oh well, she'll get over it. Then again she will never really know what happened to you, will she? No one will."

Tess panicked; she lunged at the man, digging her nails into his face, ripping and tearing. He let out a howl, turned on her, and hit her as hard as he could. Tess flew back against the wall. A sickening sound came from her when her head hit the wall. Time seemed to stand still. The man wheezed from the effort. Blood ran down his face where Tess had torn his skin. He looked down on her, waiting for her to move, but she didn't. Her head was twisted in a bizarre manner, verifying what he already knew.

"Well, sweet, I had hoped to have a little fun before killing you, but the ending is still the same." Justin leaned the torch against the wall. Kneeling, he picked up her lifeless body. He went back into the small room she had first been taken to and laid her on the plank. She could lay there and rot. Who would ever know? He turned to leave, never giving her a second glance. He walked out, angry over his own wounds. He hadn't expected her to fight. Wiping the blood from his face, he cursed her and walked away.

The once-promising life of the young woman was over. Her father, mother, husband, and all who knew her would never know what happened to their beloved Tess. The consequences for her past had killed her future. Her friend, Katie, had given her a gift worth much more than one lifetime; she had shared Christ with Tess. And now Tess was home.

Tess was missing from her cell. No one knew where she had gone. A full search was done. Gaolers were questioned and threatened. Other prisoners were held in suspicion. Some speculated that she had escaped, but her family knew better. They had a full investigation launched into her disappearance. Lord and Lady Wilson spent a lot of time and money searching for her, but to no avail. They would never know how close they had come to taking their daughter home, if they had only arrived an hour earlier. If only...

Their grief and fear turned into anger for the woman who had framed her in the first place. They had Victoria Reeves taken into custody. It was the biggest scandal in years. All the people Victoria considered friends now spoke in hushed tones and biting words. All of London was buzzing about the "beautiful killer widow."

Justin Reynolds was not to be found. He had slipped away, but Lord Wilson swore he would have him hunted down. Reynolds was named in the diary as Victoria Reeves's accomplice. Lord Wilson knew they had something to do with his daughter's disappearance. He felt it in his bones. He thought Tess might even be with Reynolds. That the man had taken her out of prison and held her as his captive. Time would prove him wrong.

Victoria could only endure three days in the gaol. She was found with a scarf around her neck, hanging from a beam. The humiliation was too great. When she heard her diary had been found, she knew there was no hope. Many people asked why she would keep such a diary in the first place. Victoria asked herself that same question before stepping off the chair into eternity.

James and Katie walked the deck, looking at the beautiful sunset. It had been three days since the storm. Finally all had returned to normal. "So how are the new mum and babe doing?" James asked his wife.

"James, it's so sad. Ruth, that's her name, told me that her husband had left her right after he found out she was going to have a baby. She said they had been so happy up until that time. She had no family in London since her husband had moved them there, looking for work. She had no money or way to make a living. She ended up stealing and getting caught. She was scared to death that she would hang, but thankfully she was transported out instead. I can't speak of the men-folk, but most of the women are not criminals. Many were forced into stealing to survive, just like you! I've heard such sad stories, James. It would break your heart to hear them."

James shook his head slowly. "I can't imagine a man leaving his wife and babe like that."

"That's because you are a godly man, James."

"Also because I love you," he whispered as he hugged her. "Any man would be blessed to have a wife like you."

Katie's heart skipped a beat. "I want to help her, James. Can you imagine being all alone, not having anyone to help you? I feel we need to do something. If we were to get our own farm, do you think we could have Ruth and her baby stay with us and help?"

"We can't have every person who has problems stay with us, Katie. I think we need to wait and see if we are to get our own place. I know we've heard that capable farmers get their own land, but we really don't know if that is true. Besides, it will be a long time before that happens. I have to serve my time. It will be years before we acquire land, if ever. It doesn't hurt to dream, though." James began chuckling. "The Lord has blessed us in so many ways. Sometimes I forget that I'm still a prisoner. We really shouldn't hang all our hopes on one man's statement about farmers being needed. We can't count on that."

Katie smiled. "You're right. We sure have lofty plans, don't we, husband? Not only do we have our own land in our minds, but we have people to work with us already."

"We are getting ahead of ourselves. If God wants it for us, then it will happen. If not, then He will have something better for us."

"Know what else I want to find out about when we get there?" Katie teased him.

"What?"

"If they have a school and a church."

"School? Did you plan on teaching the women once we get settled?"

"No, I think I'm going to have my hands full with working alongside you. We will want a school for our children."

James laughed. "That's pretty far in the future. Why worry about it now?"

"It could affect us sooner than you think, James."

James stopped and looked at his wife. "You mean, you're going to have a…I mean you and I are going to…how, when?"

Katie couldn't help but giggle. "In the summertime."

"Is it a girl or a boy?"

"Yes."

"What do you mean? Both?"

"No, I mean it's a girl or a boy."

"You can't tell?"

"Of course not, James. How would a woman be able to tell that?"

"I don't know. I just thought women knew what they were going to have. I wasn't told anything different. I guess I thought women could tell somehow. Is that why you've been getting sick?"

Katie nodded. "Yes, that's why I've been sick in the mornings and no, women can't tell what the baby is."

James hugged his wife gently. "A baby! You will never know how long and hard I prayed for my own family. Thank you, Katie." He lifted her into his arms, hugging her furiously. "A baby, a baby!" Just as suddenly as he had started his jubilee, James stopped. With panic in his eyes he carefully set Katie down. "Katie, are you all right? Are you in pain? Does it hurt?"

Katie laughed so hard she held her stomach. "James, I can't believe you. You are too funny. Of course I'm fine! No, it doesn't hurt to have you hug me. I'm just happy that you are happy. I was a little worried you wouldn't be happy with the news."

"Why would you think I wouldn't be happy about us having a

baby?"

"I guess it's because we have a lot to worry about right now."

"God doesn't make mistakes, and I know children are a blessing and a miracle. Let's trust Him."

Katie nodded in agreement.

"Just think, Katie, we have our own little family already."

Katie only wished she felt peace about it all. *Help me to trust in you, Lord, no matter what...no matter what,* she prayed silently.

24

Promises Ahead

It was now the month of December. Christmas was two days away. Katie and a few of the matrons planned to make it special for the women. Because of the kindness of the captain and careful planning by Richards they would be able to serve fuller rations for Christmas dinner to the prisoners.

Katie, the matrons, and the officers' wives had made rag dolls for the little girls. James and his men worked on wooden farm animals for the boys.

Katie sat on deck, thinking of the holiday preparations and sewing baby things. Her mind went to the Christmas past. It didn't seem possible that a whole year had gone by. How different Christmas was this year. Soft, warm breezes and sunshine surrounded her. Feeling a pang of homesickness, she gazed down at her wedding ring. What a surprise it had been when she received it. She remembered the look on Mary and Maggie's faces when she opened it. She couldn't contain a giggle when she imagined Mary traipsing around the store looking at all the fine "sparklers." She fought the threat of tears. How she missed everyone, and all the Christmas cheer. She missed the tree, snow, and the smells that only Christmas held. No, she refused to cry right now over anything. The voyage had been fairly smooth even with the few storms they had run into. Three new bairns were born and doing very well. Her wee one was growing and moving within her. Only months remained before they would be at their destination. God blessed her every day, and she wanted to pass it on to others.

Katie looked up to watch some of the women prisoners exercising and playing with their children. To look at them you would never guess they were ripped from their homeland with their futures in question. They were laughing and singing old songs of Ireland. They looked haggard and wore rags, but they seemed to be coping well. Some of their voices lifted in song...

"We dance, we sing and live life in full
We fish and plant the land that pulls
Our hearts towards home and hearth and love
Green Ireland, land from above..."

The tune was a favorite of Gran's. Katie closed her eyes, listening to Gran's sweet, quivering voice singing as she baked bread or hoed the dry earth. Katie laid her sewing down, deciding to join the women and children at their play. What a beautiful day.

Captain Warwick stood off to the side, watching some of the female prisoners playing with their children. Amusement crossed his face at their laughter. Hearing more laughter lift in the air, he turned to see Mrs. Murphy chasing a small boy. When she caught him, she lifted him in the air, making the boy giggle. It was a pleasant sight, causing his heart to pull. He missed his sweet Elizabeth and their sons. He had only spent four Christmases with his family out of twelve years of marriage. It was getting harder and harder for him as the years went by.

Christmas Day finally came. Someone played the squeeze box while others danced the jig. Many voices were raised in song. Captain Warwick ordered his crew generous portions of port for their holiday celebration, all except for those on duty, of course. He and Dr. Crane stood watching the merriment. Many marines and their families joined in the Christmas celebration. When there was a lull in their merriment, they could hear the prisoners singing below. How lovely the sound of it was. It touched each and every heart. Those who sang below were locked up with uncertain futures, but they sang anyway.

"Silent night, holy night, all is calm, all is bright…"

All prisoners spent Christmas in their bays. It was easier for the crew and marines to enjoy their holiday that way.

"Round yon virgin, mother and child,
Holy infant so tender and mild…"

Katie visited each female bay singing, praying, and sharing the miracle of Christmas. The children were given their small gifts. Their eyes sparkled at the sight of the new toys. Little girls began naming their dolls while the boys played with their wooden animals. Many of the mothers sat with tears of gratitude as they watched their children enjoy Christmas.

James spent the evening with the men. Many of them seemed to open up to him more and more. He treated them with respect and genuine concern. They sang Christmas songs of past. Old memories were shared, and laughter rang out from time to time. Even the men who were considered troublemakers sat quietly and listened. A few even joined in the singing. By the time the prisoners received their evening rations of gruel with sugar and butter, bread, salt beef, and rice, most of the joyous celebrations had wound down for the night. Quiet contemplation, memories, and regrets replaced them.

It was late when James and Katie met back at their cabin. They quietly talked, sharing their stories of the prisoners. Katie went to her side of the bed and lifted the blanket, revealing a bundle of cloth.

"What's that?" James asked.

"My Christmas present to you."

"Really, what is it?"

"Open it and see."

James removed the material, pulling out a new woolen shirt and scarf.

"It's for the cold nights when you're called to work."

"Katie, thank you. It amazes me how cold it can get at night when it's so hot during the day. These will work fine for me," he said as he tried the shirt on. Taking the scarf, he tied it around his neck. "So, how do I look? When did you have time to make them?"

"Very handsome indeed, sir. When the captain called you to his cabin I would take it out and work on it for awhile. You almost caught me with it one day, but I just casually laid it aside so you wouldn't notice. I'm always sewing something."

"That you are, Katie."

James gave his wife a hug and told her to stay put. He had to run to get his gift for her. He had hidden it out in the corridor. After a few minutes he was back, holding something small in his large hands.

"Oh James, what is it?" It was Katie's turn to question.

James handed the object out to Katie, warning her to be careful for it could break. Very carefully Katie began to take off the cloth used to hide the treasure. James smiled as he watched her. She was like a child with a new toy. She took her time savoring the moment. She let in a sharp intake of breath at the sight of it. How glorious it was! It was a small globe set on a wood base; inside the globe was sparkling "snow," water, a miniature castle, and tiny shamrocks.

"Oh James, it's beautiful! Where in the world did you get it?"

"One of the marines and his wife bought some things in their travels. She asked me to build her a few small cupboards to store some things in their cabin. She wanted to pay me, but I asked if I could pick something out for you for payment. She thinks very highly of you, Mrs. Murphy. She told me she has never met anyone so kind or full of heart. I thought of you and your Gran when I saw this. I'm glad you like it. I wasn't sure how you would feel when you saw it, happy or sad."

"Definitely happy, it's perfect! Whenever I look at it, I will be reminded of Gran and her Ireland, and of my thoughtful husband."

The couple turned back the blanket and snuggled down. They prayed together, thanking the Lord for all their many blessings, especially the gift of His birth. The gentle lift of the ship, and the sound of the waves lulled them both to sleep as they lay wrapped in each other's arms.

The *Sally Mae* was headed towards the end of her long journey. Sails billowed, bringing her ever closer to her destination. Katie and Annie talked excitedly about the coming end of their voyage. Annie shared that they were heading first to Botany Bay and then to Newcastle.

Katie added, "It seems like it all happened so fast now that we're almost there. In the beginning the voyage seemed endless. Botany Bay sounds so different. Tell me about it. You said you've been there a few times. What is it like?"

"The land is strange, but beautiful indeed, and so are the people. If you are a lazy man, it is hell. If you are industrious, it holds promise for you. There are people who live there that have the color of coal to their skin. They are savages who actually wear designs on their faces and bodies. They look like they are from the devil himself. Wait until you see the animals. Some are hard to describe. You probably won't believe me unless you see them for yourself."

"Like what?"

"Well, there's a thing called a kangaroo. The only way I can describe it is to say it looks like a huge hare, the size of a man. It has a long tail, long ears, and it sits back on its haunches. It has a pocket in the front of its belly to hold its young."

"You don't say? I cannot picture it in my mind. It must look very funny. You say it's as big as a man?" Katie added.

"Aye, I thought it was the funniest looking thing I ever did see. I saw one lay a big man, like your James, out in the dirt with one kick to the gut. Its feet are huge, and the legs on it are powerful. It nearly killed the bloke."

"Oh my, are there other dangerous animals?"

"More that would give you the willies than would harm you."

"Really?"

"There are snakes called pythons. They are huge, and can weigh hundreds of pounds. Luckily, they shy away from people. The bogs are where you are likely to find them, so stay clear of them. Then there are crocodiles. Those are scariest of all, I think. They live mostly in the water but also like to lie on shore in the sun. They have a bumpy, tough hide and are low to the ground. They have teeth that can cut a man in half with one bite. They do not fear men. You will be warned where to go, and where not to go. You won't have to worry if you heed what they say."

"Are you making this up?" Katie questioned.

"No, I speak the truth. Like I said, they are the strangest creatures you will ever see."

"Annie, I'm afraid for the wee one. What if he wanders about?"

"It can cause concern for sure. Just keep your eyes and ears open. You'll both be fine. I don't mean to frighten you, Katie, but you need to know that there are dangers. There is beauty as well: birds of every color, and I saw a butterfly once that was as big as a bird. There are plants that are glossy green, and there's some that are poisonous. You will see flowers that will take your breath away when you look at them. The sun shines mostly, but it rains enough for crops. It really depends on where in Australia you are. There is desert and lush land alike. "

"Tell me more about the people and how they live. Do they suffer, or do they prosper?"

After thinking for a moment she answered, "It depends on the person, Katie. Like I said before, if you are lazy and have a bitter heart, you will hate it. If you want to work hard and make a life for yourself, you will be fine. In the old days it was much worse. People were starving and murdering each other for food. It was awful. Some of the stories I've heard can cause your hair to curl. That is why everyone has to pull together. There is no tolerance for laziness or crime. Those who don't work don't eat. It's not all bad news, though. The colonies have been established long enough that they can take care of themselves. There was a time that a ship bringing provisions determined life or death. It's not like that any longer. Women live and work in factories or are used as domestic help. The men work the farms and build roads and bridges, things like that."

"What about those people you said come from the devil himself, the natives?"

"They are called Aborigines. They are very black and have flat noses. They are all heathen. Truth be told, you have to feel sorry for them. Many have been killed off. I heard a lot of them died when the first ships arrived, carrying diseases. Over the years they have been schooled, forced to learn English, and 'we' tried to change them into 'us.' They have fought against it. They are mostly peaceful now as long as we leave them alone and stay away from them. Once in a while a small band of them are spotted, but they pretty much stay off to themselves."

"Are there large prisons there like Newgate?"

"Yes, but only the worst prisoners are there. Men and women are needed to work. It is hard enough to feed yourself, let alone keep prisoners locked up and useless."

"I suppose. Do you think James will be hired out? Will I be able to be with him?"

"I don't know, Katie. The governor tries to keep families together. It's only common sense that people are happier with their families, but I can't say for sure."

"What are the farms like?"

"The ground is rich and fertile once it's cleared. That's the hardest thing—trying to keep the wild plants out once the crops are planted. Hard work for sure, but you can yield a bounty if the rain comes when it's supposed to. A lot of Merino is raised. That is where the money is."

"Merino? What in the world is that?"

"Those are sheep. They are especially bred to withstand the harsh, hot climate. We send wool to England and other countries as well. Merinos are what mainly feed and clothe some of the colonies, along with the lumber trade."

The two women talked a great deal more until it was time to feed the prisoners.

Katie stood to follow Annie, but saw James. She walked over to him. "James, Annie has been telling me about Australia. Some of it sounds frightening, and some exciting."

"I've been hearing about it too. I guess it's like any place you go, both good and bad."

"Aye, you're right."

James tried to lighten any fears she might have. "You don't have anything to worry about, Katie darlin'. We are going to do well in the new land. I think in a few years I may be running the place!"

"Oh really, James? You plan on running the whole place? Isn't that the governor's job? I think you better ask him first if it's all right that you take over."

Both broke into laughter.

"You can always make me feel better after I talk to you." Katie hugged her husband. "I best get to work, or Annie will come looking for me," she added. Smiling back at her husband, she headed for the galley.

James thanked God for the thousandth time for his Katie and their baby. How blessed he was. He knew in his heart that God's hand protected him and Katie. He was so thankful knowing that it was God who provided the good captain, a sturdy ship, and crew. Yes, how blessed he was, and he let his Lord know how grateful he was. Some of the crew snickered when they saw a big man kneeling on deck as if in prayer. It sure was a strange sight, but some hearts were touched.

⤦⤤

As time passed, James and Captain Warwick seemed comfortable around each other. They formed a strange relationship. It was almost a friendship, but it would be denied if anyone asked about it. Captains never befriended prisoners.

"Well sir, I've never heard of Sydney. Where is it?" James asked.

"It's between Botany Bay and Newcastle. It's a great port and well-established. Beautiful too with fertile land, and built up. We will be in Botany Bay in one month's time. A man can actually find a worthwhile life there if he has a mind to. Not saying it isn't a hard life, but tell me where a man doesn't find hardship."

"That's true enough. What will happen to the prisoners when we arrive?"

"You mean what will happen to you?"

"Yes, I guess I do."

"We will stay on board for a week's time to make sure no one carries sickness, then once we go ashore the prisoners are taken to a communal hall. There you will be processed. You are checked over for health, and they look over your records. I have to hand in a report about you. How well you performed your duties and such. They will want to know what skills you may have. I don't think you have anything to worry about. The fact that you can read, write, farm, and work with your hands means a great deal."

James blurted out his next question. "Will my wife and I be able to stay together?"

"Not at first. Men and women are separated when they process you. Families are reunited before too long, though." Relief flooded James. "Murphy, I will put in a good word for you in appreciation for the fine job you have done."

"Thank you, sir." But James wondered if the captain's "good word" would be enough.

⋖⌘⋗

The night breezes caused Katie to pull her shawl tighter. James placed his arm around his wife as they stood at the ship's railing. The sea was calm, showing the bright, full moon. A low, eerie call of a whale filled the air.

"It sounds so alone," Katie spoke. "Do you think it's calling to another whale?"

"Probably," was all James said. He seemed to be deep in thought.

"It's so funny how quickly you can become used to something like the sound of whales. Not so long ago I never even heard of such a thing."

"Ah-hah," James answered.

Katie gave up on any conversation. She turned her gaze back on the sea. James seemed a million miles away. This was to be their last night of the voyage. The captain had announced the news to the matrons, warders, marines, and their families. Once anchored, they would spend a week in quarantine and make repairs on the ship. It would also give them a chance to "ready" themselves. They were warned that they wouldn't have their "land legs" for a time. It would be strange to walk without any swaying motion at first.

James thought how frightened he was—mostly for Katie—when they had first started out. He prayed the Lord would calm the new fears that gnawed at him. He kept telling Katie they needed to trust, yet he doubted.

Katie sensed his mood. She placed her hand over one of his and glanced up at him. "Look how the Lord has taken care of us, James. He will keep on doing so. I rather feel excited about our new life." Suddenly, Katie inhaled fast, as if in fear.

"What's the matter?" James asked in alarm.

"I felt the bairn kick me!" Taking James' hand, Katie placed it on her belly. "Can you feel him move?"

"No, I don't." He left his hand there for several moments, but still felt nothing.

"Maybe it is too small yet for you to feel, but I did! How strange and wonderful it is!" Tears glistened in Katie's eyes.

"Did it hurt you?"

"Not at all. It was a fluttering feeling, as if a butterfly touched my skin. It's not the first time I felt our bairn move, but each time it's a wonder."

James once again held his wife, turning back to view all of God's glory revealed in the night and the sea.

⋞⋙

The day they dropped anchor was sun-filled and kissed with soft breezes. The business of the harbor reminded Katie of London. From the ship she could see people bustling all about. Long boats were being loaded and unloaded. A few other ships were anchored off shore, but *The Clip* was not among them.

The captain barked several orders, and men jumped to do his bidding. He sounded stern, yet a light mood settled over the men. Another successful voyage under their belts, and few lives lost. It was a good sail for sure.

The prisoners were kept locked in their bays, wondering when they would see their new "home." Now that they had arrived, they felt expectant and restless. It would be a hard week of waiting before they could go on shore. The women were luckier, for they stayed busy mending and making new clothes. Everyone spoke in hushed tones, as if afraid of waking someone.

It was two days before the prisoners were allowed to come on deck to exercise. Small groups of them were told to walk around the deck. If they moved any slower, they wouldn't have been moving at all. Their interest lay solely in watching all the sights on shore.

Two nights before going on shore, all the "free souls" were called to have dinner with the captain and officers. Captain Warwick seemed in high spirits. He was heard laughing from time to time. "Ladies and gentlemen, may I present a toast?" Raising his glass of port, he continued. "It has been my great pleasure to sail with you. For those of you who have sailed with me before, you know this has been an 'easy' sail. For those of you who have never sailed before, I'm sure there were a few frightening moments, but we have come through grandly. God bless, and good luck to us all!"

Everyone stood and cheered. Once all quieted down, they sat to listen once more to the captain. "I feel saddened that a few of my passengers have lost their lives but grateful there were not more. In a couple of days we will go ashore. I want this transition to be as smooth as possible. Matrons and warders, there are specific instructions for you as to how I want the prisoners handled. See me later on this. I want to thank everyone involved who made this sail a good one. Now let's enjoy our last meal together. The next couple of evenings will be busy for all."

Later on Katie and James would remember how festive it all had been. "You would have thought we were at a family home having dinner," James replied.

Katie agreed, "Aye, it has been fun tonight. I almost feel sad about all of this ending. Isn't it funny? I mean, there has been a lot of sadness on this trip, but a lot of good memories for us too. I guess it wouldn't have been so grand, had I been locked away in one of those bays. We had our cozy cabin. I still feel blessed by all the friends we made. I feel as if we've been traveling with family."

Quietness settled on both of them as their thoughts turned inwards. After a few moments, Katie spoke as if more to herself, "We're going to be separated at first, you know."

James nodded. "I know, but it shouldn't be for too long. I have to remind myself sometimes that I am still a prisoner. I've been treated like a free man on board, but it stops as soon as we walk on land."

"Aye, I know. Have you noticed, though, that the fear we had in the beginning is now gone? I feel such hope, and a deep joy inside. I know there's going to be hard times ahead, but I feel God's peace."

"So do I."

Katie and James spent a large part of the night talking about the Lord, and their future plans. They were without home or extended family. They were about to set foot on a strange new land. They had no job or way to make a living. James didn't even have his freedom, but with all that, their joy was full.

James began quoting Jeremiah 29:11, a verse he had memorized. It had helped him in the hard times and in the good times as well:

"'For I know the thoughts that I think toward you,' saith the Lord, 'thoughts of peace, and not of evil, to give you an expected end.'"

James and Katie were blessed.

Epilogue

James was assigned to work for Anthony Keys, a hard-working Scot with a fair heart. Keys and his wife, Bonnie, ran a large sheep ranch, and were successful at it long before James and Katie came to live there. The last of the five Keys children had left Australia to "discover" the world. The older couple was grateful for James' strong back and honest heart, along with Katie's gentle and giving nature. Oh, they didn't trust the convict and his wife that easily in the beginning. It took quite some time for James to prove himself.

Anthony Keys hated "breaking in" new prisoners. His experiences in the past had proven difficult. He had been lied to, stolen from, and even attacked. If it weren't for the free labor he would have given up on the "foulers" a long time ago.

But there was something different about this man. Instead of bragging about all he could and would do, he quietly went about his work and didn't stop until it was done well.

Bonnie watched how James treated his wife. A woman could tell a lot about a man by doing that. They were a novelty since he was a convict and his wife was not. Bonnie Keys was pleased to see the respect they had for one another, and when poor Katie lost their first babe at birth, James' gentleness and care touched the older woman's heart. She encouraged her husband to watch this couple closely as they just might be the answer to their prayers.

And so it was that James and Katie came to live and take part in the lives of the Keys family, and contribute to the growth of the new land. With their lifeblood and sweat, they became as much a part of it as anyone. They lay their firstborn in the ground of Australia, soaking the grave with their tears. They plowed and planted, and grew to know more about sheep than they ever intended.

During their third year in Australia, Katie gave birth to a healthy baby girl they named Mary. After seven years spent in service to the

Keys family, James became a "freeman" and, with Katie's help, earned a small farm. They continued to manage the Keys ranch while building their own small place. They would grow and prosper, raise many more children, and have a ministry helping other prisoners.

They spoke often of going back to London to see their families but knew it would never happen. Australia was their home. As the years passed, they sent and received many letters from their loved ones.

The years stretched out and time passed as it always does. They lived their lives and become a part of the foundation of Australia.

Some called James a prisoner, an outcast, but he had never been freer in his life. God had plans and a purpose for their lives, and they lived it gloriously, walking hand in hand with each other and with Him.

Author's Note

After researching this story I have a tremendous respect and admiration for the "pioneers" of Australia—for their strength and courage in facing the voyage across the sea, as well as the challenges of that "new land."

I have kept my story historically accurate, to the best of my ability. However, I added one detail that is not a part of history but from my imagination: that men and women convicts were forced to wed.

About the Author

COLLIE MAGGIE calls herself a "throw-away" child. Abandoned by her mother after her father's death, she entered foster homes at the age of four. Seven foster homes later she created her own home when she married Jack, now her husband for 39 years.

"My one and only dream as a child was to be adopted," Collie says. "It didn't happen until I became a Christian and read Ephesians 1:5: 'He predestined us to be *adopted* as his sons through Jesus Christ, in accordance with his pleasure and will.' My heart stood still after reading that verse. My dream came true that day."

In her early teens, Collie felt a "pull" to write a book. After pushing the urge down for so many years, she finally decided to give it a try. It was important to her that her writing be a reflection of real life—the struggles and hardships along with the joys of life. Wanting to encourage those who are hurting, Collie reminds readers of the hope in Christ and the promise He gave: that He has a purpose and a plan for each one of us.

Collie works as one of the church secretaries for her home church in Green Bay, Wisconsin. She has written many songs, poems, and short stories, and is now working on her second book. She has been involved in many ministries throughout the years and has been asked to share some of her experiences at other churches.

Jack and Collie have three children—Susan, Aaron, and Jesse—as well as two grandchildren, Anthony and Olivia.

Collie loves hearing from her readers. To email her: jollie1949@yahoo.com.

For more info: **www.oaktara.com**

Printed in the United States
213600BV00002B/2/P